9—

ATTACHMENTS

ATTACHMENTS

Rainbow Rowell

DUTTON

DUTTON
Published by Penguin Group (USA) Inc.
375 Hudson Street, New York, New York 10014, U.S.A.
Penguin Group (Canada), 90 Eglinton Avenue East, Suite 700, Toronto, Ontario M4P 2Y3, Canada (a division of Pearson Penguin Canada Inc.); Penguin Books Ltd, 80 Strand, London WC2R 0RL, England; Penguin Ireland, 25 St Stephen's Green, Dublin 2, Ireland (a division of Penguin Books Ltd); Penguin Group (Australia), 250 Camberwell Road, Camberwell, Victoria 3124, Australia (a division of Pearson Australia Group Pty Ltd); Penguin Books India Pvt Ltd, 11 Community Centre, Panchsheel Park, New Delhi–110 017, India; Penguin Group (NZ), 67 Apollo Drive, Rosedale, North Shore 0632, New Zealand (a division of Pearson New Zealand Ltd); Penguin Books (South Africa) (Pty) Ltd, 24 Sturdee Avenue, Rosebank, Johannesburg 2196, South Africa

Penguin Books Ltd, Registered Offices: 80 Strand, London WC2R 0RL, England

Published by Dutton, a member of Penguin Group (USA) Inc.

First printing, April 2011
10 9 8 7 6 5 4 3 2 1

REGISTERED TRADEMARK—MARCA REGISTRADA

LIBRARY OF CONGRESS CATALOGING-IN-PUBLICATION DATA

Rowell, Rainbow.
  Attachments / Rainbow Rowell.
    p. cm.
  ISBN 978-0-525-95198-8
  I. Title.
  PS3618.Q8755A93   2011
  813'.6—dc22

                2010036696

Printed in the United States of America

PUBLISHER'S NOTE
This book is a work of fiction. Names, characters, places, and incidents either are the product of the author's imagination or are used fictitiously, and any resemblance to actual persons, living or dead, business establishments, events, or locales is entirely coincidental.

For Kai, who's better than fiction

ATTACHMENTS

CHAPTER 1

From: Jennifer Scribner-Snyder
To: Beth Fremont
Sent: Wed, 08/18/1999 9:06 AM
Subject: Where are you?

Would it kill you to get here before noon? I'm sitting here among the shards of my life as I know it, and you . . . if I know you, you just woke up. You're probably eating oatmeal and watching *Sally Jessy Raphael*. E-mail me when you get in, before you do anything else. Don't even read the comics.

<<**Beth to Jennifer**>> Okay, I'm putting you before the comics, but make it quick. I've got an ongoing argument with Derek about whether *For Better or For Worse* is set in Canada, and today might be the day they prove me right.

<<**Jennifer to Beth**>> I think I'm pregnant.

<<**Beth to Jennifer**>> What? Why do you think you're pregnant?

<<**Jennifer to Beth**>> I had three drinks last Saturday.

<<**Beth to Jennifer**>> I think we need to have a little talk about the birds and the bees. That's not exactly how it happens.

<<**Jennifer to Beth**>> Whenever I have too much to drink, I start to feel pregnant. I think it's because I never drink, and it

would just figure that the *one time* I decide to loosen up, I get pregnant. Three hours of weakness, and now I'm going to spend the rest of my life wrestling with the special needs of a fetal alcoholic.

<<Beth to Jennifer>> I don't think they call them that.

<<Jennifer to Beth>> Its little eyes will be too far apart, and everyone will look at me in the grocery store and whisper, "Look at that horrible lush. She couldn't part with her Zima for nine months. It's tragic."

<<Beth to Jennifer>> You drink Zima?

<<Jennifer to Beth>> It's really quite refreshing.

<<Beth to Jennifer>> You're not pregnant.

<<Jennifer to Beth>> I am.

Normally, two days before my period, my face is broken out, and I get pre-cramps cramping. But my skin is as clear as a baby's bottom. And instead of cramps, I feel this strangeness in my womb region. Almost a presence.

<<Beth to Jennifer>> I dare you to call Ask-A-Nurse and tell them that you've got a presence in your womb region.

<<Jennifer to Beth>> Given: This is not my first pregnancy scare. I will acknowledge that thinking I'm pregnant is practically a part of my monthly premenstrual regimen. But I'm telling you, *this is different*. I feel different. It's like my body is telling me, "It has Begun."

I can't stop worrying about what happens next. First I get sick. And then I get fat. And then I die of an aneurysm in the delivery room.

<<Beth to Jennifer>> OR . . . and then you give birth to a beautiful child. (See how you've tricked me into playing along with your pregnancy fiction?)

<<Jennifer to Beth>> OR . . . and then I give birth to a beautiful child, whom I never see because he spends all his waking hours at the day-care center with some minimum-wage slave he thinks is his mother. Mitch and I try to eat dinner together after the baby's in bed, but we're both so tired all the time. I start to doze off while he tells me about his day; he's relieved because he wasn't up to talking anyway. He eats his sloppy joe in silence and thinks about the shapely new consumer-science teacher at the high school. She wears black pumps and nude panty hose and rayon skirts that shimmy up her thighs whenever she sits down.

<<**Beth to Jennifer**>> What does Mitch think? (About the Presence in your womb. Not the new consumer-science teacher.)

<<**Jennifer to Beth**>> He thinks I should take a pregnancy test.

<<**Beth to Jennifer**>> Good man. Perhaps a common-sensical kind of guy like Mitch would have been better off with that home ec teacher. (She'd never make sloppy joes for dinner.) But I guess he's stuck with you, especially now that there's a special-needs child on the way.

CHAPTER 2

"LINCOLN, YOU LOOK terrible."

"Thanks, Mom." He'd have to take her word for it. He hadn't looked in a mirror today. Or yesterday. Lincoln rubbed his eyes and ran his fingers through his hair, trying to smooth it down . . . or maybe just over. Maybe he should have combed it when he got out of the shower last night.

"Seriously, look at you. And look at the clock. It's noon. Did you just wake up?"

"Mom, I don't get off work until one A.M."

She frowned, then handed him a spoon. "Here," she said, "stir these beans." She turned on the mixer and half shouted over it. "I still don't understand what you do in that place that can't be done in daylight. . . . No, honey, not like that, you're just petting them. Really *stir.*"

Lincoln stirred harder. The whole kitchen smelled like ham and onions and something else, something sweet. His stomach was growling. "I told you," he said, trying to be heard, "somebody has to be there. In case there's a computer problem, and . . . I don't know . . ."

"What don't you know?" She turned off the mixer and looked at him.

"I think maybe they want me to work at night so that I don't get close to anyone else."

"What?"

"Well, if I got to know people," he said, "I might . . ."

"Stir. Talk and stir."

"If I got to know people"—he stirred—"I might not feel so impartial when I'm enforcing the rules."

"I still don't like that you read other people's mail. Especially at night, in an empty building. That shouldn't be someone's job." She tasted whatever she was mixing with her finger, then held the bowl out to him. "Here, taste this . . . What kind of world do we live in, where that's a career?"

He ran his finger around the edge of the bowl and tasted it. Icing.

"Can you taste the maple syrup?"

He nodded. "The building isn't really empty," he said. "There are people working up in the newsroom."

"Do you talk to them?"

"No. But I read their e-mail."

"It's not right. How can people express themselves in a place like that? Knowing someone's lurking in their thoughts."

"I'm not in their thoughts. I'm in their computers, in the company's computers. Everyone knows it's happening . . ." It was hopeless trying to explain it to her. She'd never even seen e-mail.

"Give me that spoon," she sighed. "You'll ruin the whole batch." He gave her the spoon and sat down at the kitchen table, next to a plate of steaming corn bread. "We had a mailman once," she said. "Remember? He'd read our postcards? And he'd always make these knowing comments. 'Your friend is having a good time in South Carolina, I see.' Or, 'I've never been to Mount Rushmore myself.' They must all read postcards, all those mailmen. Mail people. It's a repetitive job. But this one was almost proud of it—gloaty. I think he told the neighbors that I subscribed to *Ms.*"

"It's not like that," Lincoln said, rubbing his eyes again. "I only read enough to see if they're breaking a rule. It's not like I'm reading their diaries or something."

His mother wasn't listening.

"Are you hungry? You look hungry. You look deficient, if you want to know the truth. Here, honey, hand me that plate." He got up and handed her a plate, and she caught him by the wrist. "Lincoln . . . What's wrong with your hands?"

"Nothing's wrong."

"Look at your fingers—they're gray."

"It's ink."

"What?"

"*Ink.*"

WHEN LINCOLN WORKED at McDonald's in high school, the cooking oil got into everything. When he came home at night, he felt all over the way your hands feel when you get done eating French fries. The oil would get into his skin and his hair. The next day, he would sweat it out into his school clothes.

At *The Courier*, it was ink. A gray film over everything, no matter how much anyone cleaned. A gray stain on the textured walls and the acoustic ceiling tiles.

The night copy editors actually handled the papers, every edition, hot off the presses. They left gray fingerprints on their keyboards and desks. They reminded Lincoln of moles. Serious people with thick glasses and gray skin. *That might just be the lighting,* he thought. Maybe he wouldn't recognize them in the sunshine. In full color.

They surely wouldn't recognize him. Lincoln spent most of his time at work in the information technology office downstairs. It had been a darkroom about five years and two dozen fluorescent lights ago, and with all of the lights and the computer servers, it was like sitting inside a headache.

Lincoln liked getting called up to the newsroom, to reboot a machine or sort out a printer. The newsroom was wide and open, with a long wall of windows, and it was never completely empty. The nightside editors worked as late as he did. They sat in a clump at one end of the room, under a bank of televisions. There were two, who sat together, right next to the printer, who were young and pretty. (Yes, Lincoln had decided, you *could* be both pretty and molelike.) He wondered if people who worked nights went on dates during the day.

CHAPTER 3

From: Beth Fremont
To: Jennifer Scribner-Snyder
Sent: Fri, 08/20/1999 10:38 AM
Subject: I sort of hate to ask, but . . .

Are we done pretending that you're pregnant?

<<**Jennifer to Beth**>> Not for 40 weeks. Maybe 38 by now . . .

<<**Beth to Jennifer**>> Does that mean we can't talk about other things?

<<**Jennifer to Beth**>> No, it means we *should* talk about other things. I'm trying not to dwell on it.

<<**Beth to Jennifer**>> Good plan.
Okay. So. Last night, I got a call from my little sister. She's getting married.

<<**Jennifer to Beth**>> Doesn't her husband mind?

<<**Beth to Jennifer**>> My other little sister. Kiley. You met her boyfriend . . . *fiancé*, Brian, at my parents' house on Memorial Day. Remember? We were making fun of the Sigma Chi tattoo on his ankle . . .

<<**Jennifer to Beth**>> Right, Brian. I remember. We like him, right?

<<Beth to Jennifer>> We love him. He's great. He's just the kind of guy you hope your daughter will meet someday at an upside-down-margarita party.

<<Jennifer to Beth>> Is that a fetal-alcoholic joke?

This wedding is your parents' fault. They named her Kiley. She was doomed from birth to marry a hunky, fratty premed major.

<<Beth to Jennifer>> Pre-law. But Kiley thinks he'll end up running his dad's plumbing supply company.

<<Jennifer to Beth>> Could be worse.

<<Beth to Jennifer>> It could hardly be better.

<<Jennifer to Beth>> Oh. I'm sorry. I just now got that this wasn't good news. What did Chris say?

<<Beth to Jennifer>> The usual. That Brian's a tool. That Kiley listens to too much Dave Matthews. Also, he said, "I've got practice tonight, so don't wait up, hey, hand me those Zig-Zags, would you, are you in the wedding? Cool, at least I'll get to see you in another one of those Scarlett O'Hara dresses. You're a hot bridesmaid, come here. Did you listen to that tape I left for you? Danny says I'm playing all over his bass line, but Jesus, I'm doing him a favor."

And then he proposed. In Bizarro World.

In the real world, Chris is never going to propose. And I can't decide if that makes him a jerk—or if maybe I'm the jerk for wanting it so bad. And I can't even talk to him about it, about marriage, because he would say that he *does* want it. Soon. When he's got some momentum going. When the band is back on track. That he doesn't want to be a drag on me, he doesn't want me to have to support him . . .

Please don't point out that I already support him—because that's only mostly true.

<<Jennifer to Beth>> Mostly? You pay his rent.

<<Beth to Jennifer>> I pay *the* rent. I would have to pay rent anyway . . . I would have to pay the gas bill and the cable bill and everything else if I lived alone. I wouldn't save a nickel if he moved out.

Besides, I don't mind paying most of the bills now, and I won't mind doing it after we're married. (My dad has always paid my mom's bills, and no one calls her a parasite.)

It isn't the who-pays-the-bills issue that's a problem. It's the acting-like-an-adult issue. It's acceptable in Chris's world for a guy to live with his girlfriend while he works on a demo. It's not as cool to chase your guitar fantasy while your wife's at work.

If you have a wife, you're an adult. That's not who Chris wants to be. Maybe that's not who I want him to be.

<<Jennifer to Beth>> Who do you want him to be?

<<Beth to Jennifer>> Most days? I think I want the wild-haired music man. The guy who wakes you up at 2 a.m. to read you the poem he just wrote on your stomach. I want the boy with kaleidoscope eyes.

<<Jennifer to Beth>> There would very likely be no more 2 a.m. tummy poems if Chris got a real job.

<<Beth to Jennifer>> That's true.

<<Jennifer to Beth>> So you're okay?

<<Beth to Jennifer>> No. I'm about to get fitted for another bridesmaid dress. Strapless. Kiley's already picked it out. I'm dog years away being from okay. But I don't think I can complain, can I? I want him. And he wants to wait. And I still want him. So I can't complain.

<<Jennifer to Beth>> Of course you can complain. That's un-alienable. On the bright side, at least you're not pregnant.

<<Beth to Jennifer>> Neither are you. Take a pregnancy test.

CHAPTER 4

JUST FOR THE record—his own internal record—Lincoln never would have applied for this job if the classified ad had said, "Wanted: someone to read other people's e-mail. Swing shift."

The Courier ad had said, "Full-time opportunity for Internet security officer. $40K+ Health, dental."

Internet security officer. Lincoln had pictured himself building firewalls and protecting the newspaper from dangerous hackers—not sending out memos every time somebody in Accounting forwarded an off-color joke to the person in the next cubicle.

The Courier was probably the last newspaper in America to give its reporters Internet access. At least that's what Greg said. Greg was Lincoln's boss, the head of the IT office. Greg could still remember when the reporters used electric typewriters. "And I can remember," he said, "because it wasn't that long ago—1992. We switched to computers because we couldn't order the ribbon anymore, I shit you not."

This whole online thing was happening against management's will, Greg said. As far as the publisher was concerned, giving employees Internet access was like giving them the option to work if they felt like it, look at porn if they didn't.

But not having the Internet was getting ridiculous.

When the newspaper launched its Web site last year, the reporters couldn't even go online to read their stories. And most readers wanted to e-mail in their letters to the editor these days, even third-graders and World War II veterans.

By the time Lincoln started working at *The Courier*, the Internet experiment was in its third month. All employees had internal e-mail now. Key employees, and pretty much everyone in the news division, had some access to the World Wide Web.

If you asked Greg, it was all going pretty well.

If you asked anyone in upper management, it was chaos.

People were shopping and gossiping; they were joining online forums and fantasy football leagues. There was some gambling going on. And some dirty stuff. "But that isn't such a bad thing," Greg argued. "It helps us weed out the sickos."

The worst thing about the Internet, as far as Greg's bosses were concerned, was that it was now impossible to distinguish a roomful of people working diligently from a roomful of people taking the What-Kind-of-Dog-Am-I? online personality quiz.

And thus . . . Lincoln.

On his very first night, Lincoln helped Greg load a new program called WebFence on to the network. WebFence would monitor everything everyone was doing on the Internet and the Intranet. Every e-mail. Every Web site. Every word.

And Lincoln would monitor WebFence.

An especially filthy-minded person (maybe Greg) had defined the program's mail filters. There was a whole list of red flags: nasty words, racial slurs, supervisors' names, words like "secret" and "classified."

That last one, "classified," beached the entire network during WebFence's first hour by flagging and storing each and every e-mail sent to or from the Classified Advertising department.

The software also flagged large attachments, suspiciously long messages, suspiciously frequent messages. . . . Every day, hundreds of possibly illicit e-mails were sent to a secure mailbox, and it was Lincoln's job to follow up on every one. That meant reading them, so he read them. But he didn't enjoy it.

He couldn't admit this to his mother, but it *did* feel wrong, what he was doing, like eavesdropping. Maybe if he were the sort of person who liked that sort of thing . . . His girlfriend Sam—his ex-girlfriend—always used to peek in other people's medicine cabinets. "Robitussin," she'd report in the car on the way home. "And generic Band-Aids. And something that looked like a garlic press."

Lincoln didn't even like *using* other people's bathrooms.

There was a whole complicated process he was supposed to follow if he caught someone actually breaking *The Courier*'s rules. But most offenses called for just a written warning, and most offenders got the message after that.

In fact, the first round of warnings worked so well, Lincoln started to run out of things to do. WebFence kept flagging e-mails, a few dozen a day, but they were almost all false alarms. Greg didn't seem to care. "Don't worry," he said to Lincoln on the first day that WebFence didn't snag a single legitimate violator. "You won't get fired. The men upstairs love what you're doing."

"I'm not doing anything," Lincoln said.

"Sure, you are. You're the guy who reads their e-mail. They're all scared of you."

"Who's scared? Who's they?"

"Everybody. Are you kidding? This whole building is talking about you."

"They're not scared of me. They're scared of getting caught."

"Getting caught by *you*. Just knowing that you're snooping around their Sent folders every night is enough to keep them following the rules."

"But I'm not snooping around."

"You could," Greg said.

"I could?"

Greg went back to what he was doing, some sort of laptop autopsy. "Look, Lincoln, I've told you. Somebody has to be here at night anyway. Somebody has to answer the phone and say, 'Help desk.' You're just sitting around, I know. You don't have enough work, I know. I don't care. Do the crossword. Learn a foreign language. We had a gal who used to crochet . . ."

Lincoln didn't crochet.

He read the newspaper. He brought in comic books and magazines and paperback novels. He called his sister sometimes, if it wasn't too late and if he felt lonely.

Mostly, he surfed the Net.

CHAPTER 5

From: Jennifer Scribner-Snyder
To: Beth Fremont
Sent: Wed, 08/25/1999 10:33 AM
Subject: This is only a test. In the case of an actual emergency . . .

It's here. Return to your usual programming.

<<**Beth to Jennifer**>> It?

<<**Jennifer to Beth**>> You know . . . *it*, the thing that tells you you're not pregnant.

<<**Beth to Jennifer**>> *It?* Do you mean your period? Your monthly? Did your aunt Ruby arrive for a five- to seven-day visit? Is it . . . *that time?*

Why are you talking like you're in a feminine napkin commercial?

<<**Jennifer to Beth**>> I'm trying to be more careful. I don't want to trigger one of those red flags and send some company watchdog computer into a frenzy, just because I sent an e-mail about *it*.

<<**Beth to Jennifer**>> I can't imagine that any of the company's red-flag words involve menstruation.

<<**Jennifer to Beth**>> So you're not worried about it?

<<**Beth to Jennifer**>> About your period?

<<Jennifer to Beth>> No, about that note we got. The one that warned us not to send personal e-mails. The one that said we could be fired for improper use of our computers.

<<Beth to Jennifer>> Am I worried that the bad guys from *Tron* are reading our e-mail? Uh, no. All this security stuff isn't aimed at people like us. They're trying to catch the pervs. The on-line porn addicts, the Internet blackjack players, the corporate spies . . .

<<Jennifer to Beth>> Those are probably all red-flag words. *Pervs. Porn. Spies.* I bet *red flag* is a red flag.

<<Beth to Jennifer>> I don't care if they *are* reading our mail. Bring it on, Tron! I dare you. Try to take away my freedom of expression. I'm a journalist. A free-speech warrior. I serve in the Army of the First Amendment. I didn't take this job for the bad money and the regressive health care coverage. I'm here for the truth, the sunshine, the casting open of closed doors!

<<Jennifer to Beth>> Free-speech warrior. I see. What are you fighting for? The right to give *Billy Madison* five stars?

<<Beth to Jennifer>> Hey now. I wasn't always a spoiled movie reviewer. Don't forget my two years covering North Havenbrook. Two years in the trenches. I bled ink all over that suburb. I went Bob Woodward on its ass.

Furthermore, I would have given *Billy Madison* six stars if they were mine to give. You know how I feel about Adam Sandler—and that I give bonus stars for Styx songs. (Two stars if it's "Renegade.")

<<Jennifer to Beth>> Fine. I surrender. Company Internet policy be d@mned: I started my period last night.

<<Beth to Jennifer>> Say it loud, say it proud. Congratulations.

<<Jennifer to Beth>> Yeah, that's the thing . . .

<<Beth to Jennifer>> What's the thing?

<<Jennifer to Beth>> When it started, I didn't feel my usual hurricane of relief and Zima cravings.

I mean, I was relieved—because, on top of the Zima drinking, I don't think I've eaten anything with folic acid in the last six months. I may even be eating things that leach folic acid from your system, so I was definitely relieved—but I wasn't ecstatic.

I went downstairs to tell Mitch. He was working on marching band diagrams, which, normally, I wouldn't interrupt, but this was important. "Just FYI," I said, "I started my period."

And he set down his pencil and said, "Oh." (Just like that. "Oh.")

When I asked him why he said it that way, he said he thought that maybe I really was pregnant this time—and that that would have been nice. "You know I want kids," he said.

"Right," I said. "*Someday.*"

"Someday soon," he said.

"Someday eventually. When we're ready."

And then he turned back to his diagrams. Not mad or impatient. Just sorrowful, which is much, much worse. So I said, "When we're ready, right?" And he said . . .

"I'm ready now. I'm ready last year, Jenny, and I'm starting to think that maybe you never will be. You don't even want to be ready. You act like getting pregnant is a disease you can catch from public toilets."

<<**Beth to Jennifer**>> What did you say?

<<**Jennifer to Beth**>> What could I say? I'm *not* ready. And maybe I misled him every time I used the words "someday" and "eventually." I can't picture myself with kids . . .

But I couldn't picture myself married, either, until I met Mitch. I always thought the kid idea would grow on me, that all Mitch's healthy desires would infect me, and one morning I'd wake up thinking, "What a beautiful world in which to bring a child."

What if that never happens?

What if he decides to cut his losses and find some perfectly normal woman who—on top of being naturally thin and never having turned to prescription antidepressants—also wants to have his babies ASAP?

<<**Beth to Jennifer**>> Like Barbie in a state of perpetual ovulation.

<<**Jennifer to Beth**>> Yes.

<<**Beth to Jennifer**>> Like the fictional new consumer-science teacher.

<<**Jennifer to Beth**>> Yes!

<<**Beth to Jennifer**>> It won't happen.

<<**Jennifer to Beth**>> Why not?

<<**Beth to Jennifer**>> For the same reason Mitch tries to grow giant pumpkins every summer—even though your yard is too small, is infested with beetles and doesn't get enough sun. Mitch doesn't want the easy thing. He wants to work a little harder to get the thing he really wants.

<<**Jennifer to Beth**>> So he's a fool. A fool whose seeds find no purchase.

<<**Beth to Jennifer**>> That's not the point. The point is, he's a fool who won't give up on you.

<<**Jennifer to Beth**>> I'm not sure that you're right, but I think I might feel better now. So, good work.

<<**Beth to Jennifer**>> Anytime.
(You know that I mean anytime after 10:30 a.m. or so, right?)

<<**Jennifer to Beth**>> (I do.)

CHAPTER 6

JENNIFER SCRIBNER-SNYDER, ACCORDING to the company directory, was a Features copy editor.

Beth Fremont, Lincoln knew. He knew *of*, anyway. He'd read her movie reviews. She was funny, and he usually agreed with her. She was the reason he'd gone to see *Dark City* and *Flirting With Disaster* and *Babe*.

By the time Lincoln realized that he hadn't sent a warning to Beth Fremont and Jennifer Scribner-Snyder—after who knew how many offenses, three? half a dozen?—he couldn't remember why not. Maybe because he couldn't always figure out what rule they were breaking. Maybe because they seemed completely harmless. And nice.

And now he couldn't send them a warning, not tonight. Not when they were actually worried about getting a warning. That would be weird, wouldn't it? Knowing someone had read an e-mail you'd written about whether someone was reading your e-mail? If you were an excessively paranoid person, it could make you wonder whether all the *other things* you were worried about were *also* true. It might make you think, "Maybe they *are* all out to get me."

Lincoln didn't want to be the bad guy from *Tron*.

And also . . . Also, he kind of liked Beth and Jennifer, as much as you can like people from reading their e-mail, only some of their e-mail.

He read through the exchange again. "Ass" was definitely a red-flagged word. So was "blackjack" and "porn." He wasn't sure about "perv" or "menstruation."

He trashed the files and went home.

———

"YOU DON'T HAVE to pack me a lunch," Lincoln told his mother. Even though he liked it when she did. He'd practically given up fast food since he moved back home. There was always something baking in his mother's kitchen, or frying or simmering or cooling on a plate. She was always pushing Pyrex containers into his hands on his way out the door.

"I'm not packing you lunch," she said. "I'm packing you dinner."

"But you don't have to," he said. He didn't mind living with his mother, but there are *degrees* of living with your mother. And he was pretty sure that letting her cook every meal for him was too many degrees. She'd started planning her days around feeding him.

"I don't *have* to do anything," she said, handing him a grocery bag with a heavy glass dish clinking inside.

"What'd you make?" he asked. It smelled like cinnamon.

"Tandoori chicken. I think. I mean, I don't have a tandoori or a tandoor, one of those ovens, and I didn't have enough yogurt, they use yogurt, don't you think? I used sour cream. And paprika. Maybe it's chicken paprikash . . . I know I don't have to make you dinner, you know. I want to. I feel better when you eat—when you eat real food, not something that comes in a wrapper. I'm already so worried about you, the way you don't sleep, and you're never in the sun . . ."

"I sleep, Mom."

"During the day. We're meant to be awake with the sun, soaking up vitamin D, and sleeping at night, in the dark. When you were a little boy, I wouldn't even let you sleep with a night-light, do you remember? It interferes with melatonin production."

"Okay," he said. He couldn't think of a time he'd argued with her and won.

"Okay, what does 'okay' mean?"

"It means, okay, I hear you."

"Oh. Well. Then that doesn't mean anything at all. Take the chicken, would you? Eat it?"

"I will." He held the bag against his chest and smiled. He tried to look like somebody she didn't need to worry about so much. "Of course I will," he said. "Thank you."

GREG WAS WAITING for Lincoln when he walked into the IT office. It was always a few degrees colder in there, for the servers. You'd think that would be nice. Refreshing. But it was more of a clammy than a cool.

"Hey, Senator," Greg said, "I got to thinking about what you were saying a few days ago, you know, about not having enough to do. So I found you something."

"Great," Lincoln said, meaning it.

"You can start archiving and compressing all the user-stored files from the last six months or so," Greg said, clearly thinking this was an inspired idea.

Lincoln wasn't so sure.

"Why would you *want* me to do that?" he said. "It's a waste of time."

"I thought that's what you were looking for."

"I was looking for . . . Well, I wasn't looking for anything. I just felt bad getting paid to do nothing."

"And now you don't have to feel bad," Greg said. "I just gave you something to do."

"Yeah, but archiving and compressing . . . That could take years. And it doesn't matter."

Greg put on his Windbreaker and gathered up a stack of folders. He was leaving early to take his kid to the orthodontist. "There's no pleasing you, is there, Lincoln? This is why you don't have a woman."

How does he know I don't have a woman, Lincoln wondered.

He spent the rest of the night archiving and compressing files, just to spite Greg. (Even though Greg would never notice that the work was done, let alone that it was done spitefully.) Lincoln archived and compressed and thought hard about quitting. He might have walked out, there and then, if anyone had been in the IT office to accept his resignation.

It was almost ten o'clock when he remembered his mother's tandoori chicken.

The container had tilted open in its paper bag, and there was a pool of bright orange sauce on the carpet under his desk. The girl who sat there during the day, Kristi, would be angry. She'd already left Lincoln a Post-it note asking him to stop eating at her workstation. She said he was getting crumbs in her keyboard.

Lincoln took what was left of the chicken up to the second-floor break room. Almost nobody used the break room at night—the copy editors ate at their desks—but it was still livelier than the empty information technology office. He liked all the vending machines, and sometimes his break would overlap with the janitors'. Not tonight. Tonight, the room was empty.

For once, Lincoln was glad to be alone. He grabbed a plastic fork and started eating his chicken at a table in the corner. He didn't bother heating it up.

Two people walked into the break room then, a man and a woman. They were arguing about something. Amicably. "Give our readers some credit," the woman said, wagging a rolled-up Sports section at the man and leaning against the coffee machine. "I can't," he said. "I've met too many of them." The man was wearing a dingy white shirt and a thick brown tie. He looked like he hadn't changed his clothes or gotten a good night's sleep since the Carter presidency. The woman was younger. She had bright eyes and broad shoulders and hair that fell to the middle of her back. She was too pretty to look at.

They were all too pretty to look at. He couldn't remember the last time he had looked a woman in the eyes. A woman who wasn't his mother. Or his sister, Eve.

If he didn't look, he didn't risk accidental eye contact. He hated that feeling—at the bank, in elevators—when you inadvertently catch someone's eye, and she feels compelled to show you she's not interested. They did that sometimes, looked away pointedly before you even realized you were looking at them. Lincoln had apologized to a woman once when their eyes had met, unintentionally, over a gas pump. She'd pretended not to hear him and looked away.

"If you don't get a date," Eve kept threatening, "I'm going to start fixing you up with nice, Lutheran girls. Hard-core Lutherans. Missouri Synod."

"You wouldn't," he told her. "If any of your church friends met Mom, it would totally ruin your rep. Nobody would want to sit next to you at adult Bible study."

The woman in the break room laughed and shook her head. "You're being perverse," she said. She was so preoccupied with her argument, it almost felt safe to watch her. She was wearing faded jeans and a soft green jacket that inched up when she bent over to get her coffee. There were freckles on the small of her back. Lincoln looked away.

"There's nothing wrong with you, Lincoln," his sister would tell him. "You've been on dates. You've had a girlfriend. There is nothing about you that is inherently un-dateable."

"Is this supposed to be a pep talk? Because all I'm hearing is 'inherently un-dateable.'"

Lincoln had been on dates. He'd had a girlfriend. He'd seen the small of a woman's back before. He'd stood at concerts and football games and basement parties with his hand on a woman's back, on Sam's back, with his fingers sliding inside her sweater. He'd felt like he was getting away with some secret intimacy, touching her like that when no one was paying attention.

Lincoln wasn't inherently un-dateable. He'd gone on a date three years ago. A friend's sister had needed a date to a wedding. She'd danced all night with one of the groomsmen, who turned out to be her second cousin, while Lincoln ate exactly thirteen cream cheese mints.

He wasn't scared, exactly, to start dating again. He just couldn't visualize it. He could imagine himself a year in, at the comfortable place, the hand-at-the-small-of-the-back place. But the meeting, the making a girl like him . . . He was useless at all that.

"I don't believe that," Eve said. "You met Sam. You made her fall in love with you."

He hadn't, actually. He hadn't even noticed Sam before she started poking him in the shoulder during tenth-grade world geography. "You have very nice posture," she'd said. "Did you know you have a mole on the back of your neck?

"I spend a lot of time looking at the back of your neck," she said. "I could probably identify your body if there was ever an accident. As long as your neck wasn't hopelessly disfigured."

It made him blush. The next day, she told him that he smelled like peaches. She was loud. And funny. (But not as funny as loud.) And it was nothing for her to look you straight in the eye—in front of people—and say, "No, really, Lincoln, you smell like peaches." And she would laugh, and he would blush.

She liked embarrassing him. She liked that she could.

When she asked him to Homecoming, he thought that it might be a joke, that she'd spend the night teasing him in front of her friends. But he said yes anyway. And she didn't.

Sam was different when they were alone. She was quiet—well, quieter—and he could tell her anything, even things that mattered. She liked to talk about things that mattered. She was wholehearted, and fierce.

He hadn't made Sam fall in love with him. She just did.

And he'd loved her back.

Lincoln looked up at the coffee machine. The man in the rumpled shirt and the girl with the freckles were gone.

CHAPTER 7

From: Beth Fremont
To: Jennifer Scribner-Snyder
Sent: Mon, 08/30/1999 11:24 AM
Subject: Who looks good in a strapless dress?

Not just strapless. A strapless sheath. Who can pull that off?

<<**Jennifer to Beth**>> Um, Joan Collins. Lynda Carter. Shania Twain . . .

<<**Beth to Jennifer**>>
1. Do you only watch the Lifetime Network? Or do you also occasionally watch *Hollywood Squares*?
2. Even those lovely ladies would look hippy standing next to my sister's bridesmaids. They're all 20 years old and have "I might not be throwing up in the Tri-Delt bathroom after dinner, but my roommate is, and I like to borrow her jeans" hips.

Maybe I could have gotten away with a strapless sheath once . . . for like one day in 1989, but that day is long gone.

<<**Jennifer to Beth**>> Ten years gone.

<<**Beth to Jennifer**>> Thanks for that. Oh, and did I tell you that the wedding might have a theme? Kiley's fiancé wants to do something with the New Millennium.

<<**Jennifer to Beth**>> What does that even mean?

<<Beth to Jennifer>> Damned if I know. I wish it meant that I could wear a silver jumpsuit.

<<Jennifer to Beth>> Maybe your sister would let you wear a wrap or a sweater or something so that you won't feel so exposed.

<<Beth to Jennifer>> That's a good idea. Maybe I could talk Gwen into wearing one, too, so that I'm not the only one.

<<Jennifer to Beth>> Your sister Gwen is in the wedding? She's not a teeny-tiny Tri-Delt. You won't be the only life-size bridesmaid.

<<Beth to Jennifer>> No, you're right. You're right. I'm not sure why I'm getting so upset about this. This dress, this wedding. I really am happy for Kiley. And for you and every other happily married lady.

Except for that I'm not happy for you. I kind of want you all to drop dead. When Kiley showed me her ring—platinum, 1.4 carats—I really wanted to say something mean about it. Who really needs a ring that big? I ask you. It was rings that big that made our grandmothers think Elizabeth Taylor was a whore.

And then I actually did say something mean, quite a few somethings mean.

We were at the bridal shop for our first fitting (yes, already), and I said that sage green is the color of dirty aquarium water. And that polyester crepe smells like B.O. even before you put it on.

And when she told us her wedding song—of course, they've already picked their wedding song, and of course, it's "What a Wonderful World" by Louis Armstrong—I said that choosing that song is the sonic equivalent of buying picture frames and never replacing the photos of the models.

<<Jennifer to Beth>> Ouch. Are you still in the wedding?

<<Beth to Jennifer>> I'm still the maid of honor.

Nobody was listening to me snipe. Kiley was trying on veils, and the other bridesmaids were too busy counting each other's ribs to pay attention.

I felt like such a lousy human being when I left that bridal shop. I felt bad for making a scene. I felt mad that no one had noticed. I felt like the sort of person who would set something on fire just to get attention. Which suddenly seemed like a really good idea . . .

Setting something on fire. Something made of polyester crepe.

I couldn't torch Kiley's dress—not yet, I won't even get it for 10 to 12 weeks—but I have a whole closet full of dead dresses. Prom dresses. Bridesmaid dresses. I was all prepared to scoop them up in big fluffy armfuls and throw them into the Dumpster outside my building. I was going to light a cigarette in their flames, like I was the cool girl in *Heathers* . . .

But I couldn't. Because I'm not that girl. I'm not the Winona Ryder character in any movie. Jo from *Little Women,* just for example, never would have started laying all those dresses out on her bed and trying them on, one by one . . .

Including the off-the-shoulder number I wore to my brother's wedding 12 years ago. It's teal (that was 1987's sage green) with puffy sleeves and peach rosettes at the waist. Of course it was too tight, and of course it wouldn't zip—because I'm not 16 anymore. That's when it hit me—*I'm not 16 anymore.*

And I don't mean that in an offhand "well, *obviously*" way. I mean it like "Jack and Diane." Like, "Oh, yeah, life goes on, long after the thrill of living is gone."

I'm not even the same person who could zip up that dress. That person thought that wearing an ugly dress on the happiest day of someone else's life was just the beginning—the line you have to stand in to get to your own happiest day.

There is no such line. There's just the waiting room scene from *Beetlejuice.* (Another movie where I'm not Winona.)

I had dresses spread all over the spare bedroom when Chris came home. I tried to come up with some normal reason to be wearing a dusty bridesmaid dress and crying. But he reeked of cigarette smoke and went straight in to take a shower, so I didn't have to explain—which was even more upsetting because what I really wanted was for someone *else* to feel sorry for me.

<<Jennifer to Beth>> I feel sorry for you.

<<Beth to Jennifer>> Really?

<<Jennifer to Beth>> Really. I think you're pathetic. It's almost painfully embarrassing to read your messages when you're like this.

<<Beth to Jennifer>> You know just what to say to a girl. Next you'll be telling me that I'll make a beautiful bride someday . . .

<<Jennifer to Beth>> You will. Of course you will. And by the time Chris gets around to asking you, I'll bet everyone will get married in silver jumpsuits.

CHAPTER 8

"WHAT DO YOU care if they pay you to sit there?" Lincoln's sister asked.

He'd called Eve because he was bored. Because he'd already read everything in the WebFence folder. He'd read some of it twice . . .

Beth and Jennifer again. He didn't send them a warning. Again. He was starting to feel like he knew them, like they were his work friends. Weird. Yet another reason to quit this job.

"I *don't* care," he said to Eve.

"You must. You called me to whine about it."

"I'm not whining," Lincoln said, a little too forcefully.

"This was supposed to be your nothing job. You told me you wanted a job that wouldn't take too much brainpower, so that you could devote all your energy to deciding what to do next."

"That's true."

"So, what do you care if they're paying you to do nothing? That sounds ideal. Use that time to read *What Color Is Your Parachute?* Start working on your five-year plan." She was practically shouting to be heard over some mechanical noise.

"Are you vacuuming?"

"I'm DustBust-ing," she said.

"Stop. It makes you sound strident."

"I am strident."

"Well, it makes you sound excessively strident," he said. "Now I don't remember what I was saying."

"You were whining about getting paid to do nothing." Eve turned off the DustBuster.

"It's just that getting paid to do nothing is a constant reminder that I'm *doing* nothing," Lincoln said. "And doing nothing takes more energy than you'd think. I'm tired all the time."

"How could you possibly be tired all the time? Every time I call, you're asleep."

"Eve, I don't get off work until one in the morning."

"You should still be awake by noon."

"I get home at one thirty. I'm wired. I mess around on the computer for another hour or two. I fall asleep at, like, four. I get up at one, one thirty. And then I spend the next three hours thinking about how there's not enough time to do anything before I go to work. I watch *Quantum Leap* reruns and mess around on the computer some more. I go to work. Rinse. Repeat. 'Second verse same as the first.'"

"That sounds awful, Lincoln."

"It is awful."

"You should quit that job."

"I should quit this job . . . ," he said, "but if I keep it, I can move out of Mom's house."

"How soon?"

"As soon as I want. The money's good."

"Don't quit," Eve said firmly. "Move out. Find a new job. *Then* quit."

He knew she would say that. In Eve's mind, all of Lincoln's problems would go away if he moved out of their mother's house. "You'll never have your own life as long as you live there," Eve told him whenever she had the chance. She'd tell him to keep a job at a meatpacking plant if it meant getting his own apartment.

But Lincoln wasn't sure he even wanted to move out. He liked his mom's house. He liked the way everything about it was already broken in. Lincoln had the whole upstairs to himself; he even had his own bathroom. And he usually didn't mind being around his mom. He wished she would give him a little more space sometimes. *Head*space.

"Don't you hate telling people that you still live at home?" Eve would ask.

"Who asks me where I live?"

"New people."

"I don't meet any new people."

"You won't *ever* meet any new people as long as you're living at home."

"Who am I going to meet if I get my own apartment? Do you see me hanging out at the pool? Starting conversations in the community weight room?"

"Maybe," she said. "Why not? You know how to swim."

"I don't like apartment complexes. I don't like the carpet and the little concrete balconies and the cabinets."

"What's wrong with the cabinets?"

"They're made of fiberboard, and they smell like mice."

"Gross, Lincoln. Whose apartments have you even been in?"

"I have friends who live in apartments."

"Gross apartments, apparently."

"Single-guy apartments. You don't know what it's like."

Eve had moved out when she was nineteen. She'd married Jake, a guy she'd met at community college. He was ten years older and in the air force. He bought her a ranch-style house in the suburbs, and Eve painted every room a different shade of cream.

Lincoln used to sleep over at their house on weekends. He was eleven, and Eve let him have his own bedroom. "You're always welcome here," she told him. "Always. For as long as you want. This is your home, too."

He liked staying at Eve and Jake's house, but he never felt like he needed to escape to it. He'd never felt like he needed to escape from their mother, not like Eve had. He didn't understand the anger between them. He didn't even recognize his mother in the stories Eve told.

"Mom never had a bong," he'd protest.

"Oh yes, she did. It was made out of a Dr Pepper bottle, and she kept it on the coffee table."

"Now I know you're lying. Mom would never drink Dr Pepper."

WHEN LINCOLN GOT to work the next afternoon, Greg was arguing with someone on the phone. He'd hired an outside consultant to take care of the newspaper's Y2K issues, and now the consultant was saying he wouldn't be able to get to *The Courier* until early February. Greg called the guy a charlatan and a one-eyed gypsy, and hung up on him.

"I can help with the Y2K stuff," Lincoln said. "I've done some programming."

"Yeah," Greg said, "we'll have you, me . . . a couple of eighth-grade magnet students . . . I'm sure it'll be fine . . ." He turned off his computer by yanking the power cord from the surge strip. Lincoln cringed. "'Despite all my rage, I am still just a rat in a cage,'" Greg said, gathering up his papers and jacket. "See you tomorrow, Senator."

Huh. Programming. Debugging. It wasn't Lincoln's favorite, but it beat archiving and compressing. At least it was a problem to solve. And it would only be for a few months, maybe less.

He checked the WebFence folder. There were only two red flags. Which meant Lincoln had anywhere from thirty seconds to five minutes of actual work to get him through the night. He'd already decided to save it for after dinner.

Tonight, he had a plan.

Well . . . a plan to make a plan. He'd gotten up early that day, at noon, and gone to the library to check out that parachute book Eve had mentioned. It was in his backpack right now with a copy of today's want ads, a yellow highlighter, a ten-year-old Mead notebook, an *Entertainment Weekly*, and a turkey sandwich that smelled so good he was having a hard time thinking about anything else.

He was done with the sandwich and the magazine by seven.

He thought about looking at the want ads next or cracking *What Color Is Your Parachute?*—but reached for the notebook instead. He laid it on the desk and carefully leafed through the pages, through notes on the Revolutionary War and the rough draft of an essay on *Brave New World*.

Lincoln knew what he was looking for; somewhere near the middle, there it was . . . Sam's handwriting. Purple ink. Too many capital letters.

"THINGS LINCOLN IS GOOD AT."

SHE'D MADE THIS list for him senior year when he was trying to choose his major. Lincoln had already known where he was going to college— wherever Sam was going.

His mother had wanted him to stay close to home. He'd been offered a regent's scholarship at the state university just forty-five minutes away. But Sam would never go there. Sam wanted to go somewhere big and important and FAR AWAY. And Lincoln wanted to go with her. Whenever his mom brought up the scholarship, how nice the state campus was, how he could come home to do his laundry . . . Lincoln would think of Sam loading her things into her dad's minivan and heading west like the last sunset. He could do his own laundry.

So he let Sam do all the school shopping. She sent away for brochures and went on weekend trips to see campuses. "I want to be near the ocean, Lincoln, the ocean! I want to feel the tides. I want to look like one of those girls who live by the ocean, with the windblown hair and the color in their cheeks. And I want mountains, too, at least one mountain. Is that too much to ask? And trees. Not a whole forest, necessarily. I'd settle for a thicket. Scenery. I want scenery!" Something to chew on, Lincoln thought.

Sam picked a college in California—not too far from the ocean, not too far from the mountains—with a tree-lined campus and a robust theater program. Lincoln was accepted, too, and offered half a dozen scholarships.

Technically, he said to his mother, it's the same amount of scholarship money the state school is offering. "Yes," she said, "but the tuition is four times as much."

"You're not paying for it," he said.

"What a mean thing to say."

"I didn't mean it to be mean." He didn't.

He knew she felt bad that she couldn't pay for college. Well, he knew that she felt bad sometimes. College was his thing. She expected him to pay for it the same way she had expected him to pay for his own Nintendo.

"You can have it if you want it, if you're willing to pay for it. Save your money."

"I don't have any money," he'd said in the ninth grade.

"Be thankful, Lincoln. Money is a cruel thing. It's the thing that stands between you and the things you want and the people you love."

"How does money come between you and the people you love?"

"It's coming between us right now."

It wasn't really the tuition that bothered his mother about California. She didn't want him to go to California because she didn't want him to go. She didn't want him to go so far. And she didn't want him to go so far with Sam.

His mother didn't like Sam.

She thought Sam was self-centered and manipulative. ("Pot. Kettle. Black," Eve said.) His mother thought Sam was loud. And pushy. And too full of opinions. She complained when Lincoln spent too much time at Sam's house. But when he brought Sam home, that was worse. Sam would do something—rearrange the spice cabinet, turn on too many lights, say that she couldn't stand green peppers or anything with walnuts or Susan Sarandon—that irritated his mother. "Is she always like that, Lincoln?"

"Like what?"

"Is she always so *much*?"

"Yes," he'd said, trying not to sound as happy as he felt. "Always."

His mother tolerated the Sam situation, mostly quietly, for about a year. Then she started talking to Lincoln about how young he was, too young to be so serious about one person. She asked him to slow down, to think about seeing other girls. She said to him, "It's like buying shirts, Lincoln. When you go shopping for shirts, you don't buy the first shirt you try on. Even if you like it. You keep looking, you keep trying things on. You make sure you find the shirt that fits you best."

"But Mom, what if the first shirt is the best shirt? And what if it's gone by the time I'm done shopping? What if I never find a shirt like that again?"

She wasn't used to him arguing with her. "This isn't about shirts, Lincoln."

She always used his name when she talked to him. No one else said his name unless they were trying to get his attention. It was like she was patting herself on the back for thinking of such a great name—or maybe trying to remind him that it was *she* who had named him. That he was her doing. Once, during those mildly turbulent teenage years, the Sam years, he had yelled at his mother, "You don't understand me!"

"Of course I understand you, Lincoln," she replied. "I'm your mother. No one will ever know you like I do. No one will ever love you like I do."

Sam had proved his mother wrong.

And then had proved her right.

But before all that, Sam had sat on his bed with a green Mead notebook and said, "Come on, Lincoln, you have to pick a major."

"You pick my major," he'd said. He'd laid his head on her lap and kept reading a paperback, something with swords and goblin queens.

"Lincoln. Seriously. You have to declare a major. It's required. Let's focus here. What do you want to do with your life?"

He set down his paperback and smiled at her until she smiled back at him. "You," he said, touching his thumb to her chin.

"You can't major in me."

He turned back to his book. "Then I'll figure it out later."

She snatched the book from his hands. "Can we please just talk about this? Seriously?"

He sighed and sat up next to her. "Okay. We're talking."

"Okay." She smiled, she was getting her way. "Now, think about it, what do you want to do for a living?"

"I don't know."

"What do you think you *might* want to do?"

"I don't know."

"What are you good at? And don't say you don't know."

He didn't say anything at all. She stopped smiling. "Fine," she said. "We'll make a list." She opened the notebook and wrote *THINGS LINCOLN IS GOOD AT* at the top of the page.

"Dangling preposition," he said. "Dubious start."

Number one, she wrote, *Grammar.*

"And spelling," he said. "I won the fifth-grade spelling bee."

2. Spelling.

3. Math.

"I'm not good at math."

"You are," she said. "You're in honors calculus."

"I'm good enough to be in honors calculus, but I'm not good at honors calculus. I'm getting a B."

She underlined "*Math.*"

"What else?" she asked him.

"I don't like this," he said.

"What. Else." She poked him in the chest with the end of her purple ink pen.

"I don't know. History. I'm good at history."

4. History.

"You're good at physics, too," she said, "and social studies. I saw your report card."

"You're making it seem like I'm good at six different things, when really it's all the same thing." He took the pen and put a line through her list. In the margin, he wrote:

1. School.

Sam took the pen back.

2. Ruining perfectly good lists.

He reached for the pen again. "No," she said, "this isn't your list anymore. It's mine."

"Fine with me." He picked up his paperback and put his arm around her waist, tucking her into his side. She kept writing. He kept reading. An hour or so later, he walked her to her car. When he got back to his room, he found the notebook open on his pillow.

THINGS LINCOLN IS GOOD AT

1. School.
2. Ruining perfectly good lists.
3. Avoiding the issue.

4. Not worrying about things he REALLY should worry about.

5. Not worrying about things he really shouldn't worry about.

6. Staying calm/Being calm/Calmness.

7. Turning the page with one hand.

8. Reading.

9. And writing.

10. Pretty much anything to do with WORDS.

11. And pretty much anything to do with NUMBERS.

12. Guessing what teachers want.

13. Guessing what I want.

14. SECOND BASE. (Ha.)

15. Laughing at my jokes.

16. Remembering jokes.

17. Remembering song lyrics.

18. Singing.

19. Unfreezing computers/Untangling necklaces.

20. Explaining confusing things/Giving good driving directions.

21. Driving in bad weather.

22. Reaching things.

23. Being helpful.

24. Being cute.

25. Making me feel cute.

26. Making me feel RAVISHING.

27. Ravishing.

28. Making me feel important.

29. And loved.

30. Listening to me when no one else can STAND to anymore.

31. Looking at me like he knows something I don't.

32. Knowing things I don't.

33. Being SMART.

34. Being SENSITIVE.
35. Being KIND.
36. Being GOOD.

The next morning, when she came to pick him up for school, Sam told Lincoln that she'd chosen a major for him. "American Studies," she said.

"What's that?"

"It's kind of everything. Like everything that's happened in America. And everything that is happening. And pop culture. It's putting things together and making them make sense."

"That sounds fascinating," he said.

"Don't be sarcastic," she said.

"I'm not. That sounds fascinating. That sounds perfect."

It was February, and Sam was wearing a puffy pink jacket and a white scarf around her neck. He tugged the scarf down to kiss her. "Perfect for me," he said.

SAM'S FAMILY THREW her a going-away party that August, just a few days before she and Lincoln left together for California. Her parents bought fireworks and rented a karaoke machine. The party was still going strong when Lincoln fell asleep on a lawn chair around midnight. He wasn't sure what time it was when Sam squeezed into the chair next to him. She smelled like the fifth of July, like sweat and spent bottle rockets.

"Did you say your good-byes?" he asked.

She nodded her head. "I said your good-byes, too. You kissed everybody full on the mouth. It was kind of embarrassing."

"Show me."

She kissed him quickly. She seemed strange, urgent and jittery. Wide-awake.

"Are you okay?" Lincoln asked.

"Umm . . . I think so, yeah. I don't know. God, I don't know what I am."

She stood up from the lawn chair and walked across her parents' deck, picking up dirty plastic cups, then setting them down again.

"I just feel . . . ready."

"Ready for what?" Lincoln sat up and tried harder to follow what she was saying. The moon was thin, he couldn't see her face.

"I'm ready for everything to change," she said. She sat down on a picnic table and started fiddling with streamers. "I feel like it already has. Like, I thought I was going to be so sad saying good-bye to everybody. I thought I was going to cry and cry—and I didn't. I didn't feel like crying at all. I felt like singing. I felt, like, God, yes, good-bye! Not good riddance, just good-bye.

"I am so ready for new people," she said, throwing the streamers into the air. "In two days, I'm going to be in a place where I can walk around without recognizing a single face. Every person will be brand-new. Just, like, fresh and full of potential. Nothing but potential. I won't know any of their stories. Nobody will be on my last nerve."

He walked over to the picnic table and sat next to her. "For thirty-six hours."

"What's that supposed to mean?"

"Just that you're very in touch with your last nerve."

She tilted her chin up. "Maybe that's about to change. I'll be brand-new, too. Maybe the new me will be patient."

"Maybe." He put his arm around her. She was so small, he felt like could hug all of her at once.

"Don't you feel it, Lincoln? Like everything is changing?"

He held her tight. "Not everything."

LINCOLN HAD DUG out this notebook a dozen times since high school. He took it out every time he changed his major, every time he started a new program or finished a degree.

He kept hoping that he would see something on the list that he'd missed all the other times, some basic truth about himself, a clue about what he should be doing. Or shouldn't be doing. How had his life gotten stuck at No. 19, unfreezing computers? Because a person couldn't make a living untangling necklaces? Why couldn't he be stuck at No. 29? Or even 27 . . .

Whenever Lincoln looked at this list, he always ended up thinking more about Sam than his career path. He didn't get to the want ads that night or to his parachute or his plan.

CHAPTER 9

From: Jennifer Scribner-Snyder
To: Beth Fremont
Sent: Wed, 09/01/1999 1:14 PM
Subject: Do you want to hang out tonight?

I need a break from Mitch. He's still in a funk about our successful use of birth control.

<<**Beth to Jennifer**>> Can't. I'm finally going to see *Eyes Wide Shut*.

<<**Jennifer to Beth**>> Ech. I don't like Tom Cruise.

<<**Beth to Jennifer**>> Me neither. But I usually like Tom Cruise movies.

<<**Jennifer to Beth**>> Me, too . . . Huh, maybe I *do* like Tom Cruise. But I hate feeling pressured to find him attractive. I don't.

<<**Beth to Jennifer**>> Nobody does. It's a lie perpetuated by the American media. Tom Cruise and Julia Roberts.

<<**Jennifer to Beth**>> Men don't like Julia Roberts?

<<**Beth to Jennifer**>> Nope. Her teeth scare them.

<<**Jennifer to Beth**>> Good to know.

CHAPTER 10

WHEN LINCOLN CAME downstairs Thursday morning, his mother was leaning over the kitchen table, scraping lime green paint off a dresser drawer. There were flakes of paint all over the table and floor. There were chips in her hair and in the butter dish. This sort of thing gave Eve a migraine. "Didn't you just paint that dresser?" Lincoln asked.

"Yes . . . I did." She frowned at the drawer.

"Why are you scraping it?"

"It was supposed to be 'Meadow Path.' That's what it said on the paint chip. This isn't 'Meadow Path.' This is lime."

"Did it look more 'Meadow Path' on the paint chip?"

"Of course it did. It said 'Meadow Path' right there, so it couldn't help but look meadow-y. But look at it, it's clearly lime."

"Mom, can I ask you something?"

"Of course. There are biscuits in the oven, and ham gravy. I'll get you some. Do you want honey? We have fresh honey from local bees. Did you know that it's better to eat honey from local bees?"

"I've never thought about it . . . ," he said, trying not to sound impatient.

"It's better. Because the bees eat the pollen from the plants that grow around you, and then, I guess you're less likely to be allergic to those plants."

"I don't think I have any allergies."

"You're so fortunate. Maybe we've been buying local honey all along."

"Mom, do you find Tom Cruise attractive?"

His mother set down her chisel. She looked at Lincoln as if she was trying to decide whether he was "Meadow Path" or lime.

"Honey, do *you* find Tom Cruise attractive?"

"Mom. No. Why would you ask that? Jesus."

"Why would *you* ask that?"

"I asked if you found Tom Cruise attractive. I didn't ask if you thought I was gay. Do you think I'm gay?"

"I didn't say that," she said. "I have thought, occasionally, that maybe, you might, but I wasn't saying that. I was just trying to help you."

"Help me what?"

"Help you tell me, if you were. Which you're not. You're saying you're not, right?"

"*Yes.* I mean, I'm not. Are you serious with this?"

"Well, Lincoln, you have to admit, it would explain a lot."

"What? What would it explain?"

"It would explain why you don't have a girlfriend. Why you haven't had a girlfriend for, you know, honey, a long time. Since Sam, right? And frankly, it would explain Sam."

"How would that explain Sam?"

"Well, she wasn't very womanly, was she?"

"She was plenty womanly."

His mother wrinkled her nose and shrugged. "She seemed boyish to me. She didn't have breasts."

Lincoln pressed a palm into one eye. "She had breasts."

"Really," his mother said flatly. She had a way of asking "really" that wasn't ever a question. It was more of a challenge.

"I'm not gay."

"Of course you're not gay."

"I was just, I was going to ask you if you found Tom Cruise attractive because I don't find Julia Roberts attractive, and I was wondering if it was maybe all a big lie perpetuated by the media."

"You don't find Julia Roberts attractive? Huh. Really."

———

ON FRIDAY, LINCOLN got up late. He caught the last half of *Quantum Leap*, helped his mom move a couch, then met his sister at the mall to help her pick out a new cell phone. They ate hot dogs afterward in the food court, and Lincoln showed Eve his library book.

"So," she asked, "what color *is* your parachute?"

"Green," he guessed. It could be green.

Eve was so pleased with this progress that she insisted on buying him an Orange Julius. Then she remembered that he was making more money than she was now and insisted that he buy *her* an Orange Julius.

That night at work, he felt like he was wearing somebody else's pants. A thinner somebody else's pants. He shouldn't have eaten two hot dogs. He should get some exercise. Maybe he could sneak a piece of exercise equipment into the office. What could he fit in his backpack? Free weights? A ThighMaster? His mom's inflatable yoga ball?

He ate three cartons of vending machine yogurt for dinner and spent four hours playing Tetris on his computer. Maybe he could sneak in his PlayStation, too. He could still see the Tetris blocks falling on the inside of his eyelids when he finally checked the WebFence folder.

CHAPTER 11

From: Beth Fremont
To: Jennifer Scribner-Snyder
Sent: Fri, 09/03/1999 2:08 PM
Subject: This weekend.

Hey, all this week's movies came out on Wednesday, so I have tonight off, and Chris has a show. Do you still need a break from your funky husband? Do you want to get together? See a movie or something?

<<**Jennifer to Beth**>> Why would you want to see a movie when you have the night off from seeing movies? I don't write headlines on my days off. (Though I do correct grammar. It gets on Mitch's nerves.)

I would love to see a movie, but tonight is North's first home game. Mitch will have already set out the blue-and-gold sweatshirt he bought me for my birthday. My evening will be spent sitting on a cold, hard bleacher, watching my husband conduct "Tequila" and "All Hail the Golden Vikings." (And weirdly enjoying it.)

Hey, why don't you join us? Come to the game. I'll even let you borrow some Vikingwear—how do you feel about stocking hats with horns?

<<**Beth to Jennifer**>> Hey, why don't I? Maybe because I'm still too cool to sit with the band kids?

I don't know . . . I guess that could be fun. I could make scandalous eye contact with hot high school guys.

<<Jennifer to Beth>> High school guys only appear hot to high school girls. It's something to do with the fluorescent lighting in the classrooms, I think. They're actually really skinny and spotty, and they have giant feet. Why don't you go to Chris's show?

<<Beth to Jennifer>> I don't go to his shows anymore. And I know you're going to ask me why not, so I'll just tell you:

In college, I never missed a show. I would spend an hour putting on eyeliner and another hour putting on Chris's eyeliner. I'd get to the club early, help them set up, sit through the first two bands, then make sure I was sitting front and left, so that when he looked up from his guitar, I would be at the center of his field of vision. Like Courteney Cox in the "Dancing in the Dark" video. It was nirvana. (Pre-Nirvana nirvana.)

And then I started working for the Entertainment section. And all of Chris's friends found out about my job and started coming up to me during shows to give me tapes and pretend that they liked me.

And then Stef and Chris got in that fight about me working for the newspaper . . .

And I work most weekend nights anyway, so . . .

It's just easier to stay home on show nights and wait up for him.

<<Jennifer to Beth>> What fight? And doesn't Chris miss you at the shows? (You never talk about college. I can just see you swooning, in full groupie mode.)

<<Beth to Jennifer>> I do so talk about college. Don't I? I loved college. I wish I could go back.

The fight was stupid: Stef was convinced that the band would get better coverage if I didn't work for *The Courier.*

<<Jennifer to Beth>> Ooo, I hate Stef. He has Yoko Ono issues.

And actually, you don't talk about college. I don't even know how you and Chris met.

<<Beth to Jennifer>> Amen on the Yoko issues. It's because he likes to think he's Paul McCartney. But Paul McCartney is a gentle soul. And a monogamist.

<<Jennifer to Beth>> And a knight.

<<Beth to Jennifer>> And an animal rights activist! The closest Stef gets to Sir Paul McCartney is by being a pothead.
You know how I met Chris. At the Student Union.

<<Jennifer to Beth>> *"At the Student Union."* That's not how you met, that's where you met. I want to know whether it was love at first sight. Who noticed whom first. The whole deal.
And you didn't answer my question: Doesn't he miss you at the shows?

<<Beth to Jennifer>> Honestly, I think it's easier for him if I don't come to watch him play. The rest of the guys in the band are wild-and-crazy single guys. I don't drink much, and I don't smoke at all, and I can't resist commenting on their totally immature and sexist behavior. I cramp their style.

<<Jennifer to Beth>> You would think that a band called Sacajawea would be more supportive of free-thinking women.

<<Beth to Jennifer>> You always say that.

<<Jennifer to Beth>> I do not, I've said it only once before, but it's so pithy, I couldn't resist repeating myself. ("Pithy," that's what I would call my band.)

<<Beth to Jennifer>> I would call your band "Pithetic."
Anyway. Thanks for the invite to the game, but I think I'm going to see a movie tonight. (More high school guys for you.) *The Matrix* is at the dollar theater. And I actually like going to movies on my night off. It's relaxing. I don't feel like I have to think critically, or even pay attention.
Maybe I'll even stop in to see Sacajawea after the movie. You're making me feel like a bad girlfriend.

<<Jennifer to Beth>> You should put on lots of eyeliner and stand up front.

<<Beth to Jennifer>> I don't know, maybe.

CHAPTER 12

LINCOLN FELT LIKE going out that weekend. Really out.

Usually, on Saturday nights, he played Dungeons & Dragons. He'd been playing with the same five or six people since college. This was another thing Eve thought was holding him back.

"It's almost like you're *trying* not to meet girls," she'd said.

"There are girls there," he'd argued. One, anyway. Christine had always been the only girl in their group. Right after college, she'd married Dave, a burly guy who liked to be Dungeon Master, and the game had permanently moved to their living room.

"Couldn't you and your Dungeons & Dragons friends do something *else* together," Eve had suggested. "Like, go somewhere where you could *all* meet girls?"

"I don't think so," Lincoln said. "All the other guys are married."

Well, except for Troy. And even Lincoln could tell that Troy wasn't the kind of guy you took to meet girls. Troy thought that everyone—really, everyone—wanted to talk about *Babylon 5*. He had a bushy yellow beard and metal-framed, math-teacher eyeglasses, and he liked to wear leather vests.

Maybe Eve was right. Maybe Lincoln needed to branch out.

He called Troy on Friday to tell him that he'd have to find another ride to this week's D&D game. (Troy didn't believe in owning a car.) And then Lincoln called Justin.

Justin was exactly the kind of guy you took to meet girls.

Lincoln and Justin had gone to high school together. They'd both played varsity golf and were chemistry lab partners, and when Lincoln transferred to Nebraska his sophomore year of college—or for what would have been his sophomore year—they'd ended up in the same dormitory.

Justin immediately welcomed Lincoln into his pack of college friends. They used to hang out in each other's rooms, playing Sega Genesis and ordering terrible pizza. Sometimes, they'd go to women's gymnastics meets. Sometimes, somebody would score a case of beer.

Justin's friends probably weren't the kind of guys Lincoln would have sought out on his own. But they accepted him without question, and he was grateful. He started wearing a baseball cap every day and got really good at "Sonic the Hedgehog."

The next year, the rest of the guys got an apartment together off campus. Lincoln stayed in the dorm because his scholarship covered it. He didn't see them as much after that . . . He hadn't talked to Justin for at least two years, which was also how long it had been since he'd been in a bar.

"Legend of Linc! Dude. What is up, you evil-fucking-genius?"

"You know, the usual." Lincoln had called Justin at the hospital where he worked in marketing. Lincoln didn't get why a hospital needed a marketing department; who did it market to, sick people?

"Are you still in school?" Justin asked.

"No, I graduated . . . again. I'm back in town, living with my mom, you know, for now."

"Hey, man, welcome home. Let's get together. Let's catch up. I'll be honest with you, I could use the company. Are you married?"

"Not even close."

"Good. I swear to God, every other fucker has flat-out deserted me. What am I supposed to do, go to the bars alone? Like some pervert? I've been partying with my little brother, and it's no fucking good. He borrows money, and he always gets the girl. He still has hair, the little shit."

"That's why I was calling, actually," Lincoln said, relieved that Justin was already taking charge. "I work a lot of nights now, so it's hard to get out, but I thought we could try to get together, maybe . . ."

"Let's do it, homeslice. Do you work tomorrow night?"

"No. Tomorrow night's great."

"I'll pick you up at nine, is that cool? Is your mom still in the same place?"

"Yeah, yeah," Lincoln said, smiling into the phone. "Same place, same house. I'll see you at nine."

JUSTIN PULLED UP in the biggest sport-utility vehicle Lincoln had ever seen. Bright yellow. Tinted windows. Justin leaned out the driver's side and shouted, "Dude, come on, you're riding shotgun."

There were three or four guys already sitting in the back. Lincoln thought he recognized Justin's little brother. He looked like Justin, but a little taller, a little fresher. Justin himself hadn't changed much since high school. A short guy with crinkly eyes and dirty-blond hair. Clean Polo shirt. No-nonsense jeans. An immaculate baseball cap. He used to have a contraption in his dorm room that would perfectly curve the bill of your cap.

"Look at you," Justin said, smiling. He could smile and talk without ever taking the cigarette out of his mouth. "Just fucking look at you."

"It's good to see you," Lincoln said, not quite loud enough to be heard over the car stereo. It was Guns N' Roses, "Welcome to the Jungle." Lincoln couldn't see the speakers, but it felt like they were under him.

"What?" Justin yelled, leaning out the window to exhale some smoke. He was always really nice about that. If you were sitting across from Justin at a table, he would always blow the smoke behind him.

"Where are the speakers?" Lincoln shouted. "Are they in the seats?"

"Hell, yes. Fucking awesome, right? It's like having Axl Rose in your asshole."

"You wish," someone shouted from the backseat. There were three backseats. Justin held up his middle finger and kept talking.

"Don't mind these shitheads. I had to bring them, it's my turn to be designated driver. They won't kill our game, though, they hang in the kiddie section."

"No worries," Lincoln said.

"What?"

"No worries!" Lincoln wasn't worried. He didn't have any game to kill.

They drove into the suburbs and stopped at a strip mall, in front of a place called The Steel Guitar.

"Isn't this a country bar?" Lincoln asked.

"It used to be, back when everybody was into line dancing. Now they only do that shit once a week. Thursdays, I think."

"What do they do the rest of the week?"

"The usual. This is where the girls go, so this is where we go."

The place was already packed. There were people on the dance floor, and loud hip-hop music was playing—the ugliest kind of hip-hop, all thumping and shouting about luxury cars. Justin found a tall table near the dance floor and motioned to one of the waitresses, a woman wearing a bandolier full of shot glasses. There were bottles of alcohol clipped to her belt. It all looked really heavy. "Two Jägermeisters, miss," Justin said. "Thank you."

He pushed a shot toward Lincoln and held his own in the air.

"To you, Lincoln. The graduate!"

Lincoln clinked his glass and managed to down the shot.

"I thought you were the designated driver," Lincoln said.

"I am." Justin lit a new cigarette.

"I thought that meant you didn't drink."

"No, that means you don't get drunk. Or you get drunk early, so it can wear off . . ." Justin was already ordering two more shots and scoping out the bar.

It was big, practically cavernous, and everything was painted black. There was a haze machine somewhere and black lights everywhere. An expensive-looking metal guitar sculpture hung in the dark above the dance floor.

That's where all the girls were. Mostly dancing by themselves or with friends. There was a bachelorette party in the middle, dancing in a circle. It was terrible music to dance to; all you could really do was nod and hunch to the music. The girls all looked like they were listening to the same sad story. *"Yes, yes, yes, that's awful. Yes, yes, yes."*

A few girls had climbed onto raised black platforms at the back of the dance floor, beneath a row of green flashing lights. They were dancing with their hips together, mechanically riding each other's thighs and arching their backs. It was unpleasantly arousing to watch. Like masturbating in a portable toilet.

Justin was watching them, too. "Nasty things," he said, shaking his head. "When we were coming up, girls wouldn't even dance with boys like that . . .

"Look over there," Justin said, pointing to a table by the door. "Those are our girls. Too much self-esteem to dry hump their best friends, but not so much that they'll turn down a drink from us."

Justin was already walking, so Lincoln followed him. They stopped at a table where two women were sitting and nodding with the music. Lincoln couldn't tell how old they were in this light. He could hardly tell them apart. They were both youngish, mostly blond, wearing the same Saturday-night costume—tank tops, candy-colored bra straps, shaggy shoulder-length hair and pale beige lips.

"Hey there," Justin was saying, "do you mind if we join you? My friend Lincoln here is buying."

The girls smiled and moved their black backpack purses out of the way. Lincoln sat in the seat Justin didn't take and smiled at the nearest girl. Strangely, he wasn't nervous. This place and this girl were so far outside his everyday life, they didn't seem quite real. Definitely less real than the women he felt avoiding him on sidewalks and in hallways. Plus, he had Justin there taking the lead, breaking the ice and ordering the drinks. What was Justin's thing with Jägermeister? And how many shots had Lincoln had so far? Two? Three? At least three.

"I'm Lisa," the girl said, holding out a small manicured hand.

"Lincoln," he said, smiling. "Can I get you something?"

"Your friend just ordered for us."

"Oh, right, sorry, yeah . . ."

"I'll take a cigarette if you have one."

"Sorry," he said, "I don't smoke."

"That's okay. Me neither. I mean, I do, but only when I'm at a bar or a party or whatever. I hate the smell. But if I'm going to smell like smoke anyway, I figure I might as well have one."

"My friend has cigarettes . . ." Lincoln turned to Justin, who was already leading his girl to the dance floor. Damn. Lincoln really didn't want to dance.

"Don't worry about it," Lisa said.

"Do you want to dance?" Lincoln asked.

"Sort of. Do you?"

"I really don't. Is that okay?"

"Totally," she said. "You can't talk out there anyway."

Now Lincoln was nervous. Justin had taken all the night's momentum with him to the dance floor. "So," he asked the girl, "what do you do for a living?"

"I'm a dental hygienist. What about you?"

"Computers."

She smiled and nodded. "Computers," she said, "that's great." Her eyes started to drift away from him. They finished their drinks, and Lincoln ordered another round, just to have something to do. He should have eaten dinner. It's too bad this wasn't still a country bar, didn't country bars always have peanuts? Or was that only in the movies, to give the actors something to do with their hands . . .

Lisa was tearing her coaster into tiny pieces and whisper-rapping along with the music. He thought about getting up, so that she'd have a chance to meet somebody else. She could definitely meet somebody else. She was pretty . . . probably. In this green and black light, she looked like a week-old bruise. Everyone did.

"This is a terrible place to meet people," Lincoln said.

"What?" Lisa leaned forward.

"This is a terrible place to meet people," he said, louder.

Lisa was sipping her drink through a tiny straw. She stopped, the straw still in her mouth, and looked at him like she was trying to decide whether to leave the table right then or to wait for her friend. It might be a long wait. Justin and the girl had moved off the dance floor into a corner. When the spotlight whipped around, Lincoln could see them kissing. Justin was still holding a lit cigarette and a bottle of beer.

"Sorry," Lincoln said. "I didn't mean that you're a terrible person to meet. I meant that this is a terrible place to meet *anyone*." Lisa's eyes were still narrow. "Do you like this place?" he asked her.

"It's okay." She shrugged. "It's like every other bar."

"Exactly. They're all terrible."

"How much have you had to drink?" she asked. "Are you one of those sad drunks?"

"I don't know, I don't get drunk that often. How can you help but be sad in here?"

"I'm not sad," she said.

"Then you're not paying attention." He was shouting to be heard over the noise, but the shouting made his words come out angry. "I mean, *look* at this place. Listen to this music."

"Don't you like rap? They do country on Thursdays."

"No," he said, shaking his head broadly. "It's not the music," he said. "It's that, well, you came here to meet somebody, right? To meet a guy?"

"Right."

"To maybe meet *the* guy, right?"

She looked down at her drink. "Right."

"Well, when you think about that guy—who, by the way, we both know isn't me—when you think about meeting him, do you think about meeting him in a place like this? In a place this ugly? This loud? Do you want him to smell like Jägermeister and cigarettes? Do you want your first dance to be to a song about strippers?"

She looked around the bar and shrugged again. "Maybe."

"Maybe? No, of course you don't."

"Don't tell me what I want," Lisa said, digging in her friend's purse for a cigarette.

"You're right," Lincoln said. "I'm sorry."

She found a cigarette and put it in her mouth. It hung there, unlit. "Where else am I supposed to meet a guy?" she asked, watching the dancers. "Like, in a garden?"

"A garden would be nice," he said. "I'd pay a cover charge at a singles garden."

"That sounds like something they'd have at my mom's church." She went back to digging in her friend's purse. "I think if I met a guy, you know, *that* guy, I wouldn't care where I was or what he smelled like. I'd just be, like, *happy* . . .

"Look," she said, standing up, "it was nice to meet you. I'm going to try to find a light."

"Oh . . . um, right . . ." He started to stand, knocked his head against a neon Bud Light sign and sat back down. "It was nice to meet you, too," he said.

He felt like apologizing again, but didn't.

And he didn't watch her walk away.

LINCOLN WAS STILL sitting at the table an hour later when Justin came back. "Dude, I need a favor. I'm too fucked-up to drive. Can you take my truck home?"

"Um, I'm not sure if . . ."

"Linc, for real"—Justin set his keys on the table—"I'm going home with Dena."

"But what about those other guys, your brother . . ."

"I think they're gone."

"What?"

"I'll pick up the truck tomorrow. Leave the keys under the mat and lock the doors."

"I really don't think . . ." Lincoln picked up the keys and tried to hand them back to Justin. But Justin was already gone.

EVE WAS SITTING at the kitchen table when Lincoln came downstairs the next afternoon. He'd spent the night in one of Justin's backseats, then driven home sometime after dawn. His neck still felt like it was folded over an armrest, and his mouth tasted like licorice and sour meat. "What are you doing here?" he asked his sister.

"Well, good morning, sunshine. I brought the boys over to play with Mom."

He looked around the kitchen, then settled heavily into the chair next to his sister.

"They're in the backyard, building a fort," she said. "There are egg rolls on the stove. And fried rice, are you hungry?"

Lincoln nodded, but didn't move. He was already thinking about all the things he was going to do when he had the energy to stand up again. Like, go back to bed. That was the first thing.

"Geez," his sister said, getting up to make him a plate. "You must have had some night."

Standing at the stove, stirring the rice, Eve looked like a younger version of their mother—an *older* younger version. At thirty-six, Eve looked like their mother at forty-five. "Being responsible gives you wrinkles," his sister would say when their mother wasn't around. "Doesn't Eve look tired?" his mother would say, whether Eve was around or not.

"Mom says you didn't come home until seven," Eve said, handing him a plate. "She's livid, by the way."

"Why is she livid?"

"Because you didn't call. Because she stayed up half the night waiting for you."

Lincoln took a bite and waited to see whether his stomach had forgiven him yet. "What's in these egg rolls?" he asked.

"Goat cheese, I think, and maybe salmon."

"They're really good."

"I know," she said, "I ate four. Now, stop stalling, and tell me where you were all night."

"I went to a bar with Justin."

"Did you meet anyone?"

"Strictly speaking?" he said with his mouth full. "Yes."

"Were you with a girl last night?"

"No. I was asleep and drunk in the back of Justin's truck. Is there still a yellow SUV in the driveway?"

"No." Eve looked disappointed.

"Why are you looking at me like that?" Lincoln was feeling better already. Maybe he'd even take a shower before he went back to bed. "Would you really rather hear that I'd spent the night having premarital sex with a girl I'd just met at The Steel Guitar?"

"You went to a country bar?"

"It's only country on Thursday nights."

"Oh. Well." Eve took one of his egg rolls. "You could have stayed up all night *talking* to a girl you'd met at The Steel Guitar. I would love to hear that."

"Okay," he said, getting up for more, "next time, that's what I'll tell you."

CHAPTER 13

From: Jennifer Scribner-Snyder
To: Beth Fremont
Sent: Mon, 09/06/1999 10:14 AM
Subject: ALL HAIL THE GOLDEN VIKINGS!

I know how you devour the Sports section, so you've probably already read how the North High Vikings *trounced* the Southeast Bunnies Friday night. The only thing missing from our coverage was the way the Viking defense rallied when the band played "Whoomp! (There it is)." You missed quite a night.

<<Beth to Jennifer>>
1. Why is every school in this city named after a direction? Would it kill them to name something after John F. Kennedy or Abraham Lincoln or Boutros Boutros-Ghali?

2. Mitch has them playing *Jock Jams*? Has he no shame?

<<Jennifer to Beth>> Well, it is a football game. Besides, the kids love that song. It's really cute, the tubas do the "Whoomp" part. How was your weekend? Did you go see Chris? Did his band play any *Jock Jams*?

<<Beth to Jennifer>> Yeah, you should hear his guitar solo on "Tootsee Roll." My weekend was good. I did stop at the Sacajawea show Friday night and ended up catching their whole set. There were a few songs I hadn't heard before.

<<Jennifer to Beth>> Was Chris surprised to see you at the show?

<<Beth to Jennifer>> Nyah.

<<Jennifer to Beth>> Nyah? You're so coy. I've been thinking about why you won't tell me how you met. I think it must be scandalous. Was he married? Are you related?

<<Beth to Jennifer>> Yes and yes.

<<Jennifer to Beth>> There you go again. Coy.

<<Beth to Jennifer>> Sorry. It's just . . .

I know how you feel about Chris. (I know how *everybody* feels about Chris.) And it feels weird telling gushy romantic stories about him. I can sense your disdain.

<<Jennifer to Beth>> *How* do I feel? And who's *everybody*?

<<Beth to Jennifer>> You don't like him.

And everybody is everybody. My parents. My siblings. You, did I mention you?

<<Jennifer to Beth>> That's not fair. I like Chris.

<<Beth to Jennifer>> But you think I can do better.

<<Jennifer to Beth>> That's not quite true.

I love you. And I want you to be happy. And you're not happy. So I look for what in your life is making you unhappy. And I think Chris sometimes makes you unhappy.

<<Beth to Jennifer>> Mitch sometimes makes you unhappy.

<<Jennifer to Beth>> That's true.

<<Beth to Jennifer>> You're thinking, "But . . ."

<<Jennifer to Beth>> I'm sorry. I don't want you to feel like you can't tell me things about Chris, gushy and romantic or otherwise. I tell you everything, and it's such an enormous comfort to have someone to tell.

Also, maybe if you told me all the gushy, romantic things about Chris, I would understand why you put up with the *other* things, the things that do make me roll my eyes.

<<**Beth to Jennifer**>> That's a good point.

<<**Jennifer to Beth**>> So . . .

<<**Beth to Jennifer**>> So?

<<**Jennifer to Beth**>> So, tell me something gushy and romantic. Tell me how you met.

Once upon a time, at a family reunion, I met a married man . . .

<<**Beth to Jennifer**>> You don't have to like him to be my friend. As long as you like me, we're cool.

<<**Jennifer to Beth**>> I want to like him.

<<**Beth to Jennifer**>> I shouldn't have said that about Mitch making you unhappy. I love Mitch. I'm sorry.

<<**Jennifer to Beth**>> No, it's okay. You were right. Mitch *does* make me unhappy sometimes, and you don't hold it against him.

Once upon a time at a family reunion . . .

<<**Beth to Jennifer**>> Okay. Well. I met Chris at the Student Union.

<<**Jennifer to Beth**>> You don't say.

<<**Beth to Jennifer**>> We both used to study there between our 9:30 and 11:30 classes.

I had seen him on campus before. He was always wearing this yellow sweatshirt and giant headphones. The kind of headphones that say, "I may not take my clothes seriously. I may not have brushed or even washed my hair today. But I pronounce the word 'music' with a capital 'M.' Like God."

Are you rolling your eyes yet?

<<**Jennifer to Beth**>> Are you kidding? I love love stories. Keep going.

<<**Beth to Jennifer**>> So I had noticed him before. He had Eddie Vedder hair. Ginger brown, tangly. He was too thin (much

thinner than he is now), and there were permanent smudges under his eyes. Like he was too cool to eat or sleep.

I thought he was *dreamy.*

I called him Headphone Boy. I couldn't believe my luck when I realized we studied in the Union at the same time.

Well, *I* studied. He would pull a paperback out of his pocket and read. Never a textbook. Sometimes, he'd just sit there with his eyes closed, listening to music, his legs all jangly and loose. He gave me impure thoughts.

<<**Jennifer to Beth**>> You're not stopping there! You can't stop with "impure thoughts."

<<**Beth to Jennifer**>> I have to. Pam just came over. One of the old movie theaters is closing. The Indian Hills. It's got one of the last Cinerama screens left in the country. I can't believe they want to close the place. (I've seen all four *Star Wars* movies there. I need to complete the series, damn it.) Pam wants a story about it by morning. So, I'm actually on deadline. Like a real reporter. I got no time for love stories.

<<**Jennifer to Beth**>> Okay, you're excused. For now. But you're finishing this story.

<<**Beth to Jennifer**>> I will, I promise.

CHAPTER 14

LINCOLN WAS NEVER going to send Jennifer Scribner-Snyder and Beth Fremont a warning.

He may as well admit that, to himself. He was never going to send them a warning. Because he liked them. Because he thought they were nice and smart and funny. Really funny—sometimes they made him laugh out loud at his desk. He liked how they teased each other and looked out for each other. He wished that he had a friend at work he could talk to like that.

Okay. So. That's how it was going to be. He was never going to send them a warning.

Ergo. Therefore. Thus . . . He technically, *ethically*, had no reason to keep reading their e-mail.

Lincoln had told himself all along that it was okay to do this job (that it was okay to be a professional snoop and a lurker) as long as there was nothing voyeuristic about it. As long as he didn't enjoy the snooping and lurking.

But now he *was* enjoying it. He found himself hoping that Beth and Jennifer's messages would get picked up by the filter; he found himself smiling every time he saw their names in the WebFence folder. Sometimes, on slow nights, he'd read their messages twice.

It had even occurred to Lincoln once or twice that he could open up their personal folders and read any of their mail, anytime, if he really wanted to.

Not that he wanted to. Not that he ever would. That would be weird.

This was weird, he thought.

He should stop reading their messages. If he was never going to send them a warning, he should stop.

Okay, Lincoln said to himself, *I'm stopping.*

CHAPTER 15

From: Jennifer Scribner-Snyder
To: Beth Fremont
Sent: Tues, 09/07/1999 9:56 AM
Subject: Nice story.

And on the front page, even. You haven't lost your chops.

<<Beth to Jennifer>> Why, thank you. It was exciting working with the news editors again. Everyone's so intense over there. I felt like Lois Lane.

<<Jennifer to Beth>> Normally, you feel like Roger Ebert, right?

Hey, guess who wrote your headline?

<<Beth to Jennifer>> Now that you mention it, it was a very clever headline. Pithy, even. It must have been Chuck.

<<Jennifer to Beth>> Funny.

<<Beth to Jennifer>> We make a great team, you and I. We should join forces and . . . start a newspaper or something.

<<Jennifer to Beth>> Mitch read your story at breakfast this morning, and he was p;ssed. He loves that theater. He saw *The Goonies* there six times. (His seventh-grade girlfriend had a crush on Corey Feldman.) He said that the Cinerama screen could make any movie look good.

<<Beth to Jennifer>>

1. Mitch had a seventh-grade girlfriend? Play on, player.

2. I hope he wasn't implying that *The Goonies* was a bad movie. I love Martha Plimpton, and Corey Feldman was excellent. He never deserved to become a punch line. Did you see *Stand By Me*? *The 'Burbs*? *The Fox and the Hound*?

3. I love picturing you guys reading the paper together over breakfast. It's so blissfully domestic.

<<Jennifer to Beth>> Not this morning, it wasn't.

I was reading the National page, and there was a story about a mother whose son tied her up because she wouldn't buy him a PlayStation, and I said, "Jesus, one more reason not to have kids." And Mitch snorted (really, he *snorted*) and said, "Are you writing these down somewhere? All the reasons we can't have kids?"

I told him not to be mean, and he said, "*You* don't be mean. I know that you're not ready for a baby. You don't have to rub it in."

"Rub it in to what?" I asked. "Are you wounded?"

Then he said that he was tired and that I should just forget it. "I love you," he said, "I'm going to work." I told him not to say it like that, like he had to say it to be excused from the table. And he asked if I would rather he left without saying "I love you."

I said: "I'd rather you said 'I love you' because you were so full of love for me that you couldn't keep it in. I would *rather* that you wouldn't leave the house mad at me."

And then he said that he wasn't mad at me, that he was mad at the situation. The kid situation. Or, rather, the lack-of-kid situation.

But I *am* the lack-of-kid situation. So I said so. "You're mad at me," I said.

"Okay," he said, "I'm mad at you. But I love you. And I have to go to work. Good-bye."

Then I worried that he'd get into a car accident on his way to work, and I'd have to spend the rest of my life thinking about how I didn't say, "I love you, too."

I purposely didn't take my folic acid pill after breakfast—to spite us both.

<<**Beth to Jennifer**>> When did you start taking folic acid?

<<**Jennifer to Beth**>> After my last pregnancy scare. It seemed like it would give me one less thing to worry about. Do you think I should call Mitch and apologize?

<<**Beth to Jennifer**>> Yes.

<<**Jennifer to Beth**>> But I don't want to. He started it.

<<**Beth to Jennifer**>> Maybe all of your pregnancy anxiety is starting to get to him.

<<**Jennifer to Beth**>> It is. I know it is. I don't blame him. But I'm no good at apologizing. I always end up making it worse. I'll say, "I'm sorry," and I'll be all sweet, and then once I'm forgiven, I'll say, "But you really did start it."

<<**Beth to Jennifer**>> That's awful, don't do that. That's exactly what your mother would say.

<<**Jennifer to Beth**>> That's exactly what my mother *has* said, to me, a *million* times.

I inherited it. I'm genetically programmed to be a terrible person.

Speaking of my mother, I foolishly told her last weekend that Mitch and I had been fighting about having a baby. And she sighed—have you heard her sigh? It's like a balloon dying—and said, "That's how it starts. You better watch yourself."

"*It*," of course, is divorce. Which she's sure I inherited along with her straight teeth and her evil apologies. She's just waiting. She keeps poking my marriage with a toothpick. *Almost done!*

So I was like "*Really*, Mom? *It* starts with fighting? And here I thought it started with my third-grade teacher."

(Which, of course, is where her divorce started. Though one could argue that my parents' divorce started the day of their shotgun wedding, that my father's affair with Mrs. Grandy was more of a symptom than a disease.)

So, after that horrible, caustic remark, my mother and I were fighting, and I said more awful things, and she finally said, "You can say what you want, Jennifer, but we both know who's going to pick up the pieces when this all falls apart."

So I hung up on her, and Mitch—who had wandered into the room, but didn't know what we were fighting about—said, "I wish you wouldn't talk to her like that. She's your *mother*."

And I couldn't tell him, "But she thinks you're going to leave me, and she's already taking your side in the divorce." So I just frowned at him.

Then on Sunday, my mom called again, and it was like we had never argued. She wanted me to take her to the mall, and she insisted on buying me a red sweater at Sears, which I'll probably end up paying for the next time she can't make her Sears card payment.

<<**Beth to Jennifer**>> Is that the sweater you're wearing today? You got that at Sears? It's really cute.

<<**Jennifer to Beth**>> Don't distract me. (Thank you. Isn't it though?)

<<**Beth to Jennifer**>> Your mom's a nut. Your marriage is nothing like hers. Your life is nothing like hers. She was already married and divorced with a 10-year-old by the time she was your age.

<<**Jennifer to Beth**>> I know, but my mother has a way of spinning those facts into a bad thing. Her take is that I'm just a late bloomer—that I'm taking forever to ruin my life, and she's running out of patience.

I remember getting past 18, the age she was when she had me, and thinking, "Whew, I did it. I made it to 19 without getting pregnant." As if getting pregnant was even an issue. At 19, I hadn't even *kissed* a guy yet.

<<**Beth to Jennifer**>> Really? How old were you when you had your first kiss?

<<**Jennifer to Beth**>> Twenty. It's pathetic. Guys don't want to kiss fat girls.

<<Beth to Jennifer>> Not true. There are all those guys on *Jerry Springer*, and there's President Clinton . . .

<<Jennifer to Beth>> Make that: no one I ever wanted to kiss wanted to kiss a fat girl.

<<Beth to Jennifer>> I'll bet you never gave anyone a chance. Mitch says you practically beat him away with a stick.

<<Jennifer to Beth>> I was trying to spare him.

<<Beth to Jennifer>> How did he win you over?

<<Jennifer to Beth>> He just wouldn't leave me alone. He kept sitting behind me in our poetry-writing class and asking me if I had plans for lunch. Like I wanted this muscle-bound blond guy to watch me *eat*.

<<Beth to Jennifer>> I can just see him. A farm boy with sexy sousaphone shoulders . . . wearing one of those hats they give out free at the grain co-op and a pair of tight Wranglers. Do you remember those bumper stickers people used to have in college, "Girls go nuts for Wrangler butts"?

<<Jennifer to Beth>> Yes. And it's the sort of memory that makes me wish I'd gone to college out of state. Someplace in Philadelphia. Or New Jersey.

<<Beth to Jennifer>> You know, if you had gone to school in New Jersey, you never would have met Mitch. You wouldn't have taken a job here. You never would have met me.

<<Jennifer to Beth>> Mitch says he was destined to meet me. He says I could go back and do my whole life over, and I'd still end up marrying him.

<<Beth to Jennifer>> See? He's nothing like your dad. He's wonderful. I wish you and I had been friends in college. Why weren't we friends?

<<Jennifer to Beth>> Probably because I was fat.

<<Beth to Jennifer>> Don't be stupid. Probably because I was too busy being Chris's girlfriend to make friends.

<<Jennifer to Beth>> Probably because I was too busy working at the *Daily*. I never met any non-journalism majors until I started hanging out with Mitch's marching-band friends.

<<Beth to Jennifer>> But I *was* a journalism major. That's another thing I never did because I was so busy being in love: I never worked at the school newspaper.

<<Jennifer to Beth>> You didn't miss anything, trust me. It was a viper pit. A drunken viper pit.

You know . . . here we are talking about college, I don't have any stories to edit, you're basking in the glow of a brilliant front-page scoop . . .

This would be a great time to complete The Romancing of Beth.

<<Beth to Jennifer>> It was more like The Romancing of Chris.

<<Jennifer to Beth>> The Romancing of Headphone Boy.

There he was, yellow sweatshirt, paperback. There you were, impure thoughts . . .

<<Beth to Jennifer>> Ahem. Well. There we were. In the Student Union. He always sat in the corner. And I always sat one row across from him, three seats down. I took to leaving my 9:30 class early so I could primp and be in my spot looking casual by the time he sauntered in.

He never looked at me—or anyone else, to my relief—and he never took off his headphones. I used to fantasize about what song he might be listening to . . . and whether it would be the first dance at our wedding . . . and whether we'd go with traditional wedding photography or black and white . . . Probably black and white, magazine style. There'd be lots of slightly out-of-focus, candid shots of us embracing with a romantic, faraway look in our eyes.

Of course, Headphone Boy already had a faraway look in his eyes, which my friend Lynn attributed to "breakfast with Mary Jane."

<<Jennifer to Beth>> And then . . .

<<Beth to Jennifer>> I know what you're thinking now. You can't believe I would knowingly get involved with a drug user.

<<Jennifer to Beth>> I knowingly got involved with a guy who plays the tuba. Finish the story.

<<Beth to Jennifer>> Well, at first, I was sure that he would feel the cosmic forces pulling us together. I wanted him so badly, I could feel my heart reaching for him with every beat. It was destiny. "He was a magnet and I was steel."

This started in September. Sometime in October, one of his friends walked by and called him "Chris." (A name, at last. "Say it loud and there's music playing. Say it soft and it's almost like praying.") One Tuesday night in November, I saw him at the library. I spent the next four Tuesday nights there, hoping it was a pattern. It wasn't. Sometimes I'd allow myself to follow him to his 11:30 class in Andrews Hall, and then I'd have to run across campus to make it to my class in the Temple Building.

By the end of the semester, I was long past the point of starting a natural, casual conversation with him. I stopped trying to make eye contact. I even started dating a Sig Ep I met in my sociology class.

But I couldn't give up my 10:30 date with Headphone Boy. I figured, after Christmas break, our schedules would change, and that would be that. I'd wait until then to move on.

<<Jennifer to Beth>> I love this, you actually have me believing that all hope is lost. Tricky.

<<Beth to Jennifer>> All my hope *was* lost.

And then . . . the week before finals, I showed up at the Union at my usual time and found Chris sitting in my seat. His headphones were around his neck, and he watched me walk toward him. At least, I thought he was watching me. He had never looked at me before, *never*, and the idea made my skin burn. Before I could solve the problem of where to sit, he was talking to me.

<<Jennifer to Beth>> Did he say, "Stop stalking me, you psychopath"?

<<Beth to Jennifer>> Nope. He said, "Hey."

And I said, "Hi."

And he said, "Look . . ." His eyes were green. He kind of squinted when he talked. "I've got a 10:30 class next semester, so . . . we should probably make other arrangements."

I was struck numb.

I said, "Are you mocking me?"

"No," he said, "I'm asking you out."

"Then, I'm saying yes."

"Good . . . ," he said, "we could have dinner. You could still sit across from me. It would be just like a Tuesday morning. But with breadsticks."

"*Now* you're mocking me."

"Yes." He was still smiling. "Now I am."

And that was that. We went out that weekend. And the next weekend. And the next. It was wildly romantic.

<<Jennifer to Beth>> Wow, what a cucumber. (Cool, I mean.) Did he know all along that you were watching him?

<<Beth to Jennifer>> Yeah, I think so. That's just Chris. He never hurries. He never shows his cards. He always hangs up first.

<<Jennifer to Beth>> What does that mean, he always hangs up first?

<<Beth to Jennifer>> Like when we first started talking on the phone, he would always be the one who got off first. When we kissed, he always pulled away first. He always kept me just on the edge of crazy. Feeling like I wanted him too much, which just made me want him more.

<<Jennifer to Beth>> That sounds excruciating.

<<Beth to Jennifer>> Excruciating and wonderful. It feels good to want something that bad. I thought about him the way you think about dinner when you haven't eaten for a day and a half. Like you'd sell your soul for it.

<<Jennifer to Beth>> I've never not eaten for a day and a half.

<<Beth to Jennifer>> Not even when you had the flu or something?

<<Jennifer to Beth>> Maybe once. What happened to your Sig Ep?

<<Beth to Jennifer>> Oh God. It was terrible. I didn't remember to dump him until Sunday afternoon. I had two boyfriends for like nine hours. Not that I called Chris my boyfriend then. I didn't want to spook him. That first year was strange. I felt like a butterfly had landed on me. If I moved or even breathed, I thought he would float away.

<<Jennifer to Beth>> Because he always hung up first?

<<Beth to Jennifer>> That. And other things, too. I never knew when I would see him or when he would call. A week might go by and I wouldn't talk to him. Then I'd find a note slid under my door. Or a leaf. Or song lyrics written on a matchbook.

Or Chris himself. Leaning against my door on a Wednesday afternoon, waiting for me to get back from economics. Maybe he'd stay for 15 minutes. Maybe he'd leave that night after I fell asleep. Or maybe he'd talk me into skipping classes for the rest of the week. Maybe we wouldn't leave the room until Saturday morning when we'd finally exhausted my supply of salsa and Popsicles and Diet Coke.

He made me nervy. I spent a lot of time looking out of windows, trying to will him to me. I rented movies about girls who chewed on their hair and had fever patches on their cheeks.

I've never been happier.

<<Jennifer to Beth>> I think I've figured out why we weren't friends in college. You were kind of scary.

<<Beth to Jennifer>> Not scary. Single-minded.

<<Jennifer to Beth>> Scarily single-minded.

<<Beth to Jennifer>> I was focused. I knew what I wanted in life. I wanted Chris. And it was such a relief not to be distracted by anything else. I had no boring subplots.

Weren't you ever like that with Mitch?

<<Jennifer to Beth>> Never like that.

I mean, I was definitely head over heels. But, if anything, he was more caught up than I was, which is probably why we're still together. I needed Mitch to wear his heart on his sleeve. I was so insecure, I needed him to bang down my door and fill my room with flowers.

<<Beth to Jennifer>> Did he actually fill your room with flowers?

<<Jennifer to Beth>> Yep. Carnations, but flowers nonetheless.

<<Beth to Jennifer>> Hmmm. In theory, I think that sounds wonderful. But in practice, I was drawn to Chris because he didn't do that sort of thing. Because he would never do anything that was romantic in a traditional sense. And not just because he was trying to be different, but because his instincts were (*are*) so different from every other guy's. It was like dating the man who fell to Earth.

<<Jennifer to Beth>> I'm glad you finally told me all this. I hated feeling like there was this major part of your life that we couldn't talk about.

That said, I don't think you ever have to worry about me running away with or making a drunken pass at Chris. He'd make me insane.

<<Beth to Jennifer>> Ditto on the being glad we talked about this. But I can't give you a ditto on the drunken pass thing. Mitch is a hottie.

<<Jennifer to Beth>> *Now* I'm rolling my eyes.

CHAPTER 16

THEY MUST BE about his age. Jennifer and Beth and Beth's boyfriend. Twenty-eight or so. Maybe they'd all been in college together. After Lincoln transferred to the state school, after Sam broke up with him, he'd stayed in school a long time, through multiple degrees. There was a good chance he'd seen Beth on campus.

So much for stopping. So much for what he technically, ethically, knew he should do.

He'd meant to throw Beth's and Jennifer's messages away, as soon as they showed up in the WebFence folder. But then . . . he didn't. He opened them, and once he was reading them, he got caught up in their stories, in their back and forth and back and forth.

I'm getting caught up, he thought to himself after he was done reading about how Beth met her boyfriend, after he'd read through the whole story a second time and spent a few minutes thinking about it, thinking about them, wondering what they all looked like . . . What she looked like . . .

I'm getting caught up, he thought. *That's not good . . . is it?*

No. But maybe it isn't exactly all bad . . .

CHAPTER 17

From: Jennifer Scribner-Snyder
To: Beth Fremont
Sent: Fri, 09/10/1999 1:23 PM
Subject: Herring cassoulet.

You shouldn't be allowed to eat fish at work. I swear to God, whenever Tony works, I go home reeking of the sea. I know he's from Rhode Island, where they eat fish all the livelong day, but he should assume that everyone around him here is disgusted by the stink of it.

<<**Beth to Jennifer**>> I've seen you eat fish sticks before. And popcorn shrimp.

<<**Jennifer to Beth**>> Both of those have protective fried coatings. I'll eat fish that's processed beyond recognition, but I would never eat it at work. I don't even pop popcorn here. I don't like to inflict my food odors on others.

<<**Beth to Jennifer**>> Very thoughtful.

I'll trade you Tony's orange roughy stench for Tim's fingernail clipping any day.

<<**Jennifer to Beth**>> I thought you stole his fingernail clippers . . .

<<Beth to Jennifer>> I did. He has new ones. I'm not sure what bothers me more . . . the constant clip-clip noises or knowing that his cubicle is completely contaminated by tiny fingernail slivers.

<<Jennifer to Beth>> If we ever need any of his DNA for a paternity test or a voodoo spell, we'll know where to look.

<<Beth to Jennifer>> If we ever need any of Tony's DNA for a paternity test, one of us deserves to be pushed off a cliff.

Hey, remember when we used to have to leave our desks to have conversations like this?

<<Jennifer to Beth>> I don't think we ever did have conversations like this. I know I never ventured into reporter land unless I had incredibly good gossip or unless I really, really needed to talk.

<<Beth to Jennifer>> Or unless somebody brought cookies.

Remember that lady who sat in the corner, who used to always bring cookies? What happened to her?

<<Jennifer to Beth>> The city hall reporter? I heard they fired her when they found out she carried a loaded gun in her purse.

<<Beth to Jennifer>> That doesn't seem fair. As long as she kept it in her purse.

<<Jennifer to Beth>> Wow. It wouldn't be 30 pieces of silver with you, would it? It would be cookies.

<<Beth to Jennifer>> No. (*Yes.* Snickerdoodles.)

CHAPTER 18

THAT AFTERNOON, GREG introduced Lincoln to college students he'd hired to take on the Y2K project. There were three of them; one from Vietnam, one from Bosnia, and one from the suburbs. Lincoln couldn't tell how old they were. Much younger than he was. "They're like an international strike force," Greg said, "and you're their commander."

"Me?" Lincoln said. "What exactly does that mean?"

"It means you have to make sure they're actually doing something," Greg said. "If I knew anything about coding, I'd be the commander. You think I don't want to be the commander?"

The Y2K kids sat at a table in the corner. They worked days mostly, between their classes, so Lincoln usually tried to meet with them as soon as he came in. He didn't do much commanding at these meetings. The college students seemed to already know what they needed to do. And they didn't talk much otherwise, to Lincoln or to each other.

After about a week, Lincoln was pretty sure that they'd hacked the firewalls and were running instant messaging and Napster on their computers. He told Greg, but Greg said he didn't give a shit as long as he still had a job on January 1.

No one on the Strike Force had interoffice e-mail, so no one was monitoring them. Sometimes Lincoln wondered if anyone was monitoring his own mail. Maybe Greg, he thought, but it didn't really matter because Greg was the only one who ever sent him messages.

CHAPTER 19

From: Beth Fremont
To: Jennifer Scribner-Snyder
Sent: Wed, 09/22/1999 2:38 PM
Subject: Roo-ah-rooo-ahhh.

Roo-ah-rooo-ahhh.

<<**Jennifer to Beth**>> What's that?

<<**Beth to Jennifer**>> It's the Cute Guy Alarm.

<<**Jennifer to Beth**>> It sounds like a bird.

<<**Beth to Jennifer**>> There's a cute guy working here.

<<**Jennifer to Beth**>> No, there isn't.

<<**Beth to Jennifer**>> I know, that was my first response, too. I thought he must have come in from the outside, a repairman, perhaps, or a consultant. That's why I waited for two confirmed sightings before sounding the Cute Guy Alarm.

<<**Jennifer to Beth**>> Is this Cute Guy Alarm something you made up with your eighth-grade friends? Do I need to be wearing Guess overalls to understand this?

Also—confirmed by whom?

<<**Beth to Jennifer**>> Confirmed by me. I know a cute guy when I see him. Remember when I told you about the cute messenger? (And I just now made up the alarm. It felt necessary.)

<<Jennifer to Beth>> Oh, that messenger *was* cute.

<<Beth to Jennifer>> And that's why he didn't last. This place can't sustain cuteness, I don't know why. It's cuteness-cursed.

<<Jennifer to Beth>> You're very cute.

<<Beth to Jennifer>> Oh, I was. Once. Before I came to this de-cuteing factory. Look around you. We journalists are a homely lot.

<<Jennifer to Beth>> Matt Lauer isn't homely.

<<Beth to Jennifer>> Now, that is a matter of opinion. (And I can't believe you went straight to Matt Lauer. Have you *seen* Brian Williams?) Regardless, TV journalists don't count; cute is their job. There's no reason to look pretty in print journalism. Readers don't care if you're cute. Especially not my readers. The only time I'm out in public, I'm sitting in the dark.

<<Jennifer to Beth>> Now that you mention it, I haven't worn lipstick to work in three years.

<<Beth to Jennifer>> And you're still too cute for the copy desk.

<<Jennifer to Beth>> Damn me with faint praise, why don't you. Tell me more about this cute guy you've imagined.

<<Beth to Jennifer>> There's not much to tell—beyond his *monumental* cuteness.

<<Jennifer to Beth>> *Monumental?*

<<Beth to Jennifer>> He's very, very tall. And strong-looking. Like the kind of guy you feel standing next to you before you actually see him, because he's blocking so much ambient light.

<<Jennifer to Beth>> Is that how you spotted him?

<<Beth to Jennifer>> No, I spotted him the first time walking down the hallway. And then I spotted him at the drinking fountain—and I thought to myself, "Now there's a tall drink of water . . . getting a drink of water." He has really nice brown hair and action-hero facial features.

<<Jennifer to Beth>> Explain.

<<Beth to Jennifer>> Manly. Kind of square. Harrison Ford-ish. The kind of guy you can picture negotiating for hostages and also jumping away from an explosion.

Do you think it's scandalous that someone in a committed relationship like mine is checking out guys at the drinking fountain?

<<Jennifer to Beth>> No. How could you *not* notice a cute guy around here? That's like spotting a passenger pigeon.

<<Beth to Jennifer>> A passenger pigeon with a sweet ass.

<<Jennifer to Beth>> Why did you have to go there?

<<Beth to Jennifer>> To bug you. I didn't even look at his butt. I never remember to do that.

<<Jennifer to Beth>> I'm going back to work now.

<<Beth to Jennifer>> You seem a little testy. Is everything okay?

<<Jennifer to Beth>> I'm fine.

<<Beth to Jennifer>> See what I mean? Testy.

<<Jennifer to Beth>> Okay, I'm not fine. But I'm too embarrassed to talk about why.

<<Beth to Jennifer>> Don't talk, then. Type.

<<Jennifer to Beth>> Only if you don't go repeating what I'm about to tell you. It makes me sound unbalanced.

<<Beth to Jennifer>> I won't. I swear. Cross my heart, needles, etc.

<<Jennifer to Beth>> All right. But this is really stupid. More stupid than usual. I was at the mall last night, walking around by myself, trying not to spend money, trying not to think about a delicious Cinnabon . . . and I found myself walking by the Baby Gap. I've never been in a Baby Gap. So, I decided to duck in. On a lark.

<<Beth to Jennifer>> Right. On a lark. I'm familiar with those. So . . .

<<Jennifer to Beth>> So . . . I'm larking through the Baby Gap, looking at tiny capri pants and sweaters that cost more than . . . I don't know, more than they should. And I get totally sucked in by this ridiculous, tiny fur coat. The kind of coat a baby might need to go to the ballet. In Moscow. In 1918. To match her tiny pearls.

I'm looking at this preposterous coat, and a Baby Gap woman comes up to me and says, "Isn't that sweet? How old is your daughter?" And I say, "Oh, no. She's not. Not yet."

And she says, "When are you due?"

And I say, "*February*."

<<Beth to Jennifer>> Whoa.

<<Jennifer to Beth>> I know. I just lied. About being pregnant. If I were *really* pregnant, I wouldn't be at the Baby Gap, I'd be sitting in a dark room, sobbing.

So Baby Gap lady says, "Well, then you'll want one for next season, size 6 to 12 months. These coats are a steal. We just marked them down today."

And I agreed that a faux fur coat for only $32.99 was indeed an irresistible deal.

<<Beth to Jennifer>> You bought baby clothes? What did Mitch say?

<<Jennifer to Beth>> Nothing! I hid it in the attic. I felt like I was hiding a body.

<<Beth to Jennifer>> Wow. I don't know what to say. Does this mean you're softening on the baby issue?

<<Jennifer to Beth>> I think it means I'm softening on the sanity issue. I'm viewing this as a dysfunctional appendage to my general psychosis about babies. I still dread getting pregnant. But now I'm buying clothes for the child I'm terrified to have, and guess what, *it's a girl*.

<<Beth to Jennifer>> Wow.

<<Jennifer to Beth>> I know.

CHAPTER 20

SOMETIME AFTER MIDNIGHT, Lincoln walked up to the newsroom. It was mostly empty. There were a few nightside copy editors left, poring over the next morning's newspaper. Someone was sitting at the city desk, listening to a crackling police scanner and working on tomorrow's crossword.

Lincoln walked to the other side of the long room, where he assumed the Entertainment staff worked. Back there, the cubicles were full of movie posters, concert flyers, promotional photos and toys.

He stopped at a printer and opened it, just to look like he had something to do. Which desk was he looking for? Maybe the one with the R.E.M. stickers. Probably not the one with the stuffed Bart Simpson and half a dozen fully poseable *Alien* action figures . . . but maybe. Maybe. Would Beth have a Page-a-Day cat calendar? A potted plant? A Sandman poster? A Marilyn Manson press pass?

A Sandman poster.

He looked back at the copy desk. He could hardly see the copy editors from here, which meant they could hardly see him. He walked over to Beth's cubicle, to what he thought was her cubicle.

A Sandman poster. A *Rushmore* poster. A three-year-old flyer for Sacajawea at Sokol Hall. A dictionary. A French dictionary. Three books by Leonard Maltin. A high school journalism award. Empty coffee cups. Starburst wrappers. Photographs.

He sat at her desk and lamely started to take apart her computer mouse.

Photographs. One was a concert photograph, a guy playing guitar. Obviously her boyfriend, Chris. In another frame, the same guy sat on a beach. In another, he wore a suit. He looked like a rock star even without the guitar. Slender and slouched over. Never quite smiling. Always looking past the camera. Shaggy. Roguish. Handsome.

There were family pictures, too, of angelic dark-haired babies and nice-looking, well-dressed adults—but none of them seemed to be Beth. They weren't the right age, or they were standing with what were clearly husbands or children.

Lincoln went back to looking at the boyfriend. Looking at his not-quite smile and his sharp cheekbones. At his long, twisting waist. He looked like he had a get-out-of-jail-free card in his back pocket. If you looked like that, a woman would forgive you. She would expect to have to forgive you now and then.

Lincoln set the mouse down and walked back to the information technology office. Lumbered back. He could see his dim reflection in the darkened office windows along the hall. He felt heavy and plain. Lumpy. Thick. Gray.

He shouldn't have done that. What he'd just done. Gone to her desk.

It felt wrong, like he'd crossed a line.

Beth was funny. She was smart. She was interesting. And she had the sort of job that made someone more interesting. The sort of job a woman would have in a movie, a romantic comedy starring John Cusack.

He'd wanted to see what she looked like. He'd wanted to see where she sat when she wrote the things he read.

He was glad he hadn't found a picture of her. It had been enough to see the pictures of people she loved. To see how he didn't fit into them.

"I THOUGHT THAT if I moved back home," Lincoln said to Eve when she called the next day, "that I'd get a life."

"Are you retarded?"

"I thought you stopped saying 'retarded' and 'gay' so that your kids wouldn't pick it up."

"I can't help it. That's how retarded you sound right now. Why would you think that? And why would you refer to it as moving *back* home? You never moved out."

"Yes, I did. I left for college ten years ago."

"And you came back every summer."

"Not every summer. There were summers when I took classes."

"Whatever," she said. "How could you think that moving in with your mother full-time would help you get a life?"

"Because it meant that I was finally done with school. That's when all my friends got lives, after they graduated. That's when they got jobs and got married."

"Okay . . ."

"I think I missed my window," he said.

"What window?"

"My get-a-life window. I think I was supposed to figure all this stuff out somewhere between twenty-two and twenty-six, and now it's too late."

"It's not too late," she said. "You are getting a life. You've got a job, you're saving up to move out. You're meeting people. You went to a bar . . ."

"And that was a disaster. Actually, everything has been a disaster since I quit school."

"You didn't quit school," she said. He could hear her rolling her eyes. "You finished your master's degree. Another master's degree."

"Everything has been a disaster since I decided my life as it was wasn't good enough."

"It *wasn't* good enough," she said.

"It was good enough for me."

"Then why have you been trying so hard to change it?"

THAT SATURDAY NIGHT, Lincoln played Dungeons & Dragons for the first time in a month.

Christine grinned when she saw him at the door.

"Lincoln, hey!" Christine was short and round with rumpled blond hair. She was carrying a baby in some sort of sling, and when she hugged Lincoln, the baby was smushed between them.

"We thought we'd lost you to the big city," Dave said, rounding the corner.

"You did," Lincoln said. "I found a group of younger, better-looking gamers."

"We all knew that would happen eventually," Dave said, clapping Lincoln on the back and leading him into house. "This game has gotten entirely too chaotic-evil without you. We tried to kill off your character last week to punish you for abandoning us, but Christine wouldn't let us, so we left you in a pit instead. Possibly a snake-filled pit. You'll have to work that out with Larry, he's the Dungeon Master this week."

"We just started playing," Christine said. "You should've called, we would've waited for you."

"You should have called," Troy said from the dining room table. "I wouldn't have had to ride my bike twelve miles to get here."

"Troy, I said I'd pick you up," Larry said. Larry was a little older than the rest of them, in his early thirties, an Air Force captain with a family and some secret job involving artificial intelligence.

"Your car smells like juice boxes," Troy said.

"Do you have any idea what you smell like?" Larry asked.

"It's sandalwood," Troy said.

"You smell like a Pier One store with body odor," Lincoln said, finding his spot in the corner. They'd saved it for him. Dave handed him a slice of pizza.

"It's a masculine scent," Troy said.

"I didn't say I didn't like it," Lincoln said. That made Rick laugh. Rick was pale and thin and never wore anything other than black. He even wore pieces of black cloth and leather tied around his wrists. If not for Rick, Lincoln would have been the Shy One in the group.

Lincoln looked around the table, wondering where that left him.

If Dave was the Intense One, and Christine was the Girl . . . And Larry was the Serious One (and the Intimidating One and the One Most Likely to Be on a Black Ops Team) . . . If Rick was the Shy One, and Troy was the Weird One, and Teddy, a surgical resident who looked like the dad in *Back to the Future*—Teddy might actually be the Nerdy One . . .

Then who was Lincoln?

All the adjectives that came to his head (lost, stunted, mother-living) brought him down.

Tonight it was enough to be one of them. To be someplace where he always had a spot at the table, where everybody already knew that he didn't like olives on his pizza, and they always looked happy to see him.

When Lincoln realized he was rewriting the theme song to *Cheers*, he decided to stop thinking and just play.

THE GAME WENT on for seven hours. Everyone made rescuing Lincoln's character—a lawful-good dwarf named 'Smov the Ninekiller—the first order of business. They defeated a nefarious wind witch. They ordered more pizza. Dave and Christine's three-year-old fell asleep on the floor, watching *Toy Story*.

Lincoln stayed after the game ended and everyone else went home. Dave opened a window, and the three of them sat on couches, breathing cool, clean air and listening to Christine's wind chimes.

"You know what we should do now?" Dave said, rubbing his 2:00 A.M. stubble.

"What?" Lincoln said.

"Axis and Allies."

Christine threw a pillow at him. "God, no."

Dave caught it. "Lincoln wants to play Axis and Allies. I can see it in his eyes . . ."

"I think Lincoln wants to tell us what he's been doing with himself lately." Christine smiled warmly at Lincoln. Everything about her was warm and soft and welcoming.

They'd kissed once, in college, in his dorm room, before Christine had started dating Dave. Lincoln had offered to help her study for a physics final. Christine didn't need to take physics; she wanted to be an English teacher. But she told Lincoln that she didn't want to live in a world she didn't understand, that she didn't want a faith-based relationship with things like centrifugal force and gravity. As she said it, she kicked off her sandals and sat Indian-style on his bed. She had long, wavy, wheaty hair that never looked brushed.

Christine told Lincoln that he explained everything so much better than her physics professor, a stern man with a Slavic accent who acted offended every time she asked a stupid question. Lincoln told her that her questions weren't stupid, and she hugged him. That's when he kissed her. It was like kissing a warm bath.

"That was nice," Christine said when he pulled away. He couldn't tell whether she wanted him to kiss her again. She was smiling. She looked happy, but that didn't mean anything. She always looked happy . . .

"Do you feel ready for your test?" he asked.

"Could we go over torque one more time?"

"Sure," he said, "yeah." Christine smiled some more. They went back to studying, and she ended up getting a B on her physics final.

Sometimes, Lincoln wished that he would have kept kissing her that night. It would be so easy to love Christine, to be in love with her. You'd never raise your voice. She'd never be mean.

But he wasn't jealous when she started dating Dave a few months later. Christine radiated happy when she was with Dave. And Dave, who could really, truly, be painfully intense sometimes—the kind of guy who leans in too far when he's making a point, who might still be snippy with you two weeks after your D&D character had bested his in a swordfight—was loose and forgiving when Christine was around. Lincoln liked their messy-warm house, their messy-round kids, their living room with too many lamps and pillows, the way their voices softened when they talked to each other.

"I think," Lincoln said, "if we started an Axis and Allies game right now, I'd fall asleep before Russia was done buying tanks."

"Is that a yes?" Dave asked.

"That's a no," Christine said. "You should sleep here, Lincoln. You look too tired to drive."

"Yeah, stay," Dave said, "we'll make blueberry pancakes for breakfast."

Lincoln stayed. He slept on the couch, and when he woke up, he helped Christine make pancakes and argued with Dave about the plot of a fantasy novel they'd both read. After breakfast, they made him promise to come to next week's game.

"We still have to catch up," Christine said.

"Yeah," Dave said. "You still haven't told us about your job."

IT WAS SUCH a good weekend that Lincoln still felt cheerful and unlonely when he got to work Monday night. He was feeling practically sunny when his sister called.

"Have you read any more of that parachute book?" she asked.

"No. It's too intimidating."

"What is?"

"The book," he said. "The future."

"So you're done with the future?"

"I'm tightening my focus."

"To what?"

"The near future," he said. "I can handle the near future. Tonight, for example, I'm going to read for pleasure. Tomorrow, I'm going to have a beer with lunch. On Saturday, I'm going to play Dungeons & Dragons. And Sunday, I might go see a movie. That's my plan."

"That isn't a plan," she said.

"It is. It's my plan. And I feel really good about it."

"Those aren't things you plan. You don't plan to read or to have a beer with lunch. Those are things you do when you have a moment between planned events. Those are incidentals."

"Not for me," he said. "That's my plan."

"You're backsliding."

"Or maybe I'm frontsliding."

"I can't talk to you anymore," Eve said. "Call me this weekend."

"I'll pencil you in."

ALL THE Y2K stuff was keeping Lincoln busier at work—he was helping with the coding and trying to keep track of Greg's strike force—but he still had hours of free time every night. On Friday night, when he told himself how lucky he was to get paid to reread Isaac Asimov's Foundation series, he mostly believed it.

Money and time, those were the two things that he always heard people complaining about, and he had plenty of both.

There wasn't anything Lincoln wanted that he couldn't afford. What did he really want, anyway? To buy new books when they came out in hardback. To not have to think about how much money was in his wallet when he was ordering dinner. Maybe new sneakers . . . And there wasn't anything he wanted to do that he couldn't make time for. What did he have to mope about, really? What more did he want?

Love, he could hear Eve saying. Purpose.

Love. Purpose. *Those* are the things that you can't plan for. Those are the things that just happen. And what if they don't happen? Do you spend your whole life pining for them? Waiting to be happy?

That night, Lincoln got an e-mail from Dave saying that Saturday's D&D game was off. One of their kids had rotavirus, which Lincoln had never even heard of. It sounded awful. He pictured a virus with rotating blades and an engine. Dave said there'd been lots of vomiting, that they'd had to go to the emergency room, and Christine was scared to death.

"We'll probably be on hiatus for the next couple weekends," Dave had written.

"No problem," Lincoln messaged back. "I hope he feels better. Get some rest."

Poor kid. Poor Christine.

This isn't a big deal, Lincoln told himself. The plan is flexible. He could still go see a movie this weekend. He could pick up his comics. He could call Justin.

There were twenty-three red-flagged messages in the WebFence folder. There might even be something in there that Lincoln should take care of. He opened it, telling himself that he may as well earn an hour of his paycheck tonight.

He opened it, hoping.

CHAPTER 21

From: Beth Fremont
To: Jennifer Scribner-Snyder
Sent: Thurs, 09/30/1999 3:42 PM
Subject: If you were Superman . . .

. . . and you could choose any alter ego you wanted, why the hell would you choose to spend your Clark Kent hours—which already suck because you have to wear glasses and you can't fly—at a newspaper?

Why not pose as a wealthy playboy like Batman? Or the leader of a small but important nation like Black Panther?

Why would you choose to spend your days on deadline, making crap money, dealing with terminally crabby editors?

<<Jennifer to Beth>> I thought we agreed not to swear in e-mails.

<<Beth to Jennifer>> We agreed that it would probably be a good idea to stop swearing in e-mails.

<<Jennifer to Beth>> Still thinking about Lois Lane?

<<Beth to Jennifer>> Sort of. I mean, I get why Lois Lane went to journalism school. I know her type. Wants to make a difference, wants to uncover great truths. Nosy. But Clark Kent . . . why not Clark Kent, sexy TV weatherman? Or Clark Kent, mayor of Cincinnati?

<<Jennifer to Beth>> Aren't you missing the point? Clark Kent doesn't want to be famous. He doesn't want people to look at him. If they really look at him, they'd see that he's just Superman with glasses.

Plus, he needs to be someplace like a newsroom, where he's the first to hear big news. He can't afford to read "Joker attacks moon" the next day in the newspaper.

<<Beth to Jennifer>> You make an excellent point. Especially for someone who doesn't know that Superman never fights the Joker.

<<Jennifer to Beth>> Especially for someone who doesn't care. I hope you're not right about life sucking for everyone who can't fly and wears glasses. That describes everyone in this room.

What are you working on?

<<Beth to Jennifer>> We *do* all wear glasses. Weird.

Another Indian Hills story. I'm not so much working as I am waiting for a phone call.

It turns out, the hospital next door to the theater already bought the land. Months ago. They're going to make it a parking lot. I'm waiting for the hospital spokesperson to call me back so that she can say, "No comment." And then I can write, "Hospital officials would not comment on the sale." And then I can go home.

Do you know how mind-numbing it is to sit around waiting for someone to call you back so that they can officially tell you nothing? I just don't think Superman would stand for it. He could be out finding lost Boy Scouts and plugging volcanoes with giant boulders.

<<Jennifer to Beth>> Superman works at a newspaper because he's trying to get with Lois Lane.

<<Beth to Jennifer>> He probably makes twice as much as she does.

CHAPTER 22

ON FRIDAY MORNING, Lincoln picked up a spring schedule from the city college. There was a professor in the anthropology department who specialized in Afghan studies. Why not take a few classes? He had plenty of time during the day, and he could always study at work. He'd love to study at work.

"What is this?" his mother asked when she saw the class schedule.

"Something that I thought I'd put in my backpack." He took the brochure from her hands. "Seriously, Mom, what are you doing in my bag? Are you steaming open my mail, too?"

"You don't get any mail." She folded her arms. You could never be offended or dismayed with her—she always beat you to it. "I was checking your bag for dirty dishes," she said. "Do those papers mean that you're going back to school?"

"Not immediately." The fall semester had already started.

"I don't know how I feel about that, Lincoln. I'm starting to think you might have a problem. With school."

"I've never had a problem with school," he said, knowing how lame that sounded, knowing that refusing to take part in the conversation wasn't the same as avoiding it.

"You know what I mean," she said. She wagged a dirty spoon at him. "A problem. Like those women who get addicted to plastic surgery. They keep going back and going back, trying to look better until there is no more better. Like they can't look better because they don't even look like themselves anymore. And then it's just about looking different, I think.

I saw this woman in a magazine who looked just like a cat. Like a cat of prey, a big cat. Have you ever seen her? She has a lot of money. I think she might be from Austria."

"No," he said.

"Well, she looks very unhappy."

"Okay," he said quietly, shoving the schedule back into his backpack. "Okay?"

"You don't want me to go back to school, or have plastic surgery to make myself look like a cat. Okay, I get it. So noted."

"And you don't want me to open your backpack . . ."

"I really don't."

"Fine," she said, walking back to the kitchen. "So noted."

THE COURIER HAD begun holding weekly Millennium Preparedness meetings. All the department heads had to attend, including Greg, who was expected to give a readiness report at each one. He usually came back from these meetings looking red-faced and hypertensive.

"I don't know what they expect of me, Lincoln. I'm one man. The publisher thinks I should have seen this Y2K thing coming. Last week, he yelled at me for sending all our old Selectrics to churches in El Salvador. Even though the board gave me a plaque for that three years ago. It's hanging in my den . . . I think I just talked them into buying backup generators."

Lincoln tried to tell Greg, again, that he really didn't think anything bad was going to happen on New Year's Eve. Even if the coding failed, Lincoln said, which it probably wouldn't, the computers wouldn't get confused and self-destruct. "*Logan's Run* isn't real," he said.

"Then why do I feel too old for this shit?" Greg asked.

That made Lincoln laugh. If he worked days, with Greg, he might not spend so much time thinking about quitting.

CHAPTER 23

From: Jennifer Scribner-Snyder
To: Beth Fremont
Sent: Tues, 10/12/1999 9:27 AM
Subject: Another nice story.

The way you were complaining last week, I had lowered my expectations. But look at you—front page, above the fold. Giant picture, nice lead, nice ending. I especially like the quote from that protester: "If the Taj Mahal had been built on 84th and Dodge, they'd tear it down for parking."

<<Beth to Jennifer>>
1. Stop, you're too nice. You're like my mother or something.
2. That protester was very cute. Lovely red hair. A pharmacy student, no less. (Now *I* sound like my mother.) We had a very nice conversation about the way this city worships good parking. I said that eventually, we'll tear down every building of interest and just run shuttles to Des Moines and Denver. We'll have a parking-based economy. He thought that was very funny, I could tell. And then, when I asked for a follow-up number, in case I had further questions, he asked for *my* number. (!!!!)

<<Jennifer to Beth>> What? That happened yesterday? Why are you holding out on me? If cute, redheaded pharmacy students ever gave me the time of day, you'd be the first to know. Not like that would ever happen. Even construction workers don't whistle at me.

<<Beth to Jennifer>> That's because you ooze preemptive leave-me-alone death rays. Besides, anyone who gets within 10 feet of you spots the giant rock on your finger.

<<Jennifer to Beth>> And also, I'm dumpy. What did you tell the cute anti-parking guy?

<<Beth to Jennifer>>

1. If you keep insisting that you're dumpy, I'll stop sharing my romantic misadventures with you. You'll have to read about them in *Penthouse* Forum like everybody else.

2. I did something weird. I lied to him.

<<Jennifer to Beth>> You didn't tell him you had a boyfriend?

<<Beth to Jennifer>> Nope. I told him I had a fiancé.

"Sorry," I said. "I can't. I'm engaged." And then he looked at my hand and blushed. (It was an adorable, redheaded blush.) And I was like, "I left it on the sink."

I felt like you at the Baby Gap, buying munchkin overalls. Just making up my life. (Actually, it was more pathetic than that—because you don't even want a baby. I want to be engaged. Somewhat desperately, let's face it.)

Last night, when Chris came home and climbed into bed, I couldn't look him in the eye.

One, because part of me really wanted to give that guy my number.

And two, because I'd lied.

<<Jennifer to Beth>> Don't overthink wanting to give out your number. You were flattered. Attracted. That's natural. I know this from reading *Glamour* and watching *The View*, of course, not from personal experience.

Did Chris notice that you couldn't face him?

<<Beth to Jennifer>> No, there was no face time. He fell asleep before I could ask him how practice went. A long night grinding the ax takes it out of you.

<<Jennifer to Beth>> Ew. Is that a euphemism for mastur-b@tion?

<<Beth to Jennifer>> No. I think it's @ euphemism for pl@ying the electric guit@r. Or @n idiom. I don't know. Do you really think "masturbation" is one of Tron's red-flag words?

<<Jennifer to Beth>> Well, it doesn't matter now. If we get fired because you insist on poking the dragon, you're going to have to support me and my pricey Baby Gap habit.

<<Beth to Jennifer>>
1. Poking the dragon. Is that another masturbation reference?
2. Baby Gap. Still?

<<Jennifer to Beth>>
1. Ha.
2. Still. Last weekend, I scored a celery green snowsuit with matching mittens for $3.99!

<<Beth to Jennifer>> Green is a smart choice—good for an imaginary girl *or* an imaginary boy. And the season isn't at all relevant with imaginary children.

<<Jennifer to Beth>> Exactly. I don't even go to the adult Gap anymore. Once you're an imaginary mother, it's hard to take time for yourself.

<<Beth to Jennifer>> I imagine.

<<Jennifer to Beth>> So, what's tomorrow's Indian Hills story about?

<<Beth to Jennifer>> There isn't one.

<<Jennifer to Beth>> There better be. You're on the morning budget for 15 inches.

<<Beth to Jennifer>> FΩck.

CHAPTER 24

SO, THIS WAS what Lincoln's romantic life had come to. Reading what women wrote about other men, other *attractive* men. Guitar gods and action heroes and redheads.

That night, after he trashed Beth's and Jennifer's messages, after he'd left *The Courier*, Lincoln got onto the freeway. It was laid out in a rough square around the city. Once you were on the freeway, you could drive as long as you wanted to without getting off, without ever really going anywhere.

It's what he and Sam used to do on nights when they didn't feel like being around their parents or sitting in some diner. Lincoln would drive, and Sam would roll down her window and lean her head against the door, singing along with the radio.

She liked to listen to a show called "Pillow Talk" on the light-rock station. It was a request show. People would call in and dedicate songs on the air. They always requested sappy songs that were ten or fifteen years old even back then, songs by Air Supply, Elton John, and Bread. Sam liked to mock their on-air dedications, but she rarely changed the station.

She'd sing along, and they'd talk. The talking came easily to him when he was driving, maybe because he didn't have to make eye contact, maybe because it gave him something to do with his hands. Because it was dark and the freeway was empty. Because of the love songs. And the wind.

"Lincoln," Sam had asked him on one of those nights, the summer before their senior year, "do you think we'll get married some day?"

"I hope so," he'd whispered. He didn't usually think about it like that, like "married." He thought about how he never wanted to be without her. About how happy she made him and how he wanted to go on being that happy for the rest of his life. If a wedding could promise him that, he definitely wanted to get married.

"Wouldn't it be romantic," she said, "to marry your high school sweetheart? When people ask us how we met I'll say, 'We met in high school. I saw him, and I just knew.' And they'll say, 'Didn't you ever wonder what it would be like to be with someone else?' And you'll say . . . Lincoln, what will you say?"

"I'll say, 'No.'"

"That's not very romantic."

"It's none of their business."

"Tell *me,* then," she said, unbuckling her seat belt and putting her arm around his waist. "Tell me now, won't you ever wonder what it would have been like to be with someone else?"

"First, buckle up," he said. She did. "I won't wonder that because I already know what it would be like to be with someone else."

"How do you know?" she said.

"I just do."

"Then, what would it be like?"

"It would be less," he said.

"Less?"

He looked over at her, just for a second, sitting sideways in her bucket seat, and squeezed the steering wheel. "It would have to be. I already love you so much. I already feel like something in my chest is going to pop when I see you. I couldn't love anyone more than I do you, it would kill me. And I couldn't love anyone less because it would always feel like less. Even if I loved some other girl, that's all I would ever think about, the difference between loving her and loving you."

Sam squirmed out of the top half of her seat belt and laid her head on his shoulder. "That is *such* a good answer."

"It's a true answer."

"What if"—her voice was soft and girlish now—"someday, someone asks whether you ever wonder what it would be like to . . . *be* with some-body else."

"Who would ask that?"

"This entire scenario is hypothetical."

"I don't even know what it's like to *be* with you." Lincoln said this quietly and without resentment.

"Yet."

"Yet," he said, focusing on the road and the gas pedal and breathing.

"So . . . won't you look at other girls and wonder what you're missing?"

"No," he said.

"No?"

"I know you want more than a one-word answer. Let me think about this for a minute, I don't want it to sound stupid or desperate."

"Do you feel desperate?" She was kissing his neck now and leaning hard against him.

"I'm feeling . . . yes. Desperate. And like I might kill us both. I can't . . . I can't keep my eyes open when you're doing that, it's like sneezing. We're almost to the next exit. Let me drive, just for a few more minutes. Please."

She sat back in her seat. "No, don't get off at this exit. Keep driving."

"Why?"

"I want you to keep talking. I want you to answer my question."

"No," he said. "*No*, I'll never wonder what it would be like to *have sex* with someone else for the same reason I don't want to kiss anyone else. You're the only girl I've ever touched. And I feel like it was supposed to be that way. I touch you and my whole body . . . rings. Like a bell or something. And I could touch other girls, and maybe there would be something, you know, like maybe there would be noise. But not like with you. And what would happen if I kept touching and touching them, and then . . . and then, I tried to touch you again? I might not be able to hear us anymore. I might not ring true."

"I love you, Lincoln," Sam said.

"I love you," he said.

"And I love you."

"I love you," he said, "*I love you.*"

"Stop driving now, okay?"

It didn't happen that night, the being with each other. But it happened that summer. And it happened in the car. It was awkward and uncomfortable and wonderful.

"Only you," he'd promised. "Only you ever."

"PILLOW TALK" WASN'T on the air anymore. There was another show in its place, a syndicated show, where people called in with their love stories, and the host, a woman named Alexis, chose the song for them. No matter what the situation was, Alexis always prescribed a current adult contemporary hit. Something by Mariah Carey or Céline Dion.

After a few minutes of Alexis, Lincoln turned off the radio and rolled down the window. He leaned his hand into the wind and his head against the door, and drove around the city until his fingers were cold and numb.

CHAPTER 25

From: Beth Fremont
To: Jennifer Scribner-Snyder
Sent: Thurs, 10/14/1999 11:09 AM
Subject: October, at last!

Callooh! Callay!

<<**Jennifer to Beth**>> At last? October is half over. And what's in October anyway?

<<**Beth to Jennifer**>> Not "what's in," what *is*. October. My favorite month. Which, by the way, has only half begun.

Some find it melancholy. "October," Bono sings, "and the trees are stripped bare . . ."

Not I. There's a chill in the air that lifts my heart and makes my hair stand on end. Every moment feels meant for me. In October, I'm the star of my own movie—I hear the soundtrack in my head (right now, it's "Suite: Judy Blue Eyes")—and I have faith in my own rising action.

I was born in February, but I come alive in October.

<<**Jennifer to Beth**>> You're a nut.

<<**Beth to Jennifer**>> A hazelnut. A filbert.

October, baptize me with leaves! Swaddle me in corduroy and nurse me with split pea soup. October, tuck tiny candy bars in my pockets and carve my smile into a thousand pumpkins.

O autumn! O teakettle! O grace!

<<**Jennifer to Beth**>> I do love tiny candy bars.

<<**Beth to Jennifer**>> Merry October!

<<**Jennifer to Beth**>> All right, Merry October! Why not?
Are there other factors in your unreasonably good mood? Non-autumnal reasons?

<<**Beth to Jennifer**>> Nope, I don't think so. I had a really crappy night last night—I went to a Sacajawea party with Chris—but I think that's actually enhancing my good mood today. I woke up thinking about how, no matter how bad everything else is, there's still October.

<<**Jennifer to Beth**>> Who has a party on a Wednesday night?

<<**Beth to Jennifer**>> Musicians.

<<**Jennifer to Beth**>> Don't most of them have day jobs?

<<**Beth to Jennifer**>> Their day jobs are night jobs. (Sometimes late-afternoon jobs.) Only the girlfriends have to get up in the morning, and mentioning that you have to get up—that you really shouldn't be partying on a school night, so to speak—is band-girlfriend blasphemy.

<<**Jennifer to Beth**>> What happens to blasphemers?

<<**Beth to Jennifer**>> As soon as you leave, dragging your man with you or not, every other lord reaches for his lady and thanks her for not being such a killjoy. She, in turn, feels special and loved and goes to work the next morning haggard, headachy, and wearing a guitar pick around her neck like an albatross.

<<**Jennifer to Beth**>> Are you a killjoy?

<<**Beth to Jennifer**>> Oh, the worst. A killjoy of mythic proportions. For starters, I won't let them party at my apartment. And I leave all their parties early, by midnight. I've stopped pretending that staying up all night, smoking, and drinking have no effect on my body.

It wouldn't be any better if I stayed. You're not allowed to po-
litely not partake in their debauchery. That's as good as passing
judgment.

Last night was especially bad. Stef got all up in my face. He was
high, and I think he was trying to impress some girl he picked up
at a show.

"Beth . . . ," he said, "why don't you have fun anymore?"

I ignored him, which he couldn't let stand. "I'm serious, Beth,
you've changed. You used to be cool."

"I haven't changed. I was never cool."

"You were. When Chris started bringing you around, the rest of
us were jealous. You had that hair down to your waist and your
tight Hüsker Dü T-shirts, and you'd get wasted and stay up all
night rewriting our choruses."

He's vile in so many ways:

1. Implying that he ever liked me.

2. Reminding me how he used to stare at my breasts.

3. Making me scramble to insult him in a way that won't insult
Chris. I mean, I can't say, "I'm an adult now" or, "There's nothing
to rewrite, you've been playing the same songs for six years . . ."

So I said, "Give it a rest, Stef, I'm tired."

Then he got all fake-sympathetic and suggested that I go home
so I would be all rested up for work in the morning. I told him that
movie reviewers never go to work before noon. Union rules.

"I think that's what changed you, Beth. Your job. The *film critic.*
Critics are parasites. They live off other people's creativity. They
bring nothing into this world. They're like barren women who steal
other people's babies in grocery store parking lots. Those who can't
do, teach, and those who can't teach, criticize."

Just when he'd settled into a fine rant, one of the other guys
decided to cut him off—"Hey, Chris, aren't you going to defend
your girlfriend?"

And Chris said, "Beth doesn't need my help defending herself.
Trust me. She's a Valkyrie."

Which sort of made me feel good. That he loves me strong

and independent. But also, I would like some defending. And also, don't Valkyries steal the souls of fallen warriors? Or maybe just escort them to heaven or Valhalla or wherever? Either way, it doesn't make me a warrior. Maybe a Valkyrie is just another parasite, reflecting the glory of the souls she claims. I don't know, it's not what I wanted him to say.

I wanted him to say . . . "Fuck off, Stef."

Or, "Beth is not a barnacle on my boat. She's the wind beneath my wings. And, without her, films like *Armageddon* and *I Still Know What You Did Last Summer* would claim scores of innocent victims, our friends and neighbors. Hers is important work, *creative* work."

Or, "That's it, I quit this stupid band. I'm going back to school. I've always wanted to be a dentist."

<<Jennifer to Beth>> A dentist? Really, a dentist?

If Chris went back to school to become a dentist, I think you would dump him.

<<Beth to Jennifer>> I would not!

<<Jennifer to Beth>> I just can't picture you married to a dentist, somebody who wears sensible shoes and always smells like fluoride treatment.

<<Beth to Jennifer>> I can . . . He'd have a comfy little neighborhood dental practice with back issues of *Guitar World* in the waiting room. I would stop in to see him some afternoons, and he'd pull down his white mask to kiss me hello. The kids would fight over a set of giant teeth, and his nice, grandmotherly dental assistant would give them each a sugar-free lollipop . . .

<<Jennifer to Beth>> Wait a minute, the kids?

<<Beth to Jennifer>> You bet. A boy and a girl. Twins maybe. With his curly hair and my grade point average.

<<Jennifer to Beth>> What about your job?

<<Beth to Jennifer>> Are you kidding? I'm married to a dentist.

<<Jennifer to Beth>> Does this dental fantasy of yours take place in, like, 1973?

<<Beth to Jennifer>> I've always thought I would stay home when my kids were young. If I have kids. If I can afford it. My mom stayed home with us, and we turned out all right. I think I could handle being a stay-at-home mom for a few years.

<<Jennifer to Beth>> Hmmm . . . I think I'd like to be a stay-at-home mom with no kids.

<<Beth to Jennifer>> You mean, you just want to stay home?

<<Jennifer to Beth>> And do stay-at-home-mom stuff. Bake. Do crafts.

<<Beth to Jennifer>> What kind of crafts?

<<Jennifer to Beth>> I could crochet sweaters and make elaborate scrapbooks. I could buy one of those hot-glue guns.

<<Beth to Jennifer>> If our foremothers could hear us, they would regret winning the sexual revolution.

<<Jennifer to Beth>> My mother didn't fight in the sexual revolution. She's not even aware it happened. My dad left 20 years ago, and she still goes on and on about The Man being the head of the household.

<<Beth to Jennifer>> So you grew up in a headless household?

<<Jennifer to Beth>> Exactly. With my mother, the housewife without a husband.

<<Beth to Jennifer>> Your mother is depressing. I'm going back to my dentist fantasy.

<<Jennifer to Beth>> And I'm going back to work.

<<Beth to Jennifer>> Killjoy.

CHAPTER 26

BETH AND JENNIFER seemed to have forgotten all about the rules and restrictions. They didn't censor themselves anymore. Beth was so careless, some of her e-mails to other coworkers ended up in the WebFence folder, too.

Beth.

Lincoln couldn't explain, even to himself, why she mattered to him. She and Jennifer were both funny, both caring, both smart as whips. But Beth's whip always caught him by the ankle.

He felt like he could hear her talking when he read her mail, like he could see her even though he still didn't know what she looked like. He felt like he could hear her laughing.

He loved the way she put on kid gloves when Jennifer talked about her marriage and Mitch. He loved the way she riffed on her siblings and her bosses and herself. He tried not to love that she could recite scenes from *Ghostbusters*, that she liked kung fu movies and could name all of the original X-Men—because those seemed like reasons a guy would fall for a girl in a Kevin Smith movie.

Falling . . . Was he falling? Or was he just bored?

Sometimes, when his shift was over, maybe once or twice a week, Lincoln would walk through the newsroom, by Beth's desk, just to see the jumble of coffee cups and notebooks. Just to see the proof of her. By 1:00 A.M., even the copy editors were usually gone, and the room was lit by streetlights. If Lincoln felt a pang of conscience on his way to the newsroom, he told himself that it wasn't very wrong what he was doing.

As long as he didn't try to see Beth herself. He told himself it was like having a crush on a girl in a soap opera, a radio soap opera. Not anything to be proud of, but harmless. Something to make the nights go faster.

On some nights, like tonight, he'd let himself stop a moment at her desk.

A coffee cup. A half-eaten Toblerone. A puddle of spilled paper clips. And something new, a concert flyer, pinned above her monitor. It was hot pink with a picture of a cartoon guitar—Sacajawea at the Ranch Bowl, Saturday night. This Saturday night.

Huh.

JUSTIN WAS UP for a concert. Justin was up for anything, always. He offered to drive, but Lincoln said they should probably just meet at the bar.

"Dude, I get it, you're a rambling man. I won't tie you down."

They met at the Ranch Bowl about a half hour before Sacajawea took the stage. Justin was clearly disappointed with the place. It was dirty and cramped, there were no tables or shot specials, and you had to squeeze behind the stage just to get to the bar. The crowd was mostly men, and the band onstage—Razorwine, according to their drum kit—sounded like somebody playing a Beastie Boys album over a table saw. Lincoln and Justin found a spot along the wall to lean against, and Justin immediately started talking about leaving. He was too discouraged even to buy a drink.

"Lincoln, come on, this place is depressing. It's a graveyard. Worse. A fucking pet cemetery. Lincoln. Dude. Let's go. Come on. Drinks on me for the rest of the night."

A guy standing near them, a bulky guy in a flannel shirt, eventually told Justin to shut up. "Some of us came to listen to the music."

"That's your own fucking problem," Justin said through clenched teeth and a puff of Camel smoke. Lincoln grabbed his friend by the sleeve and pulled him back.

"What are you afraid of?" Justin demanded. "You're a brick wall. You can take that guy."

"I don't want to take him. I just want to hear this band, the next band. I thought you liked metal."

"This isn't metal music," Justin said. "This is horseshit."

"A half hour," Lincoln said. "Then we'll go wherever you want."

The table-saw band ended their set, and Sacajawea began setting up their instruments. It wasn't hard to find him, Beth's boyfriend. He was just as good-looking in person as he was in her photos. Willowy and wild-haired. All the guys in the band had long feminine hair. They were wearing tight pants and open, flowing shirts.

"What the fuck," Justin said.

The crowd around them was shifting. The burly guys headed for the bar, and groups of women emerged from the shadows. Girls in low-rise jeans. Girls with pierced tongues and butterfly tattoos. "Where did all these belly rings come from?" Justin wanted to know. The lights dropped, and Sacajawea's set started with a blistering guitar solo.

The women pressed forward against each other, against the stage. Like Lincoln, most of the girls had eyes only for the guitarist. The singer—that would be Stef, Lincoln thought—had to woo them his way. He purred like Robert Plant and stomped like Mick Jagger. By the end of the first song, Stef was pulling girls onstage to grind against his mic stand. But not Chris. Chris was focused on his guitar. Every once in a while, he'd look up at the girls in the audience and smile, as if he'd just noticed them there. They loved that.

"Let's go," Lincoln said to Justin, not sure anymore what he had come to see. He'd skipped D&D for this.

"Fuck you," Justin said. "These guys rock."

They did rock, Lincoln admitted to himself. If you liked that sort of thing. Sweaty, sexy, soaring acid rock. He and Justin stayed for the rest of the show. After it was over, Justin wanted to go the Village Inn across the street. He spent twenty minutes rehashing the concert and another two hours talking about a girl, the same girl he'd gone home with the night he and Lincoln had gone to The Steel Guitar together. Her name was Dena, and she was a dental hygienist. They'd gone out or stayed in almost every night since they'd met, and now Dena wanted to be exclusive, which was stupid, Justin said, because he didn't have time to see anyone else anyway.

But being exclusive, practically speaking, Dena said, was different from being exclusive, officially speaking. The former, she argued, meant that Justin was still allowed to have sex with somebody as soon as he had fifteen minutes of free time and a willing partner. Which was exactly fucking right, Justin said. He didn't want a girlfriend. He hated the idea of being with just one person—almost as much as he hated the idea of sharing Dena with anybody else.

Lincoln ate two pieces of French silk pie and listened. "If you really wanted to be with another girl," he said finally, mulling a third piece, "you would be. You wouldn't be here with me, talking about Dena."

Justin thought for a moment. "Evil fucking genius," he said, slapping Lincoln on the arm and scooting out of their booth. "Dude. Thanks. I'll call you."

Lincoln stayed at the restaurant to finish his coffee and think about whether the universe had rewarded Justin with true love at The Steel Guitar just to punish Lincoln for saying that Cupid could never get past the bouncer there.

The Village Inn had reached its 3:00 A.M. nadir when Lincoln got up to leave. The restaurant was empty except for a man sitting in a corner booth, wearing headphones and reading a paperback. Even in the early-morning, bacon-grease light, Chris looked flawless. The waitress filling the ketchup bottles was staring at him, but he didn't seem to notice.

CHAPTER 27

"HAVE YOU BEEN up to the newsroom before?" Greg asked Lincoln when he got to work Monday afternoon.

"No." How did Greg know? What did Greg know? No, wait, nothing. There was nothing to know. "I'm sorry," Lincoln said, "what?"

"What? The newsroom," Greg said. "You've been up to the newsroom before, right?"

"Right," Lincoln said.

"Right, anyway. So you know where the copy editors sit?"

"Yeah, I think so."

"I need you to install these new towers at a few stations." Greg pointed to a stack of computer boxes and handed Lincoln a piece of paper.

"Now?"

"Yeah. They know you're coming. They've moved their people to different desks."

Lincoln loaded the boxes onto a cart and took the elevator to the newsroom. The place was hardly recognizable at four o'clock, in daylight. There were people everywhere, all typing or talking or moving around. You wouldn't think that writing and editing would make so much noise. Telephones ringing, televisions buzzing, babies crying . . .

Babies? There was a crowd of people at one end of the copy desk, all fussing over a stroller. A small boy was sitting on someone's desk, playing with a stapler.

Lincoln started disconnecting cables, untangling wires, and trying not to look too closely at any of them. Jennifer must sit over here with the other day copy editors. She might still be here. This might even be her desk. No, not unless she was obsessed with Kansas basketball. What did he know about her? That she was married. Would she look married? That she thought she was fat . . . That could be any of them. Beth could be here, too. Walking around. Talking to an editor. Cooing over that baby.

No, he told himself, *don't look.*

It took about three hours to install the new computers. The newsroom turned into its nighttime self while Lincoln worked. It got quieter and darker. The people wearing ties gave way to people wearing wrinkled T-shirts and shorts. One of the nighttime editors, a girl with a limp blond ponytail and nice blue eyes, brought in banana bread and offered him a piece.

He thanked her, then headed up to the empty IT office without looking back.

CHAPTER 28

From: Jennifer Scribner-Snyder
To: Beth Fremont
Sent: Mon, 10/18/1999 4:08 PM
Subject: This isn't a day care, you know.

It's a newsroom.

<<**Beth to Jennifer**>> What are you getting at—that I shouldn't be taking a nap? Or that I shouldn't be using a sippy cup? Because it's all part of my method.

<<**Jennifer to Beth**>> What I'm getting at is, I shouldn't have to listen to babbling and cooing when I'm trying to edit Dear Abby.

<<**Beth to Jennifer**>> Why do you have to edit Dear Abby? Doesn't all that stuff come in a package from the wire service?

<<**Jennifer to Beth**>> Someone has to write the headline. Someone has to give it a good once-over, make sure there aren't words or entire paragraphs missing. Content doesn't magically appear in the newspaper. Hence, the roomful of editors.

<<**Beth to Jennifer**>> Editors, huh? By golly . . . you're right. They're *everywhere*. What is this place? Heaven?

<<**Jennifer to Beth**>> Ha.

<<**Beth to Jennifer**>> You're supposed to say, "It's Iowa."

<<**Jennifer to Beth**>> Maybe next time.

Why do people with children bring them to work? This isn't a place for children. There are no toys here. There are no changing stations. The drinking fountains are all set at adult heights.

This is a *workplace*. People come here to get away from their kids—to get away from all talk of kids. If we wanted to work with children, we would get jobs at primary schools and puppet shows. We would walk around with peppermint sticks in our pockets.

This is a newsroom. Do you see any peppermint sticks?

<<**Beth to Jennifer**>> You alliterate when you're angry. It's adorable.

<<**Jennifer to Beth**>> You are a barrel of laughs today, an entire barrel.

<<**Beth to Jennifer**>> Speaking of adorable, I saw my cute guy again last week.

<<**Jennifer to Beth**>> Are you sure? I didn't hear the alarm. Also, when did he become *your* cute guy?

<<**Beth to Jennifer**>> No one else has claimed him. He definitely works in Advertising. I saw him sitting back there.

<<**Jennifer to Beth**>> What were you doing in Advertising? That's on the other side of the building.

<<**Beth to Jennifer**>> I was trolling for cute guys. (Also, Advertising has the only pop machine in the building that sells root beer.) He was sitting at his cute desk, typing on his cute computer, looking super-super cute.

<<**Jennifer to Beth**>> Advertising, huh? I'm pretty sure they make more than us over there.

<<**Beth to Jennifer**>> They might just *look* like they make more.

And he doesn't necessarily look like he sells advertising. He's not one of those guys with the suits and the *Glengarry Glen Ross* smiles. He doesn't look like he wears product in his hair.

<<**Jennifer to Beth**>> I want to see him. Maybe we should take a root beer break.

<<**Beth to Jennifer**>> How can someone who hates children enjoy root beer?

CHAPTER 29

BETH HAD BEEN there. At her desk. In the same room with him, at the same time. Thinking about somebody else. About somebody who worked in Advertising, no less. Lincoln hated the guys who worked in Advertising. Whenever WebFence caught a dirty joke, it inevitably originated from a guy in Advertising. Salespeople. Lincoln hated salespeople. Except Justin. And, honestly, if he didn't know Justin, he'd probably hate him, too.

One time, he'd had to rebuild a hard drive up in Advertising; it'd taken a few hours, and the next day, when Lincoln went to put on his sweatshirt, it still smelled like Drakkar Noir. *No wonder my mom thinks I'm gay.*

Jealous, he thought, as he walked by Beth's desk that night—coffee cups, Halloween candy, Discman—*I'm jealous.* And not even of the boyfriend. He felt so far from being in the same league as Chris, that he couldn't be jealous of him. But some guy who works in Advertising, some guy who tries to upsell, who makes cold calls . . .

Lincoln picked up a miniature Mr. Goodbar and unwrapped it. Beth had been sitting right here while he was working on the copy desk. He might have been able to see her if he'd looked.

From: Jennifer Scribner-Snyder
To: Beth Fremont
Sent: Tues, 10/26/1999 9:45 AM
Subject: I think I'm pregnant.

I'm serious this time.

<<**Beth to Jennifer**>> Have you been exposed to radiation? Eating a lot of tuna? Shooting heroin?

<<**Jennifer to Beth**>> No, honestly, this isn't a paranoid thing. I think I'm pregnant.

<<**Beth to Jennifer**>> Because your period is three minutes late. Because you've had to pee twice in the last hour. Because you feel a *presence* in your womb.

<<**Jennifer to Beth**>> Because I had unprotected sex while I was ovulating.

<<**Beth to Jennifer**>> Is this a joke? Am I on *Candid Camera*? Who are you really, and what have you done with my friend?

The Jennifer Scribner-Snyder I know and love would never publicly admit to having had any sex at all, and certainly wouldn't sully her fingertips by typing it out like that.

She also would never start a sentence with "because." Where's my prudish little friend? What have you done with her?

<<Jennifer to Beth>> I don't have time to mince words.

<<Beth to Jennifer>> Why not? How pregnant are you?

<<Jennifer to Beth>> Four days.

<<Beth to Jennifer>> That's a little specific. (Almost grossly specific.) How could you possibly know already? And how do you know you were ovulating? Are you one of those women who can feel their eggs moving around?

<<Jennifer to Beth>> I know I was ovulating because I bought a fertility monitor.

<<Beth to Jennifer>> Just assume that my response to your next 12 statements is, "Say what?"

<<Jennifer to Beth>> I thought that if I knew when I was ovulating, I could avoid intimate contact at those times (which, honestly, hasn't been much of an issue lately).

So, four days ago, I knew I was ovulating. On that day, I hardly talked to Mitch. He left for school while I was still asleep. When I came home from work, he was upstairs, practicing the tuba. I could have gone up to tell him I was home, but I didn't. I could have yelled up to see if he wanted a grilled cheese sandwich, but I didn't.

When he came up to bed, I was already there, watching a *Frasier* rerun. I watched him get ready for bed, and he didn't say a word to me. It wasn't like he was mad; it was more like I was a piece of debris in the middle of the road that he was driving around.

I thought to myself, "My marriage is the most important thing in my life. I would rather have a happy marriage than anything—a good job, a nice house, opposable thumbs, the right to vote, *anything*. If not wanting a baby is destroying my marriage, I'll have a baby. I'll have 10 babies. I'll do whatever I have to do."

<<Beth to Jennifer>> What did Mitch think?

<<Jennifer to Beth>> I don't know. I didn't tell him about the ovulating part. He was surprised by the unprotected part. I don't know.

<<**Beth to Jennifer**>> Okay, so you might be pregnant. But you might not.

<<**Jennifer to Beth**>> You mean, I might be infertile.

<<**Beth to Jennifer**>> No, I mean, you might have at least another month to think about whether you really want to get pregnant. Most couples have to try more than once. You might not have sealed your fate four days ago.

<<**Jennifer to Beth**>> I hope I did. I just want to get this over with.

<<**Beth to Jennifer**>> Write that down, so you'll remember to put it in the baby book.

How long before you know for sure?

<<**Jennifer to Beth**>> Not long. They have those super-sensitive pregnancy tests that can tell whether you're even thinking about getting pregnant.

<<**Beth to Jennifer**>> So, are we rooting for a positive or a negative result, here?

<<**Jennifer to Beth**>> Just root for me.

<<**Beth to Jennifer**>> I always do.

CHAPTER 31

"I HAVEN'T HEARD you complain about work for a while," Eve said. "Are you liking it better?"

She'd brought her boys over for Sunday brunch after church. Lincoln's mother had made potato casserole with eggs, turkey, tomatoes, mushrooms, dandelion greens, and three kinds of cheese.

"Work is fine," Lincoln said, taking a bite.

"You're not bored?" Eve asked.

"I guess I'm getting used to it," he said, covering his mouth.

"Are you still looking for something with better hours?"

He shrugged. "These hours will be great if I decide to go back to school."

Eve frowned. She was especially edgy this afternoon. When she'd walked into the house, their mother had asked the boys if they'd had a good conversation with their higher power.

"Jesus," Eve had said. "We call him Jesus."

"That's one of the names he answers to," her mother had said.

"So," Eve said to Lincoln now, stabbing a mushroom, "you must have enough money saved to get a place closer to campus."

"It's not a bad drive from here," he said evenly.

Their mother started giving everyone a second helping of casserole. He could see she was torn. On the one hand, she still didn't like him going back to school, on the other, she hated when Eve bullied him.

"Why are they doing that?" his mother said, frowning at her grandsons. The boys were sorting the casserole into piles on their plates.

"Doing what?" Eve asked.

"Why aren't they eating their food?"

"They don't like it when things touch," Eve said.

"What things?" his mother asked.

"Their food. They don't like it when different foods touch or mix together."

"How do you serve dinner, in ice cube trays?"

"We only eat two things, Grandma," said Eve's older son, six-year-old Jake Jr.

"What two things?" she asked.

"Like hot dogs and macaroni," Jake said. "Or hamburgers and corn."

"I don't like ketchup on my hamburger," said Ben, the four-year-old.

"I like ketchup on the side," Jake said.

"Fine," Lincoln's mom said, taking their plates and scraping them onto her own. "Are you boys still hungry? I've got fruit, I've got bananas, do you like bananas?"

"So you're staying here?" Eve turned on Lincoln with new ferocity. "You're just going to keep living here?"

"For now," he said.

"Lincoln is always welcome here," their mother said.

"I'm sure he is," Eve said. "He's welcome to rot here for the rest of his life."

Lincoln set down his fork.

"Grandma," Ben said, "this banana is dirty."

"That's not dirt," she said.

"It's brown," he said.

"It's banana-colored."

"Bananas are yellow," Jake said.

"Lincoln is not rotting," their grandmother said.

"He isn't living," Eve said.

"Don't tell me how to raise my son."

"He's twenty-eight years old," Eve said. "Your job is done. He's risen."

"Like Jesus," Jake said.

"Not like Jesus," Eve said.

Lincoln stood up from the table. "Would anyone else like juice? Ben? Jake?" His nephews ignored him.

"You're never done raising your children," his mother said. "You'll see. You're not done until you're dead."

"Jesus died when he was thirty-three," Jake said.

"Stop talking about Jesus," Eve said.

"Jesus!" Ben said.

"I'm still Lincoln's mother. I'm still your mother. Whether you like it or not, I'm not done raising either of you."

"You never started raising me," Eve said.

"Eve . . ." Lincoln winced.

"You're excused, boys," Eve said.

"I'm still hungry," Ben said.

"Can we go to Wendy's?" Jake asked.

"Tell me more about how to be a good mother," Eve's mother said.

"I'll tell you this," Eve said. "My boys are going to have lives of their own. They're going to go on dates and get married and move out. I'm not going to make them feel like they aren't allowed to say good-bye to me."

"I never made you feel that way."

"You came to kindergarten with me for the first month."

"You asked me to."

"I was five," Eve said. "You should have told me no."

"You were scared."

"I was *five*."

"I didn't send Lincoln until he was seven, and I'm so glad. He was so much more prepared."

Lincoln had been prepared for kindergarten. He could already read and do some addition and subtraction. He'd ended up skipping the first grade.

"Oh my God"—Eve slammed her fork on the table—"can't you even hear yourself?"

"Don't talk about Jesus, Mommy," Ben whispered.

"Come on, boys," Lincoln said, "let's go outside. Let's play soccer."

"You're a very bad soccer player," Jake said.

"I know," Lincoln said. "You can teach me."

The kitchen windows were open. Even after Lincoln took his nephews outside, they could still hear his sister and mother shouting.

"Food touches!" Lincoln heard his mother say. "The world touches!"

After about twenty minutes, Eve leaned out the back door and told the boys to come say good-bye to Grandma. Eve looked frustrated and angry, and she'd been crying.

"We're going to Wendy's," she said to Lincoln. "Do you want to come?"

"No, I'm full."

"I'm not sorry about anything I said," she said. "It was all true. You are rotting here."

"Maybe," he said. "Maybe I'm ripening."

Eve slammed the back door closed.

CHAPTER 32

WHEN LINCOLN GOT to work on Monday, Greg took him aside to talk about the millennium project.

"It seems like they're working, right?" Greg asked, looking over at the Y2K kids' corner. "I mean, they're putting in a shit-ton of hours."

Lincoln decided not to tell Greg that his International Strike Force stayed pretty late some nights, playing Doom. (Right in front of Lincoln. You'd think they'd at least ask him to play.)

"They're so quiet," Greg said. Lincoln nodded. "Sometimes, I look over at them, and their screens are full of code, and I think about the time I had my appendix out and woke up on the operating table . . . I mean, they could be doing *anything* in there."

"I think they're just writing code," Lincoln said.

"Fucking millennium," Greg said.

CHAPTER 33

From: Jennifer Scribner-Snyder
To: Beth Fremont
Sent: Wed, 11/10/1999 10:13 AM
Subject: Positive.

Well, I took the test last night, and I've felt like I was going to throw up ever since . . . Not because I have morning sickness, I think it's too early for that.

<<**Beth to Jennifer**>> Oh my God. CONGRATULATIONS!!! Congratulations, congratulations! OH MY GOD!!!

<<**Jennifer to Beth**>> I don't feel like being congratulated right now. I told you, I feel like throwing up. I think I might have made a huge mistake. As soon as I saw that blue line, I remembered how much I don't want to have kids, the baby shaking, etc. . . .

<<**Beth to Jennifer**>> Are we talking about actual baby shaking or figurative baby shaking?

<<**Jennifer to Beth**>> Potential. Don't I seem like the type?

<<**Beth to Jennifer**>> Don't be stupid. You're going to be fine. You're going to be wonderful. Does Mitch know?

<<**Jennifer to Beth**>> I told him last night. He was ecstatic. Seriously, he was so happy that he almost started crying. He couldn't stop hugging me. It was creepy.

<<Beth to Jennifer>> That doesn't sound creepy. That sounds nice.

<<Jennifer to Beth>> Says the woman who *isn't* incubating a parasitic organism.

<<Beth to Jennifer>> You make it sound like you have a tapeworm.

<<Jennifer to Beth>> Wait until it starts kicking.

<<Beth to Jennifer>> Have you told your parents?

<<Jennifer to Beth>> Mitch called his parents. They were also creepy-excited. I'm not telling my mother, ever.

<<Beth to Jennifer>> She might notice when you start to show.

<<Jennifer to Beth>> She'll just tell me that I look fat.

<<Beth to Jennifer>> I'm so happy for you. I'm creepy-happy. I'm totally throwing you a baby shower.

<<Jennifer to Beth>> That sounds terrible.

<<Beth to Jennifer>> Terribly awesome. I'll be like a shower expert by the time you have a baby. I have to go to three bridal showers for my sister in the next six weeks, and I'm hosting one.

<<Jennifer to Beth>> Three showers? Isn't that excessive?

<<Beth to Jennifer>> One of them is a personal shower.

<<Jennifer to Beth>> Oh, I hate those. If it's personal, it shouldn't be a shower. Who wants to open lingerie in front of their friends and relatives?

<<Beth to Jennifer>> Lingerie is mild. My cousin got sex toys at her personal shower. And her bridesmaids made her try on her skimpy new underwear so she could give us a fashion show. My aunt kept saying, "Sexy, sexy!"

<<Jennifer to Beth>> Why did you tell me that? Now I'm going to be making the "ew" face for the rest of the day.

<<Beth to Jennifer>> I'm going for a more refined vibe at the shower I'm hosting for her. We're having a tea party. I'm making tea sandwiches.

<<Jennifer to Beth>> I love tea sandwiches.

<<Beth to Jennifer>> Who doesn't? You know . . . I could throw you a tea party *baby* shower.

<<Jennifer to Beth>> With no games?

<<Beth to Jennifer>> Oh, there'll be games. That's nonnegotiable. But no sexy underwear, I promise.

<<Jennifer to Beth>> I'll consider it.
Enough about me and my tapeworm. How are you?

<<Beth to Jennifer>> You can't tell me you're pregnant and then change the subject.

<<Jennifer to Beth>> This is all anyone is going to talk to me about for the next nine months. It's all anyone is going to talk to me about for the rest of my life. *Please*, can we change the subject? How are you? How is Chris?

<<Beth to Jennifer>> Chris is . . . Chris. I guess. He's in one of his distant phases. He's gone a lot, and when he is home, he turns up the stereo too loud to talk. Or he sits in the bedroom with his guitar. I ask him if he wants to go out, and he says he doesn't feel like it. But when I get home, he's gone.

<<Jennifer to Beth>> Are you worried?

<<Beth to Jennifer>> Not really.

<<Jennifer to Beth>> You don't think he's seeing someone else?

<<Beth to Jennifer>> No. Maybe I should think that.
I think he just gets like this sometimes. Like he needs to pull away. I think of it like winter. During winter, it isn't that the sun is gone (or cheating on you with some other planet). You can still see it in the sky. It's just farther away.

<<Jennifer to Beth>> That would drive me crazy. I'd lose my temper—or get pregnant—just to shake things up.

<<Beth to Jennifer>> Losing my temper wouldn't help. I can't imagine what would happen if I got pregnant. Then he probably *would* leave.

<<**Jennifer to Beth**>> Don't say that. He wouldn't leave.

<<**Beth to Jennifer**>> Actually, I think he would. Or he wouldn't expect me to keep it.

<<**Jennifer to Beth**>> That's terrible.

<<**Beth to Jennifer**>> Do you really think so? You know what it's like to not want children, to want your relationship to stay a certain way. I don't think Chris would feel responsible for me getting pregnant. He would see it as my deal, my choice. And it would be, wouldn't it?

<<**Jennifer to Beth**>> Let's change the subject again.

<<**Beth to Jennifer**>> Gladly. Congratulations!!

CHAPTER 34

LINCOLN HAD SEEN Beth's boyfriend half a dozen times now. Justin had really taken to Sacajawea after that first show. Now he called Lincoln whenever the band was playing. Dena, Justin's girlfriend, would come, too. They usually ended up at the Village Inn afterward. They'd all order pie and listen to Justin dissect the night's show.

"How are these guys not fucking rock stars?" Justin always asked. "Why aren't they on MTV instead of all that Backstreet bullshit?"

Lincoln shrugged.

"Look," Dena said, nodding toward the smoking section, "there's the guitarist again."

Chris was sitting in a booth, eating a breakfast skillet and reading.

"How does a guy like that not have a girlfriend?" Dena asked.

"Maybe he does," Lincoln said.

"No way," Dena said. "Guys with girlfriends don't spend Friday nights eating alone at the Village Inn."

"He should be out nailing groupies," Justin said.

"He's always by himself," Dena said.

"If I looked like that," Justin said through a mouthful of meringue, "I'd be banging a different girl every night."

"You were doing that anyway," Dena said, rolling her eyes, "looking like you do."

"You're right," Justin said. "If I looked like that, I'd be banging *two* different girls every night."

"Maybe he has a girlfriend," Lincoln said.

"Then I feel sorry for his girlfriend," Dena said.

"Maybe he has a boyfriend," Justin said.

"Then I feel sorry for his boyfriend," Dena said.

"They have another show tomorrow," Justin said. "We should go."

"I'm playing D & D tomorrow night," Lincoln said.

"Talk about things you do when you don't have a girlfriend," Justin said.

Justin was always needling Lincoln to go out more. To be around women. To try. Maybe because Justin had known Sam in high school. Because he remembered the days when Lincoln was the one who always had a beautiful girl on his arm. "A little mouthy for my taste," Justin had said once during golf practice. "But hotter than a jalapeño milkshake."

After California, when Lincoln showed up at the state university a year behind everybody else, Justin never asked what happened with Sam. Lincoln had even tried to tell him about it one night, over Papa John's pizza and a six-pack of Dr. Diablo, but Justin had cut him off.

"Dude. Let it go. Good riddance to bad rubbers."

CHAPTER 35

IN THE END, Lincoln hadn't told anyone what happened with Sam in California. (Even though his mother had asked and asked and eventually confronted Sam's mother at the grocery store.)

He didn't talk about it because talking about would have been conceding it. Giving in to it. And because if he told someone, he knew it wouldn't sound that bad. That it was really a fairly standard teenage heartbreak. That the saddest part of the whole story was that he missed a semester of school and lost all his scholarships. That would be the saddest part to someone else, to an outside observer.

He didn't talk to his mom about it, not once, not ever, because he knew how happy it would make her to be right.

When he first left for college, she called him twice a week.

"I've never even been to California," she said.

"Mom, it's fine. It's a nice campus. It's safe."

"I don't know what it looks like," she said. "I can't picture you there. I try to think about you and to send you positive energy, but I don't know which way to send it."

"West," he said.

"That's not what I mean, Lincoln. How am I supposed to visualize good things happening for you if I can't visualize you?"

He missed her, too. He missed the Midwest. All the scenery Sam had wanted was making his head hurt. Northern California was impractically beautiful. Everywhere you looked there were trees and streams, waterfalls, mountains, the ocean. . . . There was nowhere to look just to look, just to think. He'd been spending a lot of time in the campus library, a place without windows.

Sam had been spending a lot of time at the school theater. She wasn't taking classes in the drama department yet, but she'd gone out for a few plays and landed small roles. Back in high school, when Sam went to rehearsals, Lincoln would go with her. He'd bring his homework and sit in the back row of the auditorium. He could study just fine that way. He could block out the talking and the noise. He liked to hear Sam's voice occasionally pealing through his chemistry problems.

Lincoln would have happily studied at the college theater while Sam rehearsed, but she felt like he was drawing too much attention to her there. "You're reminding them that I'm other," she said. "That I'm a freshman, that I'm not from around here. I need them to look at me and see my role. To see my talent and nothing else. You're reminding them that I have this cloying Heartland backstory."

"What's cloying?" he asked.

"The adoring-Germanic-farm-boy thing."

"I'm not a farm boy."

"To them, you are," she said. "To them, we both just fell off the tomato truck. They think it's funny that we're from Nebraska. They think the *word* Nebraska is funny. They say it like, 'Timbuktu' or 'Hoboken.'"

"Like 'Punxsutawney'?" he asked.

"Exactly. And they think it's hilarious that we came to college together."

"Why is that funny?"

"It's too sweet," she said. "It's exactly what two kids who just fell off the tomato truck would do. If you keep coming to rehearsals, I'm never going to get good parts."

"Maybe they'll do *Pollyanna*."

"Lincoln, please."

"I want to be with you. If I don't come to the theater, I won't ever see you."

"You will see me," she said.

He didn't.

Only when they met for breakfast in the dorm cafeteria. Only when she came to his room late after rehearsals to get help with an assignment or to cry about what was happening at the theater. She wouldn't stay over, not with his roommate there. He felt hungry for her all the time.

"We spent more time alone when we lived with our parents," he complained to her on a rare Friday afternoon she spent in his room, letting him hold her.

"We had nothing but time in high school," she said.

"Why does everyone else around here have so much time?" he asked.

"Who?"

"Everyone but you," he said. "Everywhere I go, I see people being together. They're in each other's rooms. They're in the lounge and the student union. They're taking walks." That's how he thought it would be when they got to college. He'd pictured himself lying next to Sam on narrow dormitory mattresses, holding her hand on the way to classes, winding up with her on benches and coffeehouse couches. "I have time for that."

"Then maybe you should spend your time with everyone else," she said. She was pulling away from him, buttoning her black cardigan, sweeping her hair into a barrette.

"No. I want to spend it with you."

"I'm with you now," she said.

"And it's wonderful. Why can't it be like this more? Even once a week?"

"Because it can't, Lincoln."

"Why not?" He hated himself for sounding like such a baby.

"Because I didn't come to this school to spend all my time with my high school boyfriend. I came here to start my career."

"I'm not your high school boyfriend," he said. "I'm your boyfriend."

"There are probably half a dozen girls on this floor alone who would love to spend the next four years cuddling with you. If that's what you want."

"I want you."

"Then be happy with me."

SAM DIDN'T WANT to come home for winter break. She wanted to stay on campus and be in a local production of *A Christmas Carol*. (She was pretty sure she could land the role of Tiny Tim.) But her father cashed in some frequent flyer miles and sent her a first-class ticket home. "I've never flown first class before," she told Lincoln excitedly. "I'm going to wear something Betty Grable, something with wrist gloves, and order gin and tonics." Lincoln was taking the Greyhound, which Sam said would be fascinating. "Very American-experience. I'll make you sandwiches."

She didn't. She said she couldn't see Lincoln off at the bus station because she had a theater meeting that afternoon. He told her that was okay, that he didn't want her to come anyway. A girl who could pass for Tiny Tim shouldn't walk home alone from the bus station.

But Lincoln hated that, between the bus trip and Christmas, he'd have to go a week without seeing her. At least they'd both be home. And they'd have the week after Christmas together, and New Year's. Maybe it would do them some good, to see each other back in their natural habitat. He decided to leave a note for Sam, telling her that he'd miss her, before he caught his bus. He bought an inexpensive bouquet of flowers at the convenience store across from his dormitory and wrote on a piece of college-ruled paper:

> Sam,
> *Lo, though I travel through the Valley of Death,*
> *My heart flies first class.*
>   Love, Lincoln

That sounds romantic, he thought as he walked to her building. And geographic. And vaguely biblical. He stopped on her floor, in the elevator lobby, to add a postscript: *I love you and I love you and I love you.* As he finished writing the last "you," one of the elevators opened.

Lincoln almost smiled at the sight of Sam. Almost. She was standing on tiptoe, her whole body arching upward, her arms cast triumphantly around another man's neck. The two of them were kissing too . . . too *enthusiastically* to notice that their elevator had arrived. The man had a handful of Sam's black curls, and a handful of her short skirt. The wrongness of the tableau didn't fully register with Lincoln until the doors were closing. *They must be rehearsing,* he actually thought. Didn't he recognize this guy from the theater?

Lincoln reached out and pressed the down button. The doors opened again.

Sure, he recognized him. Marlon. He was small and dark and from someplace else. Brazil. Or maybe Venezuela. He was the kind of guy who always had a crowd of people around him at wrap parties. The kind of guy who was always standing on a table to toast something. *Marlon.* He and Sam had been in a play together back in September, *The Straw.*

Sam took a deep kissing breath. Lincoln could see her tongue.

"Marlon?" he said out loud.

Sam turned abruptly. Her face fell as the doors closed a second time.

Lincoln started pressing the button angrily. The elevator opened again, but he ignored it. He wanted the other elevator now. He wanted, suddenly and desperately, to leave.

"Lincoln," he heard Sam say.

He ignored her. Kept punching the button.

"Let me explain," she said.

Punch, punch, punch. Down, down, down.

"It won't come as long as we're here," Sam said. She was standing in the elevator still. Marlon was holding the door open.

"Then go," Lincoln said.

"You can have this elevator," Marlon said in his sexy south-of-Ricky-Ricardo voice.

Punch, punch, punch.

"Lincoln, stop, you'll hurt your hand," Sam said.

"Oh, of course," Marlon said, "this is *Lincolon.*" He held his hands up in recognition. *Like he's going to hug me,* Lincoln thought. *No, like he's going to toast me. Ladies and gentleman, Lincolon!* The elevator doors started to close again. Sam stepped into the doorway.

"Get out of the elevator," Lincoln said. "Let me go."

"No," she said, "no one's going anywhere. Lincoln, you're scaring me."

He hit the lit down button hard. The light went out.

"Let's calm down," Marlon said, "we are all adults here."

No, Lincoln thought, *you're an adult. I'm only nineteen. And you're ruining the rest of my life. You're kissing it. You're spoiling it with your tiny, expressive hands.*

"It's not what you think," Sam said sternly.

"It's not?" Lincoln asked.

"Well . . . ," Marlon said diplomatically.

"It's not," Sam said. "Let me explain."

Lincoln might have let her explain, then, but he was crying. And he didn't want Marlon to watch. "Just let me go," Lincoln said.

"You could use the stairs," Marlon suggested.

"Oh," Lincoln said. "Right."

He tried not to run to the stairs. The crying was embarrassing enough. Crying down eight flights through the girls' dormitory. Crying alone at the bus station. Crying through Nevada and Utah and Wyoming. Crying into the sleeves of his plaid flannel shirt like the world's saddest lumberjack. Trying to think of all the times he'd promised Sam that he could never love anyone else. Did that change now? Did she get to turn them both into liars? If he believed in true love, didn't that trump everything? Didn't that trump Marlon? Lincoln was going to let her explain. When he got home. No, he wouldn't even ask her to explain.

Somewhere in Colorado, Lincoln started writing Sam a letter. "I don't believe you cheated on me," the letter said. "And even if you did, it doesn't matter. I love you more than anything else matters."

Eve picked him up at the bus station.

"You look terrible," she said. "Did you get rolled by hobos?"

"Can we drive by Sam's house on the way home?"

"Sure."

When they got there, Lincoln asked Eve not to pull into the driveway. Sam's room was the one over the garage. Her light was on. Lincoln thought about going to the door, but dropped the letter in the mailbox instead. He hoped Eve wouldn't ask him about it on the way home.

CHAPTER 36

LINCOLN CALLED SAM the next morning and the next. Her mother kept saying that Sam wasn't home. She didn't call him back until New Year's Eve.

"I got your letter," she said. "Can you meet me at the park?"

"Now?" he asked.

"Now."

Lincoln borrowed his sister's car and drove to a little playground near Sam's house. It was where they went when they didn't have any money or gas. It was empty when he got there, so he sat on the merry-go-round to wait. It hadn't been a white Christmas—the ground was bare and brown—but it was still cold. Lincoln kicked the merry-go-round into motion and let it spin slowly until he saw Sam walking toward him, still a block away. She was wearing bright pink lipstick and a flowery mini-dress over thermal underwear. No coat.

He hoped she'd sit next to him.

She did. She smelled like gardenias. He wanted to touch her, jump on her. Cover her like a hand grenade.

Sam exhaled matter-of-factly. "I thought we should probably talk," she said, "I thought that I should explain . . ."

"You don't have to," Lincoln said, already shaking his head.

She tucked her skirt under her legs.

"Are you cold?" he asked.

"I want you to know that I'm sorry," she said.

"You can have my jacket."

"Lincoln, *listen*." She turned to face him. He told himself not to look away. "I'm sorry," she said. But I feel like what happened probably happened for a reason. It forced everything to the surface."

"What everything?"

"Everything between us," she said, getting impatient. "Our relationship."

"I told you, we don't have to talk about this."

"Yes, we do. You saw me with another man. Don't you think that's worth talking about?"

Jesus. *Another man.* Why'd she have to say it that way?

"Lincoln . . . ," she said.

He shook his head, and kicked at the ground again until they were moving.

"I didn't mean for this to happen," she said after two or three go-rounds. "I got to know Marlon when we were rehearsing *The Straw*. We were together all the time, and it just turned into something more."

"But that play was in September," Lincoln said. With new distress.

"Yes."

"That was right after we got to California."

"I should have told you sooner."

"No," Lincoln said, "you should have . . . not done this."

They were both quiet for a few moments. Lincoln kept kicking, making the playground equipment turn faster, until Sam grabbed his arm. "Stop," she said. "I'm getting dizzy."

He dug his heels into the cold, hard dirt and hugged one of the metal handholds.

"How did you think our relationship was going to end?" Sam asked when they stopped. She seemed angry now. "And don't say that you didn't think it was going to end. You're not that naïve."

He was.

"These things end," she said. "They always end. Nobody marries their first love. First love is just that. First. It's implied that something else will follow."

"I never thought I'd hear you make the case against *Romeo and Juliet*," he said.

"They would have broken up if they'd lived for the sequel."

"I love you," he said. It came out too close to a whine. "Say that you don't love me."

"I won't say that." Her face was cold.

"Then say that you do."

"I'll always love you," she said, factually. She wasn't looking at him.

"Always," he said. "But not now. Not enough . . ."

"If I was meant to be with you," Sam said, "I wouldn't have fallen in love with Marlon."

Once, when Lincoln was playing croquet with his sister, she'd accidentally cracked him in the temple with a mallet. In the moment before he fell to the ground, he'd thought to himself, *I might die now. This might be it.* That's how he felt when Sam told him she was in love with Marlon.

"You make it sound like it *happened* to you," he said. "Like you had nothing to do with it. You make infidelity sound like a hole in the sidewalk. You had a choice."

"Infidelity?" She rolled her eyes. "Fine. Then I guess I chose to be unfaithful. Do you still want to be with me, knowing that?"

"Yes."

She threw back her head in disgust.

Lincoln moved closer to her. There was a cold steel bar between them (exactly the kind you're not supposed to lick).

"Why did you want me to come to California with you?" he asked. "If you knew we were going to break up?"

"I didn't plan it this way," she said. Less angry now, and maybe a little ashamed. "I didn't know *when* we were going to break up."

"I didn't know we were *ever* going to break up," he said. "If you had told me that it was a foregone conclusion, I wouldn't have followed you across the country . . ." He stopped talking and looked at her. Even in the dark, even in January, even breaking his heart, she was pink and radiant. She reminded him of a rosebush flowering in stop-motion. "God . . . ," he said, "you know what? I probably would have."

They were both quiet again. Lincoln couldn't trust himself to speak. Everything he wanted to say was wrong. Everything he wanted to say would make her want him less.

"I wanted you to come with me," Sam finally said, "because I was scared to go by myself. And I told myself that it was okay, letting you follow me . . . because it was what you wanted. And because you didn't have any other plans. And . . . because I guess I wasn't ready to say good-bye to you."

They were quiet for another long while.

"It's not like I fell out of love with you," Sam said. "I'm just not the same person that I was when I fell in love with you."

Quiet.

"People change," she said.

"Stop talking to me like that," he said.

"Like what?"

"Like I'm Lord Greystoke, and I need to be educated in the ways of man. I know that people change. I thought . . . I thought we were going to change together. I thought that's what it meant to be in love."

"I'm sorry."

More quiet. Sam watched her breath turned to frost. She leaned back on her elbows and made her face look distant. Then stricken. Then pained. She stuck with pained. Lincoln had seen her do this so many times, try on faces, that it didn't bother him.

"Earlier," Lincoln said. "You said you didn't plan it this way. How did you plan it?"

"I didn't plan it," she said. "I hoped that we would both just know when it was time . . . That we'd have one of those moments. Like in the movies, foreign movies, when something small happens, something almost imperceptible, and it changes everything. Like there's a man and a woman having breakfast . . . and the man reaches for the jam, and the woman says, 'I thought you didn't like jam,' and the man says, 'I didn't. Once.'

"Or maybe it isn't even that obvious. Maybe he reaches for the jam, and she just looks at him like she doesn't know him anymore. Like, in the moment he reached for that jar, she couldn't recognize him.

"After breakfast, he'll go for a walk, and she'll go to their room and pack a slim brown suitcase. She'll stop on the sidewalk and wonder whether she should say good-bye, whether she should leave a note. But she won't. She'll just get into the taxi and go.

"He knows as soon as he turns onto their walk that she's gone. But he doesn't turn back. He doesn't regret a single day they spent together, including this one. Maybe he finds one of her ribbons on the stairs . . ."

Sam lay back onto the merry-go-round. She'd talked herself into a looser place. Lincoln lay down beside her, so that their heads almost touched in the center.

"Who's playing me in your movie?" he asked gently.

"Daniel Day-Lewis," she said. She smiled. Lincoln could probably kiss her now if he wanted. Instead he leaned toward her ear so that she could hear him whisper.

"There's never been a moment," he barely said, "when I didn't recognize you."

She wiped her eyes. Her mascara smeared. He nudged the merry-go-round into motion. He could kiss her now. If he wanted.

"I'd know you in the dark," he said. "From a thousand miles away. There's nothing you could become that I haven't already fallen in love with."

He could kiss her.

"I know you," he said.

Even as she turned toward him, even as her hand came to his cheek, Lincoln knew that this didn't mean Sam had changed her mind. She was saying yes to the moment, not to him. He tried to tell himself that this was enough, but he couldn't. It wasn't. Now that she was in his arms, he needed her to tell him that everything was going to be okay.

"Tell me you love me," he said between kisses.

"I love you."

"Always," he said. It came out like an order.

"Always."

"Only."

She kissed him.

"Only," he said again.

"Don't," she said.

"Sam . . . ," he said.

"I can't."

He sat up. Stepped jaggedly off the merry-go-round.

"Lincoln," she said. "Wait."

He shook his head. He wanted to cry again, but not in front of her. Not in front of her again. He started walking to his car.

"I don't want you to go," Sam said. She was upset. "I don't want it to end like this."

"You don't get to choose," Lincoln said. "It's just happening."

CHAPTER 37

SHE'D DUMPED HIM. That's all. It wasn't that bad. It shouldn't have been. It's not like they were married. It's not like she abandoned him at the altar, or made off with his best friend and their retirement savings.

People get dumped all the time. Especially in college. They don't drop out of school. They don't drop out of life. They don't spend the next decade thinking about it every time they get a chance.

If Lincoln's freshman year had been an episode of *Quantum Leap*, Scott Bakula would have gotten back on the Greyhound bus after Christmas, finished the school year like a man, and started making calls to the financial aid office at the University of Nebraska. Or maybe he wouldn't have transferred at all. Maybe Scott Bakula would have stayed in California and asked that pretty girl in Lincoln's Latin class if she wanted to see a Susan Sarandon movie.

"DO YOU LIKE basset hounds?"

Lincoln was sitting in *The Courier* break room eating homemade potato soup and still thinking about Scott Bakula and Sam when Doris interrupted him. She was loading Diet Pepsi into the machine behind him.

Lincoln wasn't exactly sure what Doris's job was. Whenever he saw her, she was stocking the vending machines, but that didn't seem like it should be a full-time job. Doris was in her sixties with short, curly gray hair, and she wore a red vest, sort of a uniform, and large eyeglasses.

"Excuse me?" he asked, hoping he sounded polite, not confused.

"Basset hounds," she said, pointing to the open newspaper in front of him. There was a photo of a basset hound sitting on a woman's lap.

"I'd never have a basset hound if I lived so close to the ocean," she said. Lincoln looked at the photo. He didn't see any ocean. Doris must think he'd already read the story.

"They can't swim, you know," she said. "They're the only dogs who can't swim. They're too fat, and their legs are too short."

"Like penguins," Lincoln said thickly.

"I'm pretty sure penguins can swim," Doris said. "But a basset hound will drown in the bathtub. We had one named Jolene. Oh, she was a pretty little girl. I cried all night when we lost her."

"Did she drown?" Lincoln asked.

"No," Doris said. "Leukemia."

"Oh," he said, "I'm sorry."

"We had her cremated. Put her in a nice copper urn. It's only this big," Doris said, holding up a can of Wild Cherry Pepsi. "Can you believe it? A full-grown dog like Jolene in a tiny, tiny urn? There's not much to any of us once you take out all the water. How much is left in a person, do you think?" She waited for an answer.

"Probably less than a two-liter," Lincoln said, still feeling like it would be rude to act as if this was anything other than normal conversation.

"I'll bet you're right," Doris said sadly.

"When did she pass?" he asked.

"Well, it was when Paul was alive, let's see, sixteen years ago. We got two more basset hounds after that one, but they weren't as sweet . . . Honey, do you need any change while I've got this thing open?"

"No," Lincoln said. "Thank you."

Doris locked up the Pepsi machine. They talked a bit more about Jolene and about Doris's late husband, Paul, whom Doris missed but didn't get all choked up about the way she did Jolene. Paul had smoked and drank and refused to eat vegetables. Not even corn.

By the time she got to Dolly, her first basset, and Al, her first husband, Lincoln had forgotten that he was talking to Doris just to be polite.

———

HE STAYED HOME from work the next day. He went to his sister's house instead and helped her bring Christmas decorations down from the attic. "Why aren't you at work?" she asked, untangling a chain of plastic cranberries. "Did you just feel like taking a break?"

He shrugged and reached for another box. "Yeah. A break from taking a break."

"What's wrong?" she asked.

He'd come to Eve's house because he knew she'd ask him that. And he'd hoped that when she did ask, he'd have an answer. Things tended to come into focus when she was around.

"I don't know," he said. "I just feel like I have to do something."

"Do what?"

"I don't know. That's what's wrong. Or part of what's wrong. I feel like I'm sleepwalking."

"You look like you're sleepwalking," she said.

"And I don't know how to wake up."

"Do something," she said.

"Do what?"

"Change something."

"I have," Lincoln said. "I moved back. I got a job."

"You must not have changed the right thing yet."

"If I were in a movie," he said, "I'd fix this by volunteering with special-needs kids or the elderly. Or maybe I'd get a job in a greenhouse . . . or move to Japan to teach English."

"Yeah? So are you going to try any of those things?"

"No. I don't know. Maybe."

Eve looked at him coolly.

"Maybe you should join a gym," she said.

CHAPTER 38

From: Beth Fremont
To: Jennifer Scribner-Snyder
Sent: Tues, 11/16/1999 2:16 PM
Subject: My Cute Guy.

We're not calling him My Cute Guy anymore.

<<Jennifer to Beth>> I don't think I ever called him that.

<<Beth to Jennifer>> We're calling him My Very Cute Guy. Or maybe My Very Cute, Kind, and Compassionate—and Also Sort of Funny—Guy.

<<Jennifer to Beth>> Not very catchy. Does this mean you have new cute-guy information to share?

<<Beth to Jennifer>> Duh. Yes. I worked kind of late last night, and when I went to the break room around 9 for a delicious packet of Cheez-Its, guess who was sitting right there for all the world to see? My Cute Guy. He was eating his dinner and talking to Doris.

<<Jennifer to Beth>> Doris, the vending machine lady?

<<Beth to Jennifer>> None other. She was talking to him about her dog. Her dead dog, I think. Actually, there's a chance she was talking about a dead child, but I don't think so. Anyway. Doris was talking about her dog, and My Cute Guy was listening attentively and asking follow-up questions, nodding his head. (It was very involved. I don't think they even noticed me ogling.) He could not have been nicer.

<<Jennifer to Beth>> Maybe he just likes to talk about dead dogs.

<<Beth to Jennifer>> Or cuter. He could not have been cuter.

<<Jennifer to Beth>> And funny? How was he funny?

<<Beth to Jennifer>> It's hard to explain. Doris was asking him if a dead body would fit into a can of Pepsi, and he said it would probably fit better into a two-liter.

<<Jennifer to Beth>> That sounds gruesome. Has anyone seen Doris today?

<<Beth to Jennifer>> In context, it wasn't gruesome. I think she was talking about cremating her dog. I was eavesdropping, not taking notes. The important thing is, he was nice—really, really nice.

<<Jennifer to Beth>> And really, really cute.

<<Beth to Jennifer>> Oh my God, yes. You have got to see this guy. You know how I said he looked like Harrison Ford? I've had a better look now. He's Harrison Ford plus the Brawny paper towel guy. He's just massive.

<<Jennifer to Beth>> Like Mr. Universe massive?

<<Beth to Jennifer>> No . . . he's more like the guy they would have cast as the Hulk if they'd made a live-action Hulk movie in the forties or fifties, back when powerful didn't mean chiseled. Like if you saw John Wayne with his shirt off, he wouldn't have had a six-pack, he'd just look like the kind of guy you'd want on your side during a fight. Like maybe this guy, My Cute Guy, lifts weights. Dumbbells in his garage or something. But he'd never touch a protein shake.

You know what? We might have to start calling him My Handsome Guy. He's a little deeper than cute.

<<Jennifer to Beth>> Okay, I can see him now. Harrison Ford plus John Wayne plus the Hulk plus the Brawny guy.

<<Beth to Jennifer>> Plus Jason Bateman.

<<Jennifer to Beth>> Who's Jason Bateman?
Also, why were you still here last night at nine o'clock?

<<Beth to Jennifer>>
1. Jason Bateman was the best friend on *Silver Spoons*.
2. You know I like to work late.

<<Jennifer to Beth>>
1. The guy from *Fresh Prince*?
2. I just can't understand why you wouldn't rather be home.

<<Beth to Jennifer>>
1. The other best friend. The white guy. With the crinkly eyes and the interesting nose. His sister was on *Family Ties*.
2. I like to work late because I don't like to work early—and I have to work sometime.

If I get here first thing in the morning, I feel like I have to iron my clothes. But by 2 o'clock, nobody cares. And by 7, nobody's here. (Well, except copy editors, and they only half count.) Besides, it's kind of cool, being here at night. It's like being in the mall after it closes. Or at school on a Saturday. Plus, sometimes I legitimately have to work late. Like, if I have to write a review on opening night or something.

<<Jennifer to Beth>> I guess *I* just don't like being here that late. The year I worked on the nightside desk was the loneliest year of my life.

And I guess I know who Jason Bateman is. I've just never thought of him as cute.

<<Beth to Jennifer>> Well, think again. And My Cute Guy is even cuter.

CHAPTER 39

NO, NO, NO, Lincoln thought.

CHAPTER 40

NO.

It couldn't be . . .

She couldn't mean . . .

He stood up from his desk, walked around the empty information technology office. Sat back down. Reread the e-mail. Cute, she'd said. Massive, she'd said. Oh my God, she'd said.

Handsome.

No. It must be a mistake, she couldn't have meant . . . No.

He stood up again. Sat down. Stood up. Started walking toward the men's bathroom. Was there a mirror in there? What did he need to look at, anyway? To see if he still looked like himself? There was a mirror. Full-length. He looked at his reflection. Massive, he asked himself. Really? Massive?

Definitely big. In high school, the football coach was always trying to recruit him, but Lincoln's mother had forbidden it. "No, you're not joining the head-injury team," she'd say. He laid his hand on his stomach. You'd call it a beer gut if Lincoln drank beer more often than once a month. Massive.

But cute, she'd said. Handsome, she'd said. Crinkly eyes.

He leaned his forehead against the mirror and closed his eyes. It was embarrassing to see himself smile like that.

CHAPTER 41

THE NEXT MORNING, Lincoln joined a gym. The person on the tread-mill next to him was already watching *Quantum Leap* on one of the big televisions. It felt like a sign.

On his way home he stopped by the bank where Eve worked. She had one of those offices in the lobby with the glass cubicle walls.

"Hey," she said, "do you need to open a savings account? Yuck. Why are you all sweaty?"

"I joined a gym."

"You did? Well, good for you. Does that mean you're listening to my advice now? I wish I would have told you to get your own apartment. Get your own apartment!"

"Can I ask you a weird question?"

"If you make it quick," she said. "All those people sitting over there on the couches actually do want to open savings accounts."

"Do I look like Jason Bateman?"

"Who's Jason Bateman?"

"The actor. He was on *Silver Spoons* and *The Hogan Family*."

"The guy who played Teen Wolf?"

"That's Michael J. Fox," Lincoln said. "Never mind. This wasn't sup-posed to be a whole conversation."

"The guy who played Teen Wolf in *Teen Wolf Too*?"

"*Yes*," Lincoln said. "Him."

Eve squinted.

"Yeah," she said. "Actually, you do kind of look like him. Now that you mention it, yeah."

Lincoln smiled. He hadn't stopped smiling.

"Is that a good thing?" Eve said. "Do you want to look like Jason Bateman?"

"It isn't good or bad. It just confirms something."

"You're a lot bigger than he is."

"I'm leaving," Lincoln said, walking away.

"Thanks for choosing Second National," she called after him.

IT TOOK FOREVER for the IT office to clear that night. Everyone was getting pretty intense about the millennium bug. Kristi, Lincoln's desk-mate, wanted to stage a practice New Year's Eve, to see if their code patch would work. But Greg said that if they were going to shut down the newspaper and maybe cause a six-block blackout, they might as well wait until the real New Year's Eve when it would be less embarrassing. The members of the International Strike Force stayed out of the argument. They just sat in the corner, coding, or maybe hacking into NORAD.

Lincoln was still trying to monitor their progress and to help, but they avoided him. He was pretty sure they knew he wasn't one of them, that he'd never actually taken a computer course, and that he'd scored higher on the verbal section of the SAT. The IT kids all wore off-brand Polo shirts and New Balance tennis shoes and the same smug look. Lincoln refused to ask for their help with the digital color printer upstairs, even though he was at his wit's end with the damn thing. Every few days it would have a crazy spell and start spitting out page after page of bright magenta.

"How can we prepare for the worst-case scenario," Kristi was saying, "if we don't understand the worst-case scenario?"

Lincoln was itching to open the WebFence folder. *Dying* to open it.

Greg said he didn't have to drive his Nissan into the river to know it would be a fucking disaster.

"That doesn't even compare," Kristi said, and then she said she wished Greg wouldn't curse. Right at the moment, Lincoln was wishing that the system really would fail at 12:01, January 1. That it would fail spectacularly. And that he'd be fired and replaced by one of the Strike Force, probably the Bosnian. But first, he wanted to check the WebFence folder. *Now.*

Maybe he didn't have to wait for everyone to leave . . . It wasn't a secret that he checked the WebFence folder. *It's nothing*, he told himself, *checking WebFence is my job.* Which was such a lame rationalization that he decided not to let himself check it, even after everybody else went home.

When he finally opened the folder, sometime after midnight, he told himself not to expect a revelation like last night's. What were the chances that Beth would be talking about him again? What were the chances that she'd seen him again? If she had seen him, would she have noticed that he was wearing a nice shirt and that he'd spent twenty minutes that afternoon combing his hair?

From: Beth Fremont
To: Jennifer Scribner-Snyder
Sent: Thurs, 11/18/1999 10:16 AM
Subject: You.

Hey, how are you feeling?

<<**Jennifer to Beth**>> Fine. Normal. The same.

<<**Beth to Jennifer**>> Really?

<<**Jennifer to Beth**>> Really? No.
Really, I feel a little bit like a suicide bomber. Like I'm walking around pretending to be normal, all the while knowing that I'm carrying something that is going to change—possibly destroy—the world as I know it.

<<**Beth to Jennifer**>> "Destroy" seems like kind of a strong word.

<<**Jennifer to Beth**>> Everyone keeps telling me that everything is going to change when the baby gets here, that my whole life will be different. That, I think, implies that the life I have now will be gone. Destroyed.

<<**Beth to Jennifer**>> When you fell in love with Mitch, he changed your whole life, right? He didn't destroy it.

<<**Jennifer to Beth**>> Sure, he did, but that was okay. My life before Mitch sucked.

<<**Beth to Jennifer**>> So gloomy. If you had bunked next to the Little Orphan Annie, *Annie* wouldn't have been a musical.

<<**Jennifer to Beth**>> Would anyone really miss it?

CHAPTER 43

OKAY, SO SHE hadn't written more about him. But at least she hadn't written, "I got a better look at that guy, and he's not as cute as I thought. Not by half." He played online Scrabble until his shift was up and fell asleep as soon as his head hit the pillow.

"You're up early," his mother said, when he came downstairs the next morning at nine.

"Yeah, I think I'm going to go work out."

"Really."

"Yes."

"Where are you going to do that?" she asked suspiciously, as if the answer might be "the casino" or "a massage parlor."

"The gym," he said.

"Which gym?"

"Superior Bodies."

"*Superior* Bodies?" she asked.

"It's right up the street."

"I know. I've seen it. Do you want a bagel?"

"Sure." He smiled. Because that was all he did lately. And because he'd given up on asking her not to feed him, especially after the confrontation with Eve. Food had always been something good between him and his mom. Something without strings. "Thanks."

She started fixing him a bagel, thick with cream cheese, smoked salmon, and red onions. "Superior Bodies," she said again. "Isn't that one of those meat markets?"

"I don't know," he said. "I've only been there once, and there were mostly elderly people there. Maybe the meat market starts when people get off work."

"Hmmm," his mother said, looking obviously thoughtful. Lincoln pretended not to notice.

"It's just," his mother said, "that name. It puts so much emphasis on the body. As if that's why people should exercise, to have a good body. Not even a good body. A *superior* body. As if people should go around looking at each other and thinking, 'My body is so far superior to yours.'"

"I love you, Mom," he said. He meant it. "Thanks for breakfast. I'm going to the gym."

"Do you shower there? Don't use the shower. Imagine the fungus, Lincoln."

"I will now."

IT WASN'T HARD going to the gym, as long as he went as soon as he woke up, before he had time to think about not going. Those morning workouts made him feel like he was starting his day like a pinball, with a giant shot of momentum. The feeling sometimes didn't wear off until six or seven at night (when it was usually overtaken by the feeling that he was just bouncing haplessly from one situation to the next without any real purpose or direction).

Lincoln liked all the machines at the gym. He liked weights and pulleys and instructional diagrams. It was easy to spend an hour or two going from machine to machine. He thought about trying the free weights, just to live up to Beth's impression of him. But he would have had to ask someone for help, and Lincoln didn't want to talk to anyone at the gym. Especially not the personal trainers who were always gossiping at the front desk when he picked up a towel.

He liked how clean he felt when he left. How loose his legs and arms were. How cold the air felt when his hair was wet. He found himself moving even when he didn't have to, running across the street even if there wasn't a car coming, bounding up the steps just because.

———

THAT WEEKEND, AT Dungeons & Dragons, Lincoln made Rick laugh so hard that Mountain Dew came up his nose. It was an orc joke, hard to explain, but Christine giggled for the rest of the night, and even Larry laughed.

Maybe Lincoln was the Funny One.

From: Beth Fremont
To: Jennifer Scribner-Snyder
Sent: Mon, 11/29/1999 1:44 PM
Subject: The next time my sister gets married . . .

Remind me that I hate weddings. And my sister.

<<Jennifer to Beth>> I happen to know that you love weddings—that you give movies a one-star upgrade for even having a wedding scene. Wasn't that the rule that forced you to give *Four Weddings and a Funeral* four stars even though you thought Andie MacDowell was a disaster?

<<Beth to Jennifer>> You're right. I love weddings. I hate my sister.

<<Jennifer to Beth>> Why?

<<Beth to Jennifer>> Basically . . . because she's getting married before me. I'm like the petty older sister in a period drama. "But Papa, she can't get married before me. *I'm* the eldest."

<<Jennifer to Beth>> Oh, I love period dramas, especially period dramas starring Colin Firth. I'm like Bridget Jones if she were actually fat.

<<Beth to Jennifer>> Oh . . . Colin Firth. He should *only* do period dramas. And period dramas should *only* star Colin Firth.

(One-star upgrade for Colin Firth. Two stars for Colin Firth in a waistcoat.)

<<Jennifer to Beth>> Keep typing his name, even his name is handsome.

<<Beth to Jennifer>> I think we've discovered the only guy we'd ever fight over at an airport bar.

<<Jennifer to Beth>> You're forgetting about Ben Affleck.

You're also forgetting to complain to me about your sister's wedding.

<<Beth to Jennifer>> Ben Affleck! Are you sure I can't talk you into Matt Damon? We could double-date . . .

I didn't forget. I just figured you were trying to change the subject because I was being ridiculous. I don't have anything real to complain about. My complaint is: I always thought I'd be married by now.

<<Jennifer to Beth>> That's not so ridiculous.

<<Beth to Jennifer>> No, it is. I had this whole plan when I graduated from high school:

I was going to go to college, date a few guys, and then meet *the* guy at the end of my freshman year, maybe at the beginning of my sophomore year. We'd be engaged by graduation and married the next year. And then, after some traveling, we'd start our family. Four kids, three years apart. I wanted to be done by the time I was 35.

<<Jennifer to Beth>> Four kids? Isn't that a little extreme?

<<Beth to Jennifer>> It doesn't matter. It's no longer mathematically possible.

I'm not married. I'm not even close. Even if I were to break up with Chris tomorrow and meet someone new the very next day, my plan still wouldn't be salvageable. It would take a year or two to figure out whether we were right for each other, at least six months to be engaged . . . That puts me at 31, 32 before I can get pregnant.

And that's being overly optimistic. If I broke up with Chris tomorrow, I'd be a mess for a year (30). Then it might take another year to meet somebody else (31). It might take six years to meet somebody else (36). How can I plan around those variables?

<<**Jennifer to Beth**>> I'm confused. I thought you were 28.

<<**Beth to Jennifer**>> Maybe my plan was never possible. Maybe I would have figured all this out sooner if I hadn't spent trigonometry passing notes to my 10th-grade boyfriend.

That's the thing of it—the really petty thing of it—I can't help but feel like this wasn't supposed to happen to me. I've never worried about finding a guy.

In sixth grade, I dated the nicest cute boy in class. We talked on the phone twice over six months and held hands at an afternoon showing of *Superman III*. I always had a date, the right date, for every dance. I fell in love for the first time in the 10th grade with the guy I was supposed to fall in love with. I broke up with him after a year, and that was supposed to happen, too.

I was pretty sure I would never have to worry about finding *the* right guy. I thought it would happen for me the way it happened for my parents and for my grandparents. They got to the right age, they found the right person, they got married, they had kids.

<<**Jennifer to Beth**>> You're kind of making me hate you.

<<**Beth to Jennifer**>> For being the kind of girl who always had a boyfriend?

<<**Jennifer to Beth**>> Kind of . . . I never had a date to any dance. I never took it for granted that any guy would ever fall in love with me. Let alone, the right guy.

<<**Beth to Jennifer**>> I don't blame you for kind of hating me. But I kind of hate you, too. You *did* meet exactly the right person at exactly the right time. You *married* the nicest cute boy in class. And now you're pregnant.

<<**Jennifer to Beth**>> But you met the right person, too, didn't you?

<<**Beth to Jennifer**>> I don't know if I even believe in that anymore. The right guy. The perfect guy. The one. I've lost faith in "the."

<<**Jennifer to Beth**>> How do you feel about "a" and "an"?

<<**Beth to Jennifer**>> Indifferent.

<<**Jennifer to Beth**>> So you're considering a life without articles?

<<**Beth to Jennifer**>> And true love.

CHAPTER 45

LINCOLN ATE DINNER in the break room at the same time every night now, thinking that might increase his chances of seeing Beth. Doris appreciated the company. She liked to take her break at nine sharp. She always brought a turkey sandwich on white bread and bought herself a Diet Slice from the machine.

"Does your girlfriend make you those huge dinners?" she asked one night as he was heating up a plate of spinach-and-potato pizza.

"My mom does," he said. Sheepishly.

"No wonder you're so big," Doris said.

He took his plate out of the microwave and looked at it. It really was an awful lot of pizza. He'd heard people say their appetite decreased when they exercised a lot, but he was hungrier than ever. He'd started taking bananas with him to the gym so that he'd have something to eat in the car as soon as he left.

"She must be a good cook, your mother. It always smells like a fancy restaurant when you're in here."

"Definitely. She's a great cook."

"I've never been much in the kitchen. I can make meat loaf and pork chops and green-bean casserole, but Paul had to cook for himself if he wanted something fancy. What is that? It looks like a giant sandwich."

"It's pizza," Lincoln said. "Double-crust, spinach and potato. I think it's an Italian thing. Would you like to try some?"

"If you're offering," Doris said eagerly. He pulled off a slice of his pizza for her. There was still plenty left on his plate.

"Oh, that's good," Doris said after a bite, "and I don't even like spin-ach. Are you Italian?"

"No," he said, "German mostly, a little Irish. My mom just likes to cook."

"Lucky you," she said, taking another big bite.

"Do you have children?" Lincoln asked.

"Nyah. Paul and I never had kids. I guess we did the same thing as everybody else does, but nothing ever happened. In those days, if you didn't have kids, you didn't have kids. You didn't go to a doctor to see who was responsible. My sister was married for fifteen years before she got pregnant. I thought that might happen to us, too, but it never did . . . Just as well, I guess."

They both chewed in silence. Lincoln didn't trust himself to make more small talk. He hadn't meant to ask such a personal question.

"My mom made carrot cake this morning," he said, "and she gave me way too much. Do you want to split it?"

"Sure, if you're offering."

They were just finishing their cake when a young woman walked into the break room. Lincoln sat up extra straight until he recognized her as one of the copy editors, the small girl who'd offered him banana bread. She smiled nervously at him.

"You're the IT guy, right?" she asked.

He nodded.

"I'm sorry to interrupt your dinner. We tried calling your office, but you weren't there. A couple of us can't get on the server. We're sort of on deadline. I'm sorry"—the girl looked at Doris—"I know you're on break."

"Don't apologize to me, honey," Doris said. "It won't be the first time a man has left me for a younger woman."

Lincoln was already standing. "That's okay, let me see if I can help."

"I really am sorry," the girl said as they walked to the newsroom.

"It's okay," he said, "really. It's my job."

"I'm sorry I called you the IT guy. I didn't—nobody on the desk knows your name."

"I answer to IT guy, don't worry about it."

She nodded, uncomfortably.

"But my name is Lincoln," he said, holding his hand out to her.

"It's nice to meet you," she said, relieved, taking his hand. "I'm Emilie."

They were at her computer now. "Can you show me what it's doing?" he asked. She sat down and tried to log on to the server. An error message popped up.

"That happens every time," she said.

"That's an easy fix," he said, leaning over to take her mouse. Her hand was still there. Both of their hands jumped, and he felt himself blushing. If this was how he acted around a girl he wasn't at all attracted to, how would he act if he ever had to fix Beth's computer? He might throw up on her.

"Maybe I should sit down," he said.

Emilie stood up, and he sat in her chair. It was set so high, her feet must not touch the ground. She was standing behind him now, and they were practically the same height. Against his will, Lincoln thought of Sam. Sam, so small he could pick her up with one arm. Sam, curled up next to him at the drive-in. Sam, slow dancing with her cheek on the third button of his shirt.

"There," he said to Emilie, "you're in. That shouldn't happen again. But give me a call if it does. Or . . . I guess you know where to find me. Did you say someone else was having problems?"

Lincoln helped two more copy editors get on the network. When he walked away, Emilie was standing by a printer. She was pretty, in a pale, unassuming way.

"Hey," she said, "Lincoln."

He stopped.

"We usually eat around now," she said, "at our desks. On Fridays, we order pizza. You should come up and hang out. I mean, not that you wouldn't want to eat with Doris. She's really nice."

"Sure," Lincoln said, imagining himself hanging out upstairs, then glancing nervously at the back of the newsroom. "Thanks."

CHAPTER 46

From: Beth Fremont
To: Jennifer Scribner-Snyder
Sent: Fri, 12/03/1999 1:35 PM
Subject: Short people got no reason to live.

Why are tall guys always attracted to short women? Not just moderately short women, either . . . Tiny women. Polly Pockets. The tallest guys always-always-always go for the shortest girls. Always.

It's like they're so infatuated with their own height that they want to be with someone who makes them feel even taller. Someone they can tower over. A little doll that will make them feel even bigger and stronger.

Whenever I see a really tall guy with a really short girl, I always want to take him aside and say, "You realize your sons will never play basketball, right?"

It wouldn't be so bad if short guys were incredibly attracted to tall women. But they're not. They don't want anything to do with us.

<<Jennifer to Beth>> Is this about Chris? Is he two-timing you with Holly Hunter?

<<Beth to Jennifer>> Holly Hunter?

<<**Jennifer to Beth**>> That's the only short woman I could think of. How about Rhea Perlman?

<<**Beth to Jennifer**>> "Two-timing"? Who says "two-timing"?

<<**Jennifer to Beth**>> Don't turn on me. I'm not the one who's seeing Crystal Gayle on the side.

<<**Beth to Jennifer**>> Crystal Gayle isn't short.

<<**Jennifer to Beth**>> Isn't that why her hair looks so long?

<<**Beth to Jennifer**>> I'm not talking about Chris. Chris isn't interested in anyone, including me. I'm talking about My Cute Guy.

<<**Jennifer to Beth**>> The Brawny Man? He's cheating on you with Mary Lou Retton?

<<**Beth to Jennifer**>> Worse. I saw him talking to that Emilie on the nightside desk.

<<**Jennifer to Beth**>> The little blond one?

<<**Beth to Jennifer**>> That's her, all right.

<<**Jennifer to Beth**>> She's not just short. She's like a normal-size person who's been miniaturized so that everything about her is still in perfect proportion. She's like something you'd find in an elaborate dollhouse, so tiny and yet so lifelike.

Have you ever noticed her waist? It's infinitesimal.

<<**Beth to Jennifer**>> I could put my hands around her waist. If standing next to her makes *me* feel strong and masculine, she must make My Cute Guy feel like a god.

<<**Jennifer to Beth**>> She's Lilliputian.

<<**Beth to Jennifer**>> They wouldn't let her ride Splash Mountain.

<<**Jennifer to Beth**>> You know what I don't like about her? The way she spells her name with an "ie." Everyone knows that Emily is spelled "Emily." It's not cute to spell it with an "ie." It doesn't make you unique. It doesn't set you apart from all the other Emilys in the world. It's pointlessly confusing.

<<Beth to Jennifer>> Her parents probably thought it was cute. That's not really her fault.

<<Jennifer to Beth>> Oh, right, not like her tiny, little, perfect body.

When did you see them together?

<<Beth to Jennifer>> Last night. I finished up a review, and I went over to the copy desk to tell the editors to have at it. And there they were. Talking. In front of God and everyone.

<<Jennifer to Beth>> Maybe they were talking about work.

<<Beth to Jennifer>> What work? He's not on the copy desk. What the hell *does* he do? I don't think it's advertising—he wears cargo pants. Who else has to work at night? Maybe he's security. Or a janitor.

<<Jennifer to Beth>> Maybe he works on the presses. Those guys are here at night.

<<Beth to Jennifer>> He's a not a pressman. They wear blue jumpsuits, and they all have mustaches. Besides, he wasn't talking to Emilie about work. She was laughing. And twirling that yellow ponytail of hers like a schoolgirl.

<<Jennifer to Beth>> Was he laughing?

<<Beth to Jennifer>> Not exactly. He was mostly just towering. And smiling.

Oh, curse you, Miniature Emilie, you petite seductress.

<<Jennifer to Beth>> Does this mean we have to start calling him Emilie's Cute Guy?

<<Beth to Jennifer>> Never!

<<Jennifer to Beth>> Lucky for you, you already have an extremely tall man in your life who doesn't have Thumbelina syndrome.

<<Beth to Jennifer>> Are you trying to make me feel guilty? You don't even like Chris.

<<**Jennifer to Beth**>> Sorry. I get that from my mom. I just can't resist an opportunity to make someone feel guilty. On the other hand, Chris *is* your boyfriend.

<<**Beth to Jennifer**>> Come on. It's not like I'm two-timing him.

<<**Jennifer to Beth**>> I think it would hurt my feelings if I found out that Mitch thought of someone at work as "My Cute Girl."

<<**Beth to Jennifer**>> That's different. Mitch works at a high school. With actual girls.

<<**Jennifer to Beth**>> You know what I mean.

CHAPTER 47

"WHAT ARE YOU grinning about?" Doris asked, digging into her mani-
cotti. She was thrilled when Lincoln told her he'd brought enough for
them both.

"I'm not grinning," Lincoln said. "I'm smiling. Like a normal person."

"I think this has something to do with a girl."

Lincoln grinned and took a bite.

"I don't blame you. That Emilie's a hot little number. I could tell she
liked you."

"Not Emilie," Lincoln said with his mouth full.

"It's not?" Doris asked. "Then who is it?"

"I don't know," he said, sort of honestly.

"Well, you could do a lot worse than Emilie. She's a smart girl. And
healthy. She eats a lot of carrot sticks."

"She's not my type," Lincoln said, feeling gleeful. Stupidly gleeful.
What did it really mean in the big scheme of things that Beth had seen
him, that she'd been jealous . . .

It meant that the girl he thought about most and liked the best thought
about him, too.

"Oh, she's not?" Doris asked.

"She's a little short." Lincoln laughed.

"Well, aren't we picky. Say, what kind of cheese does your mom put
in this?"

"Romano," Lincoln said.

"Hmm. It smells terrible, but it tastes delicious."

THE NEXT DAY was Saturday, and Lincoln had the gym to himself. He had his choice of treadmills and men's fitness magazines. Not that he could read right now, he couldn't focus on anything. He couldn't stop thinking about Beth's message.

Beth.

She liked him.

She didn't know him, but she liked him. She thought about him in a physical way. She thought about how much space he took up in the world.

And she was jealous. When had a girl ever been jealous over him? Not Sam, he thought, shaking his head at the thought of her, trying to shake the thought away.

Beth didn't know him. It wasn't real jealousy. It wasn't real anything.

But maybe it could be. He liked her so much, and she liked him. Well, she liked the look of him, and that was a good start. There must be a way he could make something happen, arrange to be near her, try to catch her eye or meet her.

He was getting ahead of himself on the treadmill. He turned up the speed to keep from stumbling.

Beth had a boyfriend; that was a problem. But clearly theirs wasn't a healthy relationship. (Lincoln and Justin spent more weekend nights with her boyfriend than she did.) He could walk by Beth's desk when he knew she was there . . .

What if it worked? What if she liked him? Really liked him?

He couldn't ever tell her about the e-mails. He'd have to keep that a secret. Even if they got married and had kids. Didn't people keep secrets like that all the time? One of Lincoln's uncles hadn't known his wife had been married before until her funeral, when all three of her ex-husbands showed up . . .

Lincoln would have to tell Beth.

But he couldn't tell her. This wouldn't work. This was stupid.

But still . . . she thought about him. She was jealous.

Lincoln had so much energy left after the treadmill that he walked over to the weight room. There was no one lifting, and the attendant was reading a magazine.

"Excuse me," he said. "Do I have to make an appointment to learn how to use the free weights?"

She set down her magazine. "Usually," she said, looking around the empty room. "But not today."

Her name was Becca, and she was a nutrition major. Lincoln didn't know you could major in nutrition. She was a little too muscular and a little too tan. But she was extremely patient. And she kept assuring Lincoln that he didn't look like an idiot.

She helped him set up a lifting program, and she wrote everything down in a special folder. "Once you get the hang of this, you should totally try to add some mass," Becca said. "You could get really big. You can tell by the size of your elbows."

"My elbows?"

"There's no fat on the elbow," she said, "so it's a good way to assess bone structure, how big your body can get. I've got small-to-medium elbows, so I'm really limited. I'll never be competitive." Lincoln thanked Becca sincerely when they were done, and she told him to track her down if he got bored with his program.

He felt sore all over when he walked to his car. He kept trying to look at his elbows, but it was kind of hopeless without a mirror.

THAT NIGHT, WHEN he got to Dave and Christine's house, Christine met him at the door. He could hear people arguing in the living room.

"Has the game started already?"

"No, we're waiting for Teddy to get off work. Dave and Larry are playing *Star Wars* CCG while we wait. Do you play?"

"No, is it fun?"

"Yeah, if you want to spend your kids' college money on a collectible card game."

"Our kids will get scholarships!" Dave shouted from the living room. "Lincoln, come watch. I'm crushing the Rebellion under my heel."

"No," Christine said, smiling, "come keep me company. I'm making pizza."

"Sure," Lincoln said, following her into the kitchen.

"You can cut the onions," she said. "I hate cutting onions. They make me cry, and once I'm crying, I start thinking about sad things, and then I can't stop. Here, give me your jacket."

The kitchen already smelled like garlic. Christine had the dinner ingredients—and everything else—spread out on the counter. She handed him a sharp knife and an onion. "Just clear a space."

He pushed aside two sacks of potatoes, a jug of red wine, and an electric yogurt maker. *This is the girl my mother wanted me to bring home*, he thought as he washed his hands. *Or this is the girl she'd want me to bring home if she actually wanted me to bring home a girl. A girl like this, who makes her own yogurt and breast-feeds while she's telling you about something she read in a medicinal herbs book.*

He watched Christine make her toddler a plate of raisins and banana slices. What could his mother find wrong with Christine? he wondered. Something. Eve would say that Christine smiled too much and that she should wear a more supportive bra.

He chopped the onion into clean, regular squares and started on the tomatoes. His arms still felt strange from all the lifting, and his face still felt strange from all the smiling.

"You're different, Lincoln," Christine said, clearing more space on the counter to roll out dough. She looked at him like she was doing math in her head. "What is it?"

He laughed. "I don't know. What is it?"

"You're different," she said. "I think you've lost weight. Have you lost weight?"

"Probably," he said. "I'm trying to exercise."

"Hmmm," she said, studying him, kneading the dough, "that's something. But that's not it . . . Your eyes are clearer. You're standing taller. You look like you're in flower."

"Isn't that something you'd say to a sixteen-year-old girl?"

"Does this have something to do with a sixteen-year-old girl?"

"Of course not," he said, laughing again. "Where would I even meet a sixteen-year-old girl?"

"But it is a girl," Christine said enthusiastically. "It's a girl!'

"Who's a girl?" Dave asked as he walked in. He went to the refrigerator and grabbed two beers. "Is Lincoln pregnant?"

Lincoln shook his head at Christine, which, he could tell, made her even more curious.

"Have you finished crushing the Rebellion?" she asked.

Dave frowned. "No," he said peevishly, walking back to the living room, "but I shall."

"It's a girl!" Christine whispered as soon as Dave had gone. "Our prayers are answered! Tell me all about her."

"Have you really been praying for me?" Lincoln asked.

"Of course," she said. "I pray for everyone we care about. Plus, I like to pray for things that seem possible. There are so many things that I pray for that seem almost too big even for God. It's rewarding to pray for something that might actually happen. It kind of keeps me going. Sometimes, I just pray for a bumper crop of zucchini or for a good night's sleep."

"So you think it's possible that I might meet a girl?" He felt genuinely grateful to think that Christine was praying for him. If he were God, he would listen to Christine's prayers.

"*The* girl." Christine smiled. "More than possible. It's probable even. Tell me about her."

He wanted to. He wanted to tell someone. Why not Christine? He couldn't think of anyone who would be less judgmental.

"If I do," Lincoln said, "you can't tell anyone else. Not even Dave."

Her face fell.

"Why not? Are you in trouble? Is it a bad secret? Oh my God, are you having an affair? Don't tell me if you're having an affair. Or breaking the law."

"I'm not breaking the law . . . ," he said. "But I may have employed questionable ethics."

"You have to tell me now," she said. "Or it'll just drive me crazy."

So he told her everything, from the beginning, trying not to play up the parts of the story that made him sound shady, but trying not to play them down either. By the end, Christine had nervously rolled the first pizza crust thin as tracing paper.

"I don't know what to say," she said, scrunching the dough back into a ball. He couldn't read her face.

"Do you think I'm horrible?" he asked, sure that she did.

"No," she said. "Oh no, of course not. I don't know how you could read people's e-mail without actually *reading* it, if that's your job."

"But I shouldn't have kept reading hers," he said. "There's no getting around that."

"No." Christine frowned. Even her frown looked like it wanted to be a smile. "No, that part's messy. You've really never met her? Do you even know what she looks like?"

"No," Lincoln said.

"There's something really romantic about that. Every woman wants a man who'll fall in love with her soul as well as her body. But what if you meet her, and you don't think she's attractive?"

"I don't think I care what she looks like," Lincoln said. Not that he hadn't thought about it. Not that it wasn't exciting in a weird way, not to know, to imagine.

"Oh, that *is* romantic," Christine said.

"Well," Lincoln said, feeling like he was getting off too easy, "I know that she's attractive. Her boyfriend is the kind of guy who dates attractive women. And I know that she's had other boyfriends . . ."

"It's still romantic," Christine said, "falling in love with someone for who she is and what she says and what she believes in. It's actually much more romantic than her crush on you, which would have to be almost completely physical. You might be nothing like she thinks you are."

Lincoln had never thought of it like that.

"Oh, not that she would be disappointed," Christine said reassuringly. "How could she be?"

"It's felt like enough," he said, "that she thinks I'm cute."

"*Lincoln*," she said quietly. "Cute has never been your problem."

Lincoln didn't know what to say then. Christine smiled and handed

him two green peppers. "Your problem," she said, "at least in the imme-
diate sense, is that you have to stop reading this woman's e-mail."

"If I stopped, do you think I could try to meet her?"

"I don't know," Christine said, rolling out the dough again, "you'd
have to tell her about the e-mail, and she might not be able to get
over it."

"Could you get over something like that?"

"I don't know . . . It would seem pretty weird. David stole my dice one
summer, before we started dating, so that he would have something of
me to keep near him over break. He carried them in his pocket. That
seemed kind of romantic, but kind of weird, and this is much weirder
than that. You'd have to tell her about how you've gone to her boyfriend's
concerts and how you walk by her desk. I don't know . . ." Christine
started spreading tomato sauce with her fingers in bright red swirls on
the dough.

"You're right," Lincoln said. It didn't matter that Christine wasn't as
judgmental as Eve or his mother or anyone else he could have told about
Beth. There was no one he could tell, no one he respected, who would tell
him that this was going to work. "I guess I ruined it the moment I decided to keep reading her e-mails. The thing is, I never really decided
that. It wasn't like a formal decision."

"Just think," Christine said, putting the first crust in the oven, "if you
had never read her mail, she would still have a big crush on you. She'd
still be gossiping about you to her girlfriend. That should make you feel
good."

It didn't.

THAT NIGHT, LINCOLN played his character so recklessly, the poor dwarf
lost three toes and was cursed with blindness. Lincoln ate too much
pizza, drank two big mugs of Dave's home brew, and slept fitfully on the
couch.

The next morning, Christine made him oatmeal and tried to tell
him to hold on to the momentum in his life, to try to channel it into a

healthier direction. "Remember," she said, "not all those who wander are lost."

He thanked her for breakfast and for everything else and hurried out, hoping she wouldn't see how irritated he was. It seemed like such a pointless, flaky thing to say. Even if it was his favorite line from *The Lord of the Rings*.

From: Jennifer Scribner-Snyder
To: Beth Fremont
Sent: Mon, 12/06/1999 9:28 AM
Subject: I'll bet you're the kind of girl who's already picked out baby
names.

Am I right? What are they?

<<**Beth to Jennifer**>> Like I'm going to tell you. A pregnant
person.

<<**Jennifer to Beth**>> I'm not going to steal them.

<<**Beth to Jennifer**>> That's what they all say. Are you starting
to pick out names?

<<**Jennifer to Beth**>> I'm not. Mitch is. Actually, he already has
a name that he likes: Cody.

<<**Beth to Jennifer**>> For a girl or a boy?

<<**Jennifer to Beth**>> Either.

<<**Beth to Jennifer**>> Hmm.

<<**Jennifer to Beth**>> Go ahead. I know it's awful.

<<**Beth to Jennifer**>> It really is. For either a boy or a girl.

<<**Jennifer to Beth**>> I know.

<<**Beth to Jennifer**>> That name feathers its bangs.

<<Jennifer to Beth>> I know.

<<Beth to Jennifer>> It collects dream catchers.

<<Jennifer to Beth>> I know.

<<Beth to Jennifer>> It cries out for the middle name "Dawn."

<<Jennifer to Beth>> I know, I know, I know.

<<Beth to Jennifer>> So, did you say, "No child of mine will be named Cody, not in this lifetime, not in the next 50 lifetimes."

<<Jennifer to Beth>> I said, "Let's wait on names until we know what we're having."

And he said, "But that's the beauty of Cody. It works for everything."

<<Beth to Jennifer>> I know it's mean to laugh at someone who might have to name her firstborn Cody, but I can't help it. *It works for everything.*

What names do you like?

<<Jennifer to Beth>> I don't know. I can't even think about it that way, like something with a name.

I feel like Mitch should get to pick out the name because he's more invested in this whole idea. It's like, when you're going out to dinner and you don't really care where you go, but the other person really wants to go to the Chinese buffet. Maybe you don't love the Chinese buffet, but it's kind of rude to argue when you don't even really care.

<<Beth to Jennifer>> Um. I think you've got a lot invested in this baby. You're the one carrying it.

<<Jennifer to Beth>> Yes, but Mitch is more attached to it.

<<Beth to Jennifer>> Your umbilical cord begs to differ.

<<Jennifer to Beth>> Do you think I have an umbilical cord already? I'm only six weeks along.

<<Beth to Jennifer>> Isn't that what feeds the baby?

<<Jennifer to Beth>> Yes, but it doesn't pop out of nowhere. It's not like you already have a cord in your uterus that's just waiting for an outlet to plug into.

<<Beth to Jennifer>> I think it forms with the baby. Isn't this covered in that *What to Expect When You're Expecting* book?

<<Jennifer to Beth>> I'm sure I wouldn't know. I can't stand books like that. Why should every pregnant woman be expected to read the same book? Or any book? Being pregnant isn't that complicated. *What to Expect When You're Expecting* shouldn't be a book. It should be a Post-it: "Take your vitamins. Don't drink vodka. Get used to empire waistlines."

<<Beth to Jennifer>> I might have to see if there's a *What to Expect When Your Crabby Best Friend is Expecting* book. I want to know about the umbilical cord.

<<Jennifer to Beth>> It's nice of you to say I'm your best friend.

<<Beth to Jennifer>> You *are* my best friend, dummy.

<<Jennifer to Beth>> Really? You're *my* best friend. But I always assumed that somebody else was your best friend, and I was totally okay with that. You don't have to say that I'm your best friend just to make me feel good.

<<Beth to Jennifer>> You're so lame.

<<Jennifer to Beth>> That's why I figured somebody else was your best friend.

CHAPTER 49

THAT NIGHT, WHEN Lincoln was changing the toner in a printer near the copy desk, he heard one of the editors complaining about some numbers that might be wrong in a story. "If journalism majors were required to take math, I might know for sure," the guy said, throwing a calculator off his desk in frustration.

Lincoln picked it up and offered to help check the math. The copy editor, Chuck, was so grateful that he invited Lincoln to go out with a bunch of the copy desk people after work. They went to a bar across the river. Bars in Iowa stayed open until 2:00 A.M.

Look at me, Lincoln thought, *I'm out. With people. New people.*

He even made plans to play golf with a few of the guys the next day. Chuck told Lincoln that copy editors do everything together because "the shitty hours keep you from meeting regular people." And also, another editor said, from figuring out that your wife is sleeping with some guy she met at church.

The copy editors drank cheap beer and seemed kind of bitter. About everything. But Lincoln felt at home with them. They all read too much, and watched too much TV, and argued about movies like they were things that had actually happened.

The little blond one, Emilie, sat next to Lincoln at the bar, and tried to get him to talk to her about *Star Wars*. Which worked. Especially after she bought him a Heineken and said she didn't notice any differences between the original movie and the special edition.

Everything about Emilie—her button nose, her delicate shoulders, her ponytail—reminded Lincoln of everything Beth had written about her. Which made him laugh and flush more than he meant to.

AT THE NEXT weekend's D&D game, Christine pulled Lincoln aside to ask about his situation at work. "Did you stop reading that woman's e-mail?" Christine asked.

"No," Lincoln said, "but I didn't walk by her desk this week."

Christine bit her lip and rocked the baby nervously. "I'm not sure that counts as progress."

From: Jennifer Scribner-Snyder
To: Beth Fremont
Sent: Mon, 12/13/1999 9:54 AM
Subject: How was the shower?

Your tea party shower for Kiley was this weekend, right?

<<Beth to Jennifer>> Ugh. Yes. Don't ask.

<<Jennifer to Beth>> You have to tell me about it. This is all about you proving you've got what it takes to throw my baby shower.

<<Beth to Jennifer>> I don't want to think about showers right now. I might not even take showers anymore.

<<Jennifer to Beth>> What happened? Did you pour tea into someone's lap?

<<Beth to Jennifer>> Uh. No. Somebody would have had to have given me the opportunity to actually pour tea for that to happen. Apparently, Tri-Delts don't drink tea. They drink Diet Coke—Diet Pepsi in a pinch—but hot tea? Not so much.

I had five varieties of tea, I had my grandmother's china, I had sugar cubes and real cream. But it hadn't occurred to me to buy Diet Coke when I was shopping for my tea party.

I had to send Chris to Kwik Shop.

<<Jennifer to Beth>> Chris came to the shower?

<<Beth to Jennifer>> He didn't really come. He just didn't leave. Which was awesome because I hadn't considered that tea sandwiches are about eight times more complicated than regular sandwiches. Chris sliced English cucumbers and blanched asparagus and spent probably an hour trimming crusts.

Again, not that anyone noticed. You know what else Tri-Delts don't really like, besides hot tea? Bread. One of Kiley's bridesmaids actually said, "I never eat bread on the weekends. I save my carbs for partying."

<<Jennifer to Beth>> What kind of parties does she go to—cupcake parties?

<<Beth to Jennifer>> I think she meant beer.

<<Jennifer to Beth>> Oh, right. So, what did you do?

<<Beth to Jennifer>> What could I do? Chris went to buy Diet Coke. They all loved him, by the way. They thought nothing of refusing my tea, spurning my sandwiches, and flirting with my boyfriend.

<<Jennifer to Beth>> Did he flirt back?

<<Beth to Jennifer>> Not exactly. He was very solicitous. He brought out ice, glasses, a bottle of rum, and all the extra vegetables from the kitchen. And every once in a while, he'd run his fingers through his hair as he was refilling their drinks, which made them just swoon. If he hadn't slipped out while Kiley was opening presents, those girls never would have left.

<<Jennifer to Beth>> That was really nice of him to help you. I'm sorry the shower was such a disaster.

<<Beth to Jennifer>> It *was* nice of him. He was nice all day. He came back home about an hour after they cleared out, and I was still sitting on the couch, feeling sorry for myself and thinking about how every one of those idiotic girls is going to get married before me, and about how Diet Coke and rum is the most moronic drink of all time. They should call it a Moron, so that girls who order it would have to call themselves out at the bar.

Chris walked in and sat next to me, and was all, "don't worry about it" and "pearls to swine" and "you don't even want to impress girls like that." And I pointed out that they seemed to like *him* well enough.

"What does that say about me?" he said. "That I'm attractive to women who drink rum and Diet Coke?"

"Isn't that the stupidest drink of all time?" I said. "Their faces lit up when you offered it to them."

"I can spot a Skinny Pirate–drinker a mile away."

And I was, like, "Huh. So there's already a name for that."

Then he reminded me that there were dozens of sandwiches left in the kitchen, most of them containing cream cheese. So we drank tea and each ate enough finger sandwiches to feed an entire sorority.

<<Jennifer to Beth>> Sometimes, I really like him.

<<Beth to Jennifer>> Me, too. If he was always the person that he was on Saturday, I would be leading a charmed life.

<<Jennifer to Beth>> Who is he usually?

<<Beth to Jennifer>> It's not like he's somebody else. It's like he's usually nobody at all.

That sounds terrible. I shouldn't say that.

<<Jennifer to Beth>> Do you feel like he ignores you?

<<Beth to Jennifer>> No. I feel like he doesn't see me. Or anything. I'd say it was like living with a ghost, but ghosts haunt you, right? Chris doesn't usually do anything that engaging.

<<Jennifer to Beth>> Do you think he's that way with everybody?

<<Beth to Jennifer>> No. I think he makes more of an effort with strangers. When he's performing, he sort of pretends to interact with the crowd . . . I think that wears him out. I think he's relieved to come home to someone who doesn't expect him to fake it. Who doesn't expect anything.

Anyway. How are you? How was your weekend?

\<\<Jennifer to Beth>> I have some news: I broke Mitch the bad news about Cody.

\<\<Beth to Jennifer>> I thought you were going to ignore that and hope it went away.

\<\<Jennifer to Beth>> I was going to, but he started calling my stomach "Little Cody." I couldn't handle it, I had to tell him to stop. I had to tell him that no part of my body—or anything that came from my body—would ever be called Cody.

"What about Dakota?" he asked.

"Never. I'm sorry."

"Well, it doesn't have to be Cody . . . ," he said. "What names do you like better?"

I told him that I didn't know, but that I liked names that are classic, distinguished, like Elizabeth for a girl. Or Sarah with an H. Or Anna. And for a boy, John or Andrew or even Mitchell. I told him that I love the name Mitchell.

He wasn't disappointed at all, that I could tell. He said he liked all those names. It was such a relief. I like this baby better already, knowing that it won't be called Cody.

Mitch is so happy that this is happening, I think he'll let me pick whatever name I want. He was being so sweet that I almost told him that Dakota might work for a middle name . . .

Then I decided I needed to start thinking like a mother with a child to protect.

\<\<Beth to Jennifer>> I knew your maternal instinct would kick in eventually.

CHAPTER 51

LINCOLN READ THIS exchange more than once. More than twice. More than he should have. And every time he read it, his stomach knotted a little tighter.

He still couldn't see this girl. This woman. But he could picture Chris clearly, and for the first time since—well, since all this had started—Lincoln was angry.

He hated to think of Chris being so tender with Beth. Making her tea, soothing her nerves. Preferring her. And he hated, too, to think of Chris neglecting her, being nobody with her. He hated to think of their eight years together. Lincoln hated to think that even if he *could* talk to Beth, even if it was possible, even if he hadn't backed himself into this corner, she would still be in love with somebody else.

He was so agitated at dinner that he let Doris eat his share of pumpkin cake.

"This lemon icing is wonderful," she said, "so sour. Who would have thought to put lemon icing on pumpkin cake? Your mother should open a restaurant. What does she do for a living?"

"She doesn't work," he said. His mother had never worked, as long as he could remember. She still got a little money from Eve's dad, who she'd divorced years before Lincoln was born. And she was a licensed massage therapist. That had been a somewhat serious gig for a while. Sometimes in the summertime, she did chair massages at flea markets. His mom never seemed to be short of money. But Lincoln should probably be paying rent, he thought, or at least helping with the groceries . . . especially now that his mom was feeding Doris, too.

"What about your dad? What does he do?"

"I don't know," Lincoln said. "I've never met him."

Doris clucked and choked on her cake. She put her hand on his shoulder. Lincoln hoped that Beth wasn't about to walk in. "You poor kid," Doris said.

"It's really not so bad," he said.

"Not so bad? It's a terrible thing to grow up without a father."

"It wasn't," Lincoln said, but maybe it was. How would he know? "It was fine."

Doris patted him a few times before she pulled her hand away.

"No wonder your mother cooks for you."

Lincoln went back to his desk after dinner and tried to think about his dad. (Who he really had never met. Who might not even know that Lincoln existed.) He ended up thinking about Sam instead. She used to tell Lincoln that he should "work the fatherless boy thing."

"It's very romantic," she'd said. They were at the park. Sitting on top of the monkey bars. "Very James Dean in *East of Eden*."

"James Dean is a motherless boy in *East of Eden*." Lincoln hadn't seen the movie, but he'd read the book. He'd read everything by Steinbeck.

"What about *Rebel Without a Cause*?"

"I think he had both parents in that one."

"Details," Sam said. "James Dean reeked of fatherless boy."

"How is that romantic?" Lincoln had asked.

"It makes you seem unpredictable," she said, "like a sad chasm could emerge in your personality at any moment."

He'd laughed then, but now it didn't seem so funny. Maybe that's where he was stuck. In the sad chasm.

"MOM SAYS YOU'VE been acting weird," Eve said when he met her for lunch the next day at Kentucky Fried Chicken. (Eve's choice.)

"What kind of weird?"

"She says you're up and down all the time and that you're losing weight. She thinks you might be taking diet pills. She compared you to Patty Duke."

"I'm losing weight because I joined a gym," he said, setting down his spork. "I told you about it already. I go before work."

"Actually," she said, "I can tell. You look nice. You're standing straighter. And your beer gut is receding."

"I don't drink that much beer."

"It's a figure of speech," she said. "You look nice."

"Thank you."

"So, why are you acting so weird?"

He almost argued that he wasn't, but that seemed pointless and like a lie.

"I don't know," he said instead. "Sometimes, I think I'm really happy. I feel better, physically, than I have in a long time. And, socially, I feel better. Like I'm connecting with people. Like I'm talking to new people, and it isn't as hard as it used to be."

That was true, even though the new people probably weren't the sort of people Eve was hoping he'd connect with . . .

Doris.

And Justin and Dena, who weren't exactly new.

And the copy editors, who were an awful lot like D&D players who didn't play D&D. They still counted as new. A bunch of them were even girls—not girls Lincoln was interested in, but girls.

Beth and Jennifer seemed to count. Even though they obviously didn't.

"I feel like I'm finally getting over things," Lincoln said. "That sounds stupid, doesn't it?"

His sister was watching his face closely. "No," she said, "that all sounds really good."

He nodded. "But I still feel really hopeless sometimes. I don't like my job. And I've stopped thinking about finding another one. And, even though I hardly ever think about Sam anymore, it still seems impossible that I might have something like that again. A relationship, I guess."

If he had made that confession to his mother, she would have burst into tears. But Eve looked at Lincoln the way he looked at people when they were explaining their computer problems. He felt partly responsible for that line between her eyebrows.

"Okay," she said. "I think this is good."

"How is it good?"

"Well, you've just told me about all these good things in your life," she said. "Big improvements from just six months ago."

"Yeah."

"So, what if, instead of thinking about solving your whole life, you just think about adding additional good things. One at a time. Just let your pile of good things grow."

"This is investment advice, isn't it? You're personal-bank-ing me."

"It's good advice," she said.

He was quiet for a moment. "Eve, do you think it was damaging to grow up without a father?"

"Probably," she said, stealing his biscuit. "Is that what's bothering you?"

"I'm just trying to figure out what's wrong with me."

"Well, stop," she said. "I told you, figure out what's right with you."

Before they left, she talked him into taking her older son to see the Pokemon movie that weekend. "I can't take him," Eve said, "I'm allergic to Pikachu." Then she said, "Get it? Pikachu? *Pikachu.* It sounds like I'm sneezing." When they walked out of the KFC, Lincoln stopped Eve on the sidewalk to hug her. She let him hold on to her for just a moment. Then she patted him stiffly on the back. "Okay, that's enough," she said. "Save it for Mom."

LINCOLN MET JUSTIN and Dena at the Ranch Bowl Saturday night. Lincoln wore his new denim jacket. He'd had to buy new jeans that week, smaller jeans, and the jacket had been an impulse buy. He'd worn one like it in junior high, and that had been the last time he'd ever come close to feeling like a badass. He forgot to take the price tag off, so Justin called him "Minnie-fucking-Pearl" and "XXLT" all night. They stayed out so late, Lincoln slept in and didn't have time to shower before he picked up his nephew the next afternoon.

"You smell like cigarette smoke," Jake Jr. said, climbing into Lincoln's car. "Do you smoke?"

"No. I went to a concert last night."

"With smoking?" the six-year-old asked. "And drinking?"

"Some people were smoking and drinking," Lincoln said, "but not me."

Jake shook his head sadly. "That stuff'll kill you."

"That's true," Lincoln said.

"I hope I don't get any of this smoke on me. I have to go to school tomorrow."

The Pokemon movie was even worse than Lincoln had expected. It was almost a relief every time Jake Jr. had to go to the bathroom. "My mom says I can't go alone," Jake whispered. "She says I'm so cute, someone might try to take me."

"My mom used to tell me the same thing," Lincoln said.

From: Beth Fremont
To: Jennifer Scribner-Snyder
Sent: Mon, 12/20/1999 1:45 PM
Subject: My Cute Guy has a kid.

Can you believe it? A kid! And probably a wife, too. How could he do this to me?

<<Jennifer to Beth>> ???

<<Beth to Jennifer>> My thoughts exactly.

<<Jennifer to Beth>> What I meant by that was: give me the information that you have and I don't—that is making you talk like a crazy person.

<<Beth to Jennifer>> I saw him (them) yesterday at Cinema Center. I was going to see *Fight Club* again, and as I was buying my ticket, I saw My Cute Guy getting in line for popcorn. So—don't judge—I got in line behind him (them), right behind him, and just sucked in his presence for three and a half minutes.

<<Jennifer to Beth>> I'm still confused. You saw him with his wife and kid? And then you sucked in his presence? What does that even entail?

<<Beth to Jennifer>>
1. Just the kid. Like a 5-to-10-year-old kid.

2. And "sucking in his presence" entails:

Standing. Exalting. Inhaling. Trying not to bite his shoulder.

Realizing that my mouth is the exact height as his shoulder.

Memorizing what he was wearing—camouflage pants, hiking boots, a Levi's jean jacket. (Like a very 1985 Levi's jean jacket. Hard to explain, but very, very cute.)

Noticing that his shoulders might be the broadest shoulders I've ever seen on someone who isn't a lumberjack. Marveling that I'm the kind of girl who finds a thick neck ridiculously attractive. (Is it thick necks in general? Or just his? I don't know.)

Imagining that if I were standing this close to him somewhere else, like at a grocery store or a restaurant, people might think we were together.

Deciding that his hair is about three shades lighter than mine. Cadbury colored.

Thinking I could probably bump into him and make it seem like an accident.

Wondering what his name is. And whether he's as nice as he seems. And whether he likes piña coladas and getting caught in the rain . . .

<<Jennifer to Beth>> Hmmm. I'm judging. I can't help it.

<<Beth to Jennifer>> But I didn't really *do* anything. He was there. And I was there. And we both like popcorn . . .

<<Jennifer to Beth>> You didn't have to exalt.

<<Beth to Jennifer>> Au contraire, mon frere. It would have been impossible to do anything but.

<<Jennifer to Beth>> How do you know it was his kid? Maybe it was his little brother. Or his Little Brother.

<<Beth to Jennifer>> No, they were acting like father and son. I had 75 minutes to evaluate the situation. I ended up—remember, don't judge—following them into their theater, *Pokemon: The First Movie*, and sitting about six rows behind them. McG sat with his arm around the kid's chair the whole time. He even got up three

times to take him to the bathroom. And when the movie was over, he really carefully put the boy's scarf on.

<<**Jennifer to Beth**>> So, you stayed in there for the entire movie? You didn't go to *Fight Club*? (*So* judging right now.)

<<**Beth to Jennifer**>> Do you think I was going to miss a chance to sit in the dark with My Cute Guy for an hour and a half? I already know who Tyler Durden is. (And I went back to catch the last showing of *Fight Club* after I followed My Cute Guy home.)

<<**Jennifer to Beth**>> Take it back. You didn't follow him home.

<<**Beth to Jennifer**>> I tried. I lost him on the freeway.

<<**Jennifer to Beth**>> That's something a scary person would do.

<<**Beth to Jennifer**>> Really? It felt more nosy than scary.

<<**Jennifer to Beth**>> How did you lose him? Was he driving evasively?

<<**Beth to Jennifer**>> No. Have you ever followed somebody in a car before? It's really hard, even though he drives a pretty distinctive car, a Toyota Corolla. (An ancient Toyota Corolla, the kind people drove back when it was still embarrassing to drive a Japanese car.) I'm hoping that means he's divorced and can't afford a decent car. But that might be an evil thing to hope; there *is* a child involved. I wish I knew whether he wore a wedding ring . . .

<<**Jennifer to Beth**>> I wouldn't guess Emilie would be throwing herself at him if he wore a wedding ring.

<<**Beth to Jennifer**>> Good point. Even so . . . I'm just not sure I'm ready to be a stepmother.

<<**Jennifer to Beth**>> It's a lot to think about.

<<**Beth to Jennifer**>> It is.

<<**Jennifer to Beth**>> You're not going to try to follow him again, are you? Now that you know what kind of car he drives?

<<**Beth to Jennifer**>> Hmmm. Probably not. But I'm still going to hang out in the break room a lot, hoping I'll run into him.

<<Jennifer to Beth>> That's fair. I don't think you can get arrested for that. What would you do if you *did* run into him?

<<Beth to Jennifer>> If I literally ran into him? I'm not sure. But it might involve never washing this sweater again.

<<Jennifer to Beth>> Would you talk to him? Would you flirt with him?

<<Beth to Jennifer>> Are you kidding? What kind of a floozy do you take me for? I have a boyfriend. More than a boyfriend. I'm living in sin.

<<Jennifer to Beth>> You are a complicated woman.

<<Beth to Jennifer>> No. Doy.

CHAPTER 53

LINCOLN DIDN'T WALK by Beth's desk that night. The next time he saw Christine, he wanted to be able to tell her that he still hadn't. But at the end of the night, before he left, he printed out the paragraph that Beth had written about him. He figured this was crossing yet another line. (How many lines do you get?) But it was the closest Lincoln had ever come to getting a love letter—even though he didn't really get it, he took it—and he wanted to be able to read it again. He tucked the paragraph into his wallet.

THE NEXT NIGHT, Lincoln parked his Corolla right next to *The Courier*'s front door.

I'm here, he thought. *Find me. Follow me. Make this inevitable.*

CHAPTER 54

From: Beth Fremont
To: Jennifer Scribner-Snyder
Sent: Tues, 12/21/1999 11:46 AM
Subject: They're tearing down the Indian Hills in March.

I just got a call from the old owner. They're having a big farewell weekend right before they start tearing out the seats. They're expecting people to come in from out of town for it. Cinerama fans.

<<Jennifer to Beth>> That's too bad. Every time I drove by and saw that the building was still there, I thought that maybe they were going to change their minds.

<<Beth to Jennifer>> Me, too.

At least they're having a big party to say good-bye. That's nice. And the proceeds are going to some film preservation charity. I'm writing a story about it.

<<Jennifer to Beth>> Will you be done by lunch?

<<Beth to Jennifer>> Probably, why?

<<Jennifer to Beth>> I was going to see if you could give me a ride. I'm meeting Mitch at the midwife's office. It's our first regular, prenatal visit. We're supposed to be able to hear the heartbeat.

<<Beth to Jennifer>> Of course I can give you a ride. That's so exciting! It's like it's *real* now. Aren't you getting excited? Even a little?

<<Jennifer to Beth>> I think I must be. I finally told my mom that I'm pregnant. Only an excited (or stupid) person would do that.

<<Beth to Jennifer>> Was she happy? I'll bet she was happy.

<<Jennifer to Beth>> She was. I'd just taken her to pay her gas bill, and we were having dinner at Hardee's. I blurted it out, and she about choked on a curly fry. She was like, "A baby? We're having a baby? Oh, *a baby*. Our very own baby." I thought her response was weirdly possessive, but it was definitely positive. She kept trying to hug me.

Then she said, "Oh, I hope it's a little girl, little girls are so much fun." I think she meant to add "to screw up," but whatever.

A full 45 minutes passed before she said something evil: "You better try not to gain all that weight back. Mitch never knew you when you were fat." Which isn't even true. I was a size 18 when Mitch and I started dating. I didn't lose weight until *years* later. I told her so, and she said, "You were a size 18? At your height? I never knew it had gotten that bad."

<<Beth to Jennifer>> Sometimes I feel really sorry for your mom . . . and sometimes I just hate her.

<<Jennifer to Beth>> Welcome to the last 20 years of my life. It's like she thinks she did me a favor by raising me to believe that the entire world was out to get me, by making sure I never get my hopes up.

When I got home, Mitch was fixing the light in the spare bedroom. (I know he's turning it into a nursery, but I'm not ready to talk about it.) It's always weird to go from my mom to Mitch. It doesn't seem like I should have been able to get to this life from my old one, like there aren't even roads between those two places.

Anyway, I walked in, and Mitch—who obviously didn't now what hell I'd just traversed—said something so nice, I was able to let it all go.

<<Beth to Jennifer>> What did he say?

<<Jennifer to Beth>> It's kind of personal.

<<Beth to Jennifer>> I'm sure it's deeply personal. But you can't just say, "And then Mitch said something so wonderful, it healed the tubercular ill that is my mother" without telling me what he said.

<<Jennifer to Beth>> It's not that profound. He just said, instead of hello, that I looked beautiful—and that, when we got married, he never realized that I would look more beautiful to him every year. He said it had nothing to do with me glowing. "Even though you are." He was standing on a ladder when he said it, which made it seem almost Shakespearean.

<<Beth to Jennifer>> If you die in a freak combine accident, I'm going to marry Mitch and live happily ever after. (I'm going to live happily ever after because Mitch is the best husband ever. Mitch, however, will spend the rest of his life pining for his one true love. You.)

<<Jennifer to Beth>> My appointment is at 12:30.

<<Beth to Jennifer>> I'll be ready to go by noon.

CHAPTER 55

CHUCK THE COPY editor had invited Lincoln to join the nightside breakfast club. A few editors and a few people from paste-up got together every Wednesday at noon at a diner downtown. Chuck told him the paste-up people were a cross between copy editors and artists, but with knives. He'd taken Lincoln down to the production room one night to watch them work.

The Courier still didn't paginate on computers, so all the stories were printed out in long columns, then cut and pasted down with wax on master pages, different masters for each edition. Lincoln had watched a paste-up artist rebuild the front page on deadline, slicing and waxing columns, and rearranging them like puzzle pieces.

The paste-up artists and the copy editors were pretty sure they could still get the newspaper out on time New Year's morning, even if the computers failed them.

"When do they not fail us?" Chuck said through a mouth full of club sandwich. "No offense, Lincoln."

"None taken," Lincoln said.

"Are the computers going to fail?" one of the artists asked him, licking ketchup off her thumb. She asked it like she was hoping he'd say yes. Lincoln couldn't remember her name, but she had all-over-the-place hair and big brown eyes. He didn't like thinking about her with an X-Acto knife.

"I don't think so," Lincoln said. "It's pretty simple coding, and we've got a crack team of international computer experts working on it." He'd meant that to sound sarcastic, but it had come out pretty sincere.

"Are you talking about that Croatian kid who fixed the color printer?" Chuck asked.

"Somebody fixed the color printer?" Lincoln asked.

"I just know that I'm not taking the heat if the publisher can't read his paper while he eats his soft-boiled egg on New Year's morning," Chuck said. "I'm going to have child support by then."

Even Doris was worried about the Y2K bug.

She'd asked Lincoln that week if she should even bother coming to work on New Year's Day. When the computers all stopped, she asked, would the vending machines be affected? Lincoln had told her he didn't think that anything was going to stop. He'd offered her a slice of sweet potato pie.

"I think I might stay home that night all the same," she said. "Stock up on the basics." Lincoln imagined a refrigerator full of turkey sandwiches and closets full of Pepsi products.

"I haven't had sweet potato pie like this since I was a little girl," Doris said. "I need to write your mother a thank-you note."

Lincoln's mother couldn't decide if the millennium problem was a good thing or a bad thing. She was pretty sure it was going to be chaos, but maybe, she said, falling back would do everyone a little good.

"I don't need a global network," she said. "I don't need to need to have my produce airmailed in from other continents. We still have a hand-crank washing machine in the basement, you know. We'll get by."

Meanwhile, his sister had filled a room in *her* basement with canned goods. "It's a win-win," Eve said. "If everything's okay, I don't have to go to the grocery store for a year. If everything isn't okay, Mom will have to come to my house and live off SpaghettiOs—and she'll have to like it."

Lincoln planned on working New Year's Eve, with the rest of the IT office. But Justin and Dena wanted him to come to a big New Year's Eve party at the Ranch Bowl. Sacajawea was headlining, and there was going to be champagne on tap. Justin was calling it "millennial debauchery."

And Christine had called to invite him to a Rebirthday Party that night.

"You're not calling it that, are you?"

"Don't tease, Lincoln. New Year's is my favorite holiday. And this is the biggest New Year's ever."

"But it's a nothing holiday, Christine. It's an odometer turning over."

"People love to watch odometers turn over," she said.

"It's a number."

"It's not," she said. "It's a chance to wake up new."

From: Beth Fremont
To: Jennifer Scribner-Snyder
Sent: Wed, 12/22/1999 11:36 AM
Subject: So . . .

How was your appointment?

<<Jennifer to Beth>> Bleah. I've already gained twice as much weight as I'm supposed to, even with all the throwing up. The baby was in the wrong position to hear the heartbeat, and Mitch wouldn't stop asking the midwife questions. He wanted to know all about epidurals and episiotomies and something called "cervix ripening." Doesn't that sound vile? Now she'll think we're *both* crazy.

<<Beth to Jennifer>>
1. Why does your midwife think *you're* crazy?
2. How does one know when one's cervix is ripe? Do you thump it?

<<Jennifer to Beth>>
1. All of my most insane subjects come up in her office. Sex. Parenthood. Being naked in front of other people.
2. I don't know. I was trying not to pay attention. But it's clear that Mitch has been reading about childbirth behind my

back and that he is infatuated with the idea of a *natural childbirth*, which seems fairly ludicrous to me. I wouldn't mind a general anesthesia.

<<Beth to Jennifer>> It's too bad Mitch can't be the pregnant one.

<<Jennifer to Beth>> Oh my God, he'd love that.

CHAPTER 57

WITH EVERYONE TALKING about New Year's, Christmas came like an afterthought.

Lincoln had to work on Christmas Eve. "Someone has to work," Greg said, "and it isn't going to be me. I rented a Santa suit."

It didn't really matter. Eve was spending Christmas with Jake's family in Colorado, and Lincoln's mother wasn't big on Christmas "or any of the Judeo-Christian holidays."

Lincoln worked Christmas Eve, then went out for dinner with a bunch of the copy editors. There was a casino across the river with a twenty-four-hour buffet. "With crab legs tonight," Chuck said, "on account of Christ's birth." Miniature Emilie came along. Lincoln could tell she was watching him, but he tried not to encourage her. He didn't want to betray Beth. *They wouldn't let you ride Splash Mountain*, he thought.

He spent Christmas Day with his mom, eating fresh gingerbread cookies and watching Jimmy Durante movies on public television.

WHEN HE CAME downstairs the next morning, his mother was on the telephone, talking about butter.

"Pfft," she said, "it's real food. Real food isn't bad for you. It's everything else that's killing us. The dyes. The pesticides. The preservatives. Margarine." His mother had a special disdain for margarine. Finding out that a family kept margarine in the butter dish was like finding out their pets weren't house-trained. If margarine was such a good idea, she said, why didn't God give it to us? Why didn't He promise the Israelites to lead them into the land of margarine and honey? The Japanese don't eat margarine, she said. The Scandinavians don't eat margarine. "My parents were healthy as horses," she told whoever was on the phone, "and they drank cream right off the top of the bucket."

Lincoln grabbed the last gingerbread cookie, and went into the living room. Eve had given their mom a DVD player for Christmas, and he'd promised to hook it up. He thought he had it working—they didn't have any DVDs to test it—when his mom walked into the living room.

"Well," she said, slowly sitting down on the couch.

"What's up?" he asked. He could tell she wanted him to.

"Well . . . ," she said, "I just got off the phone with a woman named Doris."

Lincoln quickly looked up from the floor. His mother was already looking down at him like she'd just confronted him with damning criminal evidence. Like it was clear he'd done it with the candlestick in the conservatory, and she had the candlestick to prove it.

"She acted as if I should recognize her name," his mother said. "She couldn't stop thanking me."

Lincoln felt his face fall. Why would Doris call him at home? "I can explain," he said.

"Doris already did," his mother said. He couldn't tell whether she was angry. "She said you share your dinner with her almost every night."

"Well," he said carefully, "that's true."

"I know that it's true. The woman knows everything that's come out of my kitchen for the past month. She wants the recipe for your grandmother's salmon patties."

"I'm sorry," Lincoln said. "I couldn't help myself. You should see what she brings for dinner—turkey loaf on Wonder bread every single night—and you always send me with such a feast. I felt guilty eating in front of her."

"I don't mind that you share," his mother said. "I just don't know why you wouldn't tell me that you were doing it, that you were giving my food to . . . a stranger . . ."

She looked at him through narrowed eyes. "I wondered how you were eating so much and still losing weight. I thought you might be taking steroids."

"I'm not taking steroids, Mom." That made him laugh.

And that made her laugh.

"So that's all it is?" she asked. There was something in her voice still. Worry.

"What do you mean?"

"You just feel sorry for her?"

"Well," Lincoln said. He could hardly tell his mom that he ate dinner with Doris to up his chances of running into a girl he'd never met. "I guess we're friends. Doris is actually pretty funny. Not always intentionally . . ."

His mother took a deep breath, like she was steadying herself. Lincoln's voice trailed off.

"Oh, Mom, no. It's not like that. It could not be more *not* like that. Mom. *God.*"

She put her hand on her forehead and exhaled.

"Why are you always bracing for me to tell you something weird?" he asked.

"What am I supposed to think when I hear that you eat dinner with the same woman every night? And it wouldn't be that weird, you know, a number of my friends enjoy the company of younger men."

"*Mom.*"

"Are you sure that Doris understands your intentions?"

"Yes." Now his forehead was in his hands.

"You always were too generous," she said, resting her hand on his head. "Remember when you dropped your action figures in the Salvation Army kettle?" He remembered. Snaggletooth and Luke Skywalker, X-Wing pilot. It had been an impulse. He'd ended up crying himself to sleep that night when he understood the repercussions.

She pushed his hair to the side, off his forehead, and held it for a moment.

"Do you feel like waffles?" she asked abruptly, standing up. "I've already made the batter. Oh, and don't eat the rest of the lamb. I told Doris you'd bring her a chop . . ."

"Is that why she called?" he asked. "To thank you?"

"Oh no," his mother said, talking more loudly as she walked into the kitchen, "she called for you. She's moving—did you know she's moving? She said the movers showed up for her furniture and they were throwing things around like the Samsonite gorilla. She didn't trust them with her grandmother's curio cabinet, and I don't blame her. I offered to send you right over—you've got a strong, young back—but she said it could wait a few days. What do you think, whipped cream on waffles or maple syrup? Or both? We've got both."

"Both," Lincoln said. He followed her into the kitchen, smiling, but dizzy. Even when he and his mother were on the same page, Lincoln felt like he was just keeping up.

CHAPTER 58

EVERYONE IN IT stayed late that week, even the people who weren't directly helping with the code patch. Greg was racked with anxiety. He was sure that the Y2K kids were grifting him. He told Lincoln that his doctor had written him a prescription for Paxil. Lincoln kept watching the International Strike Force for signs of fear or evasion. But they just sat in the corner, staring at screens full of code, calmly punching keys and drinking Mountain Dew.

With all the company, and all the work, Lincoln didn't have a chance to obsess over the WebFence folder or hang around the newsroom. He didn't even take a real dinner break until Thursday. (T-minus twenty-seven hours.) Doris was thrilled to see him, and even more thrilled to see that he'd brought chocolate cake.

"Your mother told you about my cabinet, right? You're sure you don't mind?"

"Of course I don't mind," Lincoln said, unwrapping the cake. "Just tell me when."

"That's just what your mom said. Boy, is she a character. A real dynamo, I could tell, on top of being a good cook. I'll bet she's pretty, too. Why didn't she ever get remarried?"

"I'm not sure," he said.

He couldn't imagine his mother married, even though he knew that she had been, briefly, to Eve's dad. He'd seen a photo of her at the wedding, wearing a white lace minidress and her hair in a blond bubble. Lincoln couldn't even imagine his mother going out on a date. Eve said it was different before he was born. She remembered men and parties and strangers at breakfast . . .

"I couldn't think about dating for the first few years after my Paul died," Doris said. "But then I realized that I could live another forty years. That's longer than Paul and I were together. I don't think he'd want me moping around for forty years. I know he wouldn't."

"So you started dating?"

"Sure I did," Doris said. "I have a couple of gentlemen I see on a regular basis. Nothing serious yet, but you never know."

Lincoln was starting to wonder if he was having dinner with Doris just to be nice, or if it was the other way around.

"My mom said to tell you not to worry about your blood pressure," he said, handing Doris a plastic fork. "She made this with olive oil."

"Olive oil in a cake?" Doris said. "Is it green?"

"It's good," Lincoln said. "I've already had three pieces."

Doris took a big bite. "Oh my," she said with a mouth full of crumbs, "that is good. So moist. And the *frosting*—do you think she uses olive oil in that, too?"

"I think the frosting's made with butter," he said.

"Oh, well."

A woman walked into the break room and stepped up to the snack machine behind them. She was young, Lincoln's age, and tall. Her hair was pulled up into a thick dark bun, and she had a sweep of freckles across her face. Pretty . . .

"Hi, Doris," she said.

"Hey there, honey," Doris said, "working late?"

The woman, the girl, smiled at Doris and nodded, then smiled at Lincoln. She had broad shoulders and a high, heavy chest. Lincoln's throat tightened. He smiled back. She turned to the snack machine. He'd never seen her before, had he? She leaned over to get something out of the machine. Pieces of hair were escaping in soft coils at the back of her neck. She walked briskly toward the door. She was wearing a fitted white shirt and strawberry pink corduroy trousers. Smallish waist. Widish hips. A soft curve at the small of her back. So pretty.

"Too bad that one's got a boyfriend," Doris said as the door closed behind the woman. "She's a nice girl . . . and about your size, too. You wouldn't have to break your back kissing her good night."

Lincoln could feel his cheeks and neck turning red. Doris giggled.

"On that note," he said, standing up, "I've got to get back to work."

"Thanks for the cake, kiddo," she said.

Lincoln walked tentatively through the newsroom on his way back to the IT office.

Maybe it was her. The girl. Beth. Maybe. Maybe this was the night, his night, to talk to her. On the eve of the eve of the new millennium. She'd smiled at him. Well, she was probably smiling at Doris, but she'd looked at him while she was still smiling.

Maybe it was her. *His* her.

And maybe she'd be sitting at her desk tonight, and Lincoln would stop to say hello—the way men all over the world stop and say hello to women all the time. *Wake up new*, he told himself firmly, as the knot in his stomach tightened.

He didn't get to Beth's cubicle.

The girl from the break room was sitting at the city desk, next to the police scanner, talking on the phone. She was probably the new police reporter, Megan something; he'd seen her byline. Not Beth. Still no Beth.

He let himself look at the girl for a moment or two, even though she wasn't the one. She was so pretty, this girl. So more than pretty. He thought about her hair falling down from her bun. He thought about her smile.

CHAPTER 59

From: Beth Fremont
To: Jennifer Scribner-Snyder
Sent: Fri, 12/31/1999 4:05 PM
Subject: Yawn 2K

That's my entry for the front-page headline contest, what do you think?

<<**Jennifer to Beth**>> D@rn it. That's so much better than mine—Meh-llennium.

<<**Beth to Jennifer**>> Are you kidding? "Meh-llennium" is excellent. Derek entered, "New Year? Old hat," which is worse than no headline at all.

Is it wrong to admit that I'm actually kind of disappointed that nothing terrible has happened yet?

<<**Jennifer to Beth**>> No, I know! It's such a letdown. I feel like all the countries ahead of us are ruining the suspense.

<<**Beth to Jennifer**>> CNN should have "spoiler alert" on its crawl.

<<**Jennifer to Beth**>> It's actually less exciting than a regular New Year's Eve. I'm not even staying up for it.

<<Beth to Jennifer>> I'll stay up, I have to work. None of the special Y2K shifts have been canceled. Plus, I'm hoping to spend most of the night in the break room.

<< Jennifer to Beth>> The break room—does this have something to do with Your Cute Guy?

<<Beth to Jennifer>> Uh . . . uh-huh.

Remember when I said that, if I ever ran into McG, I wouldn't talk to him? Because that would make me a floozy or some such nonsense?

<<Jennifer to Beth>> Vividly.

<<Beth to Jennifer>> Yeah . . . I was wrong about that. If I were ever to run into him, I would definitely talk to him. I might even stand there, smiling my best come-hither smile and hoping he didn't notice that I was sucking in my stomach.

<<Jennifer to Beth>> Floozy. Did you follow him again?

<<Beth to Jennifer>> Only to the break room.

I saw him walk out of an office on the first floor, the one with the extra card reader. He must work in security, after all. Which explains why he works nights. And why I've seen him in different departments. And his tremendous size. (It doesn't actually explain his size, but his size explains why he would be hired to work security. I feel more secure just standing across the room from him.) I wonder why he doesn't wear a uniform like the guards at the front desk. Do you think he's a plainclothes officer? A detective? Like Serpico?

<<Jennifer to Beth>> Wasn't Serpico a drug dealer?

<<Beth to Jennifer>> I think you're thinking Scarface.

Anyway. I followed him to the break room, then I walked up and down the hall a dozen times, trying to decide if I should go in there and what I would do with myself if I did. And then I finally decided to throw caution to the wind.

<<Jennifer to Beth>> Caution and fidelity. Floozy.

<<Beth to Jennifer>> I walked in all casual, like, "Don't mind me, I'm just here for the vending machines," and there he was, sitting with Doris. They were both eating chocolate cake. I was all, "Hi, Doris." I smiled at them both, made eye contact with them both, gave one of them the serious come-hither, bought a piece of beef jerky and walked away.

<<Jennifer to Beth>> Beef jerky?

<<Beth to Jennifer>> I was just randomly punching buttons at that point. And, like I said, sucking in my stomach.

<<Jennifer to Beth>> Were there fireworks when your eyes met?

<<Beth to Jennifer>> On my end? Capital Yes. Roman candles. On his end? Well, he looked at me in a very pleasant way, as if to say, "Any friend of Doris's is a friend of mine."

<<Jennifer to Beth>> They were both eating chocolate cake? Were they sharing a fork?

<<Beth to Jennifer>> Don't be silly.

<<Jennifer to Beth>> Oh, I'm being silly. Right. I thought you were giving up Cute-Guy hunting because you realized it would be awkward if he actually noticed and tried to talk to you.

<<Beth to Jennifer>> I can't give him up. What would I have to look forward to?

<<Jennifer to Beth>> I refuse to talk about this anymore. It just encourages you.

Mitch just called me to gloat. I tried to talk him into going to Sam's Club last night to buy stuff for our millennium stockpile, but he refused to go. He said that he preferred Armageddon to Sam's Club.

Did you stock up on anything?

<<Beth to Jennifer>> God no. If civilization comes crashing down at midnight, the last thing I'd want is to be stuck in my apartment, living off bottled water and canned beans.

CHAPTER 60

WHEN LINCOLN GOT up to the newsroom—because that's where he went, that's where he had to go, as soon as he'd read the words "tremendous" and "Roman candles" and "I can't give him up"—the room was full and buzzing. Most of the reporters must have special Y2K shifts. They were hanging out in clumps around the newsroom, laughing and talking. Lincoln took a deep breath, the air felt like champagne in his lungs.

She was there. The girl from the break room. Beth. She was there, at her desk. Her hair was down, her glasses were pushed up over her forehead, and she was talking on the phone, twisting the cord around her fingers. There she was. Lincoln was going to say hello.

No, he was going to wait until she was off the phone. And then say hello.

No, and then he was going to kiss her.

No, he was just going to kiss her. He wasn't going to wait. She'd kiss him back. He was absolutely certain that she would kiss him back.

And then he'd tell her that he loved her.

And then he'd tell her his name.

And then and then and then . . . *what?*

"If everything goes to hell at midnight, I want you to join my savage gang of looters."

"What?" Lincoln turned around. Chuck was standing behind him. He had a blue marker in his mouth, and he was looking at a pie graph.

"Do these percentages make sense?" Chuck said, holding out the graph.

"I don't know," Lincoln said.

"I'm asking you to check them."

"Did you say something about looting?"

"Yeah," Chuck said. "But that was more of an invitation. If things get Mad Max around here later, I want you on my team. Don't ask me what's in it for you. I haven't worked that out yet."

"I can't do this right now," Lincoln said, pushing the paper away.

"Why not?"

"I . . . I have to leave."

"Are you okay?"

"No." Lincoln looked up at Beth again and started backing away from Chuck. Away from the newsroom. "I have to go."

"Do you know something about the power grid that we don't?" Chuck called after him. "What are the machines telling you?"

"I HAVE TO go home," Lincoln said when he got back to the IT office.

"You look terrible," Greg said. "But you can't go home. We're on the cusp of a new age."

"I *feel* terrible. I have to leave."

"If you leave," Greg asked, "who's going to lead the Strike Force through zero hour?"

Lincoln looked at the television on Greg's desk. People were celebrating in London. Midnight had already arrived with an anticlimactic thud in Paris and Moscow and Beijing. Even Wolf Blitzer looked bored. The members of the Strike Force were shamelessly playing Doom.

"All right . . . ," Greg said, frowning. "But you're going to miss out. We're ordering pizza."

Lincoln shut down his computer quickly and hurried out of the building to his car. He didn't even buckle his seat belt until he was on the freeway. Didn't even know where he was going until he got there. Justin's apartment. Lincoln had driven Justin home a few times, but he'd never been inside. Maybe Justin would still be there. Maybe Lincoln could still get in on the millennial debauchery.

Dena answered the door. She was wearing her work uniform, a pink smock with little white teeth printed on it. Whole teeth, roots and all. They were supposed to be cute, but he found teeth without gums disconcerting.

"Hey, Lincoln."

"Hey. Is Justin here?"

"Not yet. He had to work late. Are you okay?"

"Yeah, I'm fine. I was just thinking I'd go to the concert with you guys. If that's all right. If the offer still stands."

"Yeah, of course," she said. "Justin will be here soon. Have a seat." He did. In the only chair in Justin's living room, a giant leather recliner. "Can I get you something? A beer?"

"That'd be great."

She handed him a Mickey's big mouth. Beer, malt liquor, same difference.

"Are you sure you're okay?" she asked.

"Completely."

"I was just going to go get ready."

"Yeah. Definitely. Go ahead. Don't mind me, I'll watch TV."

"Okay," Dena said. She hesitated a moment, then walked away.

Lincoln was pretty sure that it was a mistake, coming here. But he couldn't have stayed at work. Knowing Beth was there, that she might be thinking about him. Knowing that he couldn't talk to her. That he didn't have the guts, was that it? Or was it that he knew it was wrong, that even talking to her would be like trading with insider information?

Or maybe he was just afraid to do something real.

It was worse now that he knew what she looked like. It was already worse. Now that his wandering thoughts and warm feelings had a face. And freckles. And snug strawberry corduroys. It was unbearable to think of that face searching him out in the hallways. Lighting up when she saw him. Watching him.

Maybe she was still there. At her desk. Maybe he could still catch her and kiss her and tell her . . . tell her *what*?

When Justin walked in, Lincoln wasn't sure whether he'd been waiting in the living room for a few minutes or an hour. Probably an hour.

He'd finished three Mickeys. Three Mickeys on an empty stomach. He wasn't drunk exactly, but he was fuzzy.

"What're you doing here?" Justin said happily. "I thought you had to work."

"I did. And then I didn't."

"Did something happen?"

He thought of Beth and her long brown hair and the phone cord winding around her fingers. He thought of himself standing like a moron against the wall. "No," he said, "nothing ever happens. I had to get out of there."

"Well, all right. Let me change into something I can afford for Dena to puke on, and then we'll get this motherfucker started."

Lincoln held up his empty bottle. "Cheers," he said.

Dena came to sit with Lincoln while Justin got dressed. She'd changed into going-out clothes. Tight black jeans and stacked-heel boots. She'd put on makeup that would look fine at the bar, but looked too bright and shiny in the overhead light.

"We're meeting a few of my friends at Friday's first," she said. "Are you hungry?"

"Sure," he said. "That sounds great."

"They're all single," she said.

"Single girls on New Year's," Justin shouted from the bedroom. "Double down."

"My friend Lisa will be there," Dena said. "Do you remember her? From The Steel Guitar?"

Lincoln remembered. He could still taste the licorice. Justin held out another Mickey's on the way to the door, and Lincoln took it.

T.G.I. FRIDAY'S WAS a blur. He entertained Dena's friends by ordering whatever they did, drinks with whipped cream and cherries and blinking plastic ice cubes. Even Lincoln's steak had whiskey in it. He was more than tipsy when they got to the Ranch Bowl. *Do guys get tipsy*, he wondered, *or, if you're a guy, are there just different degrees of drunk?* How

many degrees of drunk was he? What would happen if he stopped drinking now? Would he feel better or worse?

They'd timed their arrival perfectly. Sacajawea was just taking the
stage. Justin used Lincoln as a wedge to make room at the bar.

"Are you okay, big guy? Lincoln? Hey." Dena was talking to him.

Lincoln nodded. He was okay. He was fine.

The first song started with a guitar solo. All Sacajawea's songs started
with guitar solos. Justin whooped, and the girls around them screamed.
"Oh my God, look at him," said someone at Lincoln's elbow. "He's so hot."

Lincoln looked at Chris. Shimmering. Slithering at the edge of the
stage. This wasn't a good idea. Coming here. *Look at him*, Lincoln
thought. *She's his. That beautiful girl. That girl I think about when I'm not
thinking about anything else. When I can't think about anything else. Look
at him. That magical girl. That light.* His. The women in the room, the
women around Lincoln, were swaying along with Chris's guitar, reaching out to him with open palms. All these girls who weren't the girl. All
these girls who weren't the only girl who mattered. Lincoln imagined
himself pushing his way through them to get to Chris. Imagined how
heavy his fist would fall on Chris's delicate face.

"This song is just as good as 'Stairway,'" Justin said emotionally. He
and Dena were standing right in front of Lincoln, close enough that he
felt like he was standing behind them in a class photo. Dena wasn't
watching Chris. She was watching Justin. Lincoln noticed Justin's hand
on Dena's waist, his fingers just under her shirt, in the small of her
back.

And then Lincoln stopped noticing anything at all.

THEY WERE HELPING him up stairs.

"We should have just left him in the car," Justin said.

"It's freezing outside," Dena said.

"Would've woken him up. Jesus Christ, it's like dragging a horse."

"One more flight."

"I can walk," Lincoln said, finding his tongue. He tried to support
himself and jerked forward.

"Let's leave him here," Justin said.

"Just a few more steps, Lincoln," Dena said.

They helped him stagger through Justin's doorway. He hit his head on the jamb.

"That's for making me miss the encore," Justin said, "you fucking giant."

"I can walk," Lincoln said. He couldn't. They dropped him on the armchair. Over it. Dena was trying to make him drink water.

"Am I going to die?" he asked.

"I hope so," Justin said.

LINCOLN WOKE UP again some time before dawn and staggered through a bedroom to find the bathroom. He fell back on the recliner face-first and pushed it all the way back, almost flat. His feet still hung off the end. The back of the chair smelled like hair gel and cigarettes. Everything smelled like cigarettes. He opened his eyes. The sun was up now. Justin was sitting on the arm of the chair, smoking a cigarette and using the chair's built-in ashtray.

"He's awake," Justin called to the kitchen. Lincoln groaned. "Dena was worried about you," Justin said, turning on the TV. "You sleep like a dead person."

"What?"

"You don't breathe," Justin said.

"Yes, I do."

"Not visibly," Dena said, handing him something red to drink.

"What is this?"

"Vodka and V-8" she said. "With A1."

"Not A1," Justin said. "Worcestershire."

"No, thank you," Lincoln said.

"You should drink something," Justin said. "You're dehydrated."

"Did I pass out last night?"

"Kind of," Dena said. "One minute you were standing up. And the next minute, you were lying down on the bar. Like you were resting your head. I haven't seen anybody drink that much since college."

"I never drank that much in college."

"Which explains why you're so bush-league," Justin said. "Honestly. A man of your size. It's embarrassing."

"I'm really sorry," Lincoln said to Dena.

"It's okay," she said. "Do you want some eggs or something?"

"Just some water." He crawled out of the chair, and Justin immediately slid into his place. The world hadn't ended. Not even just in the Central Time Zone. *SportsCenter* was on. Dena followed Lincoln into the kitchen. She was wearing a T-shirt and patterned scrubs. More teeth. She handed him a glass of tap water.

"Did you chase it away?" she asked.

"What?"

"Whatever was making you want to drink that much."

He closed his eyes. *Beth.* "No," he said, "but I might be done trying."

LINCOLN DRANK NEARLY a gallon of water before he left Justin's apartment. He stopped at the gym before he went home, thinking maybe it would make him feel better. Superior Bodies didn't close on holidays—it was even open a half day on Christmas—and plenty of people were already there, kick-starting their New Year's resolutions. Lincoln had to wait in line for a treadmill. He didn't feel sick anymore, not exactly. Just haggard and morose. He couldn't help but think about Beth, but thinking about her was like thinking himself into a corner. Like realizing toward the end of a logic puzzle that you'd made a mistake early on, and that there's no way to reach the solution without starting over. Without erasing everything. Without throwing out all of your assumptions.

Now that he knew what Beth looked like, he couldn't remember what it was like to have not known. He couldn't remember picturing her any other way. She was nothing like Sam, physically. And Sam was his only frame of reference. What would it be like to be with a girl, a woman, who could just barely tuck her head under his chin? "Your own size"—was that what Doris had said? He'd loved how small Sam was. Little bird. Little slip. How he could cover her, swallow her. How it had felt to hold back so that he wouldn't break her.

What would it be like to hold a different girl? A girl whose hips and shoulders nearly met his, who wouldn't disappear beneath him. A girl whose kiss wasn't always so far out of reach.

He ended up working out too long or too hard or too hungover. He felt weak and dizzy in the shower and ended up buying three of those horrible protein bars from the front desk. The girl working there talked him into drinking something with electrolytes that was supposed to taste like watermelon. It didn't. It tasted like Kool-Aid made with corn syrup and salt.

Lincoln was embarrassed to have given in, even for a moment, to the frenzy of the new year. To have believed there were cosmic forces at work in his favor. His moment had come and gone last night in the newsroom. And Lincoln had dropped the ball.

From: Beth Fremont
To: Jennifer Scribner-Snyder
Sent: Tues, 01/04/2000 1:26 PM
Subject: Is it just me, or is the new millennium a lot less cute than the old one?

Serendipity is not my friend. It's been five days since my last Cute Guy sighting. I saw Doris in the hall yesterday, and my stomach jumped. I don't want to start getting excited about Doris sightings.

<<**Jennifer to Beth**>> My world is plenty cute. Mitch and I went crib shopping last night. We didn't plan to go crib shopping—we were supposed to be looking at dishwashers—but we walked by the cribs, and there it was. Cream-colored with a rocking horse carved into the headboard. Now we can't afford a dishwasher.

<<**Beth to Jennifer**>> A crib? Already? I wanted to help pick out the crib. Can I help pick out the bedding? You can't do all this baby stuff without me. I'm trying to have a vicarious pregnancy here.

<<**Jennifer to Beth**>> I'm sorry. It was unplanned. I'm probably picking out paint for the nursery this weekend, do you want to come?

<<**Beth to Jennifer**>> You know that I do. And that I can't. This weekend is the big wedding.

<<Jennifer to Beth>> Oh, right. Are you looking forward to it?

<<Beth to Jennifer>> Looking forward to it being over.

<<Jennifer to Beth>> Does Kiley know how cranky her maid of honor is?

<<Beth to Jennifer>> She's too deliriously happy to notice.

I picked up my dress on Sunday. It's deliriously ugly, especially with me in it, and I still haven't come up with a Kiley-approved way to hide my upper arms.

<<Jennifer to Beth>> Your arms are fine.

Wasn't this wedding supposed to have a millennium theme? Is that still happening?

<<Beth to Jennifer>> It was indeed. Kiley was going to make 2,000 paper cranes to strew about the reception, but she fizzled out at 380. Now the theme is Winter Wonderland. (Hence the strapless dresses, I guess.)

And, by the way, you only think my arms are fine because I keep them covered up. Because I've mastered the art of misdirection. All of my clothes are engineered to draw the eye away from my arm-shoulder area.

<<Jennifer to Beth>> Now that I think about it, we've known each other six years, and I've never seen you in a bathing suit. Or a tank top.

<<Beth to Jennifer>> Not a coincidence, my friend. I've got the arms of a Sicilian grandmother. Arms for picking olives and stirring hearty tomato sauces. Shoulders for carrying buckets of water from the stream to the farmhouse.

<<Jennifer to Beth>> Has Chris seen your shoulders?

<<Beth to Jennifer>> He's seen them. But he hasn't *seen* them.

<<Jennifer to Beth>> I get it, but I don't *get* it.

<<Beth to Jennifer>> No sleeveless negligees. No direct sunlight. Sometimes when I'm getting out of the shower, I shout, "Hey, look, a bobcat!"

<<Jennifer to Beth>> I'll bet he falls for that every time.

<<Beth to Jennifer>> It's Chris. So recreational drugs are a factor.

Anyway, I bought a dressy cardigan that I thought I could wear with my bridesmaid dress, but Kiley said it was too "frumpy" and that it was the wrong shade of sage. And then she said, "God, Beth, no one is going to be looking at your arms."

And my mom said, "She's right, Beth, all eyes will be on the bride."

Which just infuriated me. Why did that infuriate me? It's true. But all I could think was, if no one is going to be looking at me, then why can't I wear my fucking sweater? We were at Victoria's Secret. Did I mention that we were at Victoria's Secret? My sister wasn't happy with her strapless bra, so we *all* had to go to Victoria's Secret. I'm not happy with my strapless bra either. Because I'm not happy with my strapless dress.

While Kiley was trying on bras, my mom patted me on the arm and said, "Honey, this is Kiley's day. Just roll with it." Have I also mentioned that neither of these women have large arms? I got them from my father's mother, my own Italian grandmother, a woman who is now dead, but who, while alive, had the sense to never wear a strapless dress.

<<Jennifer to Beth>> I can wait until next week to go nursery shopping.

<<Beth to Jennifer>> Would you do that for me?

<<Jennifer to Beth>> Of course I would. I'll even let you wear your ugly green sweater.

Is Chris going to the wedding with you?

<<Beth to Jennifer>> And to the rehearsal dinner. And to Sunday brunch. He told me that he didn't think I should do anything wedding-related by myself. He said, "Every time you talk about it, you go all blurry around the edges." Which of course made me cry. He's pretty good when I cry. He doesn't get flustered.

<<Jennifer to Beth>> Well done, Chris.

<<Beth to Jennifer>> I know. Five stars. He's even letting me buy him a new jacket and real pants. Slacks. But I'm not allowed to call them slacks. That word gives him the heebie-jeebies. Normally, I'm not allowed to buy him clothes of any sort.

<<Jennifer to Beth>> I'm relieved to hear you're not the one who picks out all those tight jeans he wears. What will he do with his hair? Put it in a ponytail?

<<Beth to Jennifer>> There's nothing you can do with that hair. You just have to let go and let God.

Hey, you know what? All this talk about my cute boyfriend is diminishing my cute cravings.

<<Jennifer to Beth>> As well it should.

CHAPTER 62

BETH MISSED HIM.

Lincoln thought he'd hit bottom on New Year's, and it had been a relief. Wasn't hitting bottom the thing you had to do to knock some sense into yourself? Wasn't hitting bottom the thing that showed you which way was up?

From: Jennifer Scribner-Snyder
To: Beth Fremont
Sent: Fri, 01/07/2000 2:44 PM
Subject: Are you here?

Distract me.

<<**Beth to Jennifer**>> Distract you? Gladly. Productivity-schmoductivity.

What are you supposed to be working on?

<<**Jennifer to Beth**>> I don't know. Writing headlines, I guess. Reading the same stories over and over to make sure some idiot reporter didn't use "they're" when he should have used "their." Changing "which"es to "that"s. Arguing with someone about sequence of tenses.

<<**Beth to Jennifer**>> What on earth is sequence of tenses?

<<**Jennifer to Beth**>> It's top-secret copy editor stuff.

<<**Beth to Jennifer**>> I didn't know there was such a thing.

<<**Jennifer to Beth**>> Are you kidding? Everything about being a copy editor is top secret—by default, really—because no one else cares.

<<**Beth to Jennifer**>> Can I ask why you need distracting? Are they making you edit the sports section again?

<<Jennifer to Beth>> No, it's not work.

I've been having these strange cramps for the last few days. Not even cramps—they're more like assertive twinges. I called our midwife and described them to her, and she seemed pretty confident that nothing is wrong. She said that it's natural to feel your uterus readjusting at the end of the first trimester. "This is your first pregnancy," she said. "It's going to feel strange." She also told me that I might feel better if I talked to the baby.

<<Beth to Jennifer>> What are you supposed to say? Are you supposed to talk out loud? Or are you supposed to reach out for it on the astral plane?

<<Jennifer to Beth>> I'm supposed to talk out loud. "Relax," she said. "Put on some quiet music. Light a few candles. Tune in to the life within you." I'm supposed to tell the baby that it's welcome and wanted and that it doesn't have to worry about anything right now except getting big and strong.

I've tried it a few times, when I'm alone in the car. But I never get past small talk. I feel sort of like I'm invading the baby's space or like it's going to wonder, after two months of respectful silence, why I've suddenly decided we need to get all personal with each other.

Also, I don't want to let on that something might be wrong. So I try to keep it light. "I hope you're comfortable. I hope I'm eating enough iron. Sorry I stopped taking the expensive vitamins, they made me throw up." I usually end up crying and hoping that the baby isn't actually paying attention.

<<Beth to Jennifer>> I kind of like the idea of you talking to the baby. Even if it doesn't understand you. There's something living inside of you. It makes sense to be neighborly.

Maybe I'll start talking to my eggs. Pep talks. Like William Wallace's speech in *Braveheart*.

<<Jennifer to Beth>> I think I'll feel less ridiculous talking to it after it has ears.

<<Beth to Jennifer>> When does it get ears?

<<Jennifer to Beth>> I don't know. I'd ask Mitch, but I don't want him to know any of this.

I feel like I've known all along that something was bound to go wrong at some point in this pregnancy. It's all been too easy so far.

<<Beth to Jennifer>> Nothing is bound to go wrong. Nothing is bound, period. And the chances are so much better that everything is going to be all right.

<<Jennifer to Beth>> Easy for you to say. Easy for the midwife to say. It's so easy for someone else to say, "Don't worry. Everything's going to be all right." Why *not* say it? It doesn't cost anything. It doesn't mean anything. No one will hold you to it if you're wrong.

<<Beth to Jennifer>> Your midwife says it's going to be okay because she spends her whole life working with pregnant women. She's speaking from experience.

And I say it because I trust her, and because I believe that being miserable about some bad thing that might not ever happen won't do you any good.

<<Jennifer to Beth>> I disagree. I believe that worrying about a bad thing prepares you for it when it comes. If you worry, the bad thing doesn't hit you as hard. You can roll with the punch if you see it coming.

<<Beth to Jennifer>> Are you in pain? Maybe you should go home.

<<Jennifer to Beth>> No, it doesn't hurt. It feels more like a muscle flexing. Besides, if I go home, I will obsess powerfully, with all my might. Even I don't think that's a good idea.

So distract me. Tell me more about your cute security guard. Complain about your sister's wedding. Pick a fight with me about ending a sentence with a preposition.

<<Beth to Jennifer>> Okay, here's something distracting: I've gone to a tanning salon twice this week. My brother's wife said it would make my arms look thinner. I think it will probably just

make them look tanner—but big tan arms do seem more appealing than big pale arms, so I'm doing it.

<<**Jennifer to Beth**>> I hate to say this, because it's advice I could never follow myself—in fact, this is probably the exact opposite of how I'd behave in your situation: But maybe the best thing for you to do is to let the arm thing go. Yes, somebody might notice that your upper arms are somewhat out of proportion with the rest of your body, but let's be honest, almost nobody looks good in a strapless dress.

<<**Beth to Jennifer**>> So why has it become the dominant dress of our time? Do you know that they don't even make wedding dresses with sleeves anymore? Everyone—regardless of weight, chest size, back acne, stretch marks, hunched shoulders, or over-prominent clavicle—is forced to wear one. Why? The whole point of clothing is to hide your shame. (Genesis 3:7)

<<**Jennifer to Beth**>> Did you seriously just consult a Bible?

<<**Beth to Jennifer**>> Derek has one on his desk, it wasn't that big of a deal.

Hey, I have to go now. I'm taking off early to get ready for the rehearsal dinner. Call me this weekend if you still need distracting, okay?

<<**Jennifer to Beth**>> You'll be caught up in wedding stuff.

<<**Beth to Jennifer**>> And grateful for the interruption, I'm sure.

<<**Jennifer to Beth**>> I'll bet you're going to have a really nice time at the wedding and feel bad for having dreaded it for months.

<<**Beth to Jennifer**>> It could happen, I guess. There is an open bar.

CHAPTER 64

LINCOLN DIDN'T FEEL like going home that night after work. He kept thinking about Beth in a strapless dress. Creamy white shoulders. Freckles. Maybe he should go out with one of the girls Justin was always trying to hook him up with. Or with one of his sister's Lutherans. Or with that girl who works at the gym, Becca. She'd been spotting for Lincoln lately on the bench press, and it seemed like she touched his arms a lot when she didn't really have to. Maybe she was still impressed with his elbows.

Lincoln ended up at the Village Inn, alone. When the waitress came, he ordered two pieces of French silk pie. She brought them on separate plates, which was embarrassing for some reason.

He had a copy of the next day's paper, one of the perks of working at *The Courier*, but he was so agitated, he couldn't read it.

He was so agitated, so at loose ends, he didn't notice until his second piece of pie that Chris was sitting at the next booth. Beth's Chris. He was actually facing Lincoln, both of them sitting alone at their tables.

Lincoln remembered the last time he'd seen Chris, on New Year's Eve, and considered leaping across the table to follow up on smashing his face. But he'd lost the urge.

Chris looked different. Cleaned up. He was wearing a dress shirt, rakishly unbuttoned of course, and a jacket, and his hair looked smooth and shiny. *Like a fucking Breck commercial*, Lincoln thought. And then, *Right, for the rehearsal dinner*. And then Lincoln started to laugh. A little. Mostly on the inside.

Because he shouldn't know that, but he did. And he should hate this guy, but he didn't. He didn't want to kill Chris. He wanted to trade places with him. No, he didn't even want that. If Lincoln had been Beth's date to the rehearsal dinner tonight, he'd be home with her now. If he were her date to the wedding tomorrow, he'd be counting down the hours until she put on that dress. Until she took it off again.

He laughed again. On the outside.

Chris looked up at Lincoln then, and seemed to recognize him.

"Hey," Chris said.

Lincoln stopped laughing. Until this moment, he'd believed somehow that he was invisible to Chris. The way he was invisible to Beth. (Except that he wasn't.) "Hey," Lincoln said.

"Hey, uh, you wouldn't have a cigarette, would you?" Chris asked.

Lincoln shook his head. "Sorry."

Chris nodded and smiled. "I'm unprepared tonight. Nothing to smoke. Nothing to read." He seemed agitated, too, but he wore it better than Lincoln.

"You can have a section of my paper," Lincoln said.

"Thanks," Chris said. He got up and walked over to Lincoln's booth, leaned against it, and picked up the Entertainment section.

"I missed today's movie review," Chris said.

"Movie fan?" Lincoln said dumbly.

"Movie reviewer fan," Chris said. "My girl, she's the film critic . . . Hey, this is tomorrow's paper."

"It's today's technically . . . ," Lincoln said. "I work at *The Courier*."

"Maybe you know her, then."

"I don't know many people," Lincoln said. He felt so stiff, he couldn't believe his mouth was moving. He felt like, if he said the wrong word, he might actually turn to stone. Like he might anyway. "I work nights."

"You'd know," Chris said, nodding and looking out the window, agitated again, "you'd know if you knew her. She's a force. A force to be reckoned with. An act of God, you know?"

"Like a tornado?" Lincoln asked.

Chris laughed. "Sort of," he said. "I was thinking more . . . I don't know what I was thinking, but yeah. She's . . ." He patted his chest pocket nervously, then ran his hand through his hair. "You're single, right? I mean, I never see you at our shows with anyone."

"Right," Lincoln said. *Not only am I not invisible, I'm visibly alone.*

Chris laughed again. It was sharp. Sarcastic. It undid some of the charm of his smile.

"I can't even remember what that's like . . ." He shook his head ruefully, touched his hair again. "It's this jacket," Chris said. "I had to take my cigarettes out because you could see them poking out of the pocket. Classy, right? I can't remember when I've gone this long without . . . You ever smoked?"

"No," Lincoln said. "Never picked it up."

"No cigarettes, no girl, you're living an unencumbered life, my friend."

"That's one way to look at it," Lincoln said, looking hard at the man across from him and wishing for some sort of *Freaky Friday* miracle right there, right then.

"Oh," Chris said, abashed. He was pretty enough for that word. "Right," he said. "I didn't mean . . ." He looked down and held out the Entertainment section. "Thanks. For this. I'll let you go back . . . Normally, I wouldn't have bothered . . . It's the jacket, you know? I'm not myself."

Lincoln mustered a smile. Chris stood up.

"I'll see you," Chris said, walking back to his booth and dropping a few dollars on the table. "We're playing Sokol next week, you should say hey if you're there."

Lincoln watched Chris walk away and felt himself hoping—really and truly hoping, with the best parts of his heart—that the other man was going home to her.

CHAPTER 65

THERE WAS LESS work than ever in the IT office. The International Strike Force was long gone. Nothing left of them but a stack of blank CDs and a few cigarette burns on the table. "When the fuck did that happen?" Greg asked. Lincoln shrugged. Greg wanted Lincoln to change all the system passwords and shore up the firewalls; he was even issuing new security badges to the whole department.

"Those guys always creeped me out," Greg said. "Especially the Millard South kid . . . There's such a thing as knowing too much about computers."

Lincoln's shifts felt decades long.

There was nothing from Beth in the WebFence folder Monday night. Nothing about the wedding. Nothing at all. It was empty Tuesday night, too. And Wednesday.

Lincoln watched for her in the hallways and took long dinner breaks. He saw her byline in the paper, so he knew she was coming to work. He checked the WebFence folder every night, every few hours.

Thursday, empty. Friday, empty. Monday, nothing.

On Monday night, Lincoln walked by Beth's desk at six o'clock and then again at eight. He brought chicken-leek pie to share with Doris and sat in the break room with her for two hours, talking. Waiting. Doris told him she was going to teach him how to play pinochle. She said she and Paul used to play, and it was a real kick. "I've always wanted to learn," Lincoln said.

On Tuesday, when Beth and Jennifer still hadn't turned up, he checked the e-discipline file to see if somebody else in IT had sent them a warning. He wondered for a moment if one of the Y2K kids might be responsible. But there wasn't any sign of it. There were fresh coffee cups on Beth's desk—she hadn't disappeared completely.

On Wednesday, when the WebFence folder was empty again, Lincoln felt strangely light. Maybe this was how it was going to end. Not with a humiliating, painful confrontation. Not with self-control and discipline. Maybe he wouldn't have to make himself stop reading her e-mail. Maybe it would just stop itself.

CHAPTER 66

COULD YOUR BRAIN actually reject information? Like a foreign organ? Doris was trying to teach Lincoln to play pinochle, and the rules were bouncing off his brain. Fortunately, or maybe unfortunately, that didn't discourage her. He'd thought about eating at his desk. If he wasn't trying to run into Beth, he may as well. But that didn't seem fair to Doris, especially now that his mother sent treats specifically for the other woman. Now that Doris was the one sharing *her* cake with him.

"Some people just have trouble with games," she said. "I'll deal this time." She did tricks when she shuffled. "Say, do you have big plans this weekend?"

"No," Lincoln said. He might play D&D. He might play golf with Chuck. One of the other copy editors was having a "Happy New-ish Year" party that Lincoln was invited to. ("We always celebrate holidays a few weeks late," Chuck had explained. "Those dayside bastards won't cover for us on holidays.")

"'Cause I've still got that curio cabinet at my old apartment . . . ," Doris said. "I told the super I'd have everything out by the thirty-first."

"Oh, right," Lincoln said, "sorry. I can come by Saturday afternoon if you want."

"How about Sunday? I've got a date on Saturday."

Of course she did. Why wouldn't she?

"Sure," he said. "Sunday."

WHILE THEY PLAYED golf, Chuck tried to talk Lincoln into coming to the copy desk party.

"I don't really like parties," Lincoln said.

"It won't be much of a party anyway. Copy editors throw terrible parties."

"You're really selling it."

"Emilie will be there . . ."

"I thought I heard she was dating somebody."

"They broke up. Why you don't like Emilie? She's adorable."

"Yeah," Lincoln said, "she's cute."

"She's *adorable*," Chuck said, "and she can recite the complete list of prepositions. And she's bringing pumpkin bread and Electronic Catch Phrase."

"It sounds like *you* like Emilie."

"Not me. I'm trying to reconcile with my wife. What's your excuse?"

"I'm sort of . . . coming off a bad relationship."

"When did it end?"

"Slightly before it started," Lincoln said.

Chuck barked a laugh, little bursts of steam breaking the January air.

"Isn't it too cold to play golf?" Lincoln asked.

"Sunshine gives me a headache," Chuck said.

LINCOLN DIDN'T CHANGE his mind. He didn't feel like parties. Or games. Or people.

Three weeks. That's how long it had been since Beth and Jennifer had turned up in the WebFence folder. *This is good*, Lincoln told himself. *Even if it doesn't make sense for them to be so quiet. Even if it's wildly out of character. They're making it easy for you. Easier.*

He decided to rent a movie, *Harold and Maude*. He hadn't watched it since high school, and he wanted to watch the scene at the end where Harold drives his Jaguar off a cliff and then starts to play the banjo. He hoped nobody from the newspaper would be at Blockbuster to see him rent *Harold and Maude*. (Chuck told him that before they knew his name, everyone on the copy desk called Lincoln "Doris's Boyfriend.") He almost hid the video box when someone touched his arm.

"Lincoln. Lincoln? Is that you?"

He turned.

The strange thing about seeing someone for the first time in nine years is the way they look totally different, just for a second, a *split* second, and then they look to you the way they always have, as if no time has passed between you.

Sam looked exactly like Sam. Small. Curly brown hair—a little longer now, not in that all-over-the-place bob that had been popular in college. Wide sparkling eyes, so dark you could hardly see her pupils. Black clothes that looked like she'd bought them out of state. Silver rings on her fingers. A pink necktie tied at her waist like a belt.

She was still touching him. She'd taken hold of both his arms.

"Lincoln!" she said.

Lincoln didn't move or speak, but he felt like Keanu Reeves in that scene from *The Matrix*, when he slows down time to dodge a hail of bullets.

"I just can't believe it's you." She squeezed his arms, grabbed the front of his jacket, pressed her palms on his chest. "Oh my God. You look exactly the same."

She pulled his jacket toward her. He didn't come with it.

"You even smell the same," she said, "peaches! I can't believe it's you. How are you?" She tugged at his jacket again. "How *are* you!"

"I'm good," he said. "Just fine."

"It's kismet that I'm running into you," Sam said. "I just moved back last month, and I've been thinking about you every day. I don't think I have a memory of this city that doesn't include you. Every time I go to my folks' house or get on the freeway, my head's like, 'Lincoln, Lincoln, Lincoln.' God, it's good to see you. How *are* you? *Really?* I mean, the last I heard, well . . ." She made a sad face. She touched his arms, his shoulders, his chin. "But that was years ago . . . How are you? How are you now? Tell me everything!"

"Oh, you know," he said. "I'm here. Working. I mean, I work. With computers. Not *here*-here. Around." What else could he say? That he still lived with his mom? That he was renting a movie that he'd probably watched with Sam the first time? That she was the Jaguar he needed to drive off the cliff?

Except she wasn't. Was she?

Lincoln felt a surge of something like strength. He set down *Harold and Maude*, surreptitiously, and picked up something else, *Hairspray*.

"What about you?" he asked. "What brought you back?"

"Oh God." Sam rolled her eyes, like it would take three hours and a Greek chorus to explain. "Work. Family. I came back because I wanted my boys to get to know their grandparents. Can you believe I'm a mom? God! And there's this job at the Playhouse. In development, fund-raising, you know, making rich people feel important. Behind the scenes, but not off the stage. I don't know, it's a big change. A big risk. Liam is staying in Dublin for six months just in case this isn't a good move. Did you know I've been in Dublin?"

"Dublin," Lincoln said. "With Liam. Your husband?"

"As such," Sam said, making another it's-an-unbearably-long-story gesture. "I swore I'd never marry another man with a foreign passport. Once bitten, et cetera." She said it in three hard syllables. Et-cet-ra. Her hands, small with perfectly manicured pink nails, flew around as she talked but kept landing on Lincoln's chest and arm.

"I'll tell you the whole adventure sometime," she said to him, "sometime *soon*. We have to catch up. I've always felt that two people who shared as much as we did and shared such important years should never have drifted apart." Her voice dropped intimately. From stage to screen. "It just isn't right.

"I've got an idea," she said, holding on to his jacket with both hands and standing on tiptoe, leaning into him. He mentally leaned back. "What are you doing *right now*?"

"Right now?" he asked.

"We'll go to Fenwick's and eat banana ice cream. And you'll tell me just *everything*."

"Everything," he said, trying to imagine what part of everything he'd ever want to tell Sam.

"Everything!" she said, tipping toward him. She smelled like gardenias. Plus something muskier, gardenias with carnal knowledge.

"Fenwick's closed a few years ago," he said.

"Then we'll just have to get in the car and keep driving until we find banana ice cream. Which way should we go," she asked, laughing, "toward Austin? Or Fargo?"

"I can't," he said. "I can't. Not tonight. I have a . . . a thing."

"A thing?" she asked, resting back on her heels.

"A party," he said.

"Oh," she said. Then she was digging in her black velvet purse. It had a bone-colored handle that looked like ivory. "Here," she said, pressing something into his palm. "Here's my card. Call me. Call me *yesterday*, Lincoln, I'm serious."

She made a serious face. He nodded and held on to the card.

"Lincoln," she said, all knowing smile and heavy eyelashes. She held on to his shoulders and kissed him quickly on both cheeks. "Kismet!"

And then she was walking away. The soles of her high heels were pink. She didn't even rent a movie.

And Lincoln . . . Lincoln was still standing.

CHAPTER 67

HE DIDN'T RENT *Hairspray* or *Harold and Maude*.

A few minutes after Sam left, after standing dumbly for a while in the *H*s, Lincoln decided he didn't feel like going home anymore. He didn't feel like sitting still or being quiet. He left the Blockbuster empty-handed and stopped just outside to toss Sam's business card into the trash. It wasn't a terribly meaningful gesture; he knew where Sam worked, and he still her knew her parents' phone number by heart. And then Lincoln took out his wallet and found Beth's e-mail about him, the one with the phrase "trying not to bite his shoulder." He read it again. And again. One more time. Then he crumpled it into a tight ball and threw it away.

And then . . . he went to a party. The Newish Year's party. Chuck had given him a flyer, and Lincoln was pretty sure it was still in his car. When he dug around for it in the backseat, he noticed that his hands were trembling. *That's OK*, he thought. *Still standing.* When he was parallel parking in front of Chuck's house, he caught himself grinning in the rearview mirror.

The party was already in full roar when he walked in.

Lilliputian Emilie was there with her pumpkin bread, and Lincoln didn't steer clear. He didn't want to. Emilie was perfectly nice, and she thought all of his jokes were funny—which actually made him tell funnier jokes, because he didn't have to worry about no one laughing. And also, she made him feel eight feet tall. Which is a very good feeling, there's no getting around it.

He kicked ass at Electronic Catch Phrase.

He drank Shirley Temples.

He brought the house down during 1999 charades with a two-minute, completely silent reenactment of *The Sixth Sense*. "When you mimed the ring falling on the ground," Chuck said, applauding, "I forgot that I already knew you were dead."

And when the clock struck midnight—it was a VCR clock, and it didn't strike so much as blink—Lincoln kissed Emilie on the cheek. That immediately seemed like a mistake, so he grabbed the crazy-eyed paste-up artist and kissed her, too. Which seemed like a bigger mistake. He quickly kissed every other girl standing in his reach, including Danielle the copy desk chief, two women he'd never met before, Chuck's estranged wife, and finally Chuck himself.

Then everyone sang "Auld Lang Syne." Lincoln was the only one who knew any lyrics beyond "should auld acquaintance be forgot" and the chorus. He belted them out in a clear tenor:

> *We two have run about the slopes,*
> *and picked the daisies fine;*
> *But we've wandered many a weary foot,*
> *since auld lang syne . . .*

CHAPTER 68

WHEN LINCOLN WOKE up, it was snowing. He was supposed to meet Doris at her apartment at ten, but he didn't get there until ten fifteen. He had to park a few blocks away, in front of a bakery. He wished he had time to go in.

There weren't many neighborhoods like this in town. A nice mix of old, expensive houses, big brick apartment buildings, and trendy shops and restaurants. Doris's building was yellow brick—four stories, with a courtyard and a small fountain.

Lincoln ran up her front steps, brushing the snow off his hair, and pressed the button by her name.

She buzzed him in. "I'm on the third floor," she yelled down. "Come on up." It smelled good in the stairwell. Dusty. Old. Lincoln wondered how Doris had made it up all these stairs every day with her bad knee. She was waiting for him in her doorway.

"I'm glad you're here," she said. "They turned off the heat already, and I'm freezing. The cabinet's right over there."

There was nothing left in the apartment but the Bubble-Wrapped cabinet. Lincoln looked around the living room, at the high tin ceiling and creamy plaster walls. The wood floors were dark and scratched, and the light fixture looked like something you'd see in an old opera house. "Have you lived here long?" he asked.

"Since I got married," she said. "Do you want the thirty-second grand tour?"

"Sure."

"Well, this is it. Back there's the bedroom." Lincoln walked through a doorway into the sun-filled bedroom. There was a tiny bathroom through another door, with a freestanding tub and an old-fashioned sink (small, with separate taps for hot and cold water).

"Over there's the kitchen," Doris said. "It's all old as sin. Those countertops have been here since World War Two. You should see my new kitchen—wall-to-wall Corian." Lincoln checked out the kitchen. The fridge was new, but the rest of the room did indeed know the difference between Red Skelton and Red Buttons. There was a rotary phone attached to the wall. Lincoln reached out to touch the Bakelite handle.

"Will you miss this place?" he asked.

"Oh, I suppose," Doris said. "Like anything." She was opening the kitchen drawers, making sure she hadn't left anything behind. "I won't miss the radiators. Or the draft. Or those goddamn stairs."

He looked out the window over the sink and down into the courtyard. "Is it hard to get into this building?"

"Well, it's secured access."

"I mean, to rent."

"Why, are you looking for a place?"

"I . . . well . . ." Was he?

No.

But if he was . . . This was exactly the sort of place he'd want.

"We can talk to Nate, the super, on the way out if you want. He's a good guy. One of those alcoholics that doesn't drink. If he forgets to fix the toilet, he'll give you an amends."

"Yeah," Lincoln said, "sure, let's talk to him."

He picked up the curio cabinet, a few bubbles popped. "Lift with your knees," Doris said.

NATE SAID A few people had asked about the apartment, but that it was available until someone wrote him a check for the deposit. Lincoln didn't carry a checkbook, but Doris did. "I know you're good for it," she said.

Nate took Doris's key and handed it to Lincoln. "That was a short day's work," Nate said.

Lincoln rode with Doris to the new retirement tower. He carried up the cabinet, met her sister, and admired their Corian kitchen. Then Doris offered him some Sara Lee pound cake, and they looked at old pictures of her and Paul with a series of basset hounds.

"Boy, this is exciting," she said, when she dropped him off at his car. "I feel like we're keeping this old place in the family. I'll have to introduce you to all the neighbors."

After she drove away, Lincoln walked back to the building, up to the third floor, and opened the door to the apartment. His apartment.

He walked through each room, trying to take everything in. Every cranny. There was a window seat in the bedroom—he'd missed that before—and lamps that reached out of the walls like calla lilies. There were tall oak-framed windows in the living room and a tiled area inside the entryway that said "welcome" in German.

He'd have to buy a couch. And a table. And towels.

He'd have to tell his mom.

CHAPTER 69

From: Beth Fremont
To: Jennifer Scribner-Snyder
Sent: Mon, 01/31/2000 11:26 AM
Subject: Have you seen Amanda?

Seriously, have you seen her today?

<<**Jennifer to Beth**>> Seen her? I feel like I have to buy her dinner.

<<**Beth to Jennifer**>> How can she walk around the newsroom, making eye contact with people, when she's practically naked to the waist?

<<**Jennifer to Beth**>> I couldn't conduct a telephone interview in a blouse like that.

<<**Beth to Jennifer**>> I'm used to her wearing low-cut shirts (or refusing to button decent ones), but seriously, I don't think I've ever seen that much of another woman's breasts. Maybe in junior high, in the locker room . . .

<<**Jennifer to Beth**>> If my mother were here, she'd offer to lend Amanda a sweater. And if she said no, my mom would tell her what happened to Queen Jezebel.

<<**Beth to Jennifer**>> What *did* happen to Queen Jezebel?

<<Jennifer to Beth>> Godly servants pushed her out a window. For being loose. (And pagan.) Amanda tried to talk to me a few weeks ago—she was wearing a cardigan sweater with nothing underneath. She started quibbling with me about a headline I'd written, and I deliberately took off my glasses. I can't even see my own breasts without my glasses.

<<Beth to Jennifer>> I don't know what she's trying to say with all that cleavage.

<<Jennifer to Beth>> I think she's saying, "Look at my chest."

<<Beth to Jennifer>> Yes, but why?

<<Jennifer to Beth>> Because when people are looking at her chest, they're not reading her boring leads?

<<Beth to Jennifer>> Heh.

<<Jennifer to Beth>> What's "heh"?

<<Beth to Jennifer>> It's like "ha," but meaner. I'm going back to work now.

<<Jennifer to Beth>> One more thing: I kind of love you for not asking me how I'm feeling.

<<Beth to Jennifer>> Feeling about what?

<<Jennifer to Beth>> Thanks.

CHAPTER 70

HUH.

There they were.

Back.

INSTEAD OF GOING home that night, Lincoln went to his new apartment.

He figured his mom wouldn't worry, that she wouldn't think to wait up for him on a Monday night. He could always tell her tomorrow that he'd crashed at Justin's house. If he had to tell her something.

Lincoln hauled in an old sleeping bag that he kept in his trunk (it smelled like gym clothes and exhaust) and tried to fall asleep on his new living room floor. Even though it was late, he could hear people moving around the apartment upstairs. Somewhere else, there was a radio. In the apartment below him, maybe, or across the hall. The more Lincoln listened for the music, the closer it seemed, until he could make out every song—all sleepy oldies from the fifties and sixties, slow dances and prom themes.

"Come Go With Me."

"Some Kind of Wonderful."

"In the Still of the Night."

Lincoln tried not to listen. He tried not to think.

What did it mean that Beth and Jennifer were e-mailing again?

Probably nothing, he decided. Probably the last few weeks of silence from them were just a fluke. Not God's way of helping Lincoln get on with his life. That had been a dumb thing for him to think. Dumb *and* grandiose.

Lincoln listened to the phantom radio long after the people upstairs went to bed. "Only You," "Sincerely." Maybe he'd try to find this station himself tomorrow night. He wondered when he'd learned all the words to "You Send Me" and whether it was *supposed* to be a sad song. And then he fell asleep.

From: Jennifer Scribner-Snyder
To: Beth Fremont
Sent: Tues, 02/08/2000 12:16 PM
Subject: You wish . . .

That you worked on the copy desk.

<<**Beth to Jennifer**>> Uh . . . No, I don't.

<<**Jennifer to Beth**>> Today, you do. Derek wrote a story about how the zoo is artificially inseminating tigers, and Danielle decided he couldn't use the word p*nis. She says it fails the breakfast test. She's making him say "male reproductive part" instead.

<<**Beth to Jennifer**>> What's the breakfast test?

<<**Jennifer to Beth**>> Are you sure you went to journalism school? The idea is that you don't want to write something so gross that people reading the paper over breakfast would be put off their cornflakes.

<<**Beth to Jennifer**>> I think I'm more likely to be put off my cornflakes by the double homicide on the front page than I am by infertile tigers.

<<**Jennifer to Beth**>> That's just what Derek said. He also said that only someone as se><ually repressed as Danielle would

find artificial tiger insemination too arousing to share with our readers.

<<Beth to Jennifer>> You make it sound like they're inseminating artificial tigers. That *is* pretty kinky.

<<Jennifer to Beth>> He just asked Danielle if she blacks out all the dirty words in her Harlequin romances.

<<Beth to Jennifer>> He's going to get fired.

CHAPTER 72

THEY WERE ALL like this lately, all of Beth's and Jennifer's messages.

They were writing each other again, but something had changed between them. They cracked jokes and complained about work, they checked in—but they didn't write about anything that mattered.

Why did that frustrate him? Why did that make him feel restless?

It was nasty outside, cold and gray, with rain that was trying hard to be snow. But Lincoln couldn't sit in the airless IT office for another six hours. He decided to drive to McDonald's for dinner. He felt like something greasy and hot.

The streets were worse than Lincoln expected. He almost got hit by an SUV that couldn't brake in time for a red light. The whole trip took most of his dinner break, and when he got back to the office, his parking space was gone. He had to park in the overflow lot a few blocks away.

When he first heard the crying, he thought that it was a cat. It was a terrible sound. Mournful. He looked around for it and saw a woman standing next to one of the last cars left in the lot. She was slumped over her car and standing in a giant mud puddle.

When Lincoln got closer, he saw the flat tire and the jack lying in the mud next her.

"Are you okay?" he asked.

"Yes." She sounded more scared than convinced. She was a small woman, solid, with blondish hair. He'd seen her a few times before, on the day shift. She was soaked through and crying hard. She wouldn't look at him. Lincoln stood there dumbly, not wanting to make her feel more uncomfortable, but not wanting to leave her alone.

She tried to steady herself. "Do you have a cell phone I could use?"

"No," he said. "I'm sorry. But I can help you change your tire."

She wiped her nose, which seemed fruitless, considering how wet she was. "Okay," she said.

He looked for a place to set down his dinner, but there wasn't one, so he handed the woman his McDonald's bag and picked up the lug wrench. She'd already gotten a few of the nuts off the tire; this wouldn't take long.

"Do you work at *The Courier*?" she asked. She was still so upset, he wished she wouldn't try to talk.

"Yeah," he said.

"Me, too, on the copy desk. My name is Jennifer. What do you do?"

Jennifer. Jennifer?

"Security," he said, surprising himself. "Systems security."

He jacked up her car and looked around for the spare. "It's still in the trunk," she said. Of course it was. Lincoln couldn't look at her anymore; what if she recognized him? Maybe it wasn't her. How many Jennifers worked on the copy desk? He let down the car, opened the trunk, grabbed the tire, jacked the car back up. He was pretty sure she was crying again, but he didn't know how to comfort her. "I have some French fries in there if you want them," he said, realizing as soon as he said it that it made him sound like a weirdo. At least she didn't seem scared of him anymore. When he glanced back at her, she was eating his French fries.

It took about fifteen minutes to change the tire. Jennifer (*Jennifer?*) didn't have a true spare, just one of those temporary tires that new cars come with. She thanked him and gave him back what was left of his dinner.

"That's just a doughnut," he said. "You should have your tire fixed as soon as you can."

"Right," she said. "I will." She didn't seem to be paying attention. He felt like she just wanted him to leave. And he wanted to leave. He waited for her to get into her car and turn on the engine before he walked away. But when he looked back, her car hadn't moved. He stopped walking.

He wondered why Jennifer—if this was Jennifer, the Jennifer—was crying, what had happened. Maybe she'd gotten into a fight with Mitch.

Maybe she'd started a fight with Mitch. But there was no sign of it in her e-mail. Maybe . . .

Oh.

Oh.

When was the last time she'd mentioned . . . Why hadn't he noticed . . . He should have guessed when the e-mails stopped, by the way they were talking, by what they weren't saying.

The baby. He should have realized.

He was so selfish. All he'd cared about was finding himself in their conversations. Not that it would have mattered if he *had* noticed. Not that he could have said he was sorry or sent her a card.

Lincoln walked back and knocked on her window. It was fogged over. She wiped a circle clear, saw him, and rolled it down.

"Are you sure you're okay?" he said.

"I'm fine."

"I really feel like I should call your husband."

"He's not home," she said.

"A friend, then, or your mom or something."

"I promise, I'll be fine."

He couldn't leave her alone. Especially now that he knew or thought he knew what was wrong. "If somebody that I cared about was crying alone in a parking lot," he said, wishing he could tell her that she *was* somebody he cared about, "at this time of night, I'd want somebody to call me."

"Look, you're right. I'm not fine, but I will be. I'm leaving now. I promise."

He wanted to tell her that she shouldn't be driving at all. The streets were a mess, she was a mess . . . But he couldn't tell her what to do. He couldn't say anything to comfort her. He handed her his McDonald's bag. "Okay. Just. Please go home."

She drove away then. Lincoln watched her leave the parking lot and get on the freeway. When she was out of sight, he ran into *The Courier* building. He was so wet and cold, he took off his muddy shoes at his desk, and tried to figure out which of the ceiling vents was putting out the most heat so he could huddle below it. He ended up eating dinner out of the vending machines. (He'd have to tell Doris that the sandwiches seemed to be going bad a few days before their expiration dates.) He wondered if Jennifer had gotten home okay and whether he was right about what happened. It might not be anything so terrible. It might not even be the same Jennifer.

LINCOLN SPENT THE night at his apartment again. It was still icy out, and it was closer to drive there than it was to drive home. He thought about calling his mom to tell her he was okay, that he hadn't been in an accident. She hadn't mentioned it yet, the fact that he wasn't coming home every night. Maybe she was trying to give him space. What if he didn't have to move out? What if he could just ease out. . . ?

CHAPTER 73

From: Jennifer Scribner-Snyder
To: Beth Fremont
Sent: Wed, 02/09/2000 10:08 AM
Subject: I think I met Your Cute Guy.

Unless there are two dark-haired, practically Herculean, cute guys wandering around this place.

<<**Beth to Jennifer**>> *Met?* You *met* him?

<<**Jennifer to Beth**>> Yes. Last night. When I was leaving work.

<<**Beth to Jennifer**>> Are you stringing this story out for your own amusement?

<<**Jennifer to Beth**>> I'm not sure I want to tell you at all. It's the kind of story that might make you worry about me, and I really don't want that.

<<**Beth to Jennifer**>> Too late. I'm already worried about you. Tell me—in detail.

<<**Jennifer to Beth**>> Well . . .
I worked a swing shift last night, which meant I had to park in the gravel lot under the freeway, and I didn't get out of here until 9, and it was cold out, and sleety and nasty, and when I finally got to my car, I had a flat tire. (Already, this sounds like the opening scene of a *Law & Order* episode, right?)

So . . . I immediately took out my phone to call Mitch, but it was dead. Right then, I should have just walked back to the building and called a tow truck or something. But instead I decided to change the tire myself. I mean, I've changed a tire before, I'm not completely helpless. As I was getting out the jack, I had this flash of "Maybe I shouldn't do this in my condition."

And then I remembered that I'm not in any kind of condition anymore.

It took me 20 minutes to get the first two lug nuts off. The third wouldn't budge. I even tried standing on the wrench. It went spinning off and slammed into my shin. I was muddy by this time and soaked through and crying. Somewhat hysterically.

Then I see this huge shadow of a person walking toward me, and all I can think is, "I hope he doesn't rape me because I'm supposed to wait six weeks before having intercourse."

The huge shadow says, "Are you okay?"

I say, "Yes," hoping he'll just keep moving. Then he gets close enough for me to see that he's cute—cute in kind of a specific, unexpected way; rough-hewn, one might say—and also wearing an unfashionable denim jacket. I immediately think, "This is Beth's Cute Guy," and I stop being scared of him, which is pretty funny when you think about it because, for all of your crushing, neither of us knows anything about this guy. And it might not have even been him.

Anyway, he changed my tire for me.

It took him eight minutes, tops. I just stood there, holding his dinner (McDonald's) and watched. And cried. I must have looked wildly pathetic because he said, "I have some French fries in there if you want them." I thought that was such a weird thing to offer, but frankly, I'm exactly the sort of person to be comforted by French fries, so I ate them.

And then—seriously, *minutes* later—he was done (and also covered in mud, the whole lot was one gray puddle). He told me that I should still get my tire fixed and walked away.

So I got into my car, turned on the heat . . . and started crying even harder than I was crying before. Harder than I'd cried since it happened. I don't know if I've ever cried like that before. (Maybe when my dad left.) I was shaking and making these horrible, hollow elephant noises. I kept thinking about the word "despair" and how I'd only ever understood it before from reading it in context.

I was pretty far gone when there was a knock at my window. Your Cute Guy. He was still standing there. He seemed embarrassed by the whole situation, almost physically pained to have to deal with me. He said, "I feel like I should call your husband," all firm and determined. (I was just a little bit hurt that he assumed I had a husband. It was kind of like being called "madame" when you still feel like a "mademoiselle.")

I kept saying that I would be fine, and then he said, "If somebody that I cared about was crying alone in a parking lot this late at night, I would want somebody to call me."

That's just what he said. Isn't that nice?

I told him that he was right, that I wasn't fine, but that I would be, and I promised to go home. For a minute, it seemed like he wasn't going to let me leave, like he was just going to keep standing there with his hand on my window. Which would have made sense—my eyes were swollen to slits, and I probably seemed like I was ready to drive off a cliff.

But he nodded his head, handed me his McDonald's bag (?) and walked away.

I did leave then. I went home and ate his two cheeseburgers (extra pickles) while I was waiting for Mitch, who, I should note, was actually relieved to see me crying. I think he was beginning to think I was either inhumanly cold or silently imploding.

I pretty much cried all night. I looked so puffy and splotchy when I came in to work this morning that I told Danielle I'd had an allergic reaction to shellfish.

<<Beth to Jennifer>> You should have stayed home.

<<Jennifer to Beth>> I don't want anyone to start wondering why I've been taking so many sick days.

<<Beth to Jennifer>> If they knew, they'd gladly give you some time off.

<<Jennifer to Beth>> I don't want anyone to feel sorry for me. Actually, that's not true, I feel like the entire world should feel sorry for me. I'm pathetic and I'm miserable. But I don't want anyone feeling sorry for me if it means they have to think about my uterus.

<<Beth to Jennifer>> Do you feel better today? Relieved to have let some of it out?

<<Jennifer to Beth>> I don't know. I still don't want to talk about it.

<<Beth to Jennifer>> But we can talk about My Cute Guy, right?

<<Jennifer to Beth>> Ad nauseam.

<<Beth to Jennifer>> I can't believe you *met* him. I've been following him around for months without making more than passing eye contact, and you actually *met* him. And you didn't just meet. You had a meet-cute. Is it warped for me to be jealous of you right now?

<<Jennifer to Beth>> What's a meet-cute?

<<Beth to Jennifer>> It's the moment in a movie when the romantic leads meet. They never just meet normally. It's never like, "Harry, meet Sally. Sally, this is Harry." They always meet in a cute way, like, "Hey, you just got chocolate in my peanut butter!" / "What are you talking about? You just got peanut butter in my chocolate!"

Having a handsome man rescue you (crying in the rain in the parking lot), change your tire, and share his French fries, that's very meet-cute.

Damn it, I was supposed to have the meet-cute.

<<Jennifer to Beth>> Your meet-cute would have gone like this, "Hey, you got chocolate in my peanut butter!" / "Sorry, I have a boyfriend."

Also, I feel like I should point out that it was freezing rain. Freezing rain isn't cute.

<<Beth to Jennifer>> You still got to see him with wet hair . . .

So, break it down for me, what was your lasting impression of him? It seems like you thought he was weird.

<<Jennifer to Beth>> I wouldn't say weird. I would say awkward, kind of shy. He seemed really uncomfortable—like only his chivalry and common decency were keeping him from walking away.

<<Beth to Jennifer>> So, awkward, chivalrous, decent . . .

<<Jennifer to Beth>> And very nice. It was a kind thing to stop and to stay until I pulled myself together. A lot of guys would have kept walking or, at best, called 911.

<<Beth to Jennifer>> Awkward, chivalrous, decent, kind . . .

<<Jennifer to Beth>> And really, really cute. You weren't exaggerating. Not Sears-model cute. More of an old-fashioned cute. And he got cuter, the more I looked at him. He's built like a tank. I half expected him to lift my car with his hands.

<<Beth to Jennifer>> Built like a tank, dressed like he just won the science fair. How cute is that guy.

<<Jennifer to Beth>> Very cute.

<<Beth to Jennifer>> So, I'm totally going to start parking in the gravel lot. You know that, right?

<<Jennifer to Beth>> Don't. That parking lot is spooky. Stick with the break room.

CHAPTER 74

I'M STILL HER cute guy, Lincoln thought, as he drove home.

He went to the gym early the next day and ran until his knees started to buckle.

I'm still hers.

"LINCOLN! DUDE! YOU'RE alive!"

"Justin, hey."

"Sorry to call you at work, but I've been calling your house so much, your mom probably thinks I'm trying to get into her pants. I feel like I haven't seen you since the sixth grade."

"Yeah," Lincoln said, "I haven't been . . ." He wasn't avoiding Justin. He was avoiding Sacajawea.

"Do you remember how big you were in the sixth grade? You were 'My Motherfucking Bodyguard.' Look, you're going out tonight. With me and Dena."

"I have to work tonight."

"We'll wait up. We don't turn into pumpkins at midnight. I don't have to work tomorrow. Dena does, but she can get by on less than eight hours . . . *Aw, you can, too,*" Justin said. Dena must be right there. "*You don't need eight straight to suck spit out of people's mouths . . . I meant with a vacuum . . .* Hey, Lincoln, we'll see you at the Village Inn, all right? I'll see if I can get our usual table."

"Yeah, all right. I can get there by one."

"One it is."

JUSTIN AND DENA were just getting their orders when Lincoln got there. They'd already ordered him his French silk.

"That pie is on me," Justin said, "and so is the next piece. We're celebrating."

"What's the occasion?" Lincoln asked.

"Show him, honey," Justin said.

Dena held up a hand with a ring the size of her knuckle. There must be money in hospital marketing.

"It's beautiful," Lincoln said. "Congratulations." He leaned over to clap Justin on the shoulder. "Congratulations."

"I'm as happy as a pig in shit," Justin said, "and part of that is thanks to you."

"No."

"Yeah. You were my wingman, first of all, and then you knocked some sense into me when I nearly let this beautiful woman slip out of my hands. Don't you remember? You called me on all my bullshit about not wanting to settle down?"

"You would have figured it out on your own," Lincoln said, "you were in love."

"Maybe so," Justin said, "but I still want to thank you, and I . . . Dena and I would like to ask you to be in our wedding."

"Really?"

"Really. Would you be a groomsman?"

"Sure," Lincoln said, surprised. And touched. "Sure, I'd love to."

"Well, all right," Justin said. He took a big bite of mashed potatoes. "All right! I haven't even told you the best part. Guess who's playing at our reception?" He didn't wait for Lincoln to guess. "Sacajawea!"

"That's the best part?" Dena asked.

"That's the best part besides the marriage part," Justin said.

"Sacajawea . . . ," Lincoln said.

"Damn straight. I got in touch with them through the manager at the

Ranch Bowl and talked to the lead singer. He said they'd play a fucking bar mitzvah if we could cover their fee."

"It's going to cost more than the open bar," Dena said.

"It's going to be awesome," Justin said.

They told him more about the wedding. It was going to be a big wedding party. Dena had lots of sorority sisters. Lincoln could see how Justin might need to dig pretty deep to round up enough groomsmen.

"When's the big day?" Lincoln asked.

"October seventh."

"We're shopping for a house now," Justin said.

"We're shopping for a barbecue," Dena said.

"A grill," Justin said, "and I don't see why that's such a big deal. I need to know what the grill looks like before we find the house, so I can picture it on the deck. I don't want to move into a house and find out six months down the line that the fucking grill won't fit. Why would you want to start our life together making compromises?"

Dena rolled her eyes and signaled to the waitress for another Diet Coke.

"We'll have you over for steak, Lincoln," Dena said.

"Fuck that," Justin said. "I'm calling you when we move. Dena's got a leather sectional that's going to take three grown men and a rhinoceros."

Lincoln figured he was the rhinoceros.

"It's not that big," Dena said.

"I'd be happy to help," Lincoln said. "Really. Congratulations. Both of you."

HE SPENT THE next three nights at his apartment. He bought a mattress and a box spring and a lamp. He bought a toothbrush cup and a soap dish and soap that smelled like vetiver. He stood for twenty minutes in the bedding aisle at Target, trying to choose a manly sheet set, then picked the ones with a violet pattern, because he liked violets and who else was ever going to see his sheets, anyway?

CHAPTER 75

From: Jennifer Scribner-Snyder
To: Beth Fremont
Sent: Wed, 02/16/2000 10:00 AM
Subject: Greetings from the most self-centered person in the world.

I realized last night, as I was lying awake telling myself what a despicable person I am, that I really *am* a despicable person. I'm at the very least a terrible friend. In all these weeks, I haven't stepped outside of my wretched self even once to ask you about Kiley's wedding. I am so sorry.

So please, tell me. How was the wedding?

<<**Beth to Jennifer**>> Why are you lying awake, thinking that you're a terrible person?

<<**Jennifer to Beth**>> To keep my mind occupied when I can't sleep. Some people count sheep. I self-loathe.

<<**Beth to Jennifer**>> I can see why you might have trouble sleeping right now, but I can't see why you would be hating yourself.

<<**Jennifer to Beth**>> You can't? Really?

<<**Beth to Jennifer**>> No. What happened was terrible, but you're not terrible.

<<**Jennifer to Beth**>> What happened happened because I'm terrible. How was the wedding?

<<Beth to Jennifer>> No, it didn't. Of course it didn't. Do you really believe that bad things happen to people because they deserve it?

<<Jennifer to Beth>> In general, no. In this case, yes.

Remember when my midwife told me to talk to the baby, that it could feel my emotions and intent? And I said that was crazy, and you said you thought there was probably something to it?

Well, I agree with you now. There was something to it.

The baby could feel what I wanted. I was sending out maternal vibes through my umbilical cord or whatever. And for the first six or seven weeks, the message I was sending was, "Go away." Go away, go away, go away. And it did.

You can disagree with me all you want and tell me that it isn't my fault, that these things just happen. But I know that underneath your loving reassurances, you know better than anyone how negative I was, how anxious and angry and mean. I know that it made you uncomfortable.

<<Beth to Jennifer>> I agree that you were conflicted and un-happy, but lots of unhappy people have children. You can't turn off a pregnancy with negative thinking.

<<Jennifer to Beth>> Not just negative. Corrosive.

<<Beth to Jennifer>> But you got through that. You ac-cepted being pregnant. You more than accepted it, you were happy about it.

<<Jennifer to Beth>> Ironic, huh? (Is that ironic or is it just sad? I get confused sometimes.)

<<Beth to Jennifer>> Please don't. Don't oversimplify every-thing you've been through like that. You had to feel those awful feelings. You had to face them down—confront your bitterness and pessimism—and decide that you didn't want to be that way anymore.

<<Jennifer to Beth>> Just in time to be horrifically disap-pointed. That's what I get.

\<\<**Beth to Jennifer**\>\> If you're determined to see what happened as some sort of universal justice, consider that the lesson here might not be to retreat into cynicism, even if that's where you feel most comfortable. Maybe the lesson is, rise up.

\<\<**Jennifer to Beth**\>\> Well, that seems a bit harsh.

\<\<**Beth to Jennifer**\>\> I thought you wanted me to be honest.

\<\<**Jennifer to Beth**\>\> If that's how you are when you're honest, I think I'd rather you stick to the usual sentiments, stuff I can file under "Encouragement," "Cope," or "Sorry something died inside of you." I don't really need "Snap out of it."

\<\<**Beth to Jennifer**\>\> That's not what I meant. I'm sorry.

\<\<**Jennifer to Beth**\>\> How is that not what you meant? That's what you said.

\<\<**Beth to Jennifer**\>\> Then I shouldn't have said it.

From: Jennifer Scribner-Snyder
To: Beth Fremont
Sent: Wed, 02/16/2000 3:15 PM
Subject: Anyway . . .

How was the wedding?

<<**Beth to Jennifer**>> Does this mean you've forgiven me for being insensitive?

<<**Jennifer to Beth**>> To be perfectly honest, no. I might not completely forgive you until one of us is on her deathbed. (I can't help it, I'm fond of a grudge.) But until I make another friend, I can't afford to be angry with you.

<<**Beth to Jennifer**>> I really am sorry. I don't want you to feel like you can't talk to me about what happened.

<<**Jennifer to Beth**>> Please. Who else am I going to talk to? Tell me about the wedding.

<<**Beth to Jennifer**>> All right. But I warn you, it's a pretty long story. It might take me longer to tell you about the wedding than it did to actually attend the wedding, Catholic Mass included. Give me a few weeks to type it out.

<<**Jennifer to Beth**>> I'll give you a few hours. I suppose I can find something to edit while I'm waiting.

<<**Beth to Jennifer**>> Are you sure we're cool? Because I can apologize some more. I give great penance.

<<**Jennifer to Beth**>> Just tell me about the wedding.

From: Beth Fremont
To: Jennifer Scribner-Snyder
Sent: Wed, 02/16/2000 4:33 PM
Subject: To have and to hold.

All right, I actually typed this out in a News document and saved it on the system so that I wouldn't lose it and have to start over. Make sure it doesn't get filed for the bulldog edition, okay?

Now, you're sure you're ready for this? It's a really long story.

And you're sure you aren't still mad at me? Do you want to talk more about the baby? Because the wedding will hold. (It's not exactly breaking news at this point.)

<<**Jennifer to Beth**>> Yes, I'm ready, and no, I'm not mad. Now, out with it!

<<**Beth to Jennifer**>> Okay, well, here goes . . .

The wedding itself was perfectly lovely.

As expected, I looked fairly monstrous in my bridesmaid dress. But I seemed to be the only one who noticed, and even I was sick of hearing me complain about it, so I put on my brave face. Which turned out to be far more attractive than the faces most of the other bridesmaids put on. They all wanted "smoky eyes"—"you know, like Helen Hunt at the Oscars." I'm pretty sure that my sister Gwen and I are the only ones who won't look like domestic abuse victims in the wedding pictures.

The ceremony had its moving moments, but it was so god-awfully long—a full Mass, like I said—that it was hard for me to concentrate on anything but trying not to lock my knees so that I wouldn't pass out. (That happened at my cousin's wedding. One of the groomsmen fell into a chair and cut his ear. He bled all over his rental tux.) I thought that if I fainted into the tiny little Tri-Delt behind me, I might crush her.

Chris was a total trouper. He sat with my parents during the ceremony, and afterward, he met every single member of my extended family. He was so charming, I started calling him Stepford Chris.

And when it was time to take the big family picture with all of the spouses and grandkids, Kiley insisted that Chris be included. She didn't even give him a chance to protest. "You've been around longer than any of these husbands," she said.

Dinner was delicious—the old Italian ladies from my parents' church made baked mostaccioli and Italian sausage with red peppers. My sister was so afraid of staining her dress that she wouldn't eat anything but garlic bread. (Did I eat her pasta? Why, yes, I did.)

Kiley and Brian were adorable dancing to Louis Armstrong. She looked gorgeous. I had to dance with one of the Sigma Chis during the wedding party dance—the theme from *Titanic*—and he was totally looking down my dress, which was mostly gross, but a little bit flattering. Apparently, I've still got it.

As soon as my official duties as bridesmaid were done, I put on my cardigan and felt a million times better. I was in a fantastic mood, actually, relieved that the hard parts were over and truly excited to spend the rest of the evening with Chris. I felt as madly in love with him as I'd ever been.

First of all, he looked dangerously handsome. He was wearing the charcoal jacket that I bought him with a floppy, blue satin bow tie-ish thing he'd found somewhere. It made him look like he should be writing French poetry. (Expressly to seduce virgins.) My mom asked him if he was wearing a scarf.

And second, I knew that he was being so engaging only because he loved me. As a favor to me. I felt like his good behavior was overwhelming proof that he cared. I shouldn't need proof, but proof can be very reassuring.

During dinner, Chris went outside to smoke and get away from my family, and when I found him outside the back door, he acted as happy to see me as I was to see him. "Are you mine now?" he asked. He told me I looked beautiful. He kissed me. He told me to take off the cardigan. "Let's go home," he said.

I told him that I couldn't go, that I'd promised my sister that I would dance. She didn't want one of those receptions where only toddlers dance, so all the bridesmaids swore to stay on the floor at least until the Chicken Dance.

"Then I guess we'll dance," he said, and he took one last drag of his cigarette. He has this way of tilting his head down and looking up at me as he inhales; I get why 12-year-olds think it's cool to smoke.

So we went back into the reception and danced to every song. Sort of danced. It was mostly holding each other and swaying and Eskimo kissing.

Remember when I was obsessed with that little Lithuanian restaurant downtown? And it was only ever open when the grumpy old woman who ran it felt like opening? I'd stop by every day for a week with no luck. And then, when I'd pretty much given up on ever tasting Napoleonas torte again, I'd drive by and see the open sign in the window.

Well, being with Chris is like trying to date that restaurant. I never know when he's going to be there and how open he'll be to me. Almost never is he *all* there, all in. Almost never do I get the Chris that I got the night of Kiley's wedding—open sign, cold cucumber soup, rouladen, poppy seed kolaches.

I found myself thinking that this is how I would want to dance at my own wedding. (Minus all the Dixie Chicks and Alan Jackson songs.) The kind of dancing that's more like touching to music. That's more like closing your eyes and trying to think how you

would tell someone that you loved him if you didn't have words or
sex.

Chris had one arm around my waist, and he was winding his
fingers in my hair. He kissed my forehead, smiling. He looked at
me, straight into me, and I felt like I was in love with the sun.

And then—it will be impossible for you not to laugh at me
now—the deejay played the song "Rocky Mountain High."

I fucking love "Rocky Mountain High." I don't much care for
eagles or lakes or Colorado. But "Rocky Mountain High" is what
euphoria sounds like. When you hear John Denver sing, "He was
born in the summer of his 27th year . . ." how can you not feel your
heart open to the cosmos?

So "Rocky Mountain High" came on, and I started kissing
Chris like I couldn't wait to get to the chorus, all adoration and
vulnerability and "I've seen it raining fire in the sky." And Chris
kissed me right back. And when he pulled away—about the time
that the songwriter is admitting to a life that's full of wonder, but a
heart that still knows fear—Chris said, "Beth, I love you. I love you
more than I ever meant to. More than I ever say."

And I started to tell him that I loved him, too, but he stopped
me, kissed me and said, "Wait, I'm not done. This is important."

Will you think I'm foolish if I tell you that I thought he might
be getting ready to propose? I wasn't sure of it. I probably would
have bet against it. But if he were ever going to propose to me, there
could never have been a more likely—a more perfect—moment.

"Sometimes," he said, "I love you so much that I can't stand it.
Sometimes, I just don't have the energy for it, to have something
this big coming out of me. And I can't stop it or turn it down.
Sometimes, I get tired just knowing that I'm going to see you."

I wasn't ready to let go of my reverie. I was thinking, "*Good*
tired, right?"

"I'll always love you," he said, "but I need you to know that I am
never going to marry you."

I must have looked like I wasn't getting it because he repeated
himself. Emphatically. "Beth. I am never going to marry you." He

was still looking at me with soft, loving eyes. If you were watching us from a few feet away, and you saw his face, you might think that he *did* just propose to me.

What I found myself thinking, at least immediately, was that there was a certain violence to putting it the way he did. That *he* wasn't going to marry *me*. Couldn't he have said that *we* were never going to get married? Couldn't he have implied that it would be a shared decision? Wouldn't that have been a bit more polite?

And then he tried to kiss me, to continue our kiss actually, with all the love and passion and John Denver that we were sharing before his pronouncement. But I felt like there was more to talk about. So I pulled back and said, "Do you mean that you'll never get married? Or that you'll never marry me?"

He thought about it. "Both," he said, stroking my hair, "but mostly the latter."

"Mostly that you won't marry *me*."

He nodded. "But not because I don't love you. I do love you. I love you too much. You're too much."

I pushed away from him then, and started to walk in a weird circle around the dance floor. I kind of wandered through the dancers and eventually out the front door. I walked around the parking lot for a minute before I realized that I didn't know where Chris had parked and that he still had my keys. (If I were the sort of person for whom falling in love meant eventually getting married, I would let my bridesmaids wear dresses with pockets.) I looked back and there he was, standing in the VFW doorway. "Don't do this," he shouted.

"I'm not doing this," I said. "You are." And then I decided I would be damned to hell if I took one step toward him. So I told him to throw me my keys. He wouldn't, he said he was going to drive me home. And I was like, "Don't come near me. Throw me my keys."

"I knew you wouldn't get this," he said. "I knew you'd take it wrong."

How was I supposed to take it?

He said I was supposed to see the *truth*. "That I love you enough to be honest with you."

"But not enough to marry me," I said.

"Too much to marry you."

Even in the state I was in, I managed to roll my eyes at that.

"I wasn't built for this," he yelled. "Look at me. You know it's true." And for the first time, maybe ever, he didn't sound cool. He sounded a little panicked. And a little angry. "I don't want to love someone so much that they take up all my head, all my space. If I knew I was going to feel this way about you, I would have left a long time ago, while I still could."

I kept yelling at him to throw me my keys. I think I called him "a great horrible bastard." Like I was swearing in a second language. He threw me the keys, and they hit the car behind me like a baseball. "Don't come home," I said. "I don't want to see you."

"I have to come home," he said. "I need my guitar."

Have you ever seen *The Goodbye Girl*? Don't watch it if you still want to enjoy romantic comedies. It makes every movie ever made starring Julia Roberts or Sandra Bullock lash itself in shame. Also, don't watch *The Goodbye Girl* if it would trouble you to find Richard Dreyfuss wildly attractive for the rest of your life, even when you see him in *What About Bob?* or *Mr. Holland's Opus*.

In *The Goodbye Girl*, at the very wonderful end, this character (Marsha Mason, looking like a bruised pixie) who has given up on true love after being abandoned by a string of loser actors, realizes that the Richard Dreyfuss character really is going to come back to her like he promised he would *because he left his guitar in their apartment*. That's how she knows that he really, truly loves her.

When Chris brought up his guitar, that's when I knew he really, truly didn't love me. That's when I lived that Marsha Mason scene in reverse.

I got in my car and drove until I thought he couldn't catch up with me on foot, even though I didn't really expect him to try. Then I pulled into an Arby's parking lot and attempted to cry, but I was still too dumbfounded. I was still stuck in that split second after you get punched in the gut, when you don't have enough breath to say, "Holy crap, that hurt." I felt tired, overwhelmingly tired, and like I couldn't go home; I was pretty sure Chris would be there. And everyone who would let me spend the night was still at the wedding. So, I checked into the Holiday Inn across from the Arby's and watched free HBO until I fell asleep.

I slept until checkout time and left that Satanic dress in the room. (I had gym clothes in the car.) Then I went back to my apartment.

Chris was there, of course, making tea. He'd just taken a shower. His hair was still damp and curly, and his T-shirt was lying over a chair. I swear he's three miles long from the bottom of his throat to the top button of his jeans. He said he'd been worried about me.

"I didn't want to see you," I said.

"Didn't?" he said, pouring hot water into two mugs.

"Don't."

"Beth . . ." His cool was back. He looked at me like he thought looking at me would be enough. "You can't walk away from what's between us. I've tried . . . We're a spell," he said. "We're magic."

I told him that I didn't want magic, that I wanted someone who wouldn't leave me if he could. Who wouldn't feel like being committed to me was such a burden.

"I'm committed," Chris said. "I've never cheated on you."

Which wasn't even what I meant. "You said you get tired when you look at me," I said.

"I said that sometimes it's too much."

"Well, I want someone who doesn't think so. I want someone whose heart is big enough to hold me."

"You want someone whose love will fit around your finger."

"You should write that down," I said. "It sounds like a song lyric."

It was a cold thing to say, but I was losing my nerve. I was looking around the kitchen, looking at him, thinking that it was a nice life, really. Thinking that it was absurd for me to break up with him for saying something out loud that, deep down, I already knew. Thinking how warm and loving he would be, what a wonderful day we could still have, if I could just let this go.

"I want you to leave," I said.

"Where am I going to go?"

"I can't let that be my problem."

"You can't? You're *unable* to care about me?"

"You can stay with Stef. Or your parents."

"This is my home, too."

"Then I'll go," I said. "You'll have to sign a new lease." That was a lousy thing to say. I know he can't afford the rent by himself.

"Beth, come on. Stop doing this. Look at me."

"I can't look at you anymore."

We argued for a while longer before he agreed to leave. I left then, so that he could pack. I went over to my parents' house.

My *parents* . . . who were jubilant when I told them what happened. I think they were happier about my breakup than Kiley's wedding. "I knew it was a mistake to let him be in the family picture," my mother said. "My smart, strong girl," my dad kept saying.

Chris called me once while he was packing to ask about the record player. It's mine, but he's the only one who ever listens to records. I told him he could take it and the rest of the stereo equipment, too. "Jesus," he said, "if I knew you were going to be so nice, I wouldn't have already packed all of your CDs." That made me laugh a little. "Yesterday," he said, "you were all mine. Every freckle. And today, we're talking about who gets the VCR."

"I get the VCR," I said.

I haven't talked to him since. He calls me, but I don't call him back. I'm too weak. He left one of his sweaters in the closet, and I've been crying into it for five weeks. I feel like I kicked one of my own kidneys out of the apartment.

Okay, I think that's it. That's what happened at my sister's wedding.

<<Jennifer to Beth>> Beth . . . I'm speechless. I'm practically type-less. Why did you wait so long to tell me?

<<Beth to Jennifer>> I tried to call you from Arby's, but you weren't home, and when I called you that Monday, I found out that you'd had an even worse weekend than I'd had. Once you told me about the baby, I couldn't tell you about Chris. I didn't want you to feel like you had to waste even a tiny little bit of energy on me.

<<Jennifer to Beth>> You're such a good friend.
I'm just shocked. I really didn't think you'd ever break up with him.

<<Beth to Jennifer>> Even though you wanted me to.

<<Jennifer to Beth>> Sometimes.

<<Beth to Jennifer>> I always knew he was selfish and self-indulgent and kind of lazy; those are practically prerequisites for playing lead guitar. I also knew that music was pretty much the only thing in life that he felt was worth the hassle. But I thought I was part of the "pretty much." How could I stay with him, once I knew that he felt like being in love with me was his cross to bear?

<<Jennifer to Beth>> You couldn't.

<<Beth to Jennifer>> The idea that he would be so overcome by love that marriage would just flatten him . . .

<<Jennifer to Beth>> It's a cop-out.

<<Beth to Jennifer>> Yeah, I know. When I think about it, which is pretty much constantly, I can't decide if . . .
a. He's capable of growing up and having a real relationship with someone. He just doesn't love *me* enough. Or . . .
b. He's not capable and also a jerk.

<<Jennifer to Beth>> Probably both.

<<Beth to Jennifer>> But mostly the latter.
Do you think I've wasted the last nine years of my life?

<<Jennifer to Beth>> Nyah, only the last two or three. You couldn't have known when you spotted him in the student union that his heart was three sizes too small.

<<Beth to Jennifer>> I think you might be humoring me. I think you think that Chris has been emotionally unavailable from day one—and that I wanted that for some awful reason.

<<Jennifer to Beth>> You're right. I do think that.

<<Beth to Jennifer>> So I brought this on myself?

<<Jennifer to Beth>> Maybe. I don't know. I don't think it matters what I think or what I did or didn't see coming. You had to see it for yourself. You had to see it through.

<<Beth to Jennifer>> Thank you for being honest.

<<Jennifer to Beth>> If I ask you a hard question, will you answer it honestly?

<<Beth to Jennifer>> Yes.

<<Jennifer to Beth>> Do you think I'm responsible for my miscarriage?

<<Beth to Jennifer>> No.
Ninety-three percent no. I don't think your attitude is to blame, but I don't think it helped.

<<Jennifer to Beth>> I'm not sure I can live with 93 percent.

<<Beth to Jennifer>> You can.

<<Jennifer to Beth>> I want to try to get pregnant again, is that awful and dysfunctional?

<<Beth to Jennifer>> I guess it depends on why.

<<Jennifer to Beth>> I think the answer to why is—because I really want to have a baby. But I don't trust myself not to have some twisted reason lurking in my subconscious. I feel like I've lost something so important. I know that I don't deserve it. I don't deserve a baby.

<<Beth to Jennifer>> Nobody deserves a baby.

<<Jennifer to Beth>> I feel like we should be having this conversation over a bottle of Blue Nun.

<<Beth to Jennifer>> My bad. I thought we were.

<<Jennifer to Beth>> The idea that you're hard to love is ludicrous.

CHAPTER 78

LUDICROUS.

It didn't change anything, knowing that Beth was single. Had been single for weeks. For practically *months*.

What did that change? Nothing, right? Nothing, really.

"Are you listening?" Doris said. They were playing cards and eating hoagie sandwiches they'd bought from the machines. (Doris never took anything for free.) Lincoln had spent the night at his apartment again and come straight to work.

"I'm trying to tell you about tens around," Doris said.

Chris wasn't ever the problem. Not the biggest problem, anyway. Not that it mattered anymore.

"It's not that complicated," Doris said.

Nothing had changed. Nothing.

"Listen," Doris said, "I need to talk to you about something. Your mother called me today."

"What?"

"She was supposed to give me the recipe for that carroty chicken thing she makes, with the celery? And the rice? Well, she ended up telling me that she was worried about you. She said you haven't been coming home at night. Now, you didn't tell me that the apartment was supposed to be a secret. You didn't tell me that you weren't going to tell your mother you were moving out."

"But I haven't moved out. I haven't moved anything."

"That's crazy talk. Is this about that girl?"

"What girl?"

"You mother told me what that girl did to you, that actress."

"Do you mean Sam? She didn't do anything to me," Lincoln said.

"Didn't she leave you high and dry for a Puerto Rican?"

"No," Lincoln said. "I mean, not exactly."

"And now she's calling your house."

"Sam's been calling my house?"

"And I don't blame your mother for not giving you the messages," Doris said. "Look at the secret you're keeping from her. Are you meeting that girl at my apartment?"

"No."

"It would explain why you've been so moony. And why you ignore everything else in a skirt."

"*No.*" It came out too high. Lincoln pressed his palm into his temple and tried not to sound like a child. "Did you tell my mom about the apartment?"

"I'm too old to be lying to other people's mothers," Doris said.

IT WAS TOO late to talk to his mother when Lincoln got home that night.

When he came downstairs the next morning, she was in the kitchen, slicing potatoes. There was a pot steaming on the stovetop. Lincoln leaned on the counter next to her.

"Oh," she said, "I didn't know you were here."

"I'm here."

"Are you hungry? I can make breakfast. But you're probably rushing off to the gym."

"No," he said, "I'm not hungry. And I'm not rushing off. I was hoping we could talk."

"I'm making potato soup," she said, "but I could spare some bacon. Do you feel like bacon and eggs?" She was already cracking eggs into a cast-iron pan, pouring milk and stirring. "I've got English muffins, too. The good kind."

"I'm really not very hungry," he said. She didn't look at him. Lincoln put his hand on her arm, and she scraped her fork against the bottom of the pan. "*Mom*," he said.

"It's so strange . . . ," she said. He couldn't tell from her voice whether she was sad or angry. "I can remember a time when you needed me for everything.

"You were just this little kitten, and you cried if I set you down even for a second. I don't know how I managed to ever take a shower or make dinner. I don't think I did. I was afraid to hold you too close to the stove."

Lincoln stared down at the eggs. He hated when she talked like this. It was like accidentally seeing her in her nightgown.

"Why do you think I can remember that," she asked, "when you can't? Why does nature do that to us? How does that serve evolution? Those were the most important years of my life, and you can't even remember them. You can't understand why it's so hard for me to hand you off to someone else. You want me to act casual."

"You're not handing me off. There's no one else."

"That girl. That terrible girl."

"There isn't a girl. I'm not seeing Sam."

"Lincoln, she calls here. There's no point in lying about it."

"I haven't talked to her. I haven't been here to get her calls. Look, I'm sorry I lied to you, that I didn't tell you about the apartment. But I'm not with Sam. I'm not with anyone. I wish I was, with somebody, I should be. I'm almost twenty-nine. You should want me to be."

She huffed.

"I want to show you the apartment," he said.

"I don't need to see it."

"I want you to. I want to show you."

"We'll talk about it after you eat."

"Mom, I told you, I'm not hungry . . ." He pulled her arm toward him, away from stove. "*Please*. Come with me?"

LINCOLN'S MOTHER GOT into his car reluctantly. She hated riding in the passenger seat, she said it made her nauseous. (Eve said letting anyone else control a situation for more than thirty seconds was what made her nauseous.) She was quiet while he drove to his new neighborhood, just a few miles away, and parked in front of the apartment building.

"This is it," he said.

"What do you want me to say?" she asked.

"I don't want you to say anything. I want you to see it."

He got out of the car before she could argue. She followed reluctantly, stopping outside the car, in the middle of the sidewalk, and at the steps. He didn't stop with her, so she followed. Into the building, quietly up the stairs, across the threshold. "Willkommen." Lincoln held the door open. His mother took a few steps inside—looked around, looked up—and then a few more steps toward the windows. Sunshine was falling into the living room in thick golden stripes. She held her hand up, open, into the light.

"I'll show you the kitchen," Lincoln said, after a moment, closing the door. "Well, what there is of it. You can pretty much see it from here. And here's the bedroom." His mother followed him into the next room, glancing down at his new mattress. "And the bathroom's right here. It's really small." She walked to the bedroom window, looked outside, then sat in the window seat.

"It's nice, right?" he asked her.

She looked up at him and nodded. "It's a beautiful space. I didn't know you could find apartments like this around here."

"Me neither," he said.

"The ceilings are so high," she said.

"Even on the third floor."

"And the windows . . . Doris used to live here?"

He nodded.

"It suits you better."

He wanted to smile and feel relieved, but there was still something about her—her voice, the way she was sitting—that told him he shouldn't.

"I just don't understand," she said, leaning back against the glass, "why."

"Why?"

"It's nice," she said, "it's beautiful. But I don't understand why you'd *want* to move out if you didn't have to. If there really isn't a girl. Why would you *choose* to be alone?"

He didn't know how to answer.

"As long as you're at home, you can save your money for other things," she said. "You have plenty of space to yourself, you can do whatever you want. I'm there if you need me . . . Why?

"And don't tell me," she said, picking up speed, "that moving away is just something that people do. Because . . . because who cares what people do? And besides, that's not even true. That's a recent development. A Western development. This dividing the family up into tiny bites.

"What if you'd had nowhere to go when you came home from California? What if I'd told you the same thing that my mother told me when I left Eve's father? 'You're on your own now,' she said. 'You're a grown woman.' I was twenty years old. And alone. I bounced around from one house to the next, sleeping on couches. With that tiny, little girl. Eve was so small . . . She slept right here"—his mother laid her hand on her chest, just below her throat—"because I was afraid of dropping her or losing her between the cushions . . .

"You'll never have to fend for yourself like that, Lincoln. You never have to be alone. Why would you *want* to?"

He leaned back against his bedroom wall and slunk down until he was sitting on the cast-iron radiator. "I just . . . ," he said.

"Just?"

"I need to live my own life."

"You aren't living your own life now?" she asked. "I certainly never tell you what to do."

"No, I know, it's just . . ."

"Just?"

"It doesn't *feel* like I'm living my own life."

"What?"

"It feels like, as long as I stay home, I'm still living in *your* life. Like I'm still a kid."

"That's silly," she said.

"Maybe," he said.

"Your own life starts the moment you're born. Before that, even."

"I just, I feel like as long as I live with you, I won't . . . I'm not . . . It's like George Jefferson."

"From the TV show?"

"Right. George Jefferson. As long as he was on *All in the Family*, he was just somebody who made Archie Bunker's story more interesting. He didn't have anything of his own. He didn't have a plot or supporting characters. I don't know if you ever even got to see his house. But after he got his own show, George had his own living room and kitchen . . . and bedroom, I think. He even had his own elevator. Places for him to exist in, for his story to happen. Like this apartment. This is something that's mine."

She looked at him suspiciously. "I don't know," she said. "I never watched *The Jeffersons*."

"What about *Rhoda*?" Lincoln asked.

She frowned. "So you're saying you want to be the star of the show now. That it's time for me to fade into old age?"

"God, no," he said. "It's not like they canceled *All in the Family* when *The Jeffersons* started."

"Stop talking about television. Stop telling me what everything is *like*."

"Okay," he said, trying to think clearly, bluntly. "I want to live my own life. And I want you to live your own life. Separately."

"But you are my life!" she said, breaking into frustrated tears. "You became my life on the day you were born. You're part of me, you and Eve, the most important part of me. How can I separate from that?"

Lincoln didn't answer. His mother walked past him out of the room. He slunk farther down, onto the floor, and held his face in his hands.

HE STAYED THAT way for twenty minutes or so, until he realized it was taking some effort to hold the position, until he felt more tired than guilty or angry.

He found his mother sitting on the living room floor, looking up at the chandelier. "You can take the couch from the sunroom," she said when he walked in, "the brown one. There's too much furniture in that room already. It would fit fine here. It'll look almost purple in this light."

He nodded.

"And I'll find you some nice dishes at the thrift shop. Don't buy any more plastic. It leaches into your food, you know," she said, "and simulates estrogen. It lives in your fat cells and causes breast cancer . . . I don't know what it does to men. I wish I'd known you needed dishes. I saw a complete set the other day at the Goodwill, with a butter dish and a gravy boat and everything. White with little blue daisies. Not exactly masculine, but still . . ."

"I'm not picky," he said.

She nodded and kept nodding. "You can have anything you want from your bedroom, of course, or you can leave it. That will always be your room. Just like your sister's. You can always come home if you need to, or even if you want to. That house is your home as long as it's mine."

"Okay," he said. "Thank you."

He walked over to her and held out his hands, pulling her to her feet. She held on to his hands, squeezed them, then started smoothing her long skirt.

"I suppose your sister knows all about this already," she said.

"No," Lincoln said.

"Oh." That was good news. "Maybe I'll call her. Maybe I'll see if she wants to help me go shopping for your kitchen."

"Sure," he said. He hugged her then, tight, and wished that he'd thought to do it sooner.

"It really is a beautiful apartment," she said.

EVE CALLED LINCOLN at work the next day. All she could say was, "Good for you" and "I'm so proud of you." She offered Jake Sr.'s help if Lincoln needed to move anything. "Just a couch," he said. "Anything," Eve said. There really wasn't much else to move besides clothes and his computer.

He went home, to his mom's house, for lunch every day of the next week. She sent him off with boxes full of cereal bowls and drinking glasses. A bookcase. A coffee table that just barely fit into his backseat. Hand-embroidered kitchen towels.

"All this stuff is so old," Eve said, when she came to see his apartment. "It's like somebody's grandmother died, and you moved in."

"I like it," he said.

"I'm buying you something made of stainless steel," she said, "something bachelor-y."

CHAPTER 79

From: Beth Fremont
To: Jennifer Scribner-Snyder
Sent: Tues, 02/29/2000 3:48 PM
Subject: I told Derek about Chris . . .

And now the entire eastern third of the newsroom knows that I'm single. Melissa came over and patted my hand for, I swear, 20 minutes. She said she's going to take me to this totally hot club—"wall-to-wall boys"—where you can get half-price appletinis after 10 o'clock on weeknights.

I told Derek that if I get cornered into drinking appletinis on a weeknight, I'm dragging his big mouth with me.

<<Jennifer to Beth>> What do you have against appletinis?

<<Beth to Jennifer>> I just don't understand why everything has to be a martini. I don't like drinking out of martini glasses, you have to pucker your mouth all weird to keep from spilling.

<<Jennifer to Beth>> How are you ever going to meet another man if you're not going to drink martinis?

<<Beth to Jennifer>> I'm not, apparently. The last time I went on a first date, I wasn't old enough to drink.

<<Jennifer to Beth>> Are you even interested in dating yet?

<<Beth to Jennifer>> I don't know. In a way, I don't really feel single. My life hasn't changed substantially since Chris left, which shows, I guess, how little I'd been seeing him. I could almost go on pretending that I'm still in a serious relationship. Derek thinks I should take down all the photos of Chris in my cubicle. (Or in his words, "Jesus Christ, Beth, even I'm tired of looking at that asshole.") What do you think?

<<Jennifer to Beth>> I think it's up to you. Does it make you sad to look at them?

<<Beth to Jennifer>> Yeah, it does. I should take them down.

<<Jennifer to Beth>> Your Cute Guy is never going to ask you out if your cubicle is full of photos of another man.

Seriously . . . there's nothing keeping you from making contact with YCG now.

<<Beth to Jennifer>> I can't have a real relationship with him. I've already been pretend-dating him for months. If we started dating, I'd have to eventually tell him about the time I followed him home from the movie theater. That doesn't seem healthy.

<<Jennifer to Beth>> But he's so nice.

<<Beth to Jennifer>> Are you saying that because he gave you French fries?

<<Jennifer to Beth>> I'm saying it because he seemed really, really nice.

<<Beth to Jennifer>> I need to date a guy I haven't already contaminated with a nickname.

CHAPTER 80

EMILIE STOPPED INTO the IT office Thursday night between editions. She did that now, a few times a week, just to say hi. Well, not *just* to say hi, Lincoln knew she was interested in him. But he hadn't decided yet what do with that knowledge.

He was interested in feeling the way he felt around Emilie. Like the brightest, shiniest thing in the room. Tall. And smart. And funny. When Emilie was around, he never fumbled his Christopher Walken impression. But he couldn't see anything in her eyes past his own reflection. And now that Beth was back, he couldn't make himself want to.

Emilie was twirling her ponytail around her fingers. "So, a few of us are going to do karaoke tomorrow night, there's a cheesy bar in Bellevue, you should totally come, it's going to be fun . . ."

"It sounds fun," Lincoln said. "But I play Dungeons & Dragons on Saturday nights. Usually." He'd missed some more games lately, he'd wanted to have the weekends to himself in his new apartment. "It's been a few weeks, so I really can't miss tomorrow night."

"Oh, you play Dungeons & Dragons?"

"Yeah . . . ," he said.

"That's cool . . . ," she said.

That made Lincoln smile. Which made Emilie smile even wider. Which made him feel kind of guilty.

DAVE ANSWERED THE door Saturday night. He looked at Lincoln and frowned.

"Either you're in the game or you're not," Dave said, after Christine had set Lincoln up with a plate of homemade tacos and a flagon (an actual flagon) of beer. "You can't just drop in now and then."

Dave pointed to Troy, who was trying not drip taco juice onto his faded Rush T-shirt. "Troy has been dragging your unconscious dwarf on an earth sled, just to keep you in the campaign. You're a constant drain on his magic."

"It's the least I can do," Troy said formally. "I've owed 'Smov a life debt since we battled side by side in the Free City of Greyhawk."

"Troy, that was seven years ago," Dave said, pained, "and that entire adventure was outside of continuity."

"I wouldn't expect a halfling like you to understand the nature of a life debt," Troy said.

"Thank you, Troy," Lincoln said, bowing his head.

"It's an honor, brother."

"I'm trying to run a campaign here," Dave said. "This isn't improv. It takes planning. I need to know who I have to work with."

"Maybe Lincoln has had a good reason to stay close to home," Christine said. She smiled at him, hopefully.

"We all have good reasons not to be here," Larry said, frowning. "Do you think I don't have anything more important to do?"

"I could be at the hospital, saving lives," Teddy said flatly.

"I could be at my high school reunion," Rick murmured.

"You guys aren't helping," Christine said. She looked back at Lincoln again, raising her eyebrows expectantly.

"Well," he said, swallowing. "Actually, I do have news." Christine clasped her hands. "I moved into an apartment."

They all looked up.

"You moved out of your mom's house?" Troy said.

"It's about damn time," Larry said.

"'Smov," Troy said, leaning in for a sandalwood-thick hug, "I'm so proud of you." Lincoln hugged him back.

Rick smiled.

"And *I'm* so proud of you," Christine said. "That isn't even the good news I was expecting."

"I don't know," Dave said, rubbing his beard. "If I could go back to living rent-free, I would."

"I never thought you'd do it, Lincoln," Larry said. "I thought you were one of those guys."

Lincoln winced.

"I never thought he'd move out of the dorms," Dave said.

"Okay," Lincoln said. "Enough." He'd wanted them to be happy for him, but not this happy. Not this surprised. He hadn't realized that everyone—even Troy, who lived in a studio apartment above an auto body shop—felt sorry for him. It was like getting congratulated for losing weight when you didn't think anyone else had noticed that you needed to.

Christine was grinning at him across the table. Even the baby in the sling was smiling. Lincoln decided to smile, too.

"Are we going to play or not?" Teddy said. "My shift starts in six hours."

"Now, we just have to find you a woman," Troy said, thumping Lincoln on the back.

"Enough," Lincoln said, "let's play."

"*And with a crack of thunder,*" Dave said, "*black clouds swept over the hills of Kara-Tur . . .*"

CHAPTER 81

From: Jennifer Scribner-Snyder
To: Beth Fremont
Sent: Mon, 03/13/2000 3:08 PM
Subject: This message was almost about Doritos.

But I don't think I have it in me. I don't have it in me to be trivial.

<<**Beth to Jennifer**>> Hush your mouth, what could you possibly mean?

<<**Jennifer to Beth**>> These days, I'm using up all my energy on matters of life and death. Everything else feels like a waste of time. Last night, I watched *60 Minutes* instead of *Grease*. I even listened to NPR this morning on the way to work.

<<**Beth to Jennifer**>> Wait, *Grease* was on? Damn.
What do you usually listen to on the way to work?

<<**Jennifer to Beth**>> Flame 98, bringing today's country hits straight to the heart of the heartland. I really like Kat and Mowzer in the morning. At least, I used to. Lately, I can't stand listening to them—or any of the other morning shows. They're all sound-and-fury, tale-told-by-an-idiot, signifying-nothing.

<<**Beth to Jennifer**>> That's got to be the first time someone has almost quoted Shakespeare in reference to Kat and Mowzer.

<<Jennifer to Beth>> I feel like I don't have time for anything trivial. Every night, when Mitch comes home, I drag him into excruciatingly deep conversations—usually about whether we should try to get pregnant again and what it means to be a parent and whether it really is better to have loved and lost than never to have loved at all.

<<Beth to Jennifer>> I've been thinking a lot about that last thing myself.

<<Jennifer to Beth>> Are you holding up okay?

<<Beth to Jennifer>> Yeah. Mostly. I had a wobbly moment at the grocery store last night when I realized I was buying a single banana. There's nothing sadder than buying bananas one at a time. It's like announcing to the world that there isn't a soul in the world who'll be breaking bread with you anytime soon. I don't even buy bread anymore. There's no way I can get through an entire loaf of bread before it starts to mold. I can't decide which is more dejecting: grocery shopping for one or sitting alone in a restaurant.

<<Jennifer to Beth>> You should come eat with us. Mitch always cooks something healthy and delicious. We had shrimp tempura last night.

<<Beth to Jennifer>> Plus, I hear the dinner conversation is scintillating.

<<Jennifer to Beth>> You're welcome anytime. Truly, why don't you come tonight?

<<Beth to Jennifer>> Only if you tell me the Dorito story right now.

<<Jennifer to Beth>> It isn't much of a story: I went to get some M&M'S from the break room today, and ended up in line behind the publisher at the snack machine. I was sure he would choose a conservative and traditional snack—perhaps mixed nuts or a great American Hershey's bar—but, no, he went right for the Salsa Verde Doritos.

<<Beth to Jennifer>> This is at odds with everything I thought I understood about our editorial policy.

<<Jennifer to Beth>> I know. How can someone who eats Salsa Verde Doritos so vehemently oppose gay marriage?

<<Beth to Jennifer>> And affirmative action.

<<Jennifer to Beth>> And traffic roundabouts.

<<Beth to Jennifer>> I can't believe you thought that was trivial.

<<Jennifer to Beth>> So . . . do *you* have any interesting break room stories to report? Have you been cruising the beef jerky machine even when you're not hungry?

<<Beth to Jennifer>> Uh, no. And since when do you advocate that sort of behavior?

<<Jennifer to Beth>> I told you. I've totally reversed my position on Your Cute Guy. You're single now, and he's the kind of guy who helps damsels in distress. Seize the day, I say. Carpe Cute Guy!

<<Beth to Jennifer>> It's still too weird. And I'm not ready to date anybody. I'm not even ready to rebound. I'd feel like I was hitting on someone at my husband's funeral.

<<Jennifer to Beth>> He wasn't your husband, and nobody died.

<<Beth to Jennifer>> Still.

CHAPTER 82

THAT NIGHT, LYING in his new bed, staring at his new ceiling, Lincoln thought furiously. The same thoughts over and over again, until trying not to think them was like trying to get a song out of his head.

Hi, I'm Lincoln. I've seen you in the break room . . .

Hi, I'm Lincoln, Doris's friend . . .

Hi, have we met before? In the break room? I'm Doris's friend . . .

Hi, I'm Lincoln. I work downstairs in the information technology office . . .

Hi, I work downstairs, in computer support, my name is Lincoln. Look, I know this might seem out of the blue, but would you like to have coffee sometime?

Would you like to get dinner sometime?

Would you like to join Doris and me in the break room? My mom cooks for us.

Would you like to go out? For a drink? Or coffee? Or dinner?

Before we go, there's something I need to tell you.

I think, before we go, I should confess something.

I have secrets, Beth, secrets that I'll never reveal, and you're just going to have to be okay with that. That's just the kind of guy I am.

What if I told you that I have a secret, one secret, that you must never ask me to share with you? Because if you ask, I'll have to tell you the truth. But if I tell you the truth, we'll never be happy. It's kind of a Beauty and the Beast/Rumpelstiltskin/Crane Wife thing . . .

Hi, my name is Lincoln, I work downstairs. Would you like to get to-gether sometime, maybe go out?

LINCOLN HAD AN apartment-warming party that weekend. Eve had suggested it. "It'll be like your coming-out party," she said, "you know, your cotillion."

"Jesus," Lincoln said, "don't put either of those on the invitations."

His mom brought dinner—lasagna and stuffed artichokes and honey ricotta pie—as well as a complete set of silverware, world music CDs, and fresh flowers. She insisted on answering the door when it buzzed.

"She's acting like she owns the place," Eve complained.

Lincoln smiled. He was already eating an artichoke. So was Eve. "Isn't it enough to know that she doesn't?"

Doris was the first unrelated guest to arrive. She brought a date, a retired pressman, and a pan of brownies, and she greeted Lincoln's mother like they were old school chums. "Maureen! Look at you!"

Chuck came. With his practically-not-estranged-anymore wife. Justin and Dena couldn't come, they were going to Vegas for the weekend. But most of the D&D players came, and Dave and Christine brought their kids. (As well as their dice, you know, just in case.)

Everyone said nice things about Lincoln's apartment and even nicer things about his mom's lasagna. After Doris and Chuck left, the party did in fact turn into a D&D session. Jake Jr. was mesmerized. He wanted to stay and learn how to play. Eve was horrified. "You're too young," she said, "and too socially adept."

"I'm buying him dice for his eleventh birthday," Lincoln said.

His mother stayed until almost midnight. She and Christine did the dishes together and had a two-hour conversation about natural childbirth and raw milk. They exchanged telephone numbers.

"Your mother is so wise," Christine said later. "There's so much I can learn from her."

When the last guest left, Lincoln imagined what it would be like to have someone standing next to him at the door. He imagined Beth gathering up glasses in the living room, falling into the bed next to him.

Hi, my name is Lincoln, we've almost met a few times in the break room. Look, I know this is kind of out of the blue, but would you like to go somewhere, sometime? And talk?

CHAPTER 83

LINCOLN GOT A haircut before work Monday night. The girl at Great Cuts asked him what style he wanted, and he told her that he wanted hair like Morrissey. He'd always wanted hair like Morrissey. She didn't know who that was. "James Dean?" he asked.

"Let me talk to my supervisor," she said.

Her supervisor was in her forties. She carried a hot pink comb with a handle as sharp as a dagger. "James Dean . . . ," she said, tapping her chin with the comb. "Are you sure you don't want George Clooney?" He didn't.

"We'll give it our best shot," she said.

Lincoln was embarrassingly pleased with the results. He bought something called styling wax and left a 75-percent tip. (Nine dollars.)

He decided to go home and change before he went to work. He put on a short-sleeved white T-shirt and tried not to flex when he checked his reflection in the mirror. Is this what women felt like when they put on miniskirts?

When he got to *The Courier*, he walked straight to the newsroom, straight to Beth's desk. He didn't know exactly what he was going to do when he got there. He wasn't thinking about that, because if he thought about it—if he thought any of this through—he wouldn't do it. And he needed to do it. More than he needed to do anything, at this moment, on this day, in this lifetime, in this incarnation, on this Monday afternoon, Lincoln needed to talk to Beth.

And he needed to be the one who started the conversation. He needed to stand at her desk, in daylight, with his shoulders back and his head up, and his hands—God, what would he do with his hands? *Don't think about it. Don't think. For once in your godforsaken life, don't think.*

Lincoln walked to Beth's cubicle, not trying to pretend he was doing something else. Not sneaking. Not furtive. (Not that anyone was probably paying attention.)

He walked right up to her cubicle.

She wasn't there.

Lincoln hadn't thought about what he would do if Beth wasn't there. So he just stood at her cubicle. With his shoulders back and his head up and everything. He looked at her desk. He looked around. He thought about the last time he'd tried to talk to her, on New Year's Eve, and how he'd run away. *I'm not running away this time*, he thought.

The man in the next cubicle—"Derek Hastings," his nameplate said—was on the phone, but watching Lincoln. After a few minutes, a conversation about the local zoo and panda bears, Derek hung up the phone.

"Can I help you?" he said.

"Uh, no," Lincoln said. "I need to talk to Beth, Beth Fremont."

"She's not here," Derek said.

Lincoln nodded.

"Can I give her a message?" Derek asked. "Is there something wrong with her computer?"

So, he knows what I do, who I am, Lincoln thought. *It's not a secret.*

"No," Lincoln said, standing his ground. Standing Beth's ground.

Derek eyed him suspiciously, and slowly unwrapped a Dum Dum sucker, the kind they give to kids in bank drive-throughs. Lincoln could handle the suspicion and the staring, but he couldn't handle the Dum Dum.

"I'll come back," he said, as much to himself as to Derek. *I can't make myself talk to her if she isn't even here*, he thought. *This doesn't count as running away.*

CHAPTER 84

From: Beth Fremont
To: Jennifer Scribner-Snyder
Sent: Mon, 03/20/2000 12:22 PM
Subject: Remember when I said it was too soon to date?

Guess I was wrong. I have a date.

<<Jennifer to Beth>> With Your Cute Guy?

<<Beth to Jennifer>> With *a* cute guy, but not My Cute Guy.
Remember last year, when I first wrote about the Indian Hills theater, and I told that cute pharmacy student I interviewed that I was
engaged?

Well, I ran into him last night at the big farewell gala.

He came over to talk to me and said that he'd been reading my
reviews since I interviewed him, and that my *Titanic* review had
made him laugh out loud. And I said that *Titanic* had made me
laugh out loud. And then we both laughed at how funny I am, and
he asked if it would be a conflict of interest if he bought me a drink.

I thought it probably would be, so I bought him a drink instead.
And we ended up sitting next to each other during the showing of
the Indian Hill's very last movie, *How the West Was Won*, one of the
last films ever made in Cinerama.

How the West Was Won is 162 minutes long, almost three hours,
plus there was an intermission. I see so many movies by myself, I'd

forgotten what it's like to sit next to a guy in the theater, a guy who keeps looking up at you every few minutes, just as you're looking up at him. I'd forgotten about the shoulder touching and the whispering and the leaning in.

Sean—that's right, he has a name, a real name, there will be no "Hot Protester Guy" or "Little Red-Haired Pharmacy Student"— and I stayed in our seats during the intermission, and talked about how we like Henry Fonda better than John Wayne, and Karl Malden best of all.

And when the movie was over, we sat all the way through the credits, then lingered in the lobby. And finally, he said, "I suppose you're probably still engaged."

"Actually," I said, "I'm not." (Some might say I never was.)

He made a really adorable surprised face, like that answer had taken him totally off his game. "Oh . . . I'm sorry, I guess?"

I shook my head. "Don't be."

And then he said that he had expected to feel miserable and defeated all night, but that instead he felt like he'd just been on "the nicest first date" of his life.

And *then* he asked if we could see each other again.

<<Jennifer to Beth>> And you said?

<<Beth to Jennifer>> I said *yes*!

But I told him we couldn't have our first official date until I was done covering the Indian Hills stuff. Conflict of interest, etc. He promised there wouldn't be any more lawsuits or protests or appeals to the Planning Board. "I am suddenly very happy to say that we are out of options," he said. "The preservation effort is utterly and absolutely over."

I told him my last story would be about the demolition.

"I'll be there," he said.

"Me, too."

And then he laughed, which made what he was about to say seem happy and nice instead of cheesy and stupid. "It's a date."

So there—I have a date!

<<**Jennifer to Beth**>> Congratulations! You're happy about this, right?

<<**Beth to Jennifer**>> I really am. I know it's soon. But, so far, I really like this guy, and he really likes me. (Really, really—I could tell.) If I said no, who knows when the next nice-guy-who-likes-me will come along? Maybe never.

Plus, as nice as he was and as cute as he is and as much as I was enjoying myself, I didn't feel like he was casting a voodoo love spell on me (i.e. Chris).

He might even be the anti-Chris. A pharmacy student? A community activist? A guy who owns a navy blue suit? And he's at least six inches shorter.

<<**Jennifer to Beth**>> Well, I did advise you to carpe cute guy. I guess you had my endorsement. When are they tearing the theater down?

<<**Beth to Jennifer**>> Saturday. Those sick people need somewhere to park.

<<**Jennifer to Beth**>> So, *technically*, you *are* going on a date with this guy before you write your last Indian Hills story. You better not try to quote him; that wouldn't be ethical.

<<**Beth to Jennifer**>> Imagine that quote:
"Do you kiss on the first date?" one protester asked.
"Are Trix for kids?" this reporter responded.

CHAPTER 85

LINCOLN DELETED THE messages. Then he dug deep into the WebFence hard drive and started scrubbing. Slashing and burning through every layer of memory, pouring bleach on every remnant of information.

When he was done, no one would be able to go back and see who WebFence had flagged and how many times and for what reason. He scrubbed his own hard drive, too, cleared his practically nonexistent e-mail history. He wiped the machine clean and reinstalled all the programs.

Then he cleaned out his desk—well, the drawer that Kristi had allotted him. There wasn't much in there. Gum. Microwave popcorn. A few CDs.

By the time he was done, it was after ten, too late to call Greg. He'd talk to Greg tomorrow. He found Doris in the break room, playing solitaire and eating bright red pistachios.

"Hey," he said.

"Hey, honey. Hey, look at you. I like your haircut. You know, we used to call that a D.A., 'cause it looks just like a duck's ass."

He tried to run his hand through his hair, to press it down, but his fingers got caught in the styling wax.

"Have you eaten yet?" She pushed the pistachios toward him.

"No, I guess I forgot. Look, Doris, I came down to tell you that . . . I think I'm going to quit tomorrow."

"Tomorrow? What happened?"

"Nothing happened," Lincoln said, and nothing was ever going to happen. "I just really hate this job."

"You do?" She looked surprised. Hadn't he ever complained to Doris about work?

"Yeah," he said. "I hate it. I hate the hours. I hate reading everybody's e-mail."

"Why do you read everybody's e-mail?"

"That's my job," he said. "And I hate it. I hate sitting in that office by myself. I hate being up all night. I don't even like this newspaper. I disagree with the editorials, and they don't run any of my favorite comics."

"You don't like *Blondie*?" she asked. "And *Fox Trot*?"

"*Fox Trot*'s okay," he said.

"You're really quitting?"

"Yeah," he said. "Yes."

"Well . . . good for you. No sense staying someplace after you realize you don't want to be there. Good for you. And good for me that you stayed this long. Do you have another job?"

"Not yet. I'll find one. I have enough in savings that I don't have to find one right away."

"We should celebrate," Doris said.

"We should?"

"Sure. We should have a going-away party."

"When?"

"Right now," she said. "We'll order a pizza, and we'll play pinochle until it's time to clock out."

He wouldn't have thought he'd feel like celebrating, but he did. *Enough is enough*, he thought. *Enough is enough is enough.* They ordered pizza from Pizza Hut—one medium Meat Lover's Pan Pizza each. And Doris won six rounds of pinochle. When it was time to go home, she got a little choked up.

"You're a good kid," she said, "and a good friend."

"We'll still see each other," he said. "I'll take you to dinner when you retire."

He stopped at Chuck's desk on the way back to the IT office. "I can't talk, I'm on deadline," Chuck said.

"I just want to tell you that I'm quitting."

"What? You can't quit," Chuck said.

"I hate working here."

"We all hate working here. That doesn't mean we quit. Only quitters quit."

"I'm quitting."

"I guess this is good-bye, then," Chuck said.

"It's not good-bye. We can still play golf."

"Piffle," Chuck said. "You'll get a day job. You'll forget us. There won't be anybody to help us do math."

"You might be right," Lincoln said.

"Bastard."

"Don't tell anybody until tomorrow."

"Bastard defector."

When he got back to his desk, Lincoln decided he wasn't coming back tomorrow to quit in person. He wasn't ever coming back. He didn't want to see Beth again. Didn't want to find himself opening the WebFence folder after he'd promised himself he wasn't going to for the four-thousandth time.

So he took out a pad of paper and wrote two notes. The first was to Greg. A quick resignation and an apology.

He slipped it into an envelope and stuck it into Greg's keyboard where Greg would see it first thing the next morning.

The second note he lingered over. He didn't have to write this one. He probably *shouldn't* write it. But he wanted to walk away from the newspaper tonight (this morning, actually) feeling truly and completely free, with his conscience as clear as he could make it without publicly crucifying himself.

"Beth," he wrote, then started over. They weren't exactly on a first-name basis.

Hello,

We've never met, but I'm the guy whose job it is to enforce the company's computer policy. Your e-mail gets flagged. A lot. I should have sent you warnings the same way I do everyone else, but I didn't—because reading your e-mail made me like you. I didn't want to tell you that you were breaking the rules because I didn't want to stop hearing from you and your friend, Jennifer.

This was an egregious invasion of your privacy and hers, and for that, I deeply apologize.

I won't blame you if you turn me in, but I'm quitting anyway. I never should have taken this job, and I don't like the person I've become here.

I'm writing this note because I owe you an apology—even a cowardly, anonymous one—and because I thought I should warn you to stop using your company computer to send personal e-mails.

I really am sorry.

He folded the note up and sealed the envelope before he could change his mind or think about rewriting it. She didn't need to know that he was in love with her. There was no point making the note any weirder than it had to be.

Lincoln was giving Beth proof, written proof, that he'd read her e-mail, but he wasn't sure what could come of that. Greg couldn't fire him, even if he wanted to. He probably wouldn't want to. Reading e-mail was Lincoln's job. Greg had pretty much given him permission to read whatever he wanted, even the stuff that didn't get flagged. In Lincoln's position, Greg probably would have done much worse.

Lincoln wanted to confess. He wanted to apologize. And he wanted to make it impossible for himself to turn back.

The newsroom was dark when he got there. He turned on the lights and walked to Beth's desk. He set the envelope on her keyboard, then decided to tape it there so that it wouldn't get knocked off. And then he left.

Enough is enough is enough.

CHAPTER 86

THE PHONE WOKE Lincoln up at seven forty-five the next morning. It was Greg. He was pissed, but he also really wanted Lincoln to change his mind.

"I'm not going to change my mind," Lincoln said, not even opening his eyes.

Greg offered him more money, a lot more money, making Lincoln wish he would have tried to quit his job a few months before he was actually ready to leave.

"You didn't even give me two weeks," Greg said.

"That was crappy of me. I'm genuinely sorry."

"Give me two weeks."

"I can't," Lincoln said. "I'm sorry."

"Do you already have another job?"

"No."

Greg yelled at him for a few minutes, then apologized and said that Lincoln could use him as a reference if he ever wanted to.

"What are you going to say I'm good at," Lincoln asked, "sitting around?"

"You weren't just sitting around," Greg said. "How many times do I have to tell you? You were keeping the home fires burning. Somebody has to answer the phone and say, 'Help desk.'"

"I'm sure you'll be able to find someone else who can handle it."

"Don't be so sure," Greg sighed, "only whack jobs apply for the night shift."

Lincoln wondered if Beth had read his note—probably not yet—and whether she would file some sort of complaint against him. That threat still didn't seem substantial enough to worry about. He hoped his note hadn't scared her; he hadn't meant to scare her. Maybe he should have thought more about that.

ON SATURDAY MORNING, Lincoln drove to Eighty-fourth Street and West Dodge Road to watch a demolition crew tear down the Indian Hills theater. They'd stripped the place the day before. All that was left was the screen and the building. There was a good-size crowd gathered in the parking lot, but Lincoln didn't get close enough to see any faces; he watched from the parking lot outside the doughnut shop across the street. After about an hour, he went inside and bought two crullers, a carton of milk, and a newspaper. He threw every section but the Classifieds away before he sat down.

Then he took out an old spiral notebook and opened it to the middle. To his list. He copied four entries in the margin of the Classifieds:

"No. 19. Unfreezing computers/Untangling necklaces."

"No. 23. Being helpful."

"No. 5. Not worrying about things he really shouldn't worry about."

And finally, "No. 36. Being GOOD."

The ads were full of computer jobs. He crossed out any listings that seemed vague or sneaky and anything that said, "Great people skills a must."

He circled one. "Senior computer technician needed. St. James University, Department of Nursing. Full-time. Tuition + benefits."

CHAPTER 87

EVE TEASED HIM about working on campus and taking almost a full load of classes. "It's like you went back to school through a loophole," she said after his first semester. "What is it with you and school? Are you addicted to the smell of musty auditoriums?"

Maybe he was. Musty auditoriums. Creaky library chairs. Wide green lawns.

Lincoln had his own desk in the Dean of Nursing's Office. He was the only man on the administrative staff and the only person younger than forty-five. His computer skills awed the office ladies. They treated him like Gandalf. He had a desk, but he didn't have to sit there. He could go to class or do whatever he needed to do to keep everything humming.

Part of his job was Internet security—but it was little more than up-dating antiviral programs and reminding people not to open suspicious attachments. His supervisor in the central IT office said that there had never been a pornography incident in the Nursing College and that, be-sides porn and gambling, people were free to go and do whatever they wanted online.

"Is there an e-mail filter?" Lincoln asked.

"Are you kidding?" the guy said. "The faculty senate would flip."

LINCOLN STILL THOUGHT about Beth. All the time, at first.

He subscribed to the newspaper so that he could read her reviews at breakfast and again at lunch. He tried to figure out how she was doing through her writing. Did she seem happy? Was she being too hard on romantic comedies? Or too generous?

Reading her reviews kept his memory of her alive in a way he probably shouldn't want. Like a pilot light inside of him. It made him ache sometimes, when she was especially funny or insightful, or when he could read past her words to something true that he knew about her. But the aching faded, too. Things get better—hurt less—over time. If you let them.

When fall classes started, Lincoln developed a crush on his medieval literature professor, a flammably intelligent woman in her mid-thirties. She had full hips and bluntly cut bangs, and she got rhapsodic when she talked about *Beowulf*. She'd underline phrases in his papers with bright green ink and write notes in the margins. "Exactly!" or "Ironic, isn't it?" He thought he might ask her out when the term ended. Or he might sign up for her advanced seminar.

One of the women in his office kept trying to fix him up with her daughter, Neveen, an advertising copywriter who smoked organic cigarettes. They went out a few times, and Lincoln liked Neveen well enough to take her to Justin and Dena's wedding.

It was held at a giant Catholic church in the suburbs. (Who knew that Justin was Catholic? And devout enough that he made Dena convert. "My kids aren't growing up Unitarian," he told Lincoln at the rehearsal dinner. "Those cocksuckers just barely believe in Jesus.")

The reception was at a nice hotel a few miles away. There was a Polish-themed buffet and a string quartet that played during dinner. Lincoln felt anxious about seeing Sacajawea play. He ate way too many pirogi.

The band took the stage after the bride and groom's dance ("My Heart Will Go On"), the wedding party dance ("Leather and Lace"), and the father-daughter dance ("Butterfly Kisses"). Justin made an announcement while they set up, warning his elderly aunts and uncles that they better take advantage of the open bar or get packing "cuz it's about to get fucking twisted in here."

The sting Lincoln expected to feel when he saw Chris never came.

Chris was still a beautiful specimen. A few of Dena's adolescent cousins clustered at Chris's end of the stage and fiddled with their necklaces. An older girl, college-aged, had come with the band. She had long blond hair and luminous skin, and she handed Chris beer and bottled water between songs.

There was no sting. Even when Chris seemed to recognize Lincoln and waved. Now—to Lincoln, anyway—Chris was just another guy who wasn't with Beth.

It's hard to dance to music that sounds like Zeppelin dragged in Radiohead, but most of Justin and Dena's friends were drunk enough to try. Including Lincoln's date. Lincoln wasn't drunk, but he still felt like jumping and shouting and singing too loud. He caught stage divers. He spun Neveen until she was dizzy. He shamelessly made devil horns at the sky.

CHAPTER 88

IT WAS COLD for October. The kids would have to wear puffy coats over their Halloween costumes, and they'd get asked at every door who they were supposed to be.

October, Lincoln thought to himself. *Callooh, callay.*

He stood at his open bedroom window, just for a moment, to let the memory pass through him. *Merry October.*

One of the nicer things about his apartment was that there was a movie theater in walking distance. An old art house called the Dundee, just about a mile away. It was the only place Lincoln knew of that served RC Cola on tap. He ended up there almost every weekend. Most of the time he didn't even care what was showing.

Tonight, Lincoln put on a thick turtleneck sweater and his jean jacket over a pair of olive green pants. He checked his hair in the mirror he'd hung inside his entryway. He'd kept the Morrissey hair—even though Eve said it made him look like Luke Perry. Or like he was trying to look like Luke Perry. "You need that?" she'd asked. "You're not tall enough already?"

"I don't need it," he said. "I like it."

Eve had invited him over tonight, but he'd passed. He was supposed to meet up with the copy deskers later, at some bar in Iowa that served tomato beer. Maybe he'd go . . . Maybe.

It was already dark outside at six thirty. That felt right. The cold felt right.

Lincoln could see people eating dinner inside the big houses on his way to the theater. It was the kind of neighborhood where people never closed the curtains on their picture windows. "You know why those old houses have big windows up front?" his mother had asked him once. "Because it used to be, when somebody in your family died, you had the wake right in your house. You needed a window big enough for the casket." Lincoln had decided to go on believing that the windows were there so that people could show off their Christmas trees.

When he got to the Dundee, an employee was changing the marquee from *Dancer in the Dark* to *Billy Elliott*.

Lincoln ducked into the small lobby to buy his ticket, an RC, and a box of buttered popcorn. The theater was nearly empty, and he took a seat near the front. A red velvet seat. This must be the only place left, now that the Indian Hills was gone, that didn't have plastic recliners or "love seats" with adjustable armrests. There were still curtains hanging in front of the movie screen that would draw back just as the previews started. Lincoln used to think that was pointless. Now it was the thing he waited for.

Just then, while he was waiting, someone at the back of the theater spilled a box of candy, something hard and loud, M&M'S or Everlasting Gobstoppers, that clattered down the sloped concrete floor. Lincoln turned around without thinking. That's when he saw her, sitting a few rows behind him and a few seats over.

Dark hair. Heart face. Freckles.

So pretty.

Beth.

Lincoln looked away as soon as he realized it was her—but she'd already recognized him. She'd looked right at him. She'd looked . . . How had she looked?

Surprised. Just surprised.

You'd think that he would have thought about this moment, as much as he'd thought about her over the last few months. It's not like they lived in Tokyo or Mumbai or a place where people could ever really lose each other. This was a small city. A small city with relatively few places you'd want to go, especially if you were a movie reviewer. Lincoln had thought of the Dundee as *his* theater, but, really, it was like he'd shown up at Beth's office.

And now he had to leave. She'd want him to, right? Especially if she'd put it all together by now. That's another thing he'd gone out of his way not to think about. Did Beth still think about him as her Cute Guy? Or had she figured out that he was the creep who read her e-mail?

He had to leave. Immediately. No. As soon as the lights went down. He couldn't bear to think of her eyes on him again.

Lincoln leaned forward in his seat, covered his face with one hand, and willed the lights to dim. After a few painful minutes, they did. The lights fell, the projector squeaked to life, the ancient curtains parted, and Lincoln started putting on his jacket.

Just as Beth sat down beside him.

He froze, one arm still in his jacket. He didn't speak. Or move. Only his autonomic nervous system chugged on.

He couldn't leave, not with her sitting next to him—why was she sitting next to him?—and he couldn't look at her. So he sat back slowly in his seat, careful not to touch her. He sat back and he waited.

But Beth didn't say anything.

And didn't say anything. And didn't move. And didn't say anything. Through the coming attractions, through the opening credits.

Finally, Lincoln couldn't keep from looking at her. He glanced over. Beth was staring at the screen like she was awaiting instructions from the Holy Spirit, eyes too wide, holding on to her ballpoint pen with both hands. Some T. Rex song was playing on the soundtrack. "Cosmic Dancer."

Lincoln looked away. He told himself to be patient, to wait for her to do something or to say something. But the wait was suffocating. Or maybe it was the sitting so close to her that was suffocating. The wanting to look at her again. More. And again.

Then Lincoln found himself saying the thing he always said to women, the thing he actually needed to say to Beth.

"I'm sorry," he whispered, looking over his shoulder.

"Don't," she said.

She was looking up at him now, direct and determined. Her jaw was set. She must know, he thought, his heart sinking into the concrete floor. She must know that he was the creep. Maybe she was even going to yell at him. Or slap him. He found himself counting the inches between them. Fifteen, sixteen tops. He'd never been close enough to see her ears before. They were perfect.

Beth raised her right hand then, still holding the pen, to his face. To his chin.

Lincoln closed his eyes. It seemed like the right thing to do, no matter what happened next. He closed his eyes and felt her fingertips touching his cheek, then his forehead, then his eyelids. He took a breath—ink and hand soap.

"I"—he heard her whisper, closer than he expected, and shaky and strange—"think I might be a very stupid girl."

He shook his head no. Just barely. So that only someone who was holding his cheek and his neck would notice.

"Yes," she said, sounding closer. He didn't move, didn't open his eyes. What if he opened his eyes and she saw what she was doing?

She kissed his cheek, and he let his head tip forward into her hands. She kissed his other cheek. And his chin. The groove below his bottom lip. "Stupid girl," she said near the corner of his mouth, sounding in-credulous, "what could you possibly be thinking?"

Lincoln found his mouth. "Perfect girl," he said so quietly that only someone with her hands in his hair and her lips all but touching his could possibly hear. "Pretty girl." He found her mouth. "Perfect." Kiss. "Magic." Kiss. "Only girl."

There are moments when you can't believe something wonderful is happening. And there are moments when your entire consciousness is filled with knowing absolutely that something wonderful is happening. Lincoln felt like he'd dunked his head into a sink full of Pop Rocks and turned on the water.

He shook his jacket onto the floor and put his arms around her.

All he could think was *Beth*. All he could do was let this dream come true.

———

HE DIDN'T HEAR the movie end. Didn't hear anything for two hours above the thunder of his heartbeat and the occasional click of her teeth against his. But Beth jumped when the lights came up. She jumped, sat up, pulled away from him. It felt like getting up from the warmest bed on the coldest morning. Lincoln pushed forward, not wanting to lose the nearness of her. Afraid that something horrible was happening, that somewhere a clock was striking midnight.

"I'm on deadline," Beth said. She touched her mouth and then her hair, her falling-down ponytail. "I . . . have to go, I have to . . ." She turned to the empty screen as if there might be something up there still that she could use. The curtains were sliding closed.

She crouched on the floor, looking for something. "My glasses," she said, "was I wearing glasses?" They were shoved back into her hair. Lincoln carefully pulled them free.

"Thank you," she said. He helped her stand, and tried to hold her for a moment, but she broke away as soon as she was upright and started hurrying out of the aisle. "I've never done this before," she said. She didn't mean him. She was looking at the screen. "Did you watch any of it? There was dancing, right? I'm sure there was dancing." Then she looked around, afraid someone had heard her. She touched her mouth again, with her palm and all four fingers, like she was checking to make sure it was still there.

And then she ran—almost ran—toward the exit, walking backward at first to watch him, then eventually turning away.

LINCOLN COULDN'T REMEMBER walking home to his apartment, and when he got there, he didn't want to go in. He didn't want to break the spell. So he sat on his front steps and kept reliving the last two hours. Bearing witness to himself—*yes* and *Beth* and *that just happened*.

"What could you possibly be thinking?" she'd asked herself.

What *could* she possibly have been thinking? She didn't even know Lincoln. Not like he knew her. He knew why he wanted to kiss her.

Because she was beautiful. And before that, because she was kind. And before that, because she was smart and funny. Because she was exactly the right kind of smart and funny. Because he could imagine taking a long road trip with her without ever getting bored. Because whenever he saw something new and interesting, or new and ridiculous, he always wondered what she'd have to say about it—how many stars she'd give it and why.

He *knew* why he'd wanted to kiss her. Why he still did. He could still feel her on his lips, on his lap. In his head like fog, like honey that buzzed. Is this what it had felt like to kiss Sam? (He couldn't remember just now, he didn't want to.) If it had been like this, maybe nine years wasn't such a long time to get over Sam, after all.

In all the time Lincoln was working at *The Courier*, reading Beth's mail, thinking about her, he'd never really believed that there was a course of events, a path ahead of him or a route through the space-time continuum that would lead to this.

Yes. Beth. That just happened.

And maybe . . . maybe it was still happening.

Lincoln jerked to his feet and checked his pocket for his car keys. How long had it been since she'd left? Thirty minutes? Forty-five? Beth would still be at *The Courier*. And Lincoln didn't have to keep a respectable distance anymore. He didn't have to wish and pine and feel guilty. He didn't have to do the honorable thing. Or maybe it was that the honorable thing had changed the moment Beth sat down next to him. Everything had changed.

Lincoln parked behind *The Courier*, by the loading dock. Half a dozen trucks were already waiting there, idling, while crews packed them with stacks of first editions. He ran in through a garage door, bypassing the employee turnstile—the guard on duty recognized him and waved—then bolted up the stairs to the newsroom like he was running for his life, like he was on deadline. Like if he stopped, he might settle into his old self, get trapped in his old loop.

Chuck looked up when Lincoln rushed past the copy desk. Lincoln nodded and kept rushing. He looked over at the city desk—no Beth. The back of the newsroom, the Entertainment section, was dark, but Lincoln kept going, trying not to think about all the nights he'd walked this path after he was sure she was gone.

She was there, on the phone. Sitting in her dark cubicle, the monitor lighting her face like a candle.

"No, I know," she said into the phone. Her hair was all-the-way down, she wasn't wearing her glasses. She still looked half dazed and overkissed. "I know," she said, rubbing her forehead. "Look, this won't ever . . ."

Lincoln stopped at the cubicle next to hers and tried not to breathe like a quarter horse. Beth glanced up, saw him, and lost the rest of her sentence.

He didn't know what to do then, so he smiled, hopefully, biting his lip.

"Thank you," she said into the phone. "I know. Thank you . . . Okay." She hung up and gaped at him.

"What are you doing here?" she asked.

"I can leave," he said, taking a step back.

"No," she said, standing. "No. I . . ."

"I thought we should talk," he said.

"Okay," she said.

"Okay." Lincoln nodded.

There were maybe two feet and a cubicle wall between them.

"Or maybe we shouldn't," Beth said, folding her arms.

"What?"

"I just feel like, if we talk about this, it could go horribly wrong. But if we leave it like it is, maybe it can go on feeling, I don't know, somehow horribly right."

"Like it is?" he asked.

"Sure," she said, talking too fast. "We can meet in dark theaters . . . and if I need to tell you something, I'll send it to someone else in an e-mail."

Lincoln stepped away from her, like she'd hit him.

She scrunched up her face and closed her eyes. "Sorry," she said. "*Sorry*. I warned you. I'm no good at talking. I'm better on paper."

She knows, was all Lincoln could think. *That I'm the creep. Not the cute guy. She knows . . . And she still sat next to me.*

"Are you done?" he asked.

"Embarrassing myself? Probably not."

"With your review."

"Such as it is."

"Then come with me."

Lincoln held out his hand to her and felt like he'd won something when, after another dazed moment, she took it. He started walking out of the newsroom, wishing he knew where to take her. It's not like *The Courier* had a romantic courtyard hidden away. Or a balcony. Or a corner booth.

They ended up at the break room.

"Wait," Beth said, as he pushed open the door. The room was dark. The tables were gone. The vending machines were still there, still lit and humming, but they were empty.

"It's closed," Beth said quietly. "There's a new one downstairs. This is going to be office space, I think, for the Web people."

She looked down the hall, nervously, and drew back her hand.

"Perfect," Lincoln said. He stepped into the break room and held the door open for her. She looked up at him, surprised, and followed. The door swished shut behind them, and Lincoln stopped for a moment to let his eyes adjust to the Pepsi machine light. There was a clear space against the wall, next to the Coffee-Mat. Beth followed him there—he kept expecting her not to—and they sank to the floor, facing each other.

He wanted to touch her, to take her hand again, but she pulled her skirt down over her knees and pressed her fists into her lap. He hadn't noticed what she was wearing before. A knee-length denim skirt, a rose-colored cardigan, periwinkle tights, and tall blue leather boots. She looked like a sunset, he thought.

"So now we talk?" she asked.

"I think so," Lincoln said.

Beth looked at her fists. "I can't think of anything to say to you that you don't already know."

"Don't say that," he said, "It's not like that."

"It isn't?" She looked angry.

"I'm sorry," he said.

"Don't apologize," she said, her voice breaking. "*Please*. I really, really don't want you to be sorry."

"You don't?"

"*No*," she said.

"What do you want me to say?"

"I want you to say something, I don't know what, but *something* that will make it perfectly explicable for me to be here." She was talking quickly, quavering, he thought she might even be starting to cry. "I mean, Jennifer's already going to go into labor when I tell her about this. She still thinks we should turn you in—but turn you in for what? And to who? She's accused me of being swayed by your vast cuteness . . . your cute vastness . . ."

"Jennifer's pregnant?" Lincoln asked, smiling out of context.

Beth wiped her eyes with her sweater and looked up at him.

"Yeah."

"That's great," he said genuinely. "That's really great."

"Yeah . . . ," she said, still staring at him, then hid her face her hands. "Oh my God, this is so weird."

"I'm sorry," he said.

"*Stop*."

"Right, sorry, *look*, would it help if I told you that I never meant to start reading your messages? Or Jennifer's or anybody's? I was just checking the filter, and you'd get flagged, you know, for breaking the rules, and those are the only messages I ever read, only the flagged messages, and only yours. I mean, maybe this makes it worse, but I wasn't regularly reading anybody else's mail. I didn't have to leave notes on anyone else's desk when I quit."

"Why did you have to leave a note on mine? I swear that note's the weirdest part."

"I wanted to apologize," he said, resisting the urge to look away.

"But *why* apologize? Why did it matter?"

"Because you mattered," he said. "I wanted to come clean with you."

"Anonymously?"

Lincoln didn't want to say he was sorry again, so he didn't say anything at all.

"I kept thinking about you," Beth said. "I kept thinking about how this would work in a book or the movies. If this were a Jane Austen novel, it wouldn't be so bad—if you were intercepting my letters, and I was peeking over your garden hedge . . . Computers make everything worse."

"I made everything worse," he said. "I shouldn't have written you that note. I mean, on top of everything else. I'm sorry it upset you."

"That's the thing . . . ," she said, "I'm not even sure that it did upset me. Maybe at first, thinking about some strange guy reading my e-mail. But it didn't take me long to figure out it was you. I wasn't seeing you around the building anymore. And I mentioned it to Derek one day—you know Derek, who sits next to me—'Whatever happened to that big guy with the brown hair who used to eat dinner with Doris?' And he was like, 'The IT guy? He quit.' And then it all came together. That you were . . . you."

Beth had stopped crying and relaxed against the wall. Her skirt had crept back up over purple-stockinged knees. Lincoln wanted to fall into her lap. They were still sitting sideways, facing each other, and she set her hand just next to his on the floor, so that their fingertips were almost touching.

"How would this work in a movie?" she asked, looking at their hands, looking softer by the syllable. "How would Meg Ryan and Tom Hanks make this situation less strange?"

"You mean, like in *Sleepless in Seattle*?" he asked.

"Right," she said, "or *You've Got Mail*. I mean, first of all, we'd have this conversation off camera. It's too messy."

"If this were a Meg Ryan and Tom Hanks movie," Lincoln said, "I'd just kiss you, probably in the middle of a sentence. That would fix everything."

She smiled. Had he ever seen her smile like that? With her whole freckled face?

"Cue Louis Armstrong," she said.

"But I'm not going to kiss you," he said. He had to force the words out.

"You're not?"

"No. Because you're right. This should be explicable. *We* should be. I want you to be able to look back on tonight, and believe that this is plausible, that this is how two people could find each other."

"Ah," Beth said. "*When Harry Met Sally.*" If she smiled any wider, she'd break him.

"*Joe Versus the Volcano*," he said.

"*Jerry Maguire*," she said.

"*The Empire Strikes Back.*"

She laughed. It was better than he could have imagined. Like a giggle falling off its chair. "I wouldn't have done what I did in the theater, if . . . Well, I asked Doris about you."

"Yeah?"

"And she said you were one of the nicest guys she'd ever met, maybe even nicer than her husband, Pete . . ."

"Paul."

"Paul," Beth said. "And that you shared your dinner with her and helped her move. She also told me that you were single—that the girls on the copy desk flirted with you, but that you were a perfect gentleman. She said you quit your job because reading people's e-mail made you feel like a Peeping Tom, and that working nights made you feel like Count Chocula."

"She told you all that?"

"Right here. Over three nights of pinochle."

"You should've stayed in reporting."

"See?" she whispered, closing her eyes, for just a moment. "*There.* What can I say for myself that you don't already know? What can I say, *knowing* what you know?"

"It isn't like that," he said again.

"Everything I wrote about you, what I called you . . ."

"I knew you weren't serious," he said, "I knew you had a boyfriend."

"Is that why you read my e-mail? Because I had a crush on you?"

"No, by the time you wrote that, I already felt . . . everything."

"I *was* serious," she said. "More than I ever would have admitted to Jennifer. I followed you whenever I could. I tried to follow you home once."

"I know," he said faintly.

She looked down. Pulled down her skirt.

"I just had this feeling about you," she said. "Is that foolish?"

"I hope not."

They were quiet.

"So, okay," Beth said, picking her face up and leaning forward, sharply, like she'd decided something. "When I was in the eighth grade, I saw part of a music video by the Sundays, this song—'Here's Where the Story Ends.' Do you know that song?"

He nodded. She pushed her hair behind her ears.

"I almost never got to watch MTV, only when I was at my friend Nickie's house and only when her parents weren't home. But I saw this video, not even the whole thing, and I just knew that it was going to be my favorite song for . . . for the rest of my life. And it still is. It's still my favorite song . . .

"Lincoln, I said you were cute because I didn't know how to say—because I didn't think I was *allowed to say*—anything else. But every time I saw you, I felt like I did the first time I heard that song."

She was throwing stars at him. It was hard to listen. It was hard to look at her. He still felt like he was stealing something.

"Lincoln?" she asked.

"Yes?"

"Do you believe in love at first sight?"

He made himself look at her face, at her wide-open eyes and earnest forehead. At her unbearably sweet mouth.

"I don't know," he said. "Do you believe in love before that?"

Her breath caught in her throat like a sore hiccup.

And then it was too much to keep trying not to kiss her.

She came readily into his arms. Lincoln leaned against the coffee machine and pulled her onto him completely. There it was again, that impossible-to-describe kiss. *This is how* 2001 *should have ended*, he thought. *This is infinity.*

The first time Beth pulled away, he pulled her back.

The second time, he bit her lip.

Then her neck.

Then the collar of her shirt.

"I don't know . . . ," she said, sitting up in his lap, laying her cheek on the top his head. "I don't know what you meant by love before love at first sight."

Lincoln pushed his face into her shoulder and tried to think of a good way to answer.

"Just that . . . I knew how I felt about you before I ever saw you," he said, "when I still thought I might never see you . . ."

She held his head in her hands and tilted it back, so she could see his face.

"That's ridiculous," she said. Which made him laugh.

"Absolutely," he said.

"No, I mean it," Beth said. "Men fall in love with their eyes." He closed his. "That's practically *science*," she said.

"Maybe," Lincoln said. Her fingers felt so good in his hair. "But I couldn't see you, so . . ."

"So, what did you see?"

"Just . . . the sort of girl who would write the sort of things that you wrote."

"*What* things?"

Lincoln opened his eyes. Beth was studying his face. She looked skeptical—maybe about more than just the last thing he said. This was important, he realized.

"Everything," he said, sitting straighter, keeping hold of her waist. "Everything you wrote about your work, about your boyfriend . . . The way you comforted Jennifer and made her laugh, through the baby and after. I pictured a girl who could be that kind, and that kind of funny. I pictured a girl who was that *alive* . . ."

She looked guarded. Lincoln couldn't tell from her eyes whether he was pushing her away or winning her over.

"A girl who never got tired of her favorite movies," he said softly. "Who saved dresses like ticket stubs. Who could get high on the weather . . .

"I pictured a girl who made every moment, everything she touched, and everyone around her feel lighter and sweeter.

"I pictured *you*," he said. "I just didn't know what you looked like.

"And then, when I did know what you looked like, you looked like the girl who was all those things. You looked like the girl I loved."

Beth's fingers trembled in his hair, and her forehead dropped against his. A heavy, wet tear fell onto Lincoln's lips, and he licked it. He pulled her close, as close as he could. Like he didn't care for the moment whether she could breathe. Like there were two of them and only one parachute.

"Beth," he barely said, pressing his face against hers until their lashes brushed, pressing his hand into the small of her back. "I don't think I can explain it. I don't think I can make it make any more sense. But I'll keep trying. If you want me to."

She almost shook her head. "No," she said, "no more explaining. Or apologizing. I don't think it matters anymore how we ended up here. I just . . . I want to stay . . . I want . . ."

He kissed her then.

There.

In the middle of the sentence.

CHAPTER 89

"I DON'T THINK your mom liked me," Beth said. They were on the way back to his apartment and she was balancing a giant pan of leftover lasagna on her lap.

"I think she loved you," he said. "That's why she looked so miserable. She would have been much happier if there was something obviously wrong with you. You should have seen her face when you said you were voting for Ralph Nader."

"I did. She looked pissed."

"Because she loves Ralph Nader."

"Why did your sister laugh?"

"Because she loves to see my mom thwarted."

Beth shook her head. It was raining outside, and her hair was wet and curling around her forehead. "That's crazy," she said.

"Now you're getting it," he said.

They'd decided not to tell his mom or Eve—or anyone—exactly how they'd met. They told them they'd met at work. ("Which is true," Beth said. "Technically.") Only Christine knew the whole truth—well, and Jennifer, of course, and probably Mitch. Beth said they could tell whomever they wanted after they'd been together long enough for it to seem like a bizarre footnote to their relationship. And not the whole freaky story.

"Well, my parents love you," she said, hugging the lasagna. "There's nothing tricky about it. My mom thinks you have a delightful sense of humor, and my dad told me he thinks you're quite handsome. 'Manly,' he said. He even commented on the size of your hands. Don't be surprised if he tries to dance with you at our wedding . . ."

Beth stopped talking abruptly. When Lincoln looked over, she'd turned her face to the window.

"I'll dance with your dad," he said, setting his hand on the back of her neck and brushing her cheek with his thumb. "As long as he leads . . . I'm not much of a dancer."

When she smiled up at him, he felt his heart swell against the inside of his chest. He felt that way all the time now. Even when he was holding her, it felt like there was something inside of him trying to burst out and embrace her.

"I didn't know it could be like this," she said later.

Not later that night. But on a night a lot like that one. A night that ended with Beth in his arms, with her everywhere against him.

Lincoln was almost asleep. "Like what?" he asked.

"I didn't know love could leave the lights on all the time. Do you know what I mean?"

"Not exactly," he said, finding a way to pull her closer. He could just make out her silhouette in the dark, her head lifted, her hair falling on his chest.

"I thought it took more naps," she said, struggling to find the right words. "Or blinked. I didn't know it could just go on and on and like this without falling off an edge. Like pi."

"What kind of pie?" he murmured.

"No, *pi* . . . ," she said.

"Lincoln . . ."

He didn't answer.

"Lincoln? Are you asleep?

"I didn't know someone could love me like this," she said. "Could love me and love me and love me without . . . needing space."

Lincoln wasn't asleep. He rolled on top of her.

"There's no air in space," he said.

Acknowledgments

Thanks to my magnificent sister, Jade, who demanded to know what happened next. Additional thanks to DeDra, for inspiration; to Brian, for encouragement; and to Erika, who flagged me down when I'd gone too far. And especial thanks to Christopher, for his advice and friendship, and for totally living up to his e-mail.

About the Author

RAINBOW ROWELL is a columnist at the *Omaha World-Herald*. She lives in Nebraska with her husband and two children. *Attachments* is her first novel.